Empires

To me it seems very certain, my very noble lord, that it is a worthy ambition for great men to desire to know and wish to preserve for posterity correct information concerning the things that have happened in distant parts, about which little is known.
–Pedro de Castañeda, c. 1545

BOOKS BY ALBERT MARRIN

The Airman's War
Overlord
Victory in the Pacific
The Secret Armies
The Sea Rovers
War Clouds in the West
Aztecs and Spaniards
The Yanks Are Coming
Struggle for a Continent
The War for Independence
Inca and Spaniard
The Spanish-American War
Cowboys, Indians, and Gunfighters
Unconditional Surrender: U. S. Grant and the Civil War
Virginia's General: Robert E. Lee and the Civil War
The Sea King: Sir Francis Drake and His Times
Plains Warrior: Chief Quanah Parker and the Comanches
Empires Lost and Won: The Spanish Heritage in the Southwest

Empires
Lost and Won

THE SPANISH HERITAGE IN THE SOUTHWEST

ALBERT MARRIN

ATHENEUM BOOKS FOR YOUNG READERS

Our thanks to Brian Butcher of the San Jacinto Museum of History, La Porte, Texas, for his careful reading of the manuscript.

Atheneum Books for Young Readers
An imprint of Simon & Schuster Children's Publishing Division
1230 Avenue of the Americas, New York, New York 10020

Book design by Patti Ratchford
The text of this book is set in Cloister
Printed in the United States of America
First edition
10 9 8 7 6 5 4 3 2 1

Library of Congress Cataloging-in-Publication Data:
Marrin, Albert.
Empires lost and won: the Spanish heritage in the Southwest/Albert Marrin.
p. cm.
Includes bibliographical references and index.
Summary: Discusses the history of the southwestern region of the United States from the sixteenth century to the Mexican War, examining the interactions between the Spanish, Indians, and American pioneers.
ISBN 0-689-80414-8
1. Southwest, New—History—To 1848—Juvenile literature. 2. Southwest, New—Discovery and exploration—Spanish—Juvenile literature. 3. Conquerors—Southwest, New—History—Juvenile literature. 4. Spaniards—Southwest, New—History—Juvenile literature. [1. Southwest, New—History—To 1848. 2. Southwest, New—Discovery and exploration—Spanish.] I. Title.
F799.M26 1997
979'.01—dc20
96-20851 CIP AC

Photo Credits:
Museum of New Mexico: title page, frontis, 37, 78, 105; New York Public Library Picture Collection: 4, 22; General Archives of the Indies, Seville: 5; Smithsonian Institution: 12, 38, 65, 69; Macmillan, London: 28, 43; Southern Methodist University, DeGolyer Library: 30; William Loren Katz: 33; Marcia Marshall: 57, 58; National Archives: 84, 153, 156, 174, 181; University of Oklahoma Library, Western History Collection: 99; San Jacinto Museum of History, Houston,Texas: 112, 119, 121, 125, 135, 137, 138-39, L42, 173, 191, 193; Texas State Library, Archives Division: 124, 126; National Portrait Gallery, Smithsonian Institution/Art Resource: 182; Library of Congress: 192. From the following publications: Códice Florentino: 11, 71, 13; Kiva, Cross, and Crown by John L. Kessell: 47, 49, 51, 61, 64, 75, 81, 104; The Heritage of the West by Charles Phillips: 87, 92, 132, 179, 197; Harpers New Monthly Magazine, 55 (1877):120; Sears Roebuck Catalog, 1897: 147. All other illustrations are from the author's collections.

CONTENTS

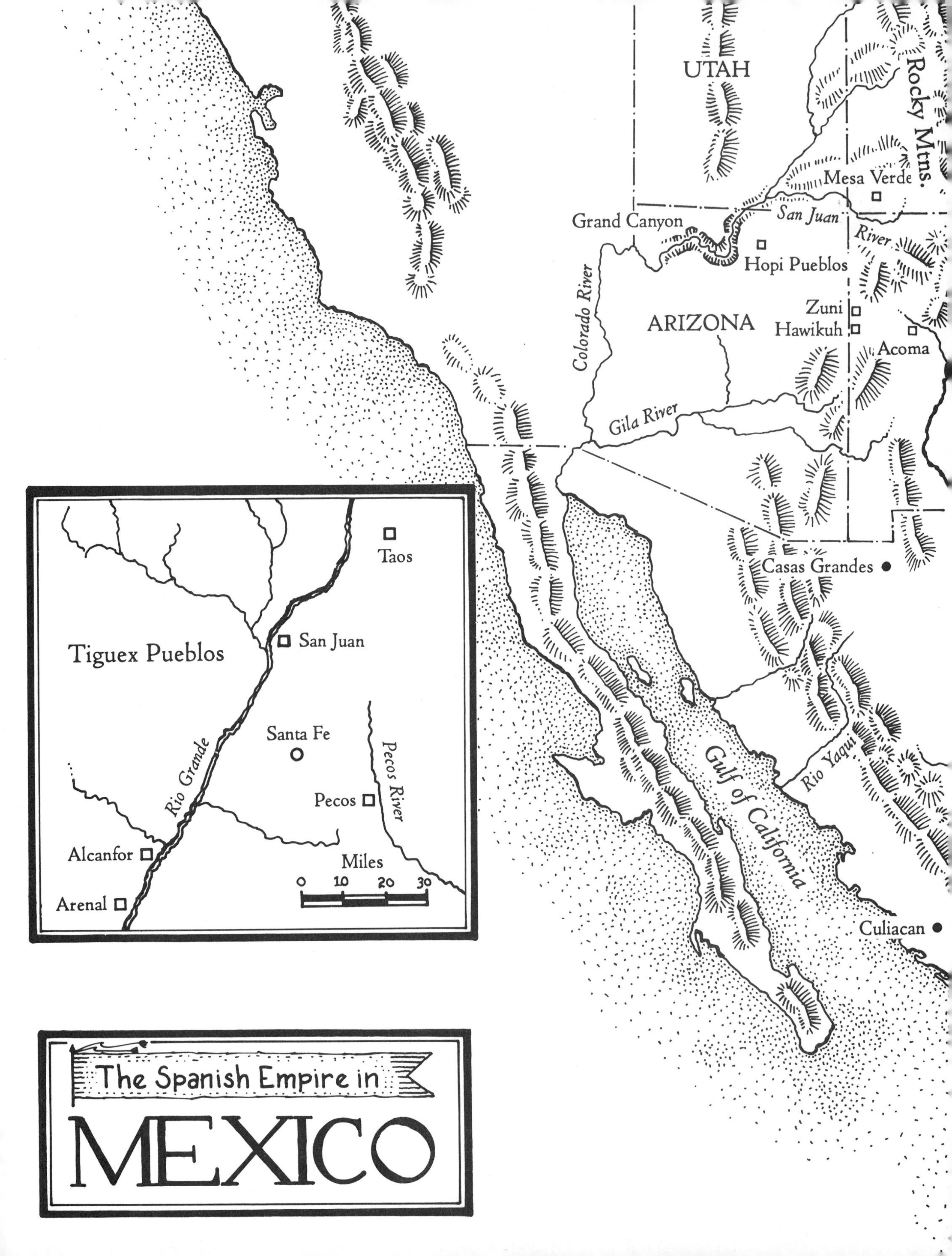
UTAH
Rocky Mtns.
Mesa Verde
Grand Canyon
San Juan
River
Hopi Pueblos
Colorado River
Zuni
Hawikuh
ARIZONA
Acoma
Gila River
Casas Grandes
Gulf of California
Rio Yaqui
Culiacan
Taos
Tiguex Pueblos
San Juan
Santa Fe
Rio Grande
Pecos River
Pecos
Alcanfor
Arenal
Miles
0
10
20
30
The Spanish Empire in
MEXICO

KANSAS (Quivira)
Missouri River
COLORADO
MISSOURI
KENTUCKY
River
TENNESSEE
Cimarron River
Arkansas River
Mississippi
Canadian River
Taos
Santa Fe
Rio Grande
OKLAHOMA
ARKANSAS
MISSISSIPPI
Fort Sumner
Fort Sill
Staked Plain
(Llano Estacado)
San Jacinto (Trinity) River
Sabine River
Red River
NEW MEXICO
Brazos River
LOUISIANA
El Paso
Juarez
Pecos River
TEXAS
Austin
Colorado River
San Antonio
Anahuac
Galveston Island
Nueces River
Goliad
Chihuahua
Rio Grande
Corpus Christi
Conchos River
Santa Barbara
Fort Brown (Brownsville)
Mier
Matamoros
Sierra Madre Mtns.
MEXICO
Monterrey
Saltillo
Gulf of Mexico
Miles
0
100
200
300
Durango
Zacatecas
Rio Panuco
Mexico City
Jalapa
Puebla
Vera Cruz

Santiago Matamoros—Saint James, Slayer of Moors—fights Spain's enemies. Saint James was the patron saint of Spain in its wars against Muslim invaders from North Africa during the Middle Ages. Drawing from Propers of the Daily Hours for Spanish Saints, a book published in Antwerp, Belgium, in 1738.

The Golden Legend

We Americans . . . abandon ourselves to the notion that our United States have been fashioned from the British Islands only, . . . which is a very great mistake.
—*Walt Whitman,* 1883

In the year A.D. 711, invaders known as Moors crossed the Mediterranean Sea to Spain from North Africa. They came in thousands and tens of thousands, a human tidal wave sweeping all that stood before it. *"Allah Akbar!"* warriors cried as they charged on sleek Arabian horses. *"Allah Akbar!"*—"God is great!" Followers of the prophet Muhammad, they were on a jihad, a holy war to destroy infidels and conquer Europe for their religion, Islam.

Unwilling to live under alien rule, seven Catholic bishops left Spain with as many Christians as could be crowded aboard a few tiny caravels, ships of about one hundred fifty tons. They sailed westward into the Atlantic Ocean, or Ocean Sea as it had been known since ancient times. It was a perilous voyage, a voyage filled with terrors worse than any nightmare could conjure. The ocean stretched before them, ending, for all they knew, at the edge of the world, over which they would tumble into the Bottomless Pit, the realm of the devil where they would suffer throughout eternity. The winds howled. The sky blackened for days on end, lit only by lightning bolts hurled by sky demons. Huge waves thundered and roared, pounding the flimsy craft as if to smash them to splinters. Writhing sea dragons threatened to turn them to ashes with their fiery breath. Yet the voyagers' faith never wavered. God heard their prayers and, in His mercy, brought them safely through the ordeal.

After many weeks an island hove into view. Antilia, as they called it, had snow-capped mountains, broad rivers, and thick forests. It abounded in everything humans needed or could ever possibly desire. Hunger was impossible in this land of plenty.

The forests teemed with game. Fertile fields yielded wheat for bread. Orchards as bountiful as the Garden of Eden bore fruit year-round. Vines heavy with grapes guaranteed the sweetest wines.

Antilia was also fabulously wealthy. Precious stones such as diamonds, rubies, and emeralds littered the ground like so many pebbles. Coastal waters teemed with clams, each containing a pearl of perfect shape and color. Whenever a farmer plowed a furrow, he turned up gold nuggets; indeed, when housewives scooped up beach sand to scour their pots and pans, it glistened with grains of gold.

Each bishop founded a city, vying with his brothers to make his the most gorgeous in the land. Church towers beckoned the faithful with crosses of pure gold as tall as hundred-year-old oak trees. The walls of public buildings were studded with gems worth a king's ransom. Poverty was unknown, for the humblest peasant dressed and lived as only a nobleman could in the Old World. Over the centuries, the cities of Antilia grew in beauty and wealth. And over the centuries Europeans never doubted their existence, as we learn from old maps of the Ocean Sea, where the island is placed in "the region away from the sunrise"; that is, in the west.

Antilia, of course, never existed. It is a legend. But like most legends it contains a kernel of truth. Spain *was* invaded by Moors, who occupied all of it except for the mountainous country in the extreme north. There the invaders faced a tough, resourceful foe bent upon winning back their land. The Spaniards began *La Reconquista,* or Reconquest, a crusade against unbelievers; indeed, it became the model for the later Crusades to retake the Holy Land from the Muslims. Spaniards had no doubt that their cause was God's, and that He fought on their side. Knights rode into battle under banners showing Christ crucified and Santiago Matamoros—Saint James the Killer of Moors, their patron saint. As they charged, they shouted *"Santiago! Santiago y a ellos!"* "Saint James! Saint James and at them!" The Reconquest continued until the Moors were expelled by the armies of King Ferdinand and Queen Isabella in 1492, only months before Christopher Columbus reached the New World.

Europeans were to believe in the Seven Cities of Antilia for over eight centuries. Columbus did; it was he who named two groups of Caribbean islands the Greater and Lesser Antilles. Giovanni Caboto, an Italian navigator who sailed for England under the name John Cabot, believed in them, too. In 1497 Cabot landed on the shores of New England and called the area the Seven Cities.

There was no reason to doubt their existence. The Age of Exploration was an age of marvels. Nothing seemed impossible, back then, or too outlandish to be believed. Columbus *had* found a new world. Spaniards *did* find gold in the West Indies, where their first settlements sprang up. Still, these discoveries were nothing compared to what awaited them on Antilia. Each discovery only fed their certainty that the golden cities would soon be found.

Gold ranked alongside God. The very word for it in Spanish, *oro,* had a magical ring. Surely, the metal could work wonders in a person's life. With enough gold, a poor fellow might return to the village of his birth as a celebrity. He could buy land, hire workers, marry a lovely lady, and enjoy his neighbor's admiration. He even might become a nobleman, or hidalgo; that is, an *hijo de algo,* a "son of someone." Why, gold had the power to open the gates of heaven itself. Had not Columbus declared, "Gold is the metal most excellent . . . and he who has it makes and accomplishes whatever he wishes in the world and finally uses it to send souls to Paradise"?[1] Spaniards, to be sure, were not alone in this belief. Europeans of every nationality were afflicted with "gold fever."

Native Americans viewed gold differently. Apart from its decorative uses, the yellow metal was too soft for tools and weapons, and therefore of no practical value. So, when they saw its effect upon the strangers, they were astonished. Indians called gold the "crazy-making metal," because the mere mention of it seemed to drive Spaniards out of their minds. The *conquistadores,* or conquerors, would stop at nothing to obtain gold. Anyone who might have some, or know where it might be found, was tortured to give it up or reveal its whereabouts. A chief pleaded with his people to surrender all they possessed for their own sake:

We must get rid of the Spanish God!
I know him.
His name is Gold!
He is more powerful than any other god.
Wherever the Spaniards go, they seek him, and it is useless to
hide it, for they have marvelous ways to find it.
If you swallow it, they will disembowel you for it.
The bottom of the sea is the only place they will not go for it.
When we have no more gold, they will leave us alone.[2]

Forty-five-year-old Hernán Cortés at the height of his fame as conqueror of Mexico.

In 1519 the most daring adventurer of the Age of Exploration sailed from Havana, Cuba, with four hundred soldiers. Hernán Cortés burned with lust for gold. Spaniards, he used to say, had a disease of the heart that only the yellow metal could cure. Almost as soon as he set foot on the Mexican coast, he met Indians who told of a golden land to the west. That was all he needed to hear! Cortés led his men to a mountain valley seven thousand feet above sea level, where he found a city of glittering temples and palaces. It was not one of the Seven Cities, but Tenochtitlán, capital of a mighty empire. Ruled by the Emperor Montezuma II, the Aztecs, or Mexica (pronounced "mesheeca"), controlled an area larger and wealthier than Spain itself. Cortés saw what he wanted, and he took it by force. Success only convinced him that what he had done was right, since God helps those who help themselves.

The Mexica were a warlike people who assumed they would always be victorious. The Spaniards, however, had better weapons, tactics, and leadership. Best of all, they had an invisible ally that silently killed their enemies in droves. "When the Christians were exhausted from war," one of Cortés's soldiers explained, "God saw fit to send the Indians smallpox."[3] Having lived with this disease for centuries, Europeans had built up a resistance to it; most victims survived after a bout of high fever. But smallpox was new to the Indians. Lacking any immunity, entire villages were often wiped out after being infected. Thus, germs did more than bullets to defeat the Mexica.

Cortés made himself lord of Mexico, which he renamed Nueva España—New Spain. He built his own capital upon the ruins of Tenochtitlán, calling it the Very Noble, Notable, and Most Loyal City of Mexico. From the outset, it was known simply as Mexico City.

Cortés's victory spurred the search for the Seven Cities of Antilia. By the 1520s, however, the island had "shifted" position. No longer did it lay in the Ocean Sea, but, thanks to Cortés's discoveries, mapmakers placed it on the mainland of North America! Since there were no accurate maps of the continent as yet, they could put Antilia anywhere they pleased without being challenged. What mattered was that Antilia existed.

Not one to rest on his laurels, Cortés became interested in the lands north of Mexico City. Expeditions were constantly sent to find the Seven Cities, or at least others as rich as his capital. In this way, Spaniards became North America's first frontiersmen. Wherever they went, they had to adapt to different peoples and different conditions. In the process, they brought European ways, European things, and European religion to a world that had been isolated for thousands of years. These sons of the Reconquest did not accept failure easily. Deep down, they knew they were on the right track. *"Poco más allá!"* they told themselves after each disappointment. "Just a little further on" and they would reach golden Antilia.

Eventually, silver was discovered in northern Mexico. It was a bonanza, greater than anything in Europe; but the Spaniards were still not satisfied. They were after gold, and gold they would have! *"Poco más allá!"* The legend of the Seven Cities acted as a magnet, drawing them deeper into the unknown. For nearly three centuries, the Spanish frontier pushed northward and westward until it stretched from the Gulf of Mexico to San Francisco Bay.

This was not North America's only frontier. Pioneers from the British colonies, then from the United States, had been moving inland from the eastern seaboard for generations. The two frontiers finally met in the early 1800s. It happened in the Southwest, an area that consists today of the states of Texas, New Mexico, Arizona, and Oklahoma.

Portion of an old map of northern Mexico showing a line of missions established by the Spaniards to Christianize the Indians.

The meeting of the two frontiers was like tossing a match into a barrel of gunpowder. When the dust settled, an empire had been lost by one people and won by another, with disastrous consequences for the Native Americans.

The Long Walk of Cabeza de Vaca

We ever held it certain that going towards the sunset we must find what we desired.
—Alvar Núñez Cabeza de Vaca

eville, Spain. A hot spring day in the year 1505. The waterfront along the Guadalquivir River.

Ships line the wharves, their jutting prows forming an archway over the cobblestoned street that runs the length of the waterfront. Each vessel has a high stern in which are mounted small brass cannons, or "mankillers," for defense against boarding parties. The hulls are painted red, blue, yellow, or any other color that happens to strike an owner's fancy. The sails are of sturdy white canvas, each with a huge cross or saint's image painted in the center. Barefoot sailors busy themselves with the thousand and one chores necessary to keep a ship in shipshape condition.

A boy in his midteens makes his way through the bustling crowds. Although he lives in nearby Jerez de la Frontera, and often has visited Seville with relatives on business, never has he found the city dull. There are always exciting things to see, to hear, to taste, and even to smell.

The Middle Ages blended with modern times in Seville. The wars of the Reconquest were still a vivid memory, and discharged men-at-arms—foot soldiers—hung around the wine shops, offering their services for any job demanding a sharp sword and tight lips. The boy listened as veterans boasted of the good old days. They spoke of tossing the heads of Moorish warriors to gangs of village boys to use as footballs and throwing Moorish children to the packs of savage dogs that roamed every town. He visited Seville's Plaza de Quemado, or place of burning, where people were burned alive for holding "dangerous" religious beliefs. Crowds flocked to the plaza to see the wicked get their just deserts and to be entertained by the gory spectacle.

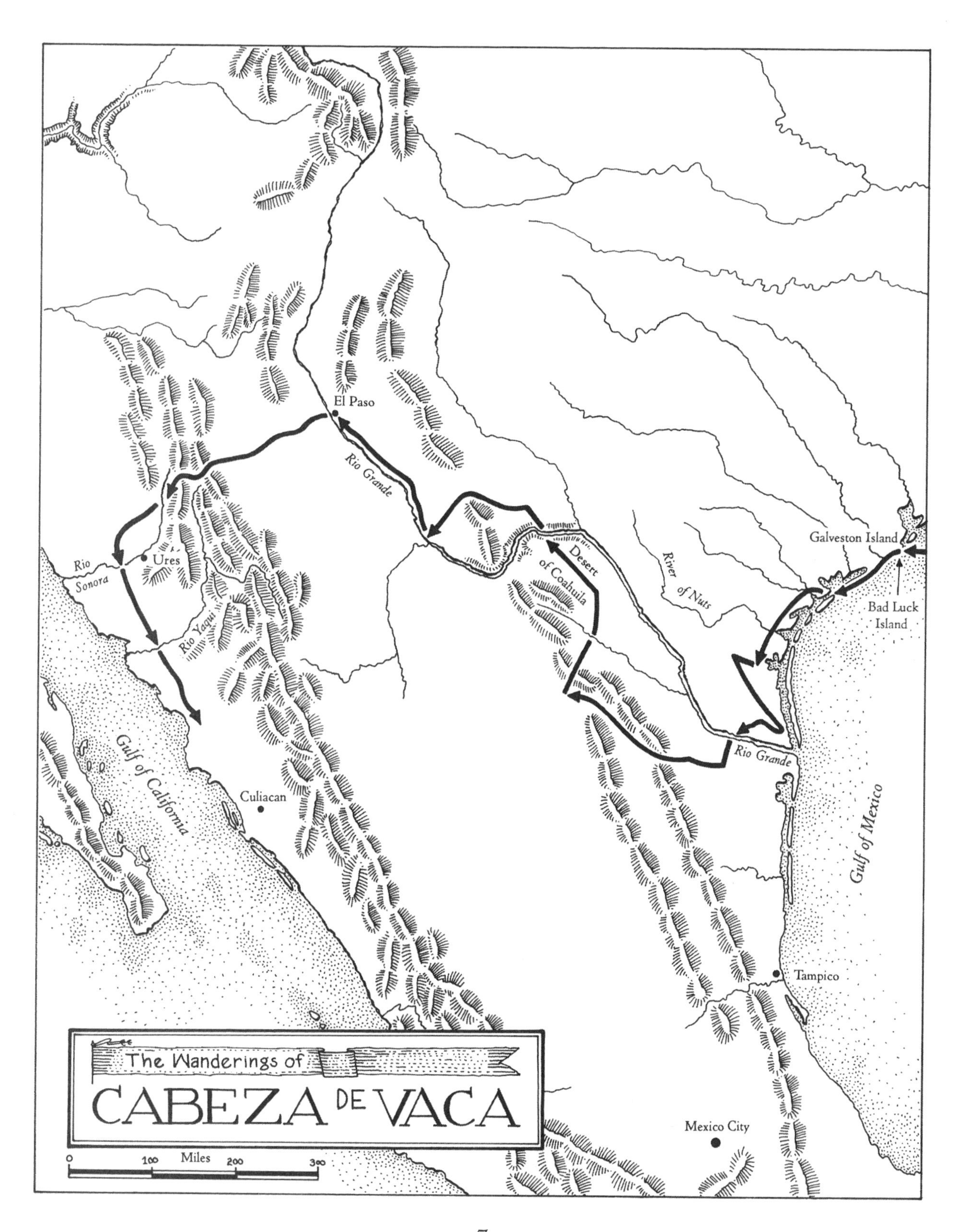
The Wanderings of
CABEZA DE VACA
El Paso
Rio Grande
Rio Sonora
Ures
Rio Yaqui
Desert of Coahuila
River of Nuts
Galveston Island
Bad Luck Island
Rio Grande
Gulf of California
Culiacan
Gulf of Mexico
Tampico
Mexico City
0
100
Miles
200
300

There, too, you could see jugglers, acrobats, puppeteers, and traveling minstrels. It was one vast open-air theater where, for a few copper coins, you need never be bored.

The waterfront, however, was the city's chief attraction. Seville held the monopoly on trade with the New World. Ships arrived weekly, bearing riches and wonders, or departed laden with trade goods, royal officials, adventurers, and Franciscan friars—priests devoted to saving the Indians' souls by converting them to Christianity. To the boy, the waterfront was a kaleidoscope of humanity. Its crowds seemed to represent every people on earth: swarthy Portuguese and Italians, fair-skinned Germans, and Dutchmen, enslaved blacks from Africa, painted Indians from the West Indies. The Indians had been kidnapped not to toil as slaves, but to learn Spanish in order to act as interpreters for future expeditions of exploration and conquest. The boy watched wide-eyed as they played *paillette,* a New World version of soccer, only more strenuous. The game's object was to get a wooden ball the size of a peach over a goal line by using only the hips, chest, shoulders, and head.

When a ship unloaded, the boy struggled to contain his excitement. Sailors came ashore with parrots, monkeys, lizards, and snakes that had bodies thick as a wrestler's thigh. Vendors offered slices of pineapple and sweet potatoes. Tobacco leaves were sold as a medicine; they were even supposed to cure cancer! Then there was the gold. It, more than anything else, captured the onlookers' attention.

Oxcarts hauled gold bars to Seville's customhouse, where they were weighed and the king's share, one-fifth of everything, was set aside to be collected by officials from the Royal Treasury. This was a heavy tax, but not an unbearable one, given the wealth that poured across the Ocean Sea. A half-million ounces of gold arrived each year just from the island of Hispaniola, shared today by Haiti and the Dominican Republic. Everyone knew about the gold nugget weighing 320 ounces found in an island stream; a roasted pig was served on it during a banquet. Whenever treasure arrived, some lucky fellows were sure to celebrate by sprinkling their food with gold dust, not for the taste, but to show how wealthy and important they had become. Yet anyone could strike it just as rich, if they were at the right place at the right time. Once Spaniards found the Seven Cities of Antilia, those others would be considered paupers!

The boy looked and listened, learned and dreamed. Little did he know that he would become one of the greatest explorers of the age. Had he known the circumstances, however, he might have begged God to spare him the "honor."

His full name was Alvar Núñez de Vera y Cabeza de Vaca. That letter *y,* Spanish for "and," tells a fascinating story. As is often the case with Spaniards, the boy had two last names joined together. The first was his father's, de Vera. The second, Cabeza de Vaca, was his mother's maiden name. That is the name he chose, and the one by which he has always been known.

It had a proud history. Until the year 1212, his mother's ancestors were peasants called "Alhaja"—"Jewel." In that year, the Reconquest nearly ended in failure at a strategic mountain pass blocked by the Moors. Unable to advance, the Spanish cause seemed lost until Martin Alhaja offered to show the army a little-used trail, which local people had marked with the skull of a cow. The Spaniards won a decisive victory. The grateful king made the peasant a nobleman, gave him land, and changed his family name in honor of his achievement. Thus, "Jewel" became Cabeza de Vaca—"Cowhead."

Alvar Núñez was born in Jerez de la Frontera around the year 1490. The eldest of four children, he grew into a fine man, intelligent, honest, and loyal. Like so many youngsters of his social class, he became a soldier. Although the Reconquest was over, there was still plenty of fighting to do. By the age of twenty-one, however, he had seen enough of war to last a lifetime. He returned from a campaign in Italy *muy destroçado,* roughly "all wiped out," by the experience. Home at last, he married; his wife's name has been lost to history, and it is not known if they had any children. Little, in fact, is known about Cabeza de Vaca's activities until he sailed for the New World.

We do know that during visits to Seville he always tried to visit the waterfront. It still held the same fascination as during his boyhood. One day a parade attracted his attention. Drummers marched along, banging as if to rouse the dead. They were followed by gaily dressed men carrying brightly colored banners with long streamers. Finally, there came the public crier, telling all able-bodied men and true Christians that an expedition to the New World was forming. Anyone who signed up would have adventures to tell his grandchildren about, make his fortune, and enjoy God's favor for helping the church convert the heathen natives.

The expedition was led by Pánfilo de Narváez. Ten years Cabeza de Vaca's senior, Narváez was a tall, heavyset man with a flaming red beard and a voice that sounded "as if it came from a cave."[1] A leader in the conquest of Cuba, he was a brave soldier and no friend of Hernán Cortés. Sent by the governor of Cuba to arrest Cortés for disobedience, he lost an eye in a surprise attack and spent three years as a prisoner in Mexico City. Released in 1523, he returned to Spain with a silk patch over the empty eye socket and a determination to conquer a land richer than New Spain.

Narváez already had such a place in mind. In 1521 Juan Ponce de León—John of the Lion's Paunch—landed in Florida, to which he gave the Spanish name for Easter—Pascua Florida, "Feast of Flowers." He had come in search of gold and the Fountain of Youth, a magical spring whose water, drunk daily, was supposed to keep a person youthful forever. But instead of the marvelous spring, Ponce de León found death on the point of an Indian arrow.

After months of haggling with the authorities, Narváez won the title of Governor of Florida. All he had to do was go there, conquer its inhabitants, and plunder their riches. Naturally, the profits must be shared with His Royal Majesty, although he, Narváez, must pay all costs and bear all losses himself. Being a conquistador had always been a gamble. Not only did you risk life and limb, but also a great deal of money. More than one conquistador ended his days in poverty.

Narváez gathered seven ships and six hundred men for the expedition, among them Cabeza de Vaca. No ordinary adventurer, Cabeza de Vaca held two important positions. As treasurer, he kept the expedition's records, seeing to it that each member got his fair share of the expected loot. As provost, the officer in charge of discipline, he enforced the expedition's rules. He must also have had a photographic memory. His book *The Journey of Alvar Núñez Cabeza de Vaca and His Companions from Florida to the Pacific, 1528–1536* was written from memory upon his return to Spain and printed in the year 1542. It is one of the finest eyewitness accounts of the Age of Exploration.

Spanish cavalry in action. These soldiers are not wearing suits of armor, but quilted leather jackets modeled upon Aztec armor, lightweight gear more suitable to the Mexican climate. Drawing from Lienzo de Tlaxcala, a book written in the Mexican city of Tlaxcala around the year 1550.

Cabeza de Vaca had joined a compact little army. Each soldier wore armor suitable to his wealth and position in society. Officers had breastplates, helmets, and armpieces of steel. Men-at-arms wore iron or leather helmets and chain-mail armor, steel links joined together to form flexible "nightshirts" reaching below the knees. Armed with a variety of weapons, they had swords; daggers; crossbows; muskets; spears; and halberds, stout poles tipped with iron points and edged with blades resembling large meat cleavers. Cavalrymen carried a sword, a lance, and a "morning star"—that is, an iron ball with spikes dangling from a length of chain. Their chief weapon, however, was the very horses they rode. Horses had once existed in the New World, but they vanished toward the close of the last Ice Age, twenty-five thousand years ago. Spaniards reintroduced the horse, and it became a decisive weapon. Never having seen such an animal, Indians were at first terrified of it; they thought it ate human flesh. On the battlefield, it gave the Spaniards speed and maneuverability. Handfuls of riders often crashed through hordes of Mexica without losing a man. Horses, too, wore armor, usually leather sheets draped over each side, with iron plates to protect the forehead.

Spanish soldiers in action, as seen by Indians. Notice their use of a combination of firearms and traditional weapons: spears and crossbows. From a drawing in Códice Florentino, around the year 1560. A codex—códice in Spanish—is the manuscript of an ancient document bound as a book.

The fleet left Seville on June 7, 1527. There was truth in the Spanish proverb "He who puts to sea, believes in God." A voyage across the Atlantic was an ordeal to test the courage of the bravest person. At best, it took seven weeks, depending on the winds, to reach the New World. At worst, a vessel might spend five months sailing against contrary winds, during which time most of the ship's company died of disease and starvation.

A ship's company was divided into two sections: sailors and landsmen. Sailors were virtual slaves. Completely under the captain's control, they could not even undress without his permission. But they did have one thing in their favor: they were the strongest of the strong, having survived past voyages. Soldiers were landsmen. Few, if any, had ever been on the ocean, or knew what lay ahead of them. They learned quickly enough.

Crowded belowdecks in dark, dank compartments reeking of sweat and mildew, they slept under goatskins on mats stuffed with dog hair. Rations were salt beef, pork, or fish; rice; honey; figs; olive oil; wine; and hardtack, a thin, flat bread baked as hard as a dog biscuit. Usually the food was rotten and crawled with worms. Not that landsmen noticed these creatures or were put off by the taste. The constant rolling of the ship, even in fair weather, made them seasick. The fortunate ones were able to lean over the deck rails in time; the less fortunate vomited where

Indians of southwest Florida await the landing of some unidentified Europeans. The explorer Ponce de León named the area Pascua Florida, for the Easter Feast of Flowers. Based on a drawing by Jacque Le Moyne Morgues, a sixteenth-century French artist.

they sat, over themselves and their neighbors. Dirt bred lice, fleas, and cockroaches as big as a man's thumb. Then there were the rats, fierce brutes with blazing eyes that bit sleepers and fought like tigers when cornered.

The fleet reached Florida after spending the winter at the Caribbean island of Hispaniola, where two hundred men deserted and two ships sank in a storm. On April 22, 1528, Narváez carried the Spanish flag ashore at Tampa Bay. Natives watching from their hiding places must have been puzzled at what happened next. No sooner did this shiny-skinned figure scramble out of a boat, when he ran to the beach and stuck the flagpole into the sand. Then he unrolled a piece of parchment and began to *read!* While soldiers stood at attention, he droned on for half an hour, his voice rising almost to a shout when he came to certain passages.

There were reasons for such behavior. Although conquistadors were often brutal, they were not outlaws. Quite the opposite; they were supposed to be acting in the name of God and their king. Narváez read from *El Requerimiento,* the Requirement, a legal document stating that he had a license to take possession of unclaimed lands for Spain. The inhabitants of this country, he read, should rejoice. His Royal Majesty, King Carlos, had generously and graciously decided to take pity upon them. Not only did he wish to protect them from enemies, he had sent priests to instruct them in "our Holy Catholic Faith" so as to win them a place in heaven. All they had to do was swear allegiance to king and church. If they refused, or later broke their oath, he, Narváez, would be ruthless.

> With the help of Our Lord I will enter with force, making war upon you from all directions. . . . I will take the persons of yourselves, your wives, and children to make slaves . . . and I will take your goods, doing you all the evil and injury I may be able.[2]

These actions were legitimate in the eyes of Christian men and holy in the eyes of their church. Every expedition was accompanied by a priest whose duty was to see that such things were done in the right way.

Had the Indians understood Narváez, they would probably have thought him insane. It would be like spacemen landing on Earth and claiming it the moment they stepped from their rocket ship! Indians (and earthlings) had inhabited their lands for ages. In their eyes, that was a just claim. The strangers disagreed. They claimed to be superior to the natives; indeed, they considered natives merely a higher form of animal, albeit an animal in human form. Natives were *gente sin razón,* Spaniards said—"people without reason." It followed, therefore, that their country was *terra nullis,* or "land belonging to no one," until Christians claimed it for themselves.

Narváez's men came to a deserted village near the beach. Searching the huts, they found something that made their hearts leap for joy. It was a golden ornament.

The villagers returned the next day and made signs that the intruders should leave immediately. Narváez made signs of his own. He held out the ornament, asking if there were any more like it. Once they understood what he wanted, the Indians smiled, pointed northward, and cried, "Apalachen! Apalachen!" Apparently, the gold came from a place with that name.

No one can say if they were telling the truth. Native Americans were definitely not *gente sin razón.* They often invented tales of fabulous lands "just a little further on" to get rid of their uninvited guests. In any case, Narváez decided to send the fleet up the coast to find a harbor, while he led the army on foot to golden Apalachen.

Cabeza de Vaca shook his head. The Spaniards had no knowledge of the country whatsoever, he said. How would the army find the ships once they anchored? Would it not be wiser to secure a harbor, send search parties inland, and then proceed with the land force? Narváez lost his temper. Perhaps, he sneered, Señor Cowhead would prefer to remain safely with the ships and the women; ten officers had brought their wives on the expedition.

It became a matter of honor. The treasurer was a gentleman, and a gentleman would rather risk his life than his good name. Cowheads were not cowards. Come what may, he must go with the land force.

The women, however, sensed that Cabeza de Vaca was right. Certain of never seeing their husbands again, they married the ships' officers as soon as they were well out to sea. Their gamble with bigamy paid off. Failing to find a harbor, the fleet returned to Tampa Bay. After cruising along the coast for nearly a year without finding their comrades, the crews sailed for Cuba. The Narváez expedition was written off as lost by the authorities. It was not the first time such a disaster had occurred, nor would it be the last, they said. Exploration, after all, was a risky business.

Meanwhile, the army marched northward, tortured by the climate. Florida is subtropical; that is, it borders on the tropics to the south. For Narváez and his men, Florida was a damp part of hell, equally hot, and with bugs. Heat waves shimmered before their eyes, and the humidity made it feel like breathing with a wet blanket over your face. Armor rubbed skin raw, causing infections. Clouds of flies the size of honeybees hovered over the column. Men's faces became masses of swollen sores; horses' sides ran with blood. Tiny gnats filled the marchers' ears and noses. Their bites felt like electrified needles. Every time a Spaniard ate, gnats flew into his mouth. Still the expedition pushed on, drawn by visions of gold.

A march of fifty-five days brought the Spaniards to Apalachen, just south of today's Florida-Georgia border. Their hearts sank. What a godforsaken place! This was not another Mexico City, but a village of forty thatch huts built on the shore of a lake fringed with forests and swamps. Its only inhabitants were frightened women and children of the Apalachee tribe; the men had fled at the strangers' approach. There was plenty of maize (Indian corn), but not a grain of gold.

Next morning the tribesmen came in a fury. The Apalachee were unlike any warriors the Spaniards had met thus far in the New World. Tall, strapping fellows, they

Timucuan Indians of northwestern Florida on their way to fight enemies, as seen by Jacque Le Moyne Morgues. In the center of the massed warriors is the tribal leader, and at the head of the force are war and religious leaders.

were born guerrilla fighters. They used a weapon similar to the English longbow, famous for driving steel-pointed arrows through suits of armor. Only their bow was more powerful than any known in Europe. Thick as a man's wrist, it could send an arrow two hundred yards with pinpoint accuracy. Although the Apalachee had no metal, they tipped their shafts with flint points. Cabeza de Vaca tells of seeing two oak trees, each the thickness of his thigh, pierced by such arrows. One whizzed past his nose, plunging six inches into a poplar tree. A well-aimed arrow could bury itself up to the feathers in a horse's body.[3]

The Apalachee shot often and well. A warrior would let off several arrows in the time it took a Spaniard to reload his musket. By the time the gun was ready to be fired, the bowman had vanished. Unlike the Mexica, who fought in masses in the open, these warriors believed in stealth. Hidden behind trees and in tall grass, they rained arrows on the enemy, retreating at the first sign of danger. Narváez's horsemen would overrun a position, only to find it deserted; the warriors had dived into a swamp, where they breathed through hollow reeds. When the coast was clear, they renewed the fight from another direction.

Narváez was disgusted. After a month of chasing shadows, he decided to return to the coast. That was when Cabeza de Vaca's warnings hit like a ton of bricks. No ships awaited them, only putrid marshes and barren sand dunes. The sea was their only hope of survival. They must build other vessels and find Pánuco, a tiny port near the present city of Tampico, Mexico. Yet that was easier said than done. Nobody knew how far they would have to sail to reach their destination. The best guess was two hundred miles; the actual distance was over a thousand miles!

There were only two craftsmen in the army, and neither knew anything about building boats. Still, necessity is the mother of invention, and they were clever fellows. The first man, a blacksmith, made the necessary tools. He began with a hole in the ground lined with clay, which he connected to a bellows of wooden pipes and deerskins. As the temperature rose inside the clay "pot," every piece of metal that could be spared—armor, muskets, spear points, halberd blades, belt buckles, spurs, stirrups, chains—was melted down. When cool, the metal was fashioned into nails, hammers, axes, and saws. These the second man, a carpenter, used to make five crude barges, each thirty-three feet in length. Split saplings became oars. Shirts were sewn together and turned into sails. The horses were killed for food and the leftovers used in any number of ways. For example, hides covered the vessels' sides; hair was woven into ropes and rigging; the skins were peeled off the legs and made into water containers.

On September 22, 1528, Narváez gave the order to sail. Slowly, the ungainly craft pulled away from shore. Crowded on board, sitting elbow to elbow, were 246 men, naked except for a threadbare covering around their waists. No longer was it a question of finding gold and ruling Indian slaves. Now their very lives hung in the balance, and they knew it. "So great is the power of need," wrote Cabeza de Vaca, "that it brought us to venture out into such a troubled sea in this manner, and without any one among us having the least knowledge of the art of navigation."[4] All they knew was how to set a southerly course and stick to it.

The sea was pitiless. A storm tossed them about, sending men to watery graves. Then the wind stopped. For a week they stood motionless, becalmed under the blazing sun. Sunburn caused excruciating pain. Water ran out, forcing wretched men to drink salt water, which drove them insane before they died. When the wind picked up, they landed, often only to be attacked again by Indians. At best, they found a few handfuls of maize and a mouthful of water to keep them going a little longer. They passed the mouth of a wide river, whose current turned the salt water fresh hundreds of yards from shore. It was the Mississippi. One by one, the barges separated at night or were blown out to sea, to be lost with all hands aboard. Finally, only Cabeza de Vaca's barge remained. As the senior officer, he was in charge. But things had slipped out of his control weeks earlier. He and his men were at the mercy of forces greater than their own.

He knew they were nearing the end. On November 6, before dawn, only he was awake; his companions had collapsed from hunger and exhaustion. "I would have hailed death with delight," he recalled, "rather than to see so many people around me in such a condition."[5]

Suddenly, he felt a strange pulling sensation. The barge began to gain speed. In the distance, he saw the dim outline of a coast. The barge went faster, faster. The roar of the breakers grew louder, louder. The undertow was so strong that, before he knew it, the barge was flung completely out of the water, landing on the beach with a bone-crunching thud. The shock awoke his companions with a start. Realizing what had happened, they used their last reserves of energy to crawl out on all fours.

They were on an island off the Texas coast, most likely Galveston Island or nearby San Luis Island. But in their condition, they could not think about geography. Hardly able to move, let alone defend themselves, they could only wait to see what fate had in store for them.

Sure enough, they had been spotted by Indian warriors. They were completely naked and seemed to be grinning oddly because each wore a piece of cane a half-finger thick through his pierced lower lip. "Our fright was such that, whether tall or little, it made them appear giants to us,"[6] Cabeza de Vaca recalled.

These were peaceful giants. When they saw the miserable castaways, they burst into tears of sympathy. Leaving arrows as a token of friendship, they returned the following day with plenty of food. Since the Spaniards were too weak to move on their own and it had grown bitterly cold, the Indians decided to take them to their village. Bonfires were built at several points along the way. After a Spaniard had warmed himself awhile, two warriors carried him to the next one so quickly that his feet barely touched the ground. How the mighty had fallen! These would-be conquerors had been reduced to such a state that they were as infants in the hands of *gente sin razón.* But instead of harming them, the natives felt their pain and were doing whatever they could to help them. It was a valuable lesson in humility; the first of many.

A surprise awaited them at the village. Not only were they treated as honored guests, they learned that other white men had come from the sea a few days earlier and were staying at a neighboring village. Instantly, Cabeza de Vaca realized that another barge had been wrecked on the island. A messenger was sent, and by evening eighty tearful Spaniards were thanking God for sparing their lives and bringing them together. But with winter approaching, it was necessary to distribute them among several villages to share the burden of feeding them. Come spring, they could decide on their next move. Meantime, they would have all they could do to survive.

Their hosts were a Stone Age people whose tools were stone axes and knives, and fishhooks of bone. They had never planted a crop, woven a piece of cloth, or raised an animal for its meat and hide. Their food consisted of fish, oysters, and the roots of edible plants that grew underwater. Still, there was a certain dignity about them. Cabeza de Vaca was impressed by their kindness toward each other. These people no longer exist, wiped out by European diseases and "progress," so his description is their only monument:

> Of all the people in the world, they are those who most love their children and treat them best, and should the child of one of them happen to die, parents and relatives bewail it, and the whole settlement, the lament lasting a full year. . . . They mourn all their dead in this way, old people excepted, to whom they do not pay any attention, saying that these have had their time and are no longer of any use, but only take space, and food from the children. . . . Their custom is to bury the dead, whom they burn, and while the fire is burning, all dance and make a big festival, grinding the bones to powder. At the end of the year, when they celebrate the anniversary, they . . . give to the relatives the pulverized bones to drink in water. [Drinking powdered bones was a way of magically capturing the power of a dead person for the use of the living.][7]

Winter held the island in its icy grip. Food became so scarce that the castaways dubbed it "Misfortune Island." The natives had schooled themselves to hunger; it had always been their lot, and they accepted it without complaint as a regular part of existence. If there was less to eat, people died; it was that simple. Spaniards, too, began to die, some in a horrible fashion. Visiting a hut outside a village, Indians found five bodies, four with the flesh peeled off the bones. The Spaniards had eaten each other one by one; the fifth man, left alone, starved when there was no one else to eat.[8] The islanders were outraged. As hungry as they might be, they never ate their own kind. Forbidding cannibalism made sense. If it were allowed in the worst of times, it might get out of hand, causing the destruction of the entire tribe. Better to have some members starve than risk the ultimate disaster. The hunger-crazed Spaniards had fewer qualms.

In April 1529 the Indians went to the Texas mainland in search of food. Cabeza de Vaca claimed that he and his companions were enslaved at this time. It probably seemed that way to them. Only fifteen Spaniards had survived the winter, thanks to their hosts' generosity. They had lived off them for five months and were now expected to earn their keep. Since they had no special skills, they were given basic tasks, like digging underwater roots with their bare hands. It was difficult work. Cabeza de Vaca's fingers became so sensitive that "the mere touch of a straw caused them to bleed."[9] Still, he was no slave. A slave is human property that may be sold at the master's whim. Nobody owned the Spaniards, who were free to leave whenever they pleased.

And that is exactly what they did. Once on the mainland, they struck out in the direction of Pánuco; all, that is, except Cabeza de Vaca, who had come down with a fever. Since he was not expected to live, his comrades left him behind. By the time the Indians returned to Misfortune Island, he had recovered. Rather than go back, he chose to stay on the mainland.

He survived by becoming a peddler, the perfect occupation for someone like himself. As an outsider, he was considered neutral by the feuding tribes. Whenever they needed anything from outside their own territory, they turned to the white stranger. Traveling deep into the interior, barefoot, a pack on his back, he carried goods from the coast: seashells for making beads, conches for knife blades, shark-oil insect repellent. These he exchanged for items desired by the coastal peoples: flint for arrow points, red ocher for dying the face and hair, deerskins for clothing. He also brought the leaves of the yaupon plant, the ingredient in the Indians' "black drink." When boiled, yaupon leaves turn water black, releasing a dose of caffeine many times stronger than coffee. Used during religious festivals, black drink made worshipers hyperactive and gave them strange visions.

Cabeza de Vaca always found a warm welcome in the villages he visited. Upon arriving, tribesmen rubbed their hands on their own breasts, then on his; as a special sign of friendship, they blew into his ear. He was so popular, thanks to his trade goods, that he had no trouble finding winter quarters.

The peddler was aided by his knowledge of the Indians' sign language. Since there were dozens of tribes, each speaking its own language, the only means of communication was by hand motions that everyone understood; those motions were to become the model for the sign language used by the deaf. His main object, however, was to learn about the mainland tribes and their country. One day he hoped to go in search of his fellow Spaniards. When that day came, the information he gained would be invaluable.

The mainland tribes, like the inhabitants of Misfortune Island, were people of the Stone Age. They did, however, enjoy a wider variety of food: spiders, ant eggs, termites, worms, salamanders, lizards, snakes. Earth, rotten wood, and, whenever available, deer manure was eaten by children as well as adults. Mothers continued to breast-feed their youngsters up to the age of twelve. Strange as it seemed to a European, this made sense in a world where you could never be sure of your next meal. It was an investment in the future, a way of seeing that the next generation survived even if adults went hungry.

Cabeza de Vaca's customers taught him a lot about human relations. Tribes fought constantly, yet violence within each tribe was strictly controlled. Weapons could not be used to settle quarrels. Anger was allowed to burn itself out, rather than spread until it involved the entire community.

> When, in any village, they quarrel among themselves, they beat and strike each other [with fists] until worn out, and only then do they separate. Sometimes their women step in and separate them, but men never interfere in these brawls. Nor do they use any bow and arrow, and after they have fought and settled the question, they take their lodges and their women and go out into the field to live apart from the others until their anger is over, and when they are no longer angry and their resentment has passed away they return to the village and are as

> friendly as if nothing had happened. There is no need of mediation. When the quarrel is between unmarried people they go to some of the neighbors, who, even if they be enemies, will receive them well, with great festivities and gifts of what they have, so that, when pacified, they return to their village wealthy.[10]

It was different in Europe. There a gentleman was expected to defend his honor with sword, dagger, and pistol. Men were touchy about their honor, dueling over the slightest "insult"; even a dispute over the spelling of a word brought a challenge. The peddler's own kin had shed plenty of blood in matters of honor. His grandfather, Pedro de Vaca, once overheard a nobleman criticize the king. He took it personally—*very* personally! He knifed the villain, tore out his tongue, and threw it at the bystanders.

Cabeza de Vaca found homosexuals among the tribes he visited. It disgusted him to see "a man married to another."[11] Homosexual couples dressed as women and did women's work, yet they used the bow and arrow and hunted. Such behavior was not uncommon in the Southwest, as elsewhere in the New World; explorers in New Mexico later described "men dressed like women who marry other men and serve as their wives."[12] As Christians, the Spaniards condemned homosexuality as a sin, certain to bring down God's wrath. Nevertheless, Indians regarded homosexuals as useful members of society, barring them only from fighting and gaining war honors.

The more Cabeza de Vaca learned, the more downcast he became. He was trapped. A person traveling alone could not possibly survive in the Texas wilderness. His only hope lay in finding other whites to share the dangers. Yet he had not seen any of his own kind for three years.

In 1532 he visited an encampment on the bank of a river. Tribesmen called it the River of Nuts, because they came there each fall to gather pecans for the winter. His arrival created a stir, which was overheard by a man working in one of the lodges. Stepping outside to see what was going on, the man came face-to-face with Cabeza de Vaca. The peddler was stunned. Here was a familiar face—a *Spanish* face! Instantly they recognized each other, embraced, and burst into tears of joy.

The man was Andrés Dorantes, a professional soldier who had served in the European wars. And he was not alone. Moments later he introduced his two companions. One was Alonso de Castillo, a doctor's son turned gambler and adventurer. The other was called Estevanico, or Little Stephen. Estevanico was anything but little. A

Cabeza de Vaca and his three companions trade with a group of Indians.

giant of a man with a bull neck and bulging muscles, he was a black Moor who had been enslaved by the Spaniards in childhood and raised as a Christian. These three, Cabeza de Vaca learned, were the last of the group that had been with him on Misfortune Island, the others having died of hunger, disease, and Indian arrows. "We gave many thanks at seeing ourselves together," he wrote, "and this was a day to us of the greatest pleasure we had enjoyed in life."[13]

They agreed to set out for Pánuco the following summer. Summer was the tuna season, when the tribes went farthest inland. The Indians' tuna was not a fish, but the prickly pear cactus, which grew in thickets covering hundreds of square miles near the present city of San Antonio. Its fruit is the size of a hen's egg and reddish black in color. Natives squeezed out the sweet juice and stuffed themselves with the ripe fruit until their bellies bulged and they could scarcely move. Tribes traveled long distances to feast on the fruit. However much they hated each other, during the harvest they observed the Truce of the Tuna. No one dared raise a weapon while the truce lasted.

The peddler continued his travels, while his comrades remained with the Indians. Unfortunately, a quarrel over a woman caused the three to leave the tuna thickets before Cabeza de Vaca arrived in 1533. After losing an entire year, the Spaniards were finally reunited in 1534. On September 21, they left together.

Before long, they came to a village of the Avavare people. The tribesmen were wary of the strangers until Cabeza de Vaca won their confidence. It so happened that one of the warriors had a splitting headache. The peddler volunteered to help. During his travels, he had watched Indian medicine men treat all sorts of illnesses. When a person fell ill, they usually rubbed the painful spot, made a cut with a sharp stone, sucked the skin around the wound and spat to the four directions. Finally, they blew on the wound and announced that the patient was cured. Sometimes patients recovered, and sometimes they did not. They probably would have recovered anyhow; most pains go away by themselves in due time. Nevertheless, a strong belief in a cure or in a curer can speed recovery.

Cabeza de Vaca decided to try his hand at curing. It was a gamble, he knew, but he realized the odds were in his favor. To increase them, he made a small but critical change in method. Combining Indian medicine with Christian belief, he began by blessing the patient and making the sign of the cross. Everyone took notice; this was not what they were used to seeing. Then he rubbed the patient's head, blew on him, and said a prayer. The warrior's headache vanished. The Avavares gave the strangers all they could eat.

A few days later, Cabeza de Vaca was asked to bring a dead man back to life. Here was a problem! If he refused to try, the Avavares might see their guests as ungrateful, even as enemies. But if he tried and failed, they might put them to death as witches. So he tried his best. Sure enough, the "corpse" was up and about next morning. We know that the man could not have died; most likely, he was in a coma or having a seizure from which he recovered naturally. Indians, however, knew nothing of comas and seizures; nor did the "doctor," who sincerely believed God was working through him. As word of the cure spread, people came from far and wide with various complaints: cramps, chills, fevers, sore throats, indigestion. Soon there more patients than he could handle, forcing his companions to learn the healer's art.[14] In the eyes of the Indians, they were no longer mortals. They were "Children of the Sun," sacred beings come from the sky.

Winter and hunger, the old enemies, returned with a vengeance. Not even Children of the Sun could be excused from work at such a critical time. Given skins to scrape and tan, they scraped deeply in order to eat the scraps. Naked except for an animal skin around the waist, they shivered in the Texas northers, frigid winds that blew from the north. Their bodies became covered with sores, and twice they shed their entire skins "like snakes." Only faith in God kept them going. "In all that trouble," wrote Cabeza de Vaca, "my only relief or consolation was to remember the passion of our Savior . . . and to ponder how much greater His sufferings had been . . . than those I was then enduring."[15] They survived, barely. By the spring of 1535, they were ready to move on.

The long walk was about to begin.

Avavare warriors took them southward to a river as wide as the Guadalquivir at Seville. It was the Rio Grande, *the* great river of the Southwest. They were the first whites to see it. Rising in the mountains of southern Colorado, it winds its way to the Gulf of Mexico nineteen hundred miles away. Next to the Saint Lawrence and the Mississippi-Missouri system, it is the longest river in North America.

Crossing the Rio Grande, they found their way blocked by mountain ranges. They could have avoided the mountains by turning east. Pánuco lay in that direction, scarcely more than three hundred miles away, but they had no idea it was so close. What they did know was that going east would bring them back to the coast, with all its evil memories. Instead they decided to follow the setting sun, a route that was to add two thousand miles to their journey. Not that they cared. They had changed during their eight months with the Avavare. Somehow they had come to see themselves differently. No longer were they castaways living a hand-to-mouth existence. Now they were explorers with a mission: to help other Spaniards who might follow in their footsteps.

The Avavare put them under the protection of friends across the Rio Grande, who escorted them through their territory before giving them into the care of those beyond, and so on from tribe to tribe. Historians disagree on their exact route. Cabeza de Vaca was confused himself, admitting, "We . . . traveled through so many sorts of people, of such diverse languages, the memory fails to recall them."[16] Apparently, they skirted the Sierra Madre mountains, moving in a northerly direction until they reached the desert of Coahuila. Food was scarce in the desert, forcing them to eat powdered straw. Recrossing the Rio Grande in the Big Bend country of Texas, they followed it to the vicinity of present-day El Paso. There they crossed the river for a third time and headed west into the Mexican state of Sonora.

Their fame raced ahead of them with the speed of a prairie fire. At sunrise each morning, scouts set out to mark the trail and hunt game for the evening meal. The Children of the Sun followed several miles behind, accompanied by three to four thousand Indians. Their bodies daubed with paint, the bearded men wore only animal skins wrapped around their waists and wooden crosses dangling from their necks on cords of braided hair. Bone-deep suntans gave them the color of dark chocolate. Estevanico was a bundle of energy, strutting along with a smile on his face and colorful feathers in his hair; he was free for the time being, the equal of any man. Nothing fazed them. They had seen it all, endured it all, and had been hardened by experiences that would have killed ordinary mortals. The Indians, Cabeza de Vaca recalled, "never saw us tired, because we were, in reality, so inured to hardships as not to feel them any more."[17] They felt indestructible.

Indian women did the heavy work, as was the custom. Lacking draft animals, everything that had to be moved had to go in their arms or on their backs. They carried the straw mats for the lodge walls, deerskin blankets, and hollow gourds filled with water. Pregnant women marched, too, and carried heavy loads as well. When they felt their time had come, they dropped out of the procession to give birth. They did so alone, by the roadside or behind a bush. An hour later, they would bring their newborns to the healers to be blessed. The babies clutched bits of food in their fists; if the holy men accepted the gifts, mothers believed they would never get sick.

By late afternoon the procession halted at a place marked by the scouts. Women set up the lodges, fetched water, and waited for the scouts to bring in the day's kill. Food was eaten raw or cooked in a gourd pot. Stones heated in a fire were dropped into a gourd filled with water. When the water boiled, meat was put in to cook. Stones were taken out as they cooled and replaced by hot ones to keep the water boiling.

No one would eat a thing unless the holy men blessed it first. Satisfying those who believed in their powers became a chore. "It was very tiresome," noted Cabeza de Vaca, "to have to breathe on and make the sign of the cross over every morsel they ate or drank."[18] And as the Spaniards ate, everyone watched them in silence, it being considered bad luck, even fatal, to disturb their meal. When, for example, a child cried, its parents took it away and scratched it with rat teeth fastened to a stick.

As they neared a village, messengers ran ahead with the wonderful news. Two things were necessary for the cures to work, the messengers said. First, those who were at war must make peace. Second, those wishing to be helped must give them, the messengers, all their belongings in payment. The Spaniards were sad when they saw the plundered villages. But the people told them not to worry; losing their possessions was a small price to pay for blessings from Children of the Sun. Besides, turnabout was fair play. When their turn came to be escorts, they would repay themselves from villages down the line.

The holy men entered on the shoulders of their escorts. Villagers poured out of their lodges, dancing, singing, and leaping as high as they could. Crowding around, they pushed and shoved—*anything* to touch their guests. Native medicine men trembled, not daring to speak until spoken to. Once a medicine man gave them two gourds filled with pebbles and painted with magical designs. Sacred objects in the Southwest, these "medicine rattles" could only be carried by those with supernatural powers; anyone else would have bad luck.

Early in 1536 they crossed the continental divide, the place separating river systems that flow to opposite sides of a continent. Until then every stream flowed in a southerly and easterly direction, toward the Gulf of Mexico and Atlantic Ocean. Now rivers flowed westward, to the Gulf of California and the Pacific Ocean. The Children of the Sun had reached Sonora. The worst was over.

For the first time since leaving Florida, they met people who grew corn, a sure sign of prosperity. At the village of Ures, they were guests at a feast in which the hearts of six hundred deer, split open, were served as the main course. Cabeza de Vaca called it "Pueblo de los Corazones"—"Village of Hearts." Natives also gave them beads of Pacific coral and five arrowheads of polished green stone—emeralds![19]

Where had the emeralds come from? the holy men asked. From another land, replied their hosts. Far to the north, beyond the great river, people lived in cities with stone houses balanced on top of each other. Indian peddlers from the south traded parrot feathers and seashells for colorful stones, hides, and other goods from the north. These northerners, we know, were the Pueblo tribes of Arizona and New Mexico. Cabeza de Vaca knew nothing of these people; nor does he say what he thought of the tales of their "cities." Others, as we shall see, would not be so cautious.

Leaving the Village of Hearts, the four traveled south to the Yaquí River. Heavy rains had caused the river to overflow its banks, forcing them to wait fifteen days to cross. During that time, hundreds of local Indians visited their encampment. It was there that Alonso de Castillo noticed a warrior with an unusual piece of jewelry: a horseshoe nail tied to the buckle of a sword belt. Castillo shouted for his companions to come at once.

Hearts pounding, they asked the owner how he had come by these things. He replied that bearded ones such as themselves had recently dropped from the sky. Cruel beyond belief, they had shiny skins, long knives of the same material as the nail, and were part of four-legged beasts that reared, pranced, and ran like the wind. After killing two Indians, they went to a sea-house that moved beneath billowy white clouds. When last seen, the house was heading into the sunset. Clearly, a Spanish vessel, most likely a slave ship, had visited the coast. And where there was one Spanish ship, there must be others!

Hurrying onward, they found the countryside in ruins. It was as if a hurricane or a plague had swept the inhabitants away. Cabeza de Vaca's words are still as moving as when they were printed nearly five centuries ago:

> We traveled over a great part of the country, and found it all deserted, as the people had fled to the mountains, leaving houses and fields out of fear of the Christians.
>
> This filled our hearts with sorrow, seeing the land so fertile and beautiful, so full of water and streams, but abandoned and the places burned down and the people, so thin and wan, fleeing and hiding; and as they did not raise any crops their destitution had become so great that they ate tree-bark and roots. Of this distress we had our share all the way along, because they could provide little for us in their indigence, and it looked as if they were going to die. They brought us blankets, which they had been concealing from the Christians, and gave them to us, and told us how the Christians had penetrated into their country before, and had destroyed and burnt the villages, taking with them half of the men and all the women and children, and how those who could escaped by flight.[20]

The four began to fear they would be blamed for the acts of their countrymen. Yet their fears proved groundless; Indians knew the difference between healers and slave catchers. They led the healers and their escorts to a secret mountain camp, where they shared what little food they had.

Messengers were sent to call the people together. Days passed without news. When the messengers finally returned, it was to report that nothing had changed. Those who had eluded the slave catchers were wise to remain in hiding. The messengers had watched them in action from behind trees. Using whips and swords, they drove lines of people in chains toward the south. Terrified, the escorts wanted to turn back. Cabeza de Vaca begged them to stay, promising his personal protection.

In this early drawing, native people are led away in chains to a life of slavery under the Spanish conquerors.

He and Estevanico went ahead with eleven Indians. After two days, they found campsites that could only have been used by mounted men; stakes for hobbling horses had been driven into the ground. The next day, March 14, they met a party of slave catchers. The horsemen were astonished to see a white person accompanied by Indians. And such a person! Except for the fact that he spoke Spanish, he appeared to be a wild man. "They stared at me for quite awhile, speechless; so great was their surprise that they could not find words to ask me anything."[21]

Their leader was a brute named Diego de Alcaraz. He listened to Cabeza de Vaca's story politely, but his face showed that he did not believe a word of it. Pánfilo de Narváez? Never heard of him! Florida? The place was on another planet, for all he cared! Cabeza de Vaca sent for his comrades, who arrived with six hundred Indians. Then Alcaraz believed.

Spaniards have been accused of being crueler than other peoples; they call it *La Leyenda Negra,* or the "Black Legend." But Cabeza de Vaca was Spanish, and he defended the Indians. He might not have done so at the start of his adventure. Yet he had grown in understanding during his eight years in the wilderness. He had come to realize that Indians were not creatures without reason. Experience had taught him that whites and Indians could live and work together, if they respected each other as human beings.

Cabeza de Vaca would not let Alcaraz seize his Indian friends. He and the slave catcher argued constantly, but he held his ground. The Indians trusted him and, as an honest man, he could not betray them without betraying himself. He won the argument, or so he thought. Alcaraz assigned a soldier to take the four to Culiacán, the nearest Spanish outpost, and promised to send the Indians back to their homes. The soldier, however, had secret instructions to prevent the four from having further contact with the Indians. He was to lead them into a waterless area and leave them to die of thirst. He did abandon them; then, fearing punishment if the truth came out, rushed to Culiacán and confessed to Melchior Díaz, the vice governor of the territory. Díaz sent a rescue party. Meantime, Alcaraz enslaved the six hundred Indians.

Melchior Díaz was a humane person. After greeting Cabeza de Vaca and his companions, he listened to their complaints about Alcaraz. He had always believed that Indians should not be enslaved unless captured in war. Yet even then, they must be treated kindly, for Christians must love their neighbors as themselves. He asked Cabeza de Vaca to send messengers to urge his Indian friends to come to Culiacán under a safe-conduct. He also ordered Alcaraz to appear at Culiacán and sent soldiers to make sure he obeyed.

A week later, three chiefs arrived at Culiacán. Speaking through an interpreter, Díaz asked them to return to their villages. They had his promise as a Christian and a gentleman that they would be safe so long as they obeyed Spanish law. Fine words, the chiefs said. But what about the six hundred held by Alcaraz?

Six hundred? Cabeza de Vaca and Díaz looked at each other in stunned silence. That was the first either had heard of Alcaraz's treachery. Díaz ordered the slave catcher to release his captives *pronto*—at once! He obeyed. The Indians, mostly from the Village of Hearts, were resettled near Culiacán, where they prospered. Alcaraz was to die miserably, his flesh rotten and peeling off in strips after being shot by a poisoned arrow in Arizona. Some said it was a divine punishment for his crimes. Cabeza de Vaca kept his opinion to himself.

During their stay with Díaz, they began to relearn the ways of civilization. It was not as easy, or comfortable, as they'd imagined in the wilderness. Spanish clothes were stiff and scratchy on bodies that had gone naked for years. Spanish wine made their heads spin. And the beds! Oh, they were torture! Having grown used to sleeping on the ground, a featherbed felt like soft, yielding jelly. For several months they slept on the floor, alongside their beds.

The four reached Mexico City on July 24, 1536. Spaniards lined the city's broad avenues, cheering and waving flags. Waiting for them in the central plaza were Hernán Cortés and Viceroy Antonio de Mendoza. Although the aging conquistador was treated with respect, the viceroy, or royal governor, held the real power in New Spain. Not that King Carlos disliked Cortés; he praised him to the sky and showered him with honors. Nevertheless, he distrusted powerful subjects ruling faraway lands. So, whenever a conquest was made, a trusted nobleman was sent to rule in the king's name. Cortés might want something done, might even demand it, but only the iron-willed Mendoza could give the order.

Don Antonio de Mendoza, viceroy of Mexico, as he appeared in the year 1539. Mendoza was a powerful Spanish nobleman who curbed many of the abuses of the early conquistadores.

Don Antonio was fascinated by his guests. Beginning with the voyage to Florida, he made them relate their experiences in minute detail. He was particularly interested in the "cities" north of the Village of Hearts. Perhaps another Mexico lay in those parts? Perhaps the golden cities of Antilia?

The viceroy asked them to lead an expedition to the lands beyond the great river. They refused, politely. All they wanted was to find good jobs and settle down. Don Antonio understood. He arranged for Dorantes and Castillo to marry rich widows; in time, each became the father of eleven children. Neither returned to Spain. Nor did Estevanico, who resumed his status as a slave. He became Mendoza's property and would have further adventures.

Cabeza de Vaca returned to Spain in 1537. We do not know whether he rejoined his wife, or, for that matter, if she was still alive. What is certain is that his fame preceded him and that His Majesty promised him high office as a reward for his achievements. After three years of waiting, he was named governor of the province of Río de la Plata in South America. From 1540 to 1543, he explored the jungles south of the equator. His humane treatment of the Indians, however, made enemies among the colonists. They had him arrested on false charges and sent back to Spain in chains. For six years he lay in a dungeon with scarcely enough light to see his hand in front of his face. Upon his release, he vanished from history. It is believed that Alvar Núñez Cabeza de Vaca spent his last years in loneliness and poverty. The date of his death is unknown. He never knew that his travels had opened a new chapter in American history.

Coronado and the Seven Cities of Gold

Granted that they did not find the riches of which they had been told,
they found a place in which to search for them and the beginning of a good country to settle in,
so as to go on farther from there.
—Pedro de Castañeda, c. 1565

abeza de Vaca's meetings with Viceroy Mendoza set tongues wagging in Mexico City. The excitement was not due to anything he actually said, but to what people told themselves he had said. He made no claims, speaking only from personal experience, which he confessed was limited. Yes, Indians had mentioned cities far to the north of New Spain; but they had spoken in sign language, which he may have misunderstood. Yes, he believed the country contained mineral wealth, particularly metals, although he brought back no samples; the "emerald" arrowheads had been lost during the march to Culiacán.

Meetings were held in secret, for Mendoza did not want to raise false hopes. Nevertheless, there were leaks as officials repeated choice bits of information. People's imaginations did the rest. Rumors became like snowballs rolling downhill. Each turn made them grow more fantastic and, oddly enough, more believable, so strong was the desire for treasure. Cabeza de Vaca and his friends had found the Seven Cities of Antilia! They had crossed streams that flowed over beds of gold! They had seen Indian children playing with precious stones the size of hen's eggs! They had passed a mountain studded with so many diamonds they dared not look at it in the sunlight for fear of going blind!

Don Antonio was a prudent man. Rather than rush into the unknown, he decided to send a small party to investigate. He had just the person for the job. Friar Marcos de Niza had already packed more adventure into his six years in the New World than most people see in a lifetime. He had been with Francisco Pizarro during his conquest of the Inca in Peru in 1532. There he saw the Inca's *coricancha,* or "golden enclosure," a temple garden of solid gold. Golden spiders, bees, butterflies, beetles, caterpillars, birds, snails, lizards, and snakes perched on golden trees, flowers, and plants. There was even a herd of golden llamas, the South American camel, guarded by golden herdsmen, and rows of golden maize plants six feet high. A friend of the Indians, the friar walked from Guatemala to Mexico City, "barefooted as was his custom," to protest the cruelties of the conquistadors.[1]

The viceroy asked Friar Marcos to serve both God and Spain. Guided by Estevanico, he must explore the country beyond the Village of Hearts. If he brought back a favorable report, Mendoza would follow up with a full-scale expedition.

On March 7, 1539, Friar Marcos left Culiacán with a line of Indian porters that stretched half a mile. What a contrast the two leaders made! The friar wore a simple gray robe and a small wooden cross; he had no personal baggage, since he owned nothing else. Not Estevanico. He dressed in gaudy clothes with armbands of parrot feathers and clusters of bells around his ankles; in his right hand he carried one of Cabeza de Vaca's medicine rattles. His baggage consisted of clothing, a tent, bedding, and four dinner plates made of green pottery. Two greyhounds trotted at his side. Several Indian girls, all beauties, prepared his meals and satisfied his other desires.

The Moor proved to be a difficult traveling companion. Although a slave, he had a mind and a will of his own. The farther they went from Culiacán, the more assertive he became. At every village he announced that a Child of the Sun had returned and that the inhabitants must give him anything he demanded. In effect, Estevanico had regained his freedom and was making the most of it. Not that he intended to escape; that would have made him an outcast forced to live out his years among the Indians. He wanted more. He realized that if he could go off on his own, he might push ahead quickly and claim for himself the glory of discovering rich lands. Surely, that would make him rich and win true freedom. Like a successful conquistador, he, too, would be a "son of someone."

Friar Marcos agreed to send him ahead. To help find treasure, Estevanico carried samples of gold, silver, and precious stones to show the Indians he met along the way. His instructions were to report anything of interest. Since he could not write, a sym-

Estevanico the Moor enters a pueblo, as portrayed in this twentieth-century mural by Jay Datus.

bol was agreed upon. If he found something interesting, he must send back a cross the size of his palm; if it was really important, a cross twice as large. Should he find something greater and finer than New Spain, he must send a large cross.

Imagine Friar Marcos's surprise when, after four days, messengers brought a cross as tall as Estevanico himself! Estevanico, they said, had fantastic news. Local Indians had told him that he was a thirty-day march from the capital of another country. Cibola, as it was called, had seven cities, each larger and wealthier than the other.

The friar could scarcely believe his ears. Seven Cities! They had to be the golden cities of the seven bishops. The Seven Cities of Antilia were none other than these Seven Cities of Cibola! Here, surely, was a gift from heaven. Friar Marcos fell to his knees and "rendered thanks to Our Lord."[2]

He hurried onward, but could not overtake the fast-moving Moor. Estevanico headed up the Sonora Valley and turned northeast. Just across the present Arizona–New Mexico line, he reached his destination. The first of the Seven Cities was called Hawikuh and was home to the Zuni, one of the Pueblo peoples. The word *pueblo* is Spanish and can mean several things: a village, a village's inhabitants, a tribe. Spaniards called people who lived in places built like Hawikuh "Pueblos," and that is how they are known to this day.

Estevanico halted and sent a messenger with his medicine rattle. That proved to be an error—a *fatal* error. The Zuni chief could read the rattle's markings like an open book. He frowned, tossed it to the ground, and stamped on it until it broke in pieces. It had been made by an enemy tribe. The strangers were spies and had better go at once, he said menacingly. The messengers ran away as fast as their legs could carry them.

When they reported to Estevanico, he laughed at their fears. The poor fellow had become trapped by his own arrogance. Boldly he walked up to the pueblo's entrance. Explaining who he was and that he expected valuable gifts, including attractive women, he announced that he spoke for white men who wished to teach the Zuni about God. The chief gave a hand signal. Warriors surrounded the Moor and hustled him into a hut outside the village, where he spent the night without food or drink. While he slept, the village elders decided his fate: He was an enemy spy. He must die.

Next morning, at sunrise, the Zuni struck. Estevanico and scores of his Indian porters were killed. To prove that he was no Child of the Sun, they cut his body to pieces. Strips of flesh were dried and sent to other pueblos with advice to kill any intruders, black or white, who appeared. Warriors kept Estevanico's bells, feathers, greyhounds, and green plates.

Friar Marcos was crossing Arizona when he met fugitives from Estevanico's party "all bloody and with many wounds."[3] After listening to their story, Marcos's guides began to desert. The intrepid friar, however, refused to turn back. He had not come so far to quit; besides, quitting would show lack of confidence in God's protection. After much talk, he persuaded two men to guide him to a place from which he could see the city.

The journey was worth the effort, he wrote Mendoza.

> The settlement is larger than the city of Mexico. At times I was tempted to go to it, because I knew that I risked only my life, and this I had offered to God the day I began the expedition. But the fact is that I was afraid, realizing my peril, and that if I should die it would not be possible to have an account of this land, which, in my opinion, is the largest and best of all those discovered.[4]

Aided by his guides, he set up a cross and took possession "of all the Seven Cities" in the name of His Royal Majesty, King Carlos.[5]

Friar Marcos returned to Mexico City a hero. His report, however, was an outright lie. Whatever he saw, it was no mighty city. Hernán Cortés had doubts from the beginning, calling him a fake; some historians believe he could not have gone within a hundred miles of Hawikuh. His reason for lying remains a mystery. Given his past, however, he may have believed he was serving a worthy cause. Marcos was a priest and an explorer. But he was a priest first; exploration was important only if it served a religious purpose. Perhaps he hoped to lure settlers and missionaries into the land of Cibola. If treasure was discovered, then that would be all to the good; both Spain and the Church would benefit. If not, at least missionaries would be in position to save Indians' souls. In any case, his report landed like a bombshell. Rumors that had been circulating since Cabeza de Vaca's arrival were suddenly "proven" to be true. Marcos's fellow priests even began to preach about the Seven Cities of Cibola from their pulpits. In November 1539 Don Antonio ordered the conquest of the new lands.

Francisco Vásquez de Coronado was chosen to lead the expedition. Born in 1510, Don Francisco was the second son of an influential family at the royal court. Soon after arriving in New Spain, he married Beatríz de Estrada, a pious woman nicknamed "the Saint." He was also a favorite of the viceroy's; Don Antonio appointed him governor of a province in the north, where he gained experience fighting Indians. A brave, capable leader, no one was more qualified than he to conquer Cibola. He took command with the rank of general.

Wealthy men seeking adventure and poor adventurers seeking wealth flocked to the general's banner. The majority were in their twenties, with several seventeen- and eighteen-year-olds; at thirty-seven, cavalryman Domingo Martín was the expedition's *viejo,* its "old man." It was an honor to serve in such an army, and those who were selected considered themselves made men. Already they could count their riches and imagine themselves living in the lap of luxury.

The army totaled 336 soldiers, mostly cavalrymen; five priests led by Friar Marcos; and eight hundred Mexican Indians, many accompanied by their families. At least three Spanish wives joined the expedition, too; since the days of the Reconquest, wives and sweethearts had followed their men to the wars. Coronado's soldiers worshiped one—María Maldonado. A tailor's wife, she mended their clothes, tended the sick, and cooked their food. Thousands of cattle, sheep, goats, and pigs were a walking supply of fresh meat.

On February 22, 1540—192 years before the birth of George Washington—the army snapped to attention at a grand review. Viceroy Mendoza was determined that the planned conquest must not be a slaughter. He reminded the soldiers that they were Christians and must behave as such. Indians were to be treated like fellow Spaniards; without saying it in so many words, he had condemned the atrocities of Cortés and Pizarro. The next day Coronado ordered the bugle to sound. The march began.

It was slow going, as we learn from Pedro de Castañeda. A common soldier, Castañeda had a talent for writing; his book, *An Account of the Expedition to Cibola which took place in the year 1540,* is our best source for the events it describes. He says that

> as each one was obliged to transport his own baggage and all did not know how to fasten the packs . . . they had a good deal of difficulty and labor during the first few days, and left many valuable things, giving them to anyone who wanted them, in order to get rid of carrying them. In the end necessity, which is all powerful, made them skillful, so that one could see many gentlemen become carriers, and anybody who despised this work was not considered a man.[6]

Impatient at the delays, Coronado divided the army into two units. Late in April he sped northward with a hundred picked men, guided by Friar Marcos.

On July 7, they reached Hawikuh. Their hearts sank as they drew near. "It is a little, crowded village," Castañeda wrote, "looking as if it had been crumpled all together."[7] Hawikuh was a typical Pueblo town but unlike any Indian town the soldiers had ever seen. It was actually a single structure built in the form of a square surrounding a central plaza. Widest on the ground floor, it consisted of adobe rooms stacked in tiers, like a modern apartment house, except that an entire family lived in a room twelve by fourteen by seven feet. Each level—Hawikuh had four—was set back several feet from the one below, like a flight of stairs. The ground floor was used for storage and defense, and it had no doors or windows; the upper stories had slots wide enough to shoot an arrow through. Entry was made by ladders placed alongside each room, leading to a hatch in the flat roof, also entered by a ladder. Ladders could be removed in time of danger, turning the town into hundreds of individual compartments that must be captured separately. Defenders were armed with bows and arrows, spears, clubs, and shields. Piles of stones were kept on the rooftops, ready to drop on attackers.

Hawikuh's inhabitants were no friendlier than they had been to Estevanico. Medicine men advanced toward the strangers with bags of sacred cornmeal. Dribbling the cornmeal between their fingers, they drew a line on the ground. Warriors were drawn up in battle formation behind the line and massed on the rooftops, waiting. Coronado was a picture of knightly glory. Clad in gilded armor, he sat erect on his white charger, sword in hand. At his nod, an aide stepped forward to read the Requirement. A flight of arrows greeted its words. *"Santiago! Santiago y a ellos!"* the soldiers shouted. So began the first pitched battle between Europeans and Indians on the soil of the present United States.

Driven by tales of fabulous wealth to be found in the mythical Seven Cities of Cibola, Coronado and his men found instead the Zuni pueblo of Hawikuh.

Coronado was a perfect target in his gilded armor. Arrows glanced off his breastplate and helmet. Stunned by a direct hit, he fell to the ground and lay there helpless. Warriors were about to drop a heavy stone on his head when Captains García López de Cárdenas and Hernando de Alvarado shielded him with their bodies, saving his life. Even so, he was covered with bruises and had an arrow lodged in his foot. Moments later, his troops drove the defenders into the pueblo. Resistance collapsed. No Spaniards died, while the Zuni lost about fifteen men.

The victors, however, were in no mood to celebrate. All they had to show for their troubles was a poor place inhabited by sullen people. That lying priest was to blame! They cursed Friar Marcos, shook their fists in his face, even threatened to kill him first chance they got. Moreover, the general had grown to hate the very sight of him. He was sent back to Mexico City in disgrace. "I can assure you that . . . he has not told the truth in a single thing that he said, but everything is the reverse of what he said," Coronado told the viceroy in a follow-up letter.[8] The friar retired to a monastery, vanishing from history.

Coronado could not turn back even had he wished to; too much money and pride

A pueblo much as Coronado and his comrades would have found it in their trek across the Southwest in 1540. From a photograph in the Smithsonian Institution, Washington, D.C.

had been invested to give up so early in the game. During the following weeks, he sent scouts in different directions. Captain Pedro de Tovar went to the northwest with a small body of horsemen. Their route led through a part of Arizona that is today a world-famous tourist attraction. This is fabulous country, at once rugged, forbidding, and beautiful. Rivers flowing from snowcapped mountains have carved up the land, exposing layer upon layer of brightly colored rock, each representing millions of years of earth's history. Other rivers have dried up, leaving only their beds as permanent scars that are visible even from space. Tabletop mountains, or *mesas,* rise from between these ancient riverbeds to form deserts. There are also isolated rock formations fashioned by wind-driven sand into towers, chimneys, and arches.

Tovar and his men were the first whites to see the Petrified Forest, thousands of ancient tree trunks turned to agates streaked with bright mineral colors, and the Painted Desert, where the rocks seem to be painted in shimmering, dazzling colors: fiery red, lavender, yellow, and every imaginable shade of brown. Eventually, they came upon the Hopi, another Pueblo group, living in villages built atop three high mesas. The people of the first village prepared to defend themselves; they had heard of the battle of Hawikuh and the shiny-skinned men "who traveled on animals which ate people."[9] But the Spaniards cried *"Santiago!"* and easily routed the defenders. Alerted by their experience, the inhabitants of the other Hopi villages met Don Pedro with pledges of peace and friendship.

Tovar returned to Hawikuh with news of a large river farther west. Another scouting party, led by Cárdenas, went to investigate. Retracing Tovar's route, twenty days beyond the Hopi villages Cárdenas halted in his tracks. He stood on the South Rim of the Grand Canyon of the Colorado River, the most colossal gash in the crust of our planet. Flowing at speeds of up to twenty miles an hour, the Colorado carries a half million tons of stone and earth through the canyon each day. Over the ages, this immense "sanding machine" has gouged a hole a mile deep, 10 to 15 miles across by 280 miles long.

Castañeda did not see the Grand Canyon himself, but he heard about it from those who had. They spoke with hesitation, as if fearing comrades would tap their fingers to their foreheads and mutter *"loco"* (crazy) at such a wild tale. They also seem not to have been impressed by the canyon's rugged beauty. That should not surprise us; to sixteenth-century Europeans, wilderness was an obstacle to be overcome, not something to delight the spirit. Cárdenas's men called the Grand Canyon a "useless piece of country,"[10] just as European travelers described the Alps mountains as "monstrous protrusions of nature."

Castañeda was the first to record the canyon's impression on the minds of white men. Viewed from the rim, the Colorado River appeared as a narrow, silvery band, easy to reach. They soon learned otherwise:

> This country was elevated and full of low twisted pines, very cold, and lying open toward the north, so that . . . no one could live there on account of the cold. They spent three days on this bank looking for a passage down to the river, which looked from above as if the water was six feet across, although the Indians said it was half a league [1.5 miles] wide. It was impossible to descend, for after these three days three men . . . made an attempt to go down at the least difficult place, and went down until those who were above were unable to keep sight of them. They returned about four o'clock in the afternoon, not

> having succeeded in reaching the bottom on account of the great difficulties which they found, because what seemed to be easy from above was not so, but instead very hard and difficult. They said that they had been down about a third of the way and that the river seemed very large from the place which they reached, and that from what they saw they thought the Indians had given the width correctly. Those who stayed above had estimated that some huge rocks on the sides of the cliffs seemed to be about as tall as a man, but those who went down swore that when they reached these rocks they were bigger than the great tower of Seville.[11]

Cárdenas faced yet another difficulty. His Hopi guides warned there was not a drop of water to be found for three or four days in any direction. When the Hopi crossed this area, they brought women who carried gourds of water, which were buried along the way for use on the return trip. Hopi men also needed less water, because, they told the Spaniards, "they travel in one day over what it takes us two days to accomplish."[12] Cárdenas abandoned his search and returned to Hawikuh. No outsider would again see the Grand Canyon until the year of the Declaration of Independence, when Friar Francisco Garcés came to convert a band of Indians living in a sheltered area on the canyon floor. No United States citizen visited the place until 1858.

While his patrols probed westward, Coronado had two visitors at headquarters. One was an elderly Indian the Spaniards called Cacique (Chief), the other a handsome fellow in his thirties with a long mustache; the soldiers nicknamed him Bigotes (Whiskers). Using sign language, they said they were chiefs who came from a village two hundred miles to the east. The village was called Pecos and lay on the bank of a river with the same name. Having heard of the Spaniards, they wished to be their friends.

The general came straight to the point: gold, silver, precious stones. The men of Pecos knew nothing of such things. Yet their country had other attractions. There were many fine villages, fields of maize, and lots of turquoise, a greenish blue stone prized throughout the Southwest. Best of all, Pecos was near the Great Plains and "the cows." One of the chiefs' party had a tattoo of the animal on his chest. The Spaniards studied it but were puzzled, since it resembled no cow they had ever seen. It had a hump on its back and was covered with coarse, tangled wool. It was an American bison, or buffalo.

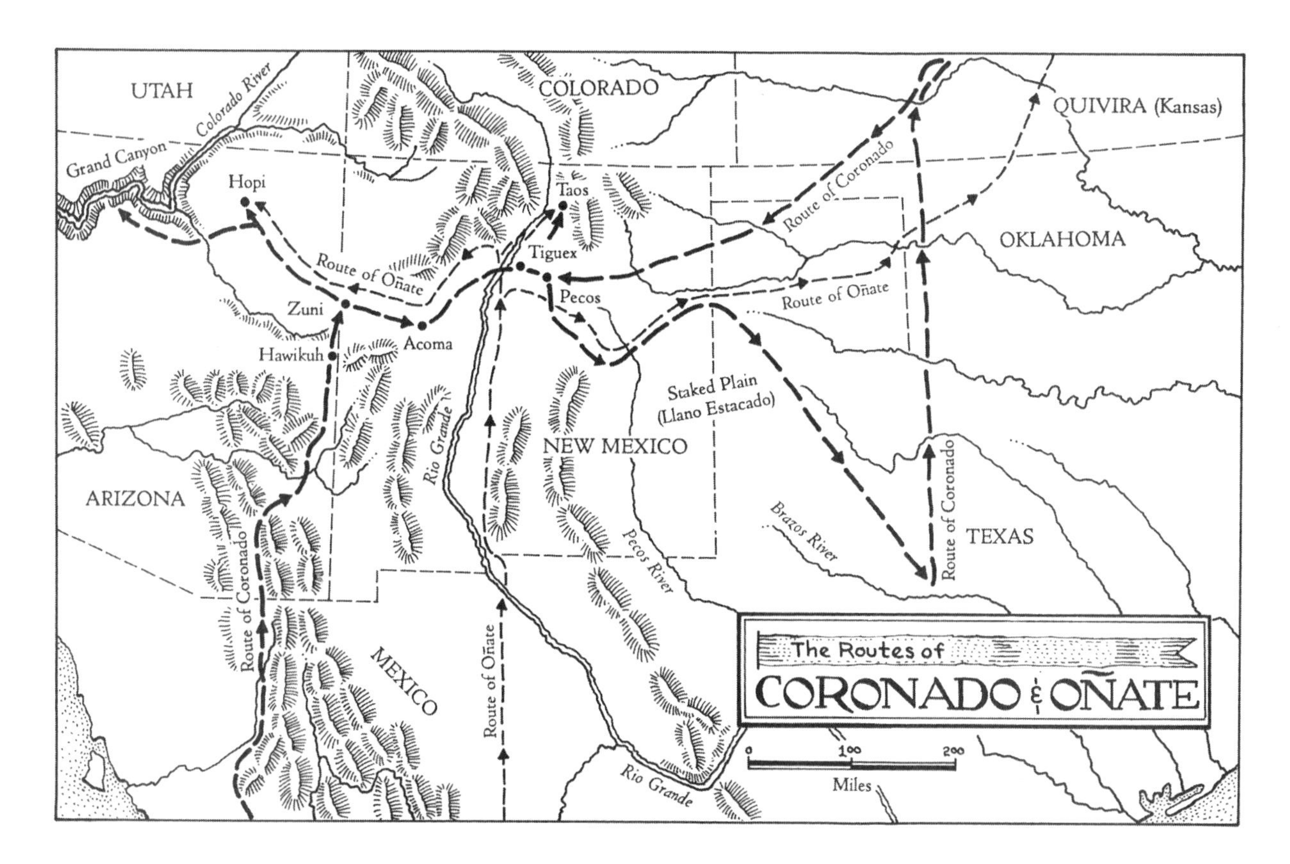

Coronado accepted the chiefs' offer to visit their country. On August 29, Captain Alvarado set out with twenty mounted men. Nine days later, after an exhausting desert journey, they reached a wide river. Since it was the birthday of the Virgin Mary, they named it Rio de Nuestra Señora—River of Our Lady. Once again Spaniards stood on the bank of the Rio Grande.

Crossing the river, Alvarado entered the land of Tiguex, a group of fifteen villages belonging to the Tigua, another of the Pueblo peoples. The Tigua knew Whiskers and greeted his companions as friends. The Spaniards were shown every courtesy, receiving gifts of turquoise jewelry and soft cotton mantles to wear over their armor. Alvarado was so impressed that he sent a message advising Coronado to take the army into winter quarters at Tiguex.

From Tiguex, the chiefs led the Spaniards to their hometown. Pecos had occupied an important position in the Southwest for centuries. It was the Indians' Seville, a port connecting different worlds, only it lay on dry land. Pecos stood between the Pueblo country, with its permanent settlements and cultivated fields, and the Great

Plains, over which roamed the buffalo herds and the nomadic tribes that hunted them for a living. Here Pueblo men passed eastward on their way to an occasional buffalo hunt. And here the plains tribes came west to trade buffalo meat and hides.

Home at last, the chiefs asked to be excused as guides; they had been away from their families longer than expected. The Spaniards, however, would not have to go on alone. Whiskers held two captives who knew the way to the buffalo. Both came from the land of Quivira far to the northeast; they were probably Wichita or Kansa Indians from the future state of Kansas. Sopete, the younger man, had circles tattooed around his eyes, giving him the appearance of a raccoon. The other's name is unknown; the Spaniards called him El Turco (the Turk) "because he looked like one."[13]

The guides led Alvarado to the plains of eastern New Mexico. Cabeza de Vaca had seen a few buffalo during his march across Texas, strays from the main herds hundreds of miles to the north. But this was something else! "There are such multitudes of them," one of Alvarado's soldiers reported, "that I do not know what to compare them to unless it be fish in the sea . . . because the plains were covered with them."[14] From horizon to horizon, the plains were practically a solid mass of buffalo. When they moved together, it was as if the ground itself were moving.

Alvarado's men held the first buffalo hunt by Europeans. Horses gave them an advantage over native hunters, who had to approach the lumbering beasts on foot. Riding up from behind, the Spaniards drove spears downward into their hearts. Nevertheless, buffalo hunting was not for the fainthearted. Buffalo bulls were short-tempered, and "they have wicked horns" that killed several horses, giving their riders the fright of their lives.[15] Indians preferred the "buffalo jump," stampeding them over the edge of a ravine or cliff. In that way scores, even hundreds, of animals were killed at once. Piles of bones at the base of ancient buffalo jumps may be seen to this very day.

Exciting as buffalo hunting was, it paled before the promise of Quivira. During the journey, the Turk learned a few Spanish words like *oro, plata,* and *metal.* Very well; if gold, silver, and metal meant so much to the strangers, he would use them to his own advantage. Quivira, he declared, was rich in all these things; his people did not value them, and every soldier could take whatever his horse could carry. Yet once burned, twice wary. The Spaniards had believed Friar Marcos, to their regret. Alvarado demanded proof. Why certainly, the Turk replied. He had been captured with a heavy gold bracelet, which had been taken by Whiskers and the Chief. Alvarado did a quick

Aperriamento, or "dogging," of the Indians by their Spanish overlords. After the conquest of Mexico and the territories to the north, the native peoples were forced to convert to Christianity and work for their new masters. Besides swords and guns, the invaders used fierce dogs called mastiffs to terrorize the Indians. Drawing from Proceso de Alvarado, a book written by a Spaniard living in Mexico around 1560.

turnaround. Cutting short the buffalo hunt, he rushed back to Pecos.

Questioned, Whiskers and the Chief said they knew nothing of a bracelet. Surely the Turk was lying, although they could not imagine why. Alvarado, however, wanted to believe the Turk's story. Blinded by greed, he put the chiefs in chains and marched them to Tiguex to let Coronado decide who was telling the truth. The people of Pecos were furious. Here they had received the strangers as friends, only to have their chiefs kidnapped. What an insult! What a breach of hospitality! Castañeda saw the episode as an evil omen. "This," he recalled, "began the want of confidence in the word of the Spaniards wherever there was talk of peace from this time on."[16]

Coronado did not help matters either. By the time they met, the Turk had perfected his story. Quivira was a fantastic country, he insisted. It had a river six miles wide and was full of fish the size of horses. The Quivirans used extra-long canoes, twenty rowers on each side, with eagle figureheads of solid gold. The Quiviran chief took his afternoon nap under a tree hung with tiny golden bells, whose tinkling lulled him to sleep. Even ordinary Quivirans ate off silver plates and drank from golden jugs and bowls. The general beamed. What a relief to know that success was within his grasp![17]

When the chiefs still denied knowing about the bracelet, Coronado tried some unfriendly persuasion. Spaniards called his method *aperriamento*—"dogging." The bound prisoners were taken into a village plaza and greyhounds set upon them. Although the prisoners were bitten all over their bodies, the dogs were pulled off before serious harm could be done; other conquistadors, such as Hernando de Soto, discoverer of the Mississippi River, had prisoners torn limb from limb. Coronado, however, was "merciful"; he might have use for his prisoners in the spring, when he set out for Quivira. Until then, it would be a cold, hard winter.

The Spaniards overstayed their welcome in Tiguex. It was one thing for the Tigua to entertain guests for a few days, another to have them settle in for several months. In November 1540 the people of Alcanfor pueblo were told the army needed their houses; they must move in with other villages. The order came so suddenly that there was only time to take the clothes on their backs. This act allowed the soldiers to spend the winter indoors and eat the food the Indians had stored. Coronado also commanded villagers to hand over warm blankets and cloaks. "Thus these people could do nothing except take off their own cloaks and give them . . . which caused not a little hard feeling,"[18] noted Castañeda.

Grievances accumulated like storm clouds. A patrol helped itself to a village's maize. A friar called a medicine man a "devil worshiper." A guard sicced his dog on a "thief." At the village of Arenal, a soldier asked the husband of a pretty woman to look after his horse while he did an errand. While the man waited below, the soldier entered his house, raped his wife, and then rode off as if nothing had happened. The family protested. An inquiry was made, but the accused said he was innocent and was set free. The husband went away angry.

The next morning a Mexican Indian who had been guarding the horse herd stumbled into Alcanfor with an arrow in his shoulder. A second guard lay dead, he cried, and the Tigua had stolen many of the horses. Without realizing it, the Tigua had made history: They had carried out the first Indian horse raid in the Southwest.

Forty horses had been taken to the pueblos of Arenal and Moho; the bodies of twenty-five others were found along the Rio Grande. They had been stolen not to ride or eat, as in later years, but to avenge the rape. Coronado, too, was out for revenge. Faced with open rebellion, he felt he must act sternly or spend the winter surrounded by enemies, who grew bolder by the day. Cárdenas was sent to drown the rebellion in blood.

Approaching Arenal, the Spaniards heard the hoofbeats of horses racing back and forth within the pueblo. Shouting warriors were chasing them around the plaza, while others lunged at them with spears from the sidelines. Warriors lined the rooftops, waving the tails of slain horses, screaming curses, and making obscene gestures with their fingers. Having killed the Spaniards' animals, they were eager to take on their masters.

The Spaniards "gave the Santiago" and charged. As riders circled the pueblo to cut off any escape, men-at-arms fired muskets while comrades advanced with battering rams and torches. Working quickly, they smashed holes through the walls of the ground floor and threw the torches inside. Flames shot upward, fanned by high winds. Smoke filled the pueblo, forcing the inhabitants onto the roofs. In the meantime, soldiers had put ladders up against the walls and were climbing onto the roofs as well. Realizing that the battle was lost, the defenders crossed their spears as a peace sign. The soldiers, who made the sign of the cross for the same purpose, promised to spare those who surrendered. Some two hundred warriors surrendered, along with their families.

The atrocity that followed began a cycle of violence that would torment the Southwest for the next three centuries. There would be other horrible scenes, but none more so than the one at Arenal.

Arenal's defenders trusted the victors' promise; keeping your word was a matter of honor with Pueblo people, something bred into them from childhood. A Pueblo would never break a promise, not even to a sworn enemy. But Cárdenas had his orders. Coronado wanted no rebels taken alive, and a Spanish soldier obeyed orders regardless of his personal feelings. Obedience was everything. If the act was criminal, the guilt was not the soldier's, but his commander's. God knew that and would deal with the criminal in His own way, they believed.

Cárdenas herded his prisoners into a large canvas tent guarded by a double ring of men-at-arms and cavalry. As they waited, not knowing that their fate had already been decided, two hundred stakes were driven into the ground and bundles of dry brush placed around each. Half the prisoners were then taken from the tent, tied to the stakes, and burned alive.

Peering out through the entrance, their friends could scarcely believe their eyes—or their noses. The burning bodies were clearly visible, the stench of charred flesh filling the air. Let Castañeda describe the rest:

> When the enemies saw that the Spaniards were binding them and beginning to roast them, about a hundred men who were in the tent began to struggle and defend themselves with what there was there and with the stakes they could seize. Our men who were on foot attacked the tent on all sides, so that there was great confusion around it, and then the horsemen chased those who escaped. As the country was

> level, not a man of them remained alive, unless it was some who remained hidden in the village and escaped that night to spread throughout the country the news that the strangers did not respect the peace they had made, which afterward proved a great misfortune.[19]

Snow began to fall, hiding the blackened ruins under a white blanket. The Spaniards wiped their weapons and marched back to headquarters through the swirling snowflakes. Arenal's women and children were enslaved.

If Coronado thought this atrocity would end resistance, he was mistaken. If anything, Indians fought harder, knowing what defeat would bring. Moho, Coronado's next objective, was the largest and strongest of the Tigua pueblos. Built on a bluff overlooking the Rio Grande, its massive walls consisted of tree trunks set in the ground and interwoven with branches plastered over with adobe. No amount of pounding with battering rams or hacking with axes could open a breach. Nor could the walls be scaled. The moment Spaniards set up ladders, they were showered with rocks. Indians "threw down such quantities of rocks upon our men," Castañeda says, "that many of [us] were laid out."[20]

Poisoned arrows were even deadlier. The Pueblos had two methods of poisoning their arrows. One was to shut rattlesnakes in baskets woven of willow twigs and poke them with arrows so that they bit the points; the venom dried, forming tiny crystals that melted in the human bloodstream. Another method was to leave a deer's liver in the sun until it putrefied. It was then ground up and mixed with rattlesnake venom. This mixture was nearly always fatal within minutes. If the victim survived the poison, he still faced blood poisoning and tetanus, an infection that causes lockjaw and unbearable pain. If, by a miracle, he survived, his flesh rotted and fell off the bones.

Coronado besieged Moho from late December 1540 to the end of March 1541. It was lack of water, not Spanish courage, that finally brought victory. Moho had just one weakness: it took its water from the Rio Grande. That supply was cut off. Winter, however, became the Indians' ally; for months they drank melted snow. But the snow was gone by March and thirst became unbearable. People with swollen tongues sucked pebbles—anything for a taste of moisture. Finally, the village elders decided to risk a breakout.

One morning, before dawn, the people left as quietly as they could. The men formed two lines, placing their families in between for protection. Unfortunately,

Spanish sentries saw them and gave the alarm. Springing into the saddle, horsemen went after the fugitives, who by then were fleeing in panic toward the Rio Grande. Riders lunged with their spears or, leaning over, swung their swords with all their strength. Indians fell, speared from behind, or had their heads lopped off by the sharp blades. The river, however, offered no safety. Flowing swift and cold, it drowned most of those who jumped in. The few who reached the other bank were captured and enslaved. Moho was destroyed.

Spanish cavalry in action, from a drawing in Lienzo de Tlaxcala. A man clad in armor riding a speeding horse was the sixteenth-century equivalent of a modern tank.

Coronado's victory was total. Some two hundred Spaniards were wounded during the Tiguex War; an unknown number, surely fewer than twenty, died. About five hundred Indians lost their lives, plus countless others injured or enslaved. After the fall of Moho, the remaining Tigua pueblos were abandoned. Villagers fled their homes, vanishing into the wilderness with their grief, pain, and rage. Spanish patrols searched the empty villages and the surrounding countryside without finding a trace of the inhabitants. It was an eerie feeling, almost as if an entire nation had been swallowed up by the earth.

Spring came. Coronado's faith in the Turk was stronger than ever. Proof or no proof, bracelet or no bracelet, he was eager to get going. On April 23, 1541, he led the army out of Tiguex and headed toward the sunrise. Now that the Tigua were enemies, he tried to patch things up with Pecos. Upon reaching the pueblo, he freed Whiskers and the Chief. Grateful at their chiefs' return, the people loaded the Spaniards with provisions, which were accepted in spite of the Turk's protests. There would be plenty of food on the plains, he insisted; besides, burdening the horses with supplies would make them too weak to bring back the treasures of Quivira!

Crossing the Pecos River, the expedition entered the Llano Estacado, or Staked Plain, a plateau covering much of southeastern New Mexico and northwestern Texas. The oldest land surface in the world, it is larger than the whole of New England and flat as a billiard table, except on its eastern edge, where the Red River and other streams have cut deep canyons.

Alvarado's men had gone a little way onto the Staked Plain the previous summer, but even they were amazed as they went farther. Having grown up in Europe, they were used to country with clear landmarks: hills, mountains, valleys, forests. The Staked Plain had none of these. It was so flat that if you saw a horseman in the distance, the sky was visible under the animal's belly. No matter where you stood, the horizon was a perfectly straight line. It gave you a giddy feeling, like standing on a gigantic blanket suspended in space and sagging slightly in the center from the weight of your own body. There was no way to measure distance, no way to know if you were reaching your destination. Every day the view was exactly the same as the day before. Like the sea, the Staked Plain closed in behind anyone who passed through, as if they had never existed.

> Who [asked Castañeda] could believe that 1,000 horses and 500 of our cows and more than 5,000 rams and ewes and more than 1,500 friendly Indians and servants, in traveling over those plains, would leave no more trace where they had passed than if nothing had been there—nothing—so that it was necessary to make piles of bones and cow dung now and then, so the rear guard could follow the army. The grass never failed to become erect after it had been trodden down, and, although it was short, it was as fresh and straight as before.[21]

The name Staked Plain may be due to the Spaniards' habit of hammering stakes into the ground to mark their route. There was no room for error, for anyone who strayed too far from camp was finished. Lost in a trackless wilderness, he would wander in circles until overtaken by heat, thirst, and exhaustion. Then the circling buzzards would indicate that a body lay below.

The Staked Plain teemed with wildlife. There were pronghorn antelope, the swiftest land animal in North America, and jackrabbits so stupid that a horseman could catch as many as he pleased on the point of his spear. Tens of millions of prairie dogs, a variety of squirrel, lived in underground "towns" spread over hundreds of square miles. Gray wolves wandered in packs, preying on anything they could catch. Yet the king of the plains was the buffalo.

Animal feo y fiero–"*an ugly and fierce animal.*" *The first European drawing of the bison appeared in Francisco Lopez de Gomara's* *Historia General de los Indias*, *a book published in Spain in 1554.*

One of nature's marvels, the buffalo, or American bison, is the largest land animal in the New World. A full-grown bull stands six feet at the shoulders, is over nine feet long, and weighs up to three thousand pounds; an adult cow weighs between twelve and fifteen hundred pounds. To Coronado's men, the buffalo was like several animals in one.

> It is to be noticed first that there was not one of the horses that did not take fright when they saw them first [wrote Castañeda in a classic description] for they have a narrow, short face, the brow two palms across from eye to eye, the eyes sticking out at the side, so that when they are running they can see who is following them. They have very long beards, like goats, and when they are running they throw their

> heads back with the beard dragging on the ground. . . . The hair is very woolly, like a sheep's, very fine. . . . They have a great hump, larger than a camel's. The horns are short and thick, so that they are not seen much above the hair. . . . They have a short tail, with a bunch of hair at the end. When they run, they carry it erect like a scorpion.[22]

In Castañeda's day, there were about sixty million buffalo on the Great Plains; today, one hundred thirty-five thousand are scattered in small herds throughout the West. Back then, the largest herds roamed the Staked Plain, feeding on the short "buffalo grass"; an adult buffalo eats up to thirty pounds of grass each day. You might cross the plains for weeks and see nothing but "cows and sky," as Coronado's men said. A herd could be fifty miles deep and twenty-five miles wide, and still be nothing special. In the 1860s a traveler saw a herd a hundred miles wide and of unknown length. Large herds often drank small streams dry.

Coronado's army once came to a weird graveyard. On the southern edge of a salt lake, they found a heap of buffalo bones fifty yards long, twelve feet high, and eighteen feet wide. This was in a area where there were no people to make such a pile. The only explanation was that countless old and weak buffalo had died when they went into the water to drink and could not get out. Over the centuries, waves whipped up by northers swept the bones to the opposite shore.

Equally fascinating were the Plains people. One day a patrol noticed parallel marks on the ground like those that would be made by dragging two spears side by side. Following the trail, the patrol overtook an Indian band and learned that the marks were caused by platforms fastened between two poles pulled by dogs. Before they had horses, Plains tribes used such platforms, or travois, to move their belongings. This band was Querechos, part of a nomadic people that hunted and raided throughout the Southwest. The Pueblos called them "Apachu"—"the Enemy." We know them as the Apache. The Querecho were Plains Apaches from eastern New Mexico and western Texas.

Everything the Querecho needed, except wood for tepee poles, spears, bows and arrows, and stone for arrowheads came from the buffalo. Their tepees, blankets, clothes, and moccasins were made of buffalo skin tanned with a mixture of buffalo brains and water. Buffalo sinew, or muscle fiber, was twisted into sewing thread and bowstrings; buffalo hair made strong rope. Buffalo bones became awls and knife

Across the Great Plains. The Coronado expedition as visualized by the American artist Frederic Remington in the year 1898.

blades, which were fastened to their handles with glue made from boiled buffalo hooves; horns were used as drinking cups and to carry lit charcoal from campsite to campsite. Because the Querecho planted no maize, their diet was almost entirely meat roasted over fires of dried buffalo dung or cut into thin strips dried in the sun. Usually they preferred their meat raw, hacked off in great chunks while the kill was still warm. In waterless country, the buffalo provided drink. "They empty a large gut and fill it with blood, and carry this around the neck and drink when they are thirsty. When they open the belly of a cow, they squeeze out the chewed grass and drink the juice that remains behind. . . ."[23] Partially digested grass contained not only water, but vegetable juices rich in vitamins.

The Turk spoke to the Querecho in sign language. Quivira, they said, lay to the east. Coronado was surprised. Back in Tiguex, the Turk had said it was to the northeast. Why the discrepancy? The Querechos could not be questioned further; having given their information, they struck camp and vanished into the vastness of the plains. The Turk was no help, either. When asked to explain, he just smiled, shrugged, and pointed eastward.

Sopete, however, was not so calm. Ever since leaving Pecos, he had marched with the army's rear guard. He disliked the Turk, and Coronado separated them to avoid trouble. But Sopete could no longer contain his anger. The Turk, he insisted, had influenced the Quechero. Both were liars who were sending the expedition on a wild-goose chase. Besides, Quivira was a poor place. Nobody paid attention to him.

Coronado halted while a search party went ahead. A few days later, the party returned with no news of Quivira. But while hunting buffalo, they had triggered the first stampede witnessed by whites. Everyone had seen cattle run wild back home in Spain, but this was something entirely different. There were so many buffalo and they moved so fast, that the ground shook under the pounding of their hooves. Coming to a ravine, the lead animals fell over the edge, pushed by those pressing from behind. Finally, the ravine filled and the rest crossed on top of the bodies. Ten horsemen got swept along and tumbled into the ravine. The riders and all but three of their mounts managed to escape. The unfortunate animals vanished into the churning, bawling mass.

Since the scouts had not found Quivira and the Turk stuck to his story, Coronado felt he must continue eastward. The army wandered as if adrift at sea, until it reached a place so barren there was not even a stone to take a bearing on. Fortunately, scouts met another Apache band. They invited the strangers to visit their camp in a canyon on the eastern edge of the Staked Plain. Some historians think it was Tule Canyon, others the Palo Duro Canyon.

A river flowing through the canyon made it an oasis. Walnuts, grapes, and other wild plants provided a welcome change in diet, although there was no getting away from buffalo meat, which by then had become monotonous. The Spaniards marveled at Apache skill with the bow and arrow. Castañeda admired the way a hunter "shot a bull right through both shoulders with an arrow, which would be a good shot for a musket."[24] Everyone was enjoying a well-earned rest when the sky suddenly turned black and a deafening roar filled the air. Tornado! Winds brought hailstones "as big as bowls."[25] The horses broke loose, except for a few that soldiers protected with their shields. It took days to round them up and treat the welts raised by the ice pellets.

The Spaniards' hosts said Quivira actually did exist, but that they were heading away from it; for it lay to the northeast. Still, they could not imagine why anyone should want to go there, as the Quivirans only grew a little maize and hunted buffalo, just as Sopete had been saying all along.

This time Coronado *would* listen! Sopete threw himself on the ground, indicating by signs that he would rather have his head cut off than continue in the wrong direction. All eyes turned to the Turk. Questioned closely, he admitted to misleading the Spaniards, although he did not say why.

Still, Coronado would not give up his golden dreams. Perhaps the Turk was still lying? Perhaps Quivira had treasure after all, and the Turk was trying to keep the Spaniards away from his homeland? Perhaps Quivira and Antilia were one in the same?

Coronado decided to divide his army rather than risk everything on a gamble that seemed unlikely to pay off. While the main force headed back to Tiguex to prepare for another winter, he would go on to Quivira with a small, mobile force composed of the best men and horses. It was an unpopular decision, for many still believed that riches lay "a little further on." Soldiers also feared that the advance force might take all the gold and leave nothing for later arrivals. Their pleas fell on deaf ears. The general had made up his mind and nothing could change it.

On June 1, 1541, Coronado set out for Quivira with thirty-six men. Sopete served as chief guide, assisted by Apache volunteers. The Turk, disgraced and knowing what lay ahead, walked at the rear of the column, enveloped in its dust. Hands tied, an iron collar fastened around his neck, a cavalryman led him by a rope, like a dog on a leash.

For four weeks Coronado's party lived entirely on buffalo meat cooked over fires of dried buffalo dung. Their route lay through the open country of northern Texas, across the Oklahoma panhandle, then eastward through south-central Kansas to the Arkansas River. Upon reaching that muddy stream, near the present town of Ford, Kansas, Sopete threw up his arms and gave a shout of triumph. He recognized the spot. Across the way lay Quivira and home.

Sopete took them over a ford used by the buffalo, then followed the river's northern bank. On July 2, they met Quiviran hunters. The Indians were taken by surprise; they had never seen bearded white men riding four-legged monsters. As they ran away, Sopete called out in his native tongue. They understood and came back without showing any sign of fear. Sopete was the Spaniards' passport, a guarantee that the strangers came in peace.

Coronado explored Quivira for twenty-five days. The results of these explorations were later sent to King Carlos in the form of a long letter. It is a sad letter, in which the author admits that he had little to show for over two years of struggle. Quivira, he said, was a beautiful land, "the best I have ever seen for growing all the products of Spain."[26] Its green, fertile meadows, watered by streams flowing into the Arkansas

River, could support countless settlers. Yet he was disappointed. The Quivirans dressed in animal skins and lived in villages of straw-thatched huts, not in cities of stone. As for gold, the expedition's main objective, "I am sure of it that there is not any gold or any other metal in all that country."[27] He blamed the Turk for leading him astray.

Snared by his own lies, the Turk tried to save himself. When his guard dismounted and walked over to another soldier, he pointed to the horse and told some Quivirans, *"Tit-ley!"*—"Kill him!" They turned away. Later he asked Quiviran warriors to attack the Spaniards, but they refused. Sopete learned of the requests and told the Spaniards.

The Turk was forced to make a full confession. Only then did Coronado realize how he had been duped by the Indian as well as by his own greed. The bracelet story was merely a hoax to get the Spaniards to take him away from Pecos and return him to Quivira, where he would escape. Unfortunately, things hadn't turned out as he expected. After Whiskers and the Chief had received dogging at the hands of the Spaniards, the Turk had been placed under close guard. The chiefs had not forgotten their humiliation, nor did they forgive it. They made the Turk promise to lead the Spaniards astray on the plains, then leave them stranded. Their provisions would soon run out, which explains why he tried to talk them out of accepting gifts of food in Pecos. Even if a few should find their way back to Pecos, they could easily be killed. Destroying the expedition, however, was not merely a matter of revenge. It was an investment in the future, a way of discouraging future Coronados.

The Turk's confession became his death warrant. That night soldiers awakened him from a deep sleep. While two held him down, the third slipped a rope around his neck and twisted it with a stick. They buried his body in an unmarked grave, which greatly pleased Sopete.

There was no need to linger in Quivira. Before leaving, Coronado gave Sopete his freedom as a reward for his loyalty. His final act was to set up a cross with this inscription: "Francisco Vásquez de Coronado, general of an expedition, reached here."[28] Other than the cross, the Spaniards left Quivira without a trace. Sopete's people would not see another white man for over half a century.

The second winter at Tiguex was a long, drawn-out ordeal. The previous year there had been a war to hold the soldiers' interest. Now there was nothing but cold, hunger, boredom, and despair. Soldiers spent their time quarreling with one another and blaming the general for their misfortunes. Needing supplies, Coronado tried to make up with the Tigua, but they despised him. Not that they admitted it in so many words; they had learned the lessons of Arenal and Moho only too well. Their politeness was merely caution bred by fear; their eyes revealed their true feelings.

Coronado suffered as much as anyone in the army. While out riding one day, he challenged his companion to a race. He was on a spirited horse, galloping at top speed, when his saddle girth snapped, throwing him directly in the path of his opponent. As the horse passed over him, it kicked him in the head. The blow knocked him out so soundly that aides feared for his life. When he awoke, he was fretful and restless. Expecting to die at any moment, he wanted only to return to his saintly Doña Beatríz.

The army left Tiguex on April 1, 1542—All Fools' Day. Two friars stayed behind to teach the Indians about Christianity. They were never heard from again. Their comrades reached Mexico early in the autumn. Few soldiers had any respect for Coronado by then. Discipline collapsed, as one group after another deserted. Viceroy Mendoza officially disbanded the remainder at Mexico City.

Don Antonio did not bear grudges. Although disappointed, as he had a right to be, he did not blame Coronado. His friend, after all, had done everything humanly possible to make the expedition a success. Two years later, Mendoza defended him against charges of incompetence and crimes against the Tigua. The charges were dropped. Captain Cárdenas, however, did not get off so easily. In his case, at least, some justice was done. Cárdenas was ordered back to Spain, arrested, and heavily fined for the massacre at Arenal. Coronado kept his official posts but had become a shadow of his former self. "He is more fit to be governed . . . than to govern,"[29] a judge wrote the king during his trial. He died in Mexico City on September 22, 1554, at the age of forty-four. No artist ever painted his portrait, and there are no descriptions of his physical appearance.

Failure that he was, Coronado had set the stage for the next chapter in the story of the Southwest. The lure of gold remained as strong as ever. Sooner or later, other explorers would follow in his footsteps.

Conquest of the Pueblos

I shall give your majesty a new world, greater than New Spain.
–Don Juan de Oñate to King Philip II, April 1, 1599

Coronado's failure to find the golden cities was a blessing for the Pueblos, preserving their freedom for another three generations. That was important. For although the Pueblos lacked certain things Spaniards took pride in—belief in one god, writing, iron weapons, gunpowder, horses—they had other qualities that made them, perhaps, more civilized than their future conquerors. Not only did they build sturdy homes, they built a sturdy society; so sturdy, in fact, that they have always kept their identity as a people.

The Pueblo Indians are not a unified tribe, but a group of peoples who live in the same region and share a similar way of life. In Coronado's time, there were at least 60 pueblos extending for 140 miles north and south along the Rio Grande and westward through Hawikuh and the Hopi villages of Arizona. The total population was approximately forty-one thousand.

Pueblo men, the Spaniards saw, were seldom taller than five feet; women were usually six to ten inches shorter. In warm weather, men wore moccasins and a breechclout, one of the most comfortable garments ever invented. A string was tied around the waist, then a piece of cloth drawn under the string in front, passed between the legs, and drawn under the string in back, the loose ends forming flaps hanging front and rear. When the weather turned cold, they put on buffalo robes or cloaks made of rabbit skin. Women wore a cotton garment that reached from the shoulders to the knees, adding warmer clothes as needed. Both sexes decorated themselves with turquoise jewelry.

The Pueblo story begins long before there was a Spanish nation. Their ancestors

A view of the Cliff Palace, Mesa Verde National Park, Colorado. Note how the overhanging rock ledge protected this ancient pueblo from the weather and enemies.

came to the Southwest about three thousand years ago, perhaps even earlier, hence their Pueblo name, Anasazi—"the Ancients." Wanderers from the north, the Anasazi found their way into the Four Corners area of New Mexico, Colorado, Arizona, and Utah. At that time there were still mastodons to hunt, not to mention bison twice the size of their modern descendants. As these animals died out, the Anasazi began to gather fruits and dig up edible roots. Somehow, probably by way of Mexico, they learned how to grow crops. Agriculture made possible a new way of life. They settled down, building villages of flat-roofed houses plastered with mud. The dried mud, or "adobe," was hard as rock and could last centuries in the dry climate.

The Anasazi planted cotton, beans, and squash. Maize, however, was their chief food. "Do we not live on corn, just as the child draws life from the mother?"[1] the Hopi still ask. It is a question that needs no answer. Maize has always been the Pueblos' staff of life, the equivalent to the Europeans' bread.

Although the corn most of us see is either yellow or white, Pueblo corn is as colorful as a fireworks display. Yellow, blue, red, pink, orange, purple, black, even speckled: All flourish in their fields. As with any crop, water is the key to growing corn. The Four Corners, however, is dry much of the year; and when it does rain, the water quickly sinks into the ground or evaporates. The Anasazi learned to make the

The inhabitants of the ancient Southwest left many petroglyphs, drawings on rocks and cliff faces. Many of these drawings are whimsical, like some of today's graffiti, done for amusement. Others chronicle events such as hunting expeditions and intertribal fights.

most of what they had. Locating their fields near dry streambeds, they captured the spring runoff in stone reservoirs. By planting seeds a least a foot deep, they also took advantage of the soil where it was still moist.

Sometime around the year A.D. 1000, disaster struck the Anasazi. Bands of nomadic hunters, ancestors of the Apache and Navajo, entered the Four Corners from the north. Unable to defend their villages, the farmers retreated into deep canyons or to high mesas. There they built fortresses that have become part of the American heritage. Take, for example, Pueblo Bonito. Located in New Mexico's Chaco Canyon National Monument, it was the largest man-made structure in the area of the United States until the skyscrapers of the twentieth century. Built of millions of stones so finely polished that a knife blade cannot be forced between them, the pueblo has eighteen hundred rooms that housed as many as five thousand people. Another example is found in Colorado's Mesa Verde National Park. Its Cliff Palace is actually a city built under the roof of an immense cave in the side of a cliff. An overhanging rock ledge made it impossible for enemies to approach from above, while the steep cliff discouraged attack from the canyon below.

In addition to houses and lookout towers, Anasazi cities had several kivas, underground chambers entered through a hatch in the roof. Kivas served as places of worship, club rooms, and boys' schools. Women were forbidden to enter them for any reason other than to bring food to their husbands and sons. A large pueblo might have as many as thirty kivas.

An artistic people, the Anasazi decorated rock walls with petroglyphs and pictographs. Petroglyphs are designs carved directly into the rock with stone chisels; pictographs are painted on rock surfaces with vegetable dyes. Visitors can still see cliffs decorated with zigzags, circles, spirals, outlines of human hands and feet, animals, and pictures of hunters killing game. These scenes are a form of magic, a way of controlling nature for human benefit. The Anasazi believed that like creates like, so by painting a hunt, or acting it out in advance, the actual hunt would be a success. They also wove cotton cloth and discovered the secret of making pottery. Originally, tightly woven baskets were used to carry water. Such baskets, they found, held water longer if the inside was smeared with clay. One day, someone may have left a basket too close to a cooking fire and forgotten about it. Meantime, the fire burned the basket away, leaving a hardened pot.

Anasazi prosperity ended in 1276. Beginning in that year, the Southwest experienced a crippling drought. Each year, for the next twenty-three years, there was less rain than the year before. The result was devastating. Crops withered and turned to dust. Hunting became poor, as game animals died of thirst or migrated to other areas. The disaster was too much even for such creative people as the Anasazi. By 1299 all their cities were abandoned. Left to the wind and the owls, they remained untouched until modern times. Fearing ghosts, Apaches and Navajos dared not go near them; Spanish explorers were interested in gold, not ruins.

Seeking a reliable water supply, the Anasazi moved close to the rivers: the San Juan, Gila, Pecos, and Rio Grande. There they built pueblos of the type Coronado saw during his expedition. Not only did pueblos look different from European towns, they were run by different rules. Land was not owned by individuals but by the community, which distributed it according to each family's needs; the larger the family, the more farmland it needed to feed itself. Under this system, no one could be rich or poor. In times of scarcity, burdens were shared equally by the community; thus, during a famine, everyone starved together.

Farming was not the only source of food. The Pueblos hunted deer, rabbits, gophers, prairie dogs, birds, and occasionally buffalo. Rabbits were killed in the open with curved wooden throwing sticks or drawn out of holes by twisting a thorny stick into their fur. The Pueblos, however, raised no animals for food. Their dogs were used for hunting, not eating, as with the Plains tribes, who liked nothing better than a newborn puppy boiled in its own juices. Before setting out, a hunting dog was fed powdered bumblebees to "sting" it into action. Turkeys were sacred birds, kept solely for their feathers.

The Pueblos led orderly, disciplined lives free from most of the cares of modern societies. There was no drug addiction, political corruption, juvenile delinquency, or unemployment. Every person knew his or her place in the scheme of things. They knew who they were, where they belonged, and what was expected of them during every waking moment. That knowledge was a source of stability, binding the community together in times of trouble.

Men did "manly" things: planted crops, hunted, dressed animal skins, dug irrigation ditches, built houses, made war. Not that the Pueblos were warlike; to be sure, the Hopi take their name from *hopitu,* their term for "peaceful ones." Nevertheless, they could fight well, if only in self-defense. Warriors who did not glorify war, the Pueblos were never the aggressor. Sadly, fighting was a man's duty, an unpleasant thing he did simply because he *was* a man. For that reason, it was sometimes better to be a woman. Warriors sang:

> *So we have bad luck*
> *For we are men.*
> *You have good luck*
> *For you are women.*
> *To Navajo camps we go*
> *Ready for war. Good-bye.*[2]

Slain enemies were scalped, a custom common to tribes throughout North America. After being torn from the top of a victim's head, the scalp was stretched on a thin wooden hoop until dry. The warriors of most tribes used scalps to decorate their clothes and advertise their bravery. The Zuni were more practical; since the dried skin became soft and pliable before it rained, scalps were used to predict the weather.

Marriage was regarded as the best way for people to live. Every girl dreamed of marrying in her early teens, having already learned everything she needed to be a wife from her mother and aunts. If a young man wished to court a girl, he asked to carry her water jug, a sure sign of his interest. Or he might weave a blanket and put it in front of her without saying a word; by placing it over her shoulders, she automatically became his wife. In Tiguex and Pecos, marriageable girls went naked. An Indian told Pedro de Castañeda why:

> I asked him especially for the reason why the young women . . . went completely naked, however cold it might be, and he told me that the

> virgins had to go around this way until they took a husband. . . . They say that if they do anything wrong then it will be quickly seen, and so they do not do it; nor do they need to be ashamed, because they go around just as they were born.[3]

The young wife ground cornmeal, cooked the meals, made the clothing, and helped her husband with certain heavy tasks. Before the spring planting, the couple worked at cleaning the irrigation ditches. While he hauled stone and timber to build their house, she did the plastering. The house became her property, and if the marriage ended in divorce, the husband had to go back to the house of his mother or older sister; single men could not live alone.

The wife also made a special dish by chewing cornmeal into a paste that her saliva changed into a sugary syrup. Water was then added and the liquid used to sweeten food or as a drink. The Pueblos had no alcoholic beverages and no drunkenness until the coming of the Spaniards.

In time, the wife became a mother. A new life was considered a blessing for the community, and so its welfare became a community concern. Even in a large village there were no strangers. Everyone knew everyone else by sight and, usually, by name. There was no such thing as "minding your own business": People were supposed to look out for one another and correct someone if necessary. Besides its birth parents, there were always caring adults—grandparents, uncles, aunts, cousins, family friends, neighbors, passersby—to keep an eye on the child.

View of a pueblo room at Zuni, showing people grinding corn. Cornmeal was to the pueblo peoples what wheat was to the Europeans: the basic food. From a drawing in Century magazine, February 1883.

Not only were they concerned with a child's safety, but also with its behavior. Children were constantly lectured and taught by example to be modest, obedient, and respectful. Naturally children, being children, misbehaved. But when they did, no one shouted at them, much less beat them. Shouting and beating were signs of weak character, frowned upon by the community. Naughty youngsters were reasoned with and if that did not help, scared by evil spirits. Scores of these ghostly beings were supposed to soar on the night winds, searching for bad boys and girls to kidnap. Just as Europeans had their boogeyman, the Pueblo had Saveyo Sendo, a wicked old man with sharp teeth and an appetite for tender young flesh. Crybabies were his special "dish." At bedtime, mothers sang:

Stop crying! Go to sleep, my little boy Primrose.
That Saveyo Sendo will take you if you cry.
Over there he will eat you, if you do not stop crying.
Right now he will eat you, if you do not stop crying.
That Saveyo Sendo in his bag he will put you,
Stop crying! Go to sleep, my little boy Primrose.
Over there he will take you, then I will be crying![4]

Children learned three basic truths. First, nature is all-powerful. Second, people are puny and weak. Third, the world is a dangerous place. Knowing these truths made the Pueblos a religious people; in fact, it is impossible to understand them without an understanding of their religious beliefs. Religion influenced everything they did: when they planted and harvested and hunted, when they built a house, when they sang and danced, when they made war and peace. In their view, so long as religious ceremonies were properly performed, nature would give them the necessities of life.

In the Pueblo tradition, life on earth began far beneath the planet's surface. Ages ago, before the memory of the grandfathers' grandfathers, people, animals, and plants lived in darkness in a vast cavern. When the time came, the gods led them to the upper world through a narrow opening in the cavern roof. The earth's surface being too soft to walk upon, the gods dried it out and gave light by creating the sun, moon, and stars. The gods taught the people practical skills, like fire making, weaving, hunting, farming, and irrigation. Moreover, they taught them about spirit. Pueblos believe that everything in the world is part of a single living force, or spirit. Mountains, caves, rivers, lakes, and plains; trees, plants, animals, birds, fish, reptiles, insects, and human beings; clouds, wind, rain, snow, hail, lightning, tornadoes, and thunder; houses, kivas, canals, reservoirs, and hunting trails; colors, lines, circles, spirals, and zigzags; thoughts, feelings, and dreams; hot and cold; the living and the dead—the list goes on and on. Different as these may seem at first glance, they are actually part of the same thing. They have spirit and are therefore related.

It follows that if the world is to continue and prosper, all things must be in harmony. In Pueblo belief, humans are not separate from nature, but part of the balance that sustains the world. The very ground they walked on is sacred. Everything in the landscape must be respected or changed in a way so as not to alter its basic character. The Europeans' belief that the natural world was merely an economic resource to be exploited was, to the Pueblo mind, not only wrong, but self-destructive. Exploitation harms "Mother Earth," who nourishes and preserves the lives of her children, including mankind. Humans are a part of the world; but they do not own it, much less rule over it.

Nor are there any "lowly creatures." The Pueblos see all living beings as fellow creatures; indeed, as family and friends. Hunting was not a sport to them, but a sacred activity. A hunter made sure to remind a rabbit that it had been put on earth to feed hungry people and to ask its forgiveness before killing it. Whenever a deer was killed, its body was decorated with ornaments, prayers were said over it, and sacred tobacco smoke was blown in its direction. The animal's spirit appreciated such respect and thought well of the hunter. When the hunter went out again, the animal's relatives would be kind and allow themselves to be killed. Pueblos even asked a tree's forgiveness before cutting it down.

Pueblo society mirrored Pueblo religion. Group harmony means everything, individual concerns nothing. A good person has no ambition other than the community's welfare. He or she is always quiet, careful, and cooperative. Anything else is unacceptable. Be they of joy, anger, or sadness, emotional outbursts are signs of bad upbringing and reflect on all the family members. Braggarts, complainers, and those quick to speak their minds disturb village harmony, weakening its unity and ultimately its ability to survive. Such people have to be kept in line. Organized gossip and public insults make them aware of the community's displeasure. The *koshare,* or clown society, uses jokes and ridicule to shame them into reforming. Yet patience had its limits. When everything else failed, malcontents were denounced as witches and killed.

Fully half the Pueblos' waking hours were given to religious activities. Individuals prayed in various ways. To speed their prayers to the gods, they tossed handfuls of white cornmeal or pinches of pollen into the air. The most common method, however, was the *paho,* or prayer stick. A short stick was painted in bright colors with turkey feathers tied to the tip. Set out in the open, the breeze stirred the feathers and attracted a god's attention, revealing what the maker had in his or her heart.

Important ceremonies were conducted by religious societies. Each society still has its own kiva, priests, and sacred objects such as masks and dance costumes. Some societies specialized in war, others in hunting, healing, clowning, and other activities. Religious societies have various names, such as Antelope, Snake, Bear, Knife, Eagle, and Spider.

Only men could belong to a religious society. Between the ages of five and nine, a boy went to school in the kiva of his father's society. There he was told the Pueblos' legends, taught how to pray, and learned the sacred dances. When he was ready, the kachinas initiated him into the society. The kachinas are good spirits that bring rain, abundant crops, and countless other blessings. Each Pueblo people has its own kachinas; the Hopis have 250 of them, each represented by a man who wears a unique mask and costume. In early ceremonies the kachinas whipped the boy until he cried. Pain was good, they said, because it drove the badness out of him and prepared him for a useful life.

Ceremonial dances were community affairs among the pueblo peoples. Here people watch dancers at Zuni. These dances are still performed today. From a drawing in Century magazine, December 1882.

Dancing is still at the heart of Pueblo religion. These dances are not for amusement or relaxation; they serve the same purpose as the chanting of priests and the Bible stories dramatized on holy days during the Middle Ages in Europe—that is, to make religion live for the onlookers. Dances still bring Pueblo communities together, reminding them of the unity and harmony of

Members of a religious society dancing with rattlesnakes in the year 1885. The pueblo peoples believe that the rattlesnake is a favorite of the rain god and that if they do the dance properly, the reptile will carry their prayers to the god, who will favor them with rain. There is no record of a dancer ever being bitten.

all beings. The most important dances are the Corn, Buffalo, Basket, Feather, Hoop, Bow and Arrow, Sun, Butterfly, Turtle, War, and Peace dances. Each dance has its own rhythm and meaning. In the Eagle Dance, for example, two men wear feathers on their arms in imitation of wings, fan-shaped tails of eagle feathers, and eagle headdresses with feathery white caps and yellow beaks. Moving gracefully, they imitate the noble bird as it soars into the heavens, carrying the people's messages to the sky gods.

Only the Hopis perform the Snake Dance. Held in late August, this dance is supposed to bring rain, since these reptiles are dear to the rain spirits. In preparation, snakes, preferably rattlers, were captured; as many as fifty were used in a dance. Priests of the Snake Society danced in pairs. The first dancer placed a snake between his teeth, carefully supporting its body with his hands. The second dancer, called the Hugger, carried a feathered wand. Staying close to his partner, he watched the snake's every movement. At the least sign of restlessness, he stroked it, soothing it and distracting its attention. When the dancer finished, he placed the snake on the ground, where a third priest grabbed it behind the neck. Before long, his hands were full of squirming, hissing snakes. When he could hold no more, another priest took over, until all the dancers were finished and all the snakes used. Then they were taken out of the village and released with these words: "Dear Elder Brothers, creep down into your holes to the underworld and ask the rain spirits to favor us."[5] It is said that no dancer ever died of snakebite. Weather reports kept over many years show that rain usually falls after a Snake Dance.

For the Pueblos, then, religion is not just a part of daily life, but the framework of life itself. Its destruction would mean the end of the Pueblos' world and of their existence as a people. They would do anything to prevent such a calamity from happening.

Coronado lay in his grave forty years before another Spaniard ventured into the land of the Pueblos. Coronado's route was nearly forgotten by then, and when his countrymen finally returned, they came a different way.

In the 1550s prospectors found large silver deposits at Zacatecas, five hundred miles north of Mexico City. Within a generation, others struck it rich at Durango and Santa Bárbara. These places lay far to the east of Coronado's route, which had followed the Pacific coast before turning inland. Santa Bárbara, New Spain's most northerly outpost, was near the headwaters of the Conchos River, a tributary of the Rio Grande, some four hundred miles south of the Pueblo country.

Spanish prospectors and settlers were frontiersmen—America's first—and there was plenty for them to do. Not only did they have to earn a living, they waged constant warfare against the northern tribes, a people known as Chichimeca ("Of the Family of the Dog") who ate raw meat, wore animal skins, and were expert with the bow and arrow. The fighting was so savage that the area became known as *una tierra de guerra*—"a land of war." Not only did the Spaniards force Indians from their villages, they enslaved hundreds each year under the most brutal conditions. Mining was dangerous, and workers were routinely killed or crippled in accidents. As a result, mine owners hired professional slave catchers to ensure a regular labor supply.

Slavers pushed northward, toward the Rio Grande. By the 1570s strange rumors were circulating in Santa Bárbara. Enslaved Indians spoke of Cibola, a land with seven towns consisting of houses built one on top of the other; apparently, Coronado's discoveries had been forgotten by the public.

Between 1581 and 1593, four small expeditions returned from the Pueblo country with encouraging reports. Expedition leaders called the land north of the Rio Grande "Nueva México"—"New Mexico." At last, they felt, they had discovered a country to match the Old Mexico of the Aztecs. Although gold had not been found, they saw no reason to believe that it wouldn't be. King Philip II agreed. Spurred by these reports, he ordered New Mexico brought into the Spanish empire.

Juan de Oñate, one of New Spain's wealthiest men, was chosen to lead the expedition on condition that he paid its costs out of his own pocket. On January 26, 1598, Oñate left Santa Bárbara with 129 soldiers, 10 friars, hundreds of Mexican Indian servants, 83 wagons, and a herd of 7,000 cattle and sheep. Expecting to become lords in New Mexico, the soldiers brought along their personal possessions. Captain Luís de Velasco needed three wagons to carry his spare saddles, cases of wine, furniture, armor, and clothing, including forty pairs of boots and shoes.

On April 30, the army reached the Rio Grande, where Oñate claimed "all the kingdoms and provinces of New Mexico" in the name of Philip II. Continuing upstream, late in May he arrived at *el paso,* "the ford," a shallow place in the river where the cities of Juárez, Mexico, and El Paso, Texas, stand today. From there, he went ahead of the army with a small escort. It was rough going, since the weather was hot and they had to cross a stretch of desert where a soldier had died of thirst; hence its name, El Jornada de Muerto—"The Dead Man's March." On July 11, Oñate set up headquarters at a pueblo he called Santo Domingo. Nine years later the first English settlers would land at Jamestown, Virginia, on the other side of the continent.

Oñate invited the local chiefs to pay him a visit. Speaking through an interpreter, he explained that he had been sent by Philip II, the most powerful ruler in the world. There was only one God, he said, and His Majesty wanted to serve Him by making the Pueblos royal subjects. If they agreed, pledging their loyalty and obedience, the king would protect them from enemies and see that they lived in peace and prosperity. Better yet, "if they were baptized and became good Christians, they would go to heaven and enjoy an eternal life of great bliss in the presence of God. If they did not become Christians, they would go to hell to suffer cruel and everlasting torment."[6] Heaven or hell: The choice was theirs. They had better choose wisely.

In the days following the speech, friars visited thirty-four pueblos. During each visit, villagers knelt before the crosses they carried and accepted Oñate's offer. Their reason for doing so is unclear. At first glance, it seems they should have resisted with every ounce of their strength. As polytheists, they believed not in one god, but in hundreds that controlled every detail of their lives. It is possible they saw the strangers' God as just another kachina to worship and impersonate in their dances. Perhaps they were simply terrified. The tale of Arenal and Moho had been repeated by village storytellers for generations. Coronado and his iron-clad horsemen were transformed into demons, always hovering in the shadows, always bloodthirsty, always ready to pounce like a swarm of Saveyo Sendos. Now they had returned. Knowing they would pay dearly for resisting Spanish demands, the Pueblo people may have decided to give in and see what happened next.

The pueblo of Acoma would have none of it. Built on an immense white rock rising 357 feet above the plain, Acoma, or "Sky City," was a natural fortress. Settled before the year 1200, it is the oldest continuously inhabited site in the Southwest; its name means "the place that always was." The only way to reach the top was by flights of uneven steps and a series of hand- and footholds carved into the rock. Natives made the climb easily; indeed, women balancing heavy water jugs on their heads scrambled up without using their hands.

Juan de Zaldívar, one of Oñate's captains, came to Sky City in search of winter supplies. After keeping him waiting for three days, on December 4, 1598, the Acomas invited him up to trade. Leaving twelve men below, he led seventeen others on the difficult climb. Zaldívar ordered them to be polite and pay for everything they took. Two soldiers, however, had their own ideas. Noticing a flock of turkeys, they grabbed a few for their cooking pots. A woman objected but had no way of telling them that turkeys were sacred. So she gave a war cry, bringing a swarm of warriors from every corner of the pueblo.

The outnumbered Spaniards resisted as best they could. His belly ripped open, one soldier slashed an enemy with his sword; both fell together, their guts mingling in the dust. In all, fourteen soldiers, including Zaldívar, died fighting. Three others ran to the edge of the rock, crossed themselves, and jumped. One struck his head on a rock and died; his companions landed in a pile of soft sand and walked away with minor bruises. Indian losses are unknown.

Oñate vowed revenge. Vincente de Zaldívar, the slain captain's brother, was sent to Acoma with seventy men and two light cannons. His orders were to offer the inhabitants peace in return for their surrender. But what a peace! The Acomas were to abandon their homes, turn themselves over to the Spaniards, and surrender their leaders for execution. Once they left the pueblo, Zaldívar was to "burn it to the ground, and leave no stone on stone, so that the Indians may never be able again to inhabit it."[7] If they resisted, he must make "war by blood and fire." That is how Europeans had always dealt with such matters. According to the laws of war, when a besieged town fell, it could be looted and its defenders slaughtered.

A view of the surrounding countryside from Acoma, or "Sky City."

The Acomas replied to Zaldívar's "peace" terms with boasts, insults, and showers of arrows. They had reason to be confident. Outnumbering the Spaniards by twenty to one, they had the added advantage of an impregnable stronghold; impregnable, that is, to attack by other Indians. It was unthinkable that anyone should climb their rock, let alone capture Sky City.

Zaldívar formulated an ingenious plan of attack. On January 22, 1599, he faked an assault on one side of the rock. While the defenders rushed to meet it, a handful of soldiers climbed up on the other side unseen. It was a harder climb than any of the town's inhabitants had ever made. Weighed down by their armor and weapons, the soldiers inched their way up the face of the cliff, hand over hand, not daring to look down. Gaining a foothold at the top, they signaled for reinforcements and hoisted up the two cannons.

"Santiago y a ellos!" The Spaniards charged, taking the defenders from behind. Cannonballs flew through the air, each one killing and maiming several Indians before

it came to rest. Soldier with swords and pikes slashed and hacked their way forward, spreading panic as they went. With resistance crumbling, they put Acoma to the torch. As flames spread from room to room, the inhabitants rushed into the open. The soldiers were merciless. Fleeing warriors were killed, along with their wives and children. Captured warriors were dragged to the edge of the rock, cut to pieces, and pitched over the side. Some Indians killed their children rather than see them fall into enemy hands. In the end, five hundred men, plus three hundred women and children, lay among Acoma's smoking ruins. Eighty men and five hundred others were taken prisoner. A few Spaniards had flesh wounds. None died.

The captives were put on trial, convicted of "treason," and sentenced by Oñate. The sentence speaks for itself. Here are his words, as preserved in the official trial record:

> I must and do sentence all of the Indian men and women from the . . . pueblo as follows:
> The males who are over twenty-five years of age I sentence to have one foot cut off and to twenty years of personal servitude [that is, slavery].
> The males between the ages of twelve and twenty-five I sentence likewise to twenty years of personal servitude.
> The women over twelve years of age I sentence likewise to twenty years of personal servitude.
> Two [Hopi] Indians . . . who were present at the pueblo of Acoma and who fought and were apprehended, I sentence to have the right hand cut off and to be set free in order that they may convey to their land the news of the punishment.
> All of the children under twelve years of age I declare free and innocent of the grave offense of which I punish their parents.[8]

These "free and innocent" youngsters were placed with Spanish families to be raised as Christians. Old men and women were given to the Apaches as slaves. The mutilations were carried out according to Oñate's order. On February 12, hands and feet were chopped off in front of an audience of horrified Indians brought from neighboring pueblos. Spaniards, however, took the scene in stride. Such punishments, and worse, had been normal in Europe for a thousand years.

Having crushed all resistance, Oñate turned to exploration. He crossed the

Staked Plain, hunted buffalo, and visited Quivira, only to find no more treasure than Coronado. He explored large stretches of New Mexico and Arizona, but again saw no precious metals. In 1607 he was dismissed as governor and ordered to answer criminal charges in Mexico City. Soldiers who had previously returned had told about Acoma. Convinced that he had only obeyed Spanish law, Oñate put up a strong defense. The court, however, thought otherwise. Convicted of crimes against the Indians, Oñate was stripped of his honors, banished from New Mexico for life, and fined six thousand ducats. Although a large sum of money, given Oñate's wealth it was merely a slap on the wrist. Zaldívar was banished from New Mexico for eight years and fined two thousand ducats.

Cutting off a culprit's hand was a standard punishment throughout Europe in early modern times. Here a Spanish soldier lops off an Indian's hand with one blow of his sword. Drawing from Códice Florentino.

The Spaniards came to New Mexico to stay. Friars built churches and missions, settlements to teach the Indians about Christianity. Each mission was self-sufficient, having a church, quarters for the friars, storehouses, and lands for farming and grazing. In 1610 Oñate's successor built a permanent capital that he called Santa Fe. (The city's full name is La Villa Real de Santa Fé de San Francisco—the Royal City of the Holy Faith of Saint Francis.) Built by forced Indian labor, Santa Fe lies on a plateau at the foot of the Sangre de Cristo (Blood of Christ) Mountains.

The number of settlers grew slowly; half a century passed before the white population reached three thousand. Santa Fe is nearly two thousand miles from Mexico City, and few were willing to make the dangerous six-month journey. Those who did prospered, for New Mexico was a good place for Spaniards. Since land was cheap, or free in certain cases, most settlers could own a hacienda, a large farm or ranch with several buildings. The main building, also called a hacienda, was built of adobe bricks and had walls a foot thick, which made it cool in summer and warm in winter.

Settlers brought new things with them. European plant foods flourished in the soil of New Mexico: wheat, oats, barley, chili peppers, onions, peas, watermelons, grapes, figs, dates, apples, cherries, peaches, apricots, lemons, oranges. European animals grazed in the pastures: horses, cattle, goats, sheep. The Pueblos learned that wool had certain advantages over cotton, their traditional fiber. Warm in winter, it did not absorb water and lasted longer than cotton. Before long, they were spinning wool in the same way as cotton and weaving it on the same looms.

These improvements, however, had a heavy cost. Spaniards had not come to New Mexico to work; working with your hands was beneath a "gentleman's" dignity. If asked to do physical labor, the settler would have replied, like Hernán Cortés: "But I came to get gold, not to till the soil like a peasant."[9] Governors, officials, soldiers, settlers: all prospered at the Pueblos' expense. Prisoners in their own land, natives had no civil rights, no economic opportunity, and no religious freedom.

Laws the Pueblo people had no part in making bound them in countless ways. Taxes were paid not in money, which Indians knew nothing about, but in goods and services. Each year, each village was required to deliver a fixed number of blankets, bushels of maize, and tanned deerskins. Indians were also assigned to the haciendas to work, without pay, at whatever tasks they were given. Serving as housekeepers, Pueblo women were often sexually abused by the owners; their children became known as mestizos, or "mixed bloods." Pueblo men were required to repair roads, dig irrigation ditches, do farmwork, and tend livestock. The least bit of resistance brought a whipping or a dogging.

The agony of the Pueblos seemed endless. Not only were they forced to work, they were expected to obey the friars and believe everything they taught. Friars were conquistadors of the spirit. Unlike conquistadors of the sword, they did not want to enrich themselves. These devoted men of God were willing, no, eager, to sacrifice their lives to convert the Indians to Christianity. By so doing, they felt they saved the Indians' souls and earned themselves a place in heaven.

Convinced that theirs was the only true faith, the friars had contempt for Pueblo beliefs. Pueblo religion, they insisted, was "idolatry and worship of the devil."[10] For the Pueblos' own good, everything that made them Pueblos had to be destroyed. Thus, the friars seized kivas and took away their contents. Kachina masks, dance costumes, and prayer sticks were burned. Religious societies were banned and their dances, "something that sounded like hu-hu-hu," outlawed.[11] Pueblo Indians were forced to take Spanish names and use only the Spanish language. Anyone who missed church services was severely punished. Women had their hair cut off, a grave insult, since hair was regarded as an outgrowth of the spirit. Men were whipped or imprisoned in tiny cells "not even large enough or decent enough for a good-sized pig,"[12] according to a

Spaniard. Some friars were cruel even by the standards of the time. One friar, for example, found a kachina mask in the house of a Hopi. He whipped the owner, smeared turpentine on the open wounds, and applied a torch. The man died screaming.[13]

Hard work and severe beatings were the lot of the pueblo peoples in colonial New Mexico. Drawing from Códice Florentino.

Pueblo people did as the friars wished, concealing their true feelings about the white man's religion. Yet they held their beliefs as strongly as ever, worshiping in the old ways at every opportunity. Their protests were quiet, as when the women of Taos, the most northern of the pueblos, offered a visiting friar tortillas—a flat, unleavened bread made of cornmeal. These tortillas, however, were seasoned with ground-up field mice and urine, which he ate with "a good appetite."[14] Other friars were less gullible. "The Indians are totally lost," one noted, "without faith, without law, and without devotion to the Church; they neither respect nor obey their ministers."[15]

Things went from bad to worse. For seven years beginning in 1667, New Mexico experienced a drought as severe as that which had driven the Anasazi from their cities. The Rio Grande became little more than a thin sheet of wetness, while smaller streams dried up altogether. Dust clouds hung in the air and wild creatures vanished as if they had returned to their homes beneath the earth.

Spaniards and Pueblos escaped starvation by eating strips of leather softened in water and then roasted over fires. Nevertheless, the Pueblos were the greatest sufferers, for not only did they lose the bulk of their crops, but the nomadic tribes struck as never before. Unable to hunt, bands of hungry Apaches and Navajos swooped down on Pueblo fields and storehouses. The result was mass starvation in which, said a Spanish report, "a great many Indians perished of hunger, lying dead in the roads, in the ravines, and in their huts."[16] The Pueblo population fell by at least half, to sixteen thousand, and dozens of villages were abandoned.

The years of turmoil and starvation raised questions in Pueblo minds. What are the Spaniards good for? Why can't their soldiers protect us from the marauders? If their God is as loving and powerful as the friars claim, why doesn't He send rain? The friars explained that God was punishing the people, Spaniards and Indians alike, for their sins. Pueblo medicine men shook their heads in disbelief. The invaders' God, they insisted, must be as weak and helpless as a newborn puppy. All He did was anger the spirits that really controlled nature. Therefore, to bring back the rain, the Pueblos must renew their faith in their own gods.

Medicine men preached this message in village after village. But as Pueblos rallied to the old faith, the Spaniards cracked down. In 1675 they arrested forty-seven medicine men on charges of witchcraft. One captive committed suicide; three were hanged; the rest were publicly whipped and thrown into jail in Santa Fe.

A delegation of seventy irate warriors from various villages demanded to see the governor. Explaining that without their medicine men the Pueblos were helpless against evil spirits, they asked for their release. When the governor refused, they gave him an ultimatum: If the medicine men were not freed, the Pueblos would join the Apaches to exterminate the Spaniards. The medicine men were set free at sundown.

The word *Apache* sent chills up the spine of any Spaniard. It hadn't always been that way, for the early explorers admired these nomads. In describing the Plains Apache, Pedro de Castañeda spoke for his comrades when he said: "They are a kind people and not cruel. They are faithful friends."[17] He might have added that they were kind only to those they respected and who respected them. In the 1620s, however, slave catchers took to raiding Apache camps. Theirs was a dirty business, but profitable and worth the risk. Apache slaves became New Mexico's chief export to New Spain. Apache men were sold to mine owners. Apache women and children were sold as domestic servants. The most attractive women and girls were forced into prostitution.

Having been wronged by some Spaniards, the Apache saw all Spaniards as enemies. New Mexico exploded in violence. War parties ambushed travelers, burned supply wagons, raided haciendas and kidnapped their residents. Spanish women and children might later be killed, or ransomed by their relatives. Often they were adopted by their captors; adoption enabled a tribe to replace members who had been lost in war or to disease. Male captives were never spared. Spanish men might be stripped naked and spread-eagled over a cactus with inch-long thorns, or buried up to their necks, scalped, their eyelids cut off, and left in the broiling sun. "The whole land is at war with the widespread heathen nations of Apache Indians, who kill all the [Christians] . . . they find," a friar wrote in 1669. "No road is safe; everyone travels at the risk of his life."[18]

Among the freed medicine men was a mysterious figure named Popé. Little is

A Plains Apache warrior as seen by J. W. Abert, a United States Army lieutenant, in the year 1845. Although fierce fighters, the Apache were no match for the hard-riding Comanche, who drove them from the southern plains.

known of Popé except that he came from San Juan pueblo, had grievances against the Spaniards, and was even less forgiving than the Apaches. He had been whipped several times for preaching about the Pueblo gods. When whipping failed to silence him, his older brother was enslaved in reprisal.

Upon his release, Popé set out to plan a revolt. Over the years, there had been isolated uprisings, all crushed by Spanish troops. The Indians' problem, Popé believed, was not lack of numbers, but lack of unity. He compared the Pueblos to the fingers of a hand, easily broken one by one, but invincible as a clenched fist. To build unity, he traveled widely, meeting in secret with village leaders. Their first duty, he explained, was to get rid of possible informers. He set the example by denouncing his son-in-law and killing him in his own house. Yet, despite every precaution, the Spaniards grew suspicious. Rather than answer their questions, Popé hid in the kiva of Taos pueblo. There he spoke to the gods and gained their approval for the revolt.

By the summer of 1680, Popé was ready. He had formed a vast alliance; not only were the Pueblos united among themselves, the Apaches and Navajos had declared a truce, pledging to join them against the common enemy. To make sure the Indians rose at the same time, Popé sent out knotted cords indicating the number of days left before the revolt. Runners traveled southward along the Rio Grande, eastward to Pecos, and westward to the Hopi and Zuni, untying one knot each day. Popé's final instructions were to guard every road and block every avenue of escape. There was to be a clean sweep. No Spaniard should be spared. Having cleared New Mexico, the rebels must erase every trace of the hated Spaniard and his religion.

August 11, 1680, was the day chosen for the revolt to start. On August 9, however, two messengers were arrested with their knotted cords. Brought to Santa Fe, they revealed the plan under some hard-fisted questioning. Governor Antonio de Otermín sprang into action. Riders were sent to alert the haciendas in the area around the capital. Every citizen of Santa Fe able to bear arms was given a weapon and assigned to a post. Trenches were dug across the main streets and cannons set up at key points. It was no use. Popé must have had an excellent spy system, for within hours of Otermín's action, he knew everything. More runners were sent, and Spaniards noticed puffs of smoke rising in the distance. Popé had decided to strike a day ahead of schedule.

The first American revolution began at sunrise on Saturday, August 10. Many settlers had not received Otermín's warning. Taken by surprise, they were cut down in their homes, fields, and churches. Hysterical refugees poured into Santa Fe with frightful stories. Even "devoted" servants were turning on their masters.

The rebels reached Santa Fe on August 15. Surrounding the town, they sent a war chief to give Otermín an offer he dared not refuse. It is not known whether or not Popé knew of the offer, or if he gave it his approval. In any case, the chief carried two small crosses, one red and one white. Holding them out, he told the governor to take his choice. If he chose white, the Spaniards would be allowed to leave New Mexico without further bloodshed. Choosing red, however, meant a war to the death. Otermín scoffed at the proposal, since a true Spaniard must fight for his honor against any odds. He countered with an offer of his own: If the Indians left peacefully, he promised to show clemency for their crimes. Now the chief scoffed. He knew about Spanish "clemency" at Arenal, Moho, and Acoma. Let it be a fight to the finish!

During the next six days, the Indians tightened their ring around Santa Fe. The Spaniards retreated through the town to the governor's palace, their main defense position. Outnumbered many times over, they charged repeatedly in efforts to keep the enemy off balance. Miraculously, only five Spaniards lost their lives during these assaults. Some three hundred Indians were killed and eighty captured; these were executed. Yet valor was useless against thirst. On the third day, rebels broke the ditch that brought water from a creek to the palace. Santa Fe's end was near, and the Indians knew it. That night, their victory cries echoed through the deserted streets. The God of the Spaniards was dead, they yelled, taunting the defenders. The Spaniards' mother, the Virgin Mary, was dead. And soon every Spaniard would also be dead.

On August 21, the entire population of Santa Fe, about a thousand people, left the doomed town. Since there were barely enough horses to haul vital supplies, let alone extra clothing and household goods, each person carried just a few personal things. As they left, they expected to be attacked at any moment.

Nothing happened. Realizing that the hated foreigners were leaving, the rebels showed mercy. Surely they knew how desperate the refugees were and how easy it would be to exterminate them. The friars had always attacked the Indians' "paganism" and "immorality," yet these "savages" let their oppressors go.

Smoke signals rose from the hilltops. Looking up, the refugees saw Indian warriors watching them come down from the Santa Fe plateau. Four hundred Spaniards had been killed the previous week and their bodies left unburied. Dozens of naked corpses lay in the roads, in the fields, in the gardens, in the haciendas. The breeze carried the odor of smoke and decaying flesh. Every church lay in ruins, their sacred objects broken or smeared with human filth. The refugees' terror comes through even in the dry language of this official report:

> The said Indians took up their arms and, carried away by their indignation, killed . . . priests, Spaniards, and women, not sparing even innocent babes in arms; and as blind fiends of the devil, they set fire to the holy temples and images, mocking them with their dances and making trophies of the priestly [garments] and other things belonging to divine worship. Their hatred and barbarous ferocity went to such extremes that in the pueblo of Sandia images of saints were found among excrement, two chalices were found concealed in a basket of manure, and there was a carved crucifix with the paint and varnish taken off by lashes [of a whip]. There was also excrement at the place of the . . . main altar, and a sculptured image of Saint Francis with the arms hacked off; and all this was in one temple only, [seen] as we were marching out. . . . We found . . . the [haciendas] sacked, and the horses, cattle, and other articles of our household goods on the mesas and . . . with the enemy guarding all of it and verbally mocking and insulting us.[19]

Crossing the Jornada de Muerto, the Santa Fe survivors halted at El Paso, where they met fugitives from other parts of the colony. New Mexico was lost.

Popé and his followers moved into the ruins of Santa Fe. The Pueblos were

Don Diego de Vargas Zapata y Lujan Ponce de León reconquered New Mexico after the great pueblo revolt. From a picture in the Museum of New Mexico.

ordered to erase all traces of Christianity, however small. Spanish names and the Spanish language were outlawed. The walls of burned-out churches were pulled down and their bells broken. Christianized Indians were plunged into rivers and "washed clean" of the alien religion.

Popé led the first American revolution, but he was no George Washington. Success went to his head, turning him into a tyrant. Having defeated the Spaniards, he aped the Spanish governors. Like them, he raised taxes, organized a personal bodyguard, and insisted that others bow in his presence. Unlike them, however, he kept a harem of beautiful girls taken by force from their home villages. The date and circumstances of his death are unknown. He may have been killed by the followers he betrayed.

The Spaniards returned in September 1692, after an absence of twelve years. Led by General Diego de Vargas, a veteran of the wars in Europe, a powerful force seized Santa Fe. To show the folly of resistance, Vargas had seventy rebel leaders shot in the town plaza; more than four hundred Indian men, women, and children were given as slaves to his soldiers and the colonists who accompanied the army. Moving out into the countryside, Vargas conquered most of the other pueblos with little difficulty. In several, he found survivors of Popé's revolt, including four Spanish women with children fathered by Pueblo warriors. In 1696 a second revolt was crushed at a cost of only twenty-six Spanish lives. After a six-month campaign, Vargas controlled every rebel village except those of the Hopis. Reinforced by refugees from the Rio Grande pueblos, the Hopi beat off every assault until the Spaniards decided to leave them alone.

Never again would the Pueblo Indians challenge Spanish rule. Nor would Spaniards, dreading another revolt, bear down as heavily as before. Taxes were reduced, Indians allowed to travel freely, and forced labor eliminated. Although religious freedom was not formally given, it existed in fact. The friars, too, had learned from their bitter experiences. Force gave way to persuasion.

The change produced results, if only on the surface. Outwardly, the Pueblos acted as Christians. They attended church services, were married by Catholic priests, and had their children baptized in the same way as Spaniards. Yet they remained true to the faith of their forefathers. Men still gathered in the kivas, kachinas still helped the people, and dancers still seemed to soar like the eagle. The Hopi, however, never pretended to be Christians. Only Awatovi, their most eastern village, allowed the friars to return. Their neighbors disapproved—*strongly.* In 1701 warriors from the other Hopi pueblos destroyed Awatovi and slaughtered its population of over seven hundred men, women, and children.

In the meantime, conqueror and conquered drew closer. Once again the Apache were on a warpath, attacking both Spaniards and Pueblos with equal boldness. To survive, it became necessary for their victims to join forces. From 1700 onward, every Spanish expedition against the Apache had a detachment of Pueblo warriors. Not only did they prove to be brave allies, Pueblos were invaluable as scouts and interpreters. Commanders reported that, man for man, the Pueblos were better soldiers than Spanish settlers.

If an Apache on foot was a dreaded foe, a mounted Apache was hell on four legs. The Spaniards, we recall, had introduced horses into the Americas. Recognizing the horse as a war-winning weapon, at first they tried to keep it to themselves. Every colony had laws against Indians owning horses and learning to ride. Nevertheless, once cattle were introduced, it became impossible to manage large herds on foot. In New Mexico, ranchers ignored the law and trained Pueblo vaqueros, or cowboys. Vaqueros worked from sunrise to sunset, and falling down on the job brought a whipping. Punishment, however, only deepened resentment. Each year, scores of vaqueros escaped to the Apaches. To make themselves welcome, they brought gifts of stolen horses and, equally important, horse knowledge. By 1650 Apaches were creeping up to corrals at night and running off with the horses. Within a generation, they had become master riders and raiders. A practical people, the Apache did not love their horses as did the Plains tribes. Horses were creatures to be used, and used up, as needed. Apaches rode their horses to death, ate them, and stole fresh mounts to take their place.

After 1680 the Pueblos took thousands of Spanish horses for their own use. Thousands more broke free and headed for the plains, where they multiplied further. Within a generation, horse herds were roaming eastern New Mexico and for hundreds of miles on either side of the Rio Grande. A traveling friar wrote in his diary that horses were so abundant north of the river "that their trails make the uninhabited country look as if it were the most populated in the world. All the grass on the vast ranges has been consumed by them, especially around the watering places."[20] The same was true of the country south of the river; Mexicans still know it as El Llano de los Caballos Mesteños, the Plain of the Wild Horses.

Spaniards call wild horses *broncos mesteños,* from which we get the English word "mustang." Without the mustang, American history would have been different; indeed, certain aspects of it, like the Indian wars fought by the United States cavalry, would be unimaginable. Scattering across the Southwest, mustangs acted as a magnet, drawing distant tribes into the region. As tribesmen learned to ride, they traded their spare mounts to neighboring tribes and shared their horse knowledge with them. By the time of the Declaration of Independence, all Great Plains tribes from the Rio Grande to Canada had become "horse Indians."

Horses became as necessary to the Plains Indians as the automobile and airplane are to modern-day Americans. Only the buffalo met their needs so completely. Both animals were worshiped as gifts of the Great Spirit. Prayers were said for the buffalo spirit, the "Mighty Bull of the Prairie," as well as for the horse, known as the "Holy Dog" and "Mystery Dog." Indians ate horse flesh, drank melted horse fat, and shampooed their hair in horse blood. Riding bareback or on a rawhide bag stuffed with grass, they traveled faster and farther than any medicine man could imagine in a dream. The horse travois allowed them to have more possessions and to carry them more easily than ever. Best of all, horses enabled them to follow the buffalo herds closely, assuring a steady supply of food.

Horses brought a different style of warfare. Speed became the rule. A brave could charge into battle like the wind, or vanish like a wisp of smoke. Controlling his mount with his legs alone, he could shoot eight well-aimed arrows in the time it took a Spaniard to load his single-shot musket. He invented tricks that would make circus performers green with envy. By the time an Indian boy was five, he had his own mount

Plains Indians used bows and arrows as well as spears in hunting buffalo. Spearing such a large animal was particularly dangerous because the hunter had to ride alongside it in order to use his weapon. Copy of a paining by J. M. Stanley in the Smithsonian Institution, Washington, D.C.

and played games like Push Him Off His Horse, in which opposing teams charged at full gallop. Bodies might be bruised and limbs broken, but riding became second nature. As a teenager, he could braid a loop of horsehair into his horse's mane, then hang over its side with one arm while shooting arrows under its neck. Acting together, two braves could pick up a fallen comrade and get him out of harm's way in a matter of seconds.

Although mounted Apaches spread terror throughout New Mexico, they were mild compared to the Comanches. This is no exaggeration. A short, stocky people with broad faces and jet-black hair, the Comanche seemed clumsy on foot. But once they threw a leg over a horse's back, they were among the finest—if not *the* finest—riders on earth. Add that to the fact that they were the most warlike of the Plains tribes, and they became a force to be feared. By the 1750s they had driven the Plains Apaches into the mountains and deserts of New Mexico. The Comanchería, or Domain of the Comanche, stretched from the Rio Grande to the Arkansas River and from the plains of eastern New Mexico halfway across Texas. Any Apache caught there was killed instantly or reserved for a lingering death by torture.

The Spaniards had double trouble. In New Mexico, Apaches and Comanches fought them constantly, while continuing their own feud. Spaniards built presidios, small forts manned by soldiers, but these had little effect; raiders bypassed them like a stream flowing around rocks. Not that the Comanche wanted total victory, since that was not in their interest. War chiefs boasted that the only reason they allowed Spaniards to survive was to raise horses for them to steal. Had they wished otherwise, they could have pushed the Spaniards completely out of the Southwest.

New Spain was not spared, either. Each fall, its northern frontier was tormented by *los indios broncos*—"the wild Indians." In September, when the desert cooled and the fall rains filled the water holes, the marauders swept down like an avalanche. Apaches from New Mexico came by way of their Great Stealing Road, a network of trails that led into the province of Sonora. The Comanche, however, were in a class by themselves. Running along the eastern edge of the Staked Plain, the Great Comanche War Trail crossed the Rio Grande and went almost to the gates of Mexico City. Word that the Comanche were coming sent people flocking to the churches, for only an act of God, and not the Mexican army, could have any effect. Even so, a "good" year was pretty bad. Comanches killed every man they met, kidnapped boys and girls for adoption or ransom, and made off with thousands of horses. Left behind were ruined haciendas, weeping families, and funeral processions.

By 1800 the Southwest had become a gigantic melting pot. Spaniards, Mexican Indians, mestizos, Pueblos, Apaches, Navajos, and Comanches led an uneasy existence in this harsh, beautiful land. Only the Americans of the new United States were absent from the mixture. And they were on the way. When they arrived, the Southwest would be changed forever.

•

Mountain Men and Santa Fe Traders

Danger, privation, heat, and cold are equally ineffectual in checking their career of enterprise and adventure.
–Augustus Storrs, St. Louis merchant, 1824

t the same time that the Spaniards were conquering New Mexico, other people were setting out on a long march from the Atlantic coast two thousand miles to the east. Anglo-Americans, English-speaking people hailing from the British Isles, were a restless breed. In the early 1600s, as Santa Fe grew, these "Anglos" began to settle in colonies stretching from Maine to Georgia. By the 1690s, however, many were feeling cramped as more immigrants arrived each year from Europe. So, for the next century, they pushed westward in small family groups into the interior of the continent; many pioneer farm families moved six or more times in a lifetime. Crossing the Appalachian Mountains, they eventually reached the Mississippi River, where they halted; for the lands beyond were part of Louisiana, a French possession.

In 1803 President Thomas Jefferson bought these lands at a bargain price. The Louisiana Purchase cost the United States fifteen million dollars, a figure that worked out to three cents per acre for an area of 828,000 square miles, more than doubling the nation's size by giving it all the territory between the Mississippi River and the Rocky Mountains.

What had Mr. Jefferson *really* bought? Plenty of nothing, critics grumbled. An empire of boundless wealth and promise, supporters boasted. Still, nobody knew for sure. In 1804 Meriwether Lewis, the president's private secretary, and William Clark, an army officer, were sent to find out. In an epic journey, the Lewis and Clark

In 1806 the United States government sent Lieutenant Zebulon Montgomery Pike to explore the Southwest. During the journey, Pike discovered a mountain in Colorado, later named after him, and spied on the Spanish colony in New Mexico.

expedition traveled four thousand miles across the northern plains and Rocky Mountains to the Pacific Ocean, returning to their starting point, St. Louis, Missouri, after an absence of two years. The explorers brought back a storehouse of information on the plants, animals, native peoples, and geography of the Northwest. In years to come, that information would be invaluable to pioneers bound for the green valleys of Oregon.

Lewis and Clark had tackled only half the problem. Still to be explored were the lands bordering New Spain in the southern part of the Louisiana Purchase. That task went to twenty-seven-year-old Lieutenant Zebulon Montgomery Pike of the U.S. Army. Officially, Pike was supposed to gather scientific data, open friendly relations with the Pawnee and Osage tribes, and follow the Arkansas River to its source. Unofficially, he had a secret mission that has remained unclear up to the present day. Historians believe Pike was a spy sent to study Spanish defenses in New Mexico in case war broke out at some future time. The truth may never be known, because his instructions were, apparently, not written down.

In July 1806 Pike left St. Louis with twenty-four men. Following the Arkansas River across Kansas into Colorado, he saw in the distance "a mountain on our right, which appeared like a small blue cloud."[1] It grew larger as they drew closer, casting an enormous shadow at certain times of the day. The lieutenant tried but failed to climb the peak that was to bear his name—Pike's Peak. Turning south, the expedition followed the Rio Grande into northern New Mexico, where they built a log fort on a bank of one of the river's tributaries. The Americans had no right to build this fort; indeed, they had no right to be in New Mexico. Like all Spanish colonies, New Mexico was closed to foreigners. No foreigner could visit without a passport or trade without a royal license. Passports and licenses were few and far between.

It was winter by then, and the Americans had nearly frozen to death in snowstorms. They were taking a well-earned rest when some travelers arrived from Santa Fe. The authorities, they said, had learned of their arrival from the Indians. A strong cavalry force was already on the way to arrest them for trespassing and would arrive in two days. Although his men wanted to "have a little dust-up with the Spaniards," Pike decided against fighting.[2] Fighting against such odds might get them all killed; besides, being captured would allow him to take a closer look at New Mexico.

The cavalrymen treated their prisoners not as criminals, but as honored guests. As they passed through villages on the way to Santa Fe, people greeted them warmly. Pike recalled:

> We were frequently stopped by the women, who invited us into their houses to eat; and in every place where we halted a moment there was a contest who should be our hosts. My poor fellows who had their feet frozen were conducted home by old men, who would cause their daughters to dress their feet, provide them victuals and drink, and at night give them the best bed in the house. In short, their conduct brought to my recollection the hospitality of the patriarchs. . . .[3]

In Santa Fe the authorities wanted to know everything about the fellow with the tongue-twister name "Mongo-Meri-Paike." Pike was closely questioned for a week and his papers taken away. Fortunately, he managed to hide the pages of his diary in the gun barrels of his men, who had been allowed to keep their weapons. Talking to him, however, was like talking to a wall: He told nothing and admitted nothing, saying only that he had lost his way and wished to be released as soon as possible. The authorities may or may not have believed him; we cannot be sure either way. What is certain is that Pike and his men were sent home in the spring of 1807.

Pike was the first Anglo-American to see the Southwest and return with detailed information about it. During his travels, he had noted its natural resources and the inhabitants' desire for American manufactured goods. He also learned of their dissatisfaction with Spanish rule and desire for independence. Not only in Mexico, but throughout Latin America, Spanish rule had become a burden. Corrupt and inefficient, it drained the colonies' wealth, giving nothing in return. In New Mexico,

Spanish officials traveled with mules loaded with wines and fine foods. Yet the common soldier was a miserable wretch dressed in rags; indeed, some were convicts serving out their sentences in frontier presidios. Their weapons were so out of date that cavalrymen carried a shield and a lance, as knights did during the Middle Ages; infantrymen had muskets and crossbows like the ones used by Coronado's troops. No wonder Apaches and Comanches held them in contempt. If war came, the Spaniards would be a pushover for the Americans, Pike thought.

The publication of Pike's diary in 1810 caused a sensation. Overnight, it focused American attention on the Southwest. So what if Spain owned it! That was just a legal technicality. Pike had found a land of promise, and nothing could keep them away.

Just as mustangs drew the Comanche into the Southwest, fur-bearing animals drew Pike's countrymen. For centuries furs had been a basic item in trade. During the Middle Ages in Europe, furs were worn not only for warmth, but as a symbol of social rank. The English kings, for example, decreed ermine a royal fur; that is, only the royal family could wear this soft white fur. Later, when European seafarers cruised along the eastern shores of North America, they traded furs with the Indians. The French founded Quebec in Canada; and the Dutch, New Netherland, as fur-trading centers. Although dealers paid handsomely for fox, muskrat, and marten, it was beaver that was the real moneymaker. For centuries no European gentleman would appear in public without his tall beaver-skin hat; indeed, it was said that going out without "your beaver" was like going out naked. A trading post called Beverwyck was named in honor of the beaver. When the English conquered New Netherland, Beverwyck became Albany, New York. From 1690 to 1756, the French and English fought four wars in North America. These "French and Indian Wars" were largely over control of the Great Lakes beaver trade. Meanwhile, Spaniards were trapping the

Mountain men as portrayed by Frederic Remington. Fur trappers such as these were the first Americans in the Southwest, opening the way for the traders, soldiers, and settlers who followed.

beaver streams in the Rocky Mountains north of Santa Fe.

The beaver is found throughout North America, from the Arctic Circle to the gulfs of Mexico and California. An average-size beaver weighs thirty to forty pounds, although some have tipped the scales at over one hundred pounds. A strong swimmer, the beaver has webbed hind feet and lives along tree-lined waterways, its thick paddlelike tail acting as a rudder to steady it while swimming. Sturdy chisel-like teeth and powerful jaws enable it to cut down large trees, whose leaves, bark, and twigs are its food. The beaver builds its nest, or lodge, in calm water, from branches woven together and cemented with mud slapped on with its tail. In fast-flowing streams, as in the Rockies, it digs into the bank to make its nest.

Mountain men in winter quarters. During the slow season, many mountain men gathered in small groups or lived with their Indian wives.

American fur trappers—mountain men, they called themselves—claimed to be as hard as nails. They had to be, particularly in the Southwest, where they were intruders. Ignoring Spanish law, they risked arrest, loss of their property, and a long stay in the Santa Fe *calabozo;* "calaboose" is still Western slang for a jail.

In 1821 New Spain became the Republic of Mexico after a bloody revolution. Independence brought a change in the hunting laws, but not enough to satisfy the mountain men. Hunting licenses were still required, and these usually went to Mexican citizens. Mountain men broke the law or got around it by bribing government officials, buying licenses from New Mexicans, or claiming citizenship by marrying Hispanic women.

James Ohio Pattie gained his license in an unusual way. A native of Kentucky, Pattie was a legend among mountain men. His 1831 book, *Personal Narrative during an Expedition from St. Louis to the Pacific Ocean,* is packed with stories that make Hollywood "action" movies seem tame. Pattie and his friends were trapping in New Mexico illegally when they saw a Comanche war party returning from a raid. Up ahead were four naked girls driving a flock of stolen sheep; Comanches stripped white captives to discourage escape attempts. In the ambush that followed, the girls were freed. It so happened that one of them, a teenager named Jacova, was the daughter of a former governor of New Mexico. Her grateful father could not do enough for the Americans. Whenever they needed a meal or a place to sleep, they were welcome at his hacienda. Better yet, he made sure they had licenses to trap anywhere in Mexican territory.[4]

The mountain man's life was governed by the seasons. When winter held the Rockies in its frozen grip, friends might band together in a sheltered valley known as a "hole," where they "holed-up" in snug log cabins. Others preferred to be alone, camping in a tepee along an isolated stream. Some loners were educated men, who spent the winter reading books. One fellow memorized the complete plays of William Shakespeare.

Many wintered with their Indian wives. An Indian women saw advantages in having a mountain man for a husband. She gained more by way of material things and was often treated with more consideration than her sisters who married within the tribe. Her man spared no expense on "fafarraw," fancy doodads for his lady. A traveler wrote:

> In the first place, she must have a horse for her own riding; but no jaded, sorry, earth-spirited hack, such as is sometimes assigned by an Indian husband for the transportation of his [wife and children]: the wife of a . . . trapper must have the most beautiful animal she can lay her eyes on. And then, as to decoration: headstall, breastbands, saddle and crupper, are lavishly embroidered with beads, and hung with thimbles, hawks' bells, and bunches of ribbons. . . . Then as to jewelry: in the way of finger-rings, earrings, necklaces, and other female glories, nothing within reach of the trapper's means is omitted that can tend to impress the beholder with the idea of the lady's high estate.[5]

Finding a willing mate was easy. If a trapper saw a young woman he liked, he went straight to her father. After some bargaining, they agreed on a "bride-price," a sum reckoned in horses, blankets, bullets, and pounds of gunpowder. The arrangement suited everyone.

The mountain man's work year began in the spring. When the ice in the streams began to melt, he set out to join his partners. In the crook of his arms he carried a rifle; his first line of defense, he kept it cleaner than his own body. From his shoulder dangled a powder horn and leather bullet pouch. Hanging from his belt were a knife and a tomahawk; unlike the Indian's stone-headed weapon, his tomahawk had an iron blade and could be thrown with deadly accuracy up to forty feet. Around his neck he wore a "possible sack," a buckskin bag containing his pipe, tobacco, and flint for making fire. A packhorse carried his traps, blankets, and strips of dried buffalo meat. This was all the mountain man brought with him. Everything else he took from the land.

Those who trapped the northern Rockies usually worked for large companies that organized them into "brigades" of fifty to a hundred men. Those who worked the Southwest were called "free trappers," because they were their own bosses and operated in bands of from three to twelve. A band of free trappers set up a base camp, where they elected a leader and drew up a set of rules that promised stiff punishment, including death, for anyone who disobeyed. So did the old-time pirates, who scoured the seas for ships to loot, and the "forty-niners," who went to California during the 1849 gold rush. The reason is simple: Even those living beyond the reach of the law must have rules if they are to survive in a hostile environment.

Small parties left the base camp each day. Following the streams, they searched for beaver. When a lodge was found, they set their traps. A steel beaver trap had jaws that snapped shut when anything touched its springed trigger. Traps were placed in three or four inches of water near the lodge entrance. A long chain was attached to the trap and held in place by a stout pole driven into the streambed. Over the trap a bait stick was set so that one end was about four inches above the water's surface. This end was smeared with castoreum, an oil given off by beavers to attract mates and waterproof their fur. The scent of castoreum is irresistible to another beaver. The instant it lifted its nose toward the bait, it raised its body and lowered its hind legs, triggering the trap. Held fast, it swam into deep water, only to drown when it could not break free; beavers, like humans and whales, are air-breathing mammals. Each morning the hunter waded into the stream to collect the previous night's catch, which might number as many as thirty beavers. The skins were then scraped clean of flesh and stretched over wooden frames for a few days. When dry, they were folded, fur side inside, and tied into bundles of ten.

Mid-June to mid-September was the shedding season, when beaver skins became worthless. Not that the trapper was sorry to get some time off. After so many months in the wilderness, he looked forward to the rendezvous, a sort of fair, held in the Southwest, at Taos or Bent's Fort on the Arkansas River. Each summer traders came from St. Louis to buy their catch. In a good year, a trapper might have four hundred pounds of skins, valued at five dollars a pound. Two thousand dollars went a long way. With that amount a man could build a small house and have enough left over to buy a farm or a country store. No wonder beaver skins were called "hairy bank notes"; they were as good as cash in the bank, provided you could sell them at a fair price and keep the money.

Traders were smooth operators. Having given the trappers gold coins with one hand, they took them back with the other. Nothing they sold was cheap; everything a mountain man bought, from guns and traps to coffee, tea, and sugar, cost him top dollar. For instance, a plug of chewing tobacco that sold for five cents in St. Louis went for three dollars in New Mexico. Cotton cloth worth six cents a yard back East sold for fifty cents, and glass beads for a dollar apiece. Woolen blankets brought sky-high profits.

After a mountain man bought the necessities, he spent plenty on fafarraw for his wife, and on gambling and drinking. It was an unusual person who could resist the temptation for a "blast," a wild spree that might last for weeks. Trappers gambled round the clock; one group used the body of a comrade killed in a shoot-out as their card table! It was common for men to leave the rendezvous penniless, having lost their money, their horses, and even their pants. Shrugging their shoulders, they'd mumble, "There goes hos and beaver!"[6] Yet it wasn't so simple. If they wished to continue trapping, they had to take a silent partner. The trader lent them supplies in return for a healthy share of future profits.

If gambling was a curse, alcohol was a killer. The trader's biggest profits came from whiskey. The idea was to get a mountain man so drunk that he could not make a good deal. Any trader who didn't leave the rendezvous with a load of prime furs and whiskey profits of at least a thousand percent wasn't worth his salt. Trader's liquor was known as "mountain dew," "red-eye," "snake poison," and "rotgut," because it was said it could rot away your insides. The usual drink was a mixture of alcohol, water, red pepper, and chewing tobacco boiled together and sold in small wooden kegs. Rotgut brought out the worst in people. Drunkards tore into each other, punching, kicking, gouging eyes, and biting off noses. Drunkards dueled with rifles at twenty paces, often falling together at the command "Fire!" Drunkards doused the hair of sleeping companions with whiskey and struck a spark, roaring with laughter as these human torches rolled on the ground, trying to smother the flames. Drunkards circled blazing bonfires, doing Indian dances and chanting:

Hi-Hi-Hi-Hi! Hi-i—Hi-i—Hi-i—Hi-i!
Hi-ya—Hi-ya—Hi-ya—Hi-ya
Hi-ya—Hi-ya—Hi-ya—Hi-ya.[7]

Broke and battered, the mountain men returned to their camps for the fall hunt. Before long they had another load of furs and another winter was upon them. Except for the rendezvous, they spent all their time in the wilderness. Slowly, probably without realizing it, they adapted to their environment. Instead of shaping it, as the farmer does, it shaped them, as it had the Indians for thousands of years.

After a few seasons, a mountain man's mother might not have recognized him. He *had* changed! Lean and wiry, long exposure to the sun had turned his face and hands a rusty brown; his body was white everywhere else, for he seldom removed his clothes even to sleep. He wore a buckskin hunting shirt with long fringes dangling from the seams. Ornamental as well as useful, when it rained, fringes acted as drains, directing the water away from his body; each piece of fringe could also become a cord to tie packages or a tourniquet to stop bleeding. He also wore buckskin trousers, a felt hat, deerskin moccasins, and a wide leather belt. Neither his body nor his clothes were washed; both stank to high heaven and crawled with lice. A mountain man was forever scratching. If lice became too pesky, he threw his clothes over an anthill so that those industrious insects could eat them clean. But he could not do the same with his hair. Unkempt and matted, it reached to his shoulders and swarmed with lice, as did his bushy beard. Every article of clothing was decorated with feathers, beads, and porcupine quills dyed every color of the rainbow.

The mountain man's speech was as colorful as his costume. Any man, to him, was a "child" or a "hoss" or a "coon" or a "nigger"; no insult intended, since he applied the last two words to whites as well as blacks. When he got hungry, he was "wolfish" and must fill his "meatbag," or stomach, with "buffler" (buffalo) meat. If "Injuns" were nearby, he had to "make tracks," otherwise some "red varmint" would "tickle his fleece" with an arrow and then "lift his ha'r" with a scalping knife. To meet a violent death was to be "rubbed out" or "sent under."[8]

Violence was accepted as a normal part of life. Yet, tough as he was, the mountain man was also human, with all the human fears. To keep up his spirits, he boasted of his greatness, portraying himself as an American superman. He claimed to have a jaw of stone, nine rows of teeth, ribs of steel, and a head so hard he could butt down the biggest tree. He could drink a lake of rotgut, belch fire, spit bullets, and sleep naked on a bed of cactus. Fearless, he had ice water in his veins instead of blood. He sang:

I'm a killer and a hater,
I'm the great annihilator.[9]

Often it was he who faced annihilation. Nature was unforgiving, and the slightest misstep spelled disaster. Mountain men were victims of accidents caused by rock slides or by their horses stepping into a hole and falling on top of them. Since there were no doctors in the wilderness, they devised their own remedies or copied those of the Indians, as Cabeza de Vaca had done. Experts at setting broken bones, they could remove arrows and amputate limbs as well as any surgeon. Scrapes, bruises, and rashes were treated with a soothing ointment of sugar, beaver fat, and castoreum. For stomachaches, they drank "bitters," a mixture of water and gall, a yellow liquid from the buffalo's gallbladder. Rattlesnake bites were cauterized; that is, the two puncture marks were joined together by a knife cut and a pinch of gunpowder burned inside the wound.

Being a fur trapper was lonesome, dangerous work, requiring months in the wilderness, where the enemies were accidents, hostile Indians, and grizzly bears.

No animal was feared more than the grizzly bear. Grizzlies roamed the southern Rockies in such numbers that one trapper counted 220 in a single day. An adult grizzly is eighteen hundred pounds of pure trouble. Towering above the tallest man, it has front paws eight inches across, armed with six-inch claws. Although its eyesight is poor, the grizzly can detect man-scent miles away. Then watch out! It came on the trappers like greased lightning, its raking claws cutting to the bone with every swipe, its teeth snapping bones as if they were dry twigs. By a miracle, trapper Hugh Glass lived to tell how a mother grizzly caught his thigh in her teeth, tore off a mouthful of flesh, and offered it to her cub.[10]

James Ohio Pattie saw a friend caught by a grizzly. The scene burned itself into his memory. He wrote years later:

> Our companion was literally torn in pieces. The flesh of his hip was torn off, leaving the sinews bare, by the teeth of the bear. His side was so wounded in three places, that his breath came through the openings; his head was dreadfully bruised, and his jaw broken. His breath came out from both sides of his windpipe, the animal in his fury having placed his teeth and claws in every part of his body.

Pattie shot the bear several times. Nothing. Then he put his rifle up against its head and pulled the trigger. Down went the grizzly, but not in time to save the man.[11]

Indians were known as "two-legged grizzlies." Beaver country was a war zone in which mercy was neither shown nor expected. War parties struck swiftly, silently, and left chilling reminders of what awaited those who violated their hunting grounds. "We found the man that the Indians had killed," wrote Pattie.

> They had cut him in quarters, after the fashion of butchers. His head, with his hat on, was stuck on a stake. It was full of arrows, which they had probably discharged into it, as they danced around it. We gathered up the parts of the body, and buried them.

Pattie later found three trappers, "their bodies cut to pieces, and spitted before a great fire, after the same fashion which is used in roasting beaver."[12]

To survive, the mountain man had to learn the Indians' ways. Like the Indian, he became so familiar with his surroundings that he blended into them. He "read" nature not only with his eyes, but with his ears, nose, and intuition. He learned that sand thrown up in piles meant young deer had been playing and, therefore, felt safe. He could touch a pile of manure and tell by its shape, hardness, and warmth what kind of animal had left it, what it had eaten, and if it was still in the vicinity. A wolf's off-key howling, or birds suddenly rising from the underbrush, told him that something unusual was happening and he had better look out. Then there was his "sixth sense," a gut feeling or hunch that put him on alert even though everything seemed normal.

The mountain man copied the Indian's fighting style, adding a few twists of his own. A master of ambush, he took advantage of every tree and rock to conceal his approach. There was no such thing as a battle, a stand-up fight between organized groups. A hail of bullets announced the trapper's presence, preferably while his foe was asleep, followed by a war whoop and a charge with knife and tomahawk. Within minutes it was all over. Then, like the Indian, he took scalps. He put his feet against his victim's shoulders for leverage, grabbed his hair with one hand, and cut a circle around it with a knife. A quick jerking motion pulled it away from the skull with a sound like *flop*. Later his wife decorated his hunting shirt by sewing clumps of hair into the seams.

Like the Indian, too, the mountain man used terror to frighten his enemies. James Ohio Pattie describes a typical incident in which a war party escaped an ambush, leaving its dead and wounded to the trappers' mercy. They showed no mercy. Instead, they killed them all and hung the bodies in trees "to dangle in terror to the rest."[13] Another time a trapper was about to shoot the only survivor of a war party when a comrade knocked his rifle aside. "Ef ye kill that Injun, ye'll do it over my carcase," he snarled. "I want that red varmint to live so's he kin drag into his village an' tell the rest o' them skunks jes' who 'twas rubbed out their war party. Otherwise they might never know. They gotta larn t' respec' decent Christians."[14]

Mountain men and Indians often went a long time between meals. Here, too, whites learned from their enemies. In a pinch, anything became food. A ravenous trapper might chew grass, gnaw tree bark, or swallow beetle grubs whole. An old-timer recalled:

> I have held my hands in an ant-hill until they were covered with ants, then greedily licked them off. I have taken the soles of my moccasins, crisped them in the fire, and eaten them. In our extremity the large black crickets which are found in the country were considered fair game. We used to take a kettle of hot water, catch the crickets and throw them in, and when they stopped kicking, eat them.

James Ohio Pattie once shot a raven, a "nauseous bird" he shared with six other men.[15]

The mountain man's ideal food was meat. No quarter-pounder hamburgers for him! In good times he ate eight or nine pounds of meat a day. As he said, there was nothing like roasted beaver tail or puppy-dog meat to make his face "shine with grease and gladness."[16] Nothing, that is, except "buffler" meat. Buffalo were usually found in the lower, or front, ranges of the Rockies. In warm weather they grazed the mountain meadows. In cold weather they sheltered in the valleys.

Every part of the buffalo was eaten except the hair, horns, hooves, and eyes. The moment a buffalo fell dead, the mountain man went down on his hands and knees to lap up the blood; it reminded him of warm milk, he said. Slicing the animal open, he reached in up to the elbows and pulled out the liver, which he seasoned with gall and ate raw. If he was lucky enough to shoot a pregnant cow, he had a real treat: the raw legs of an unborn calf. Bones were split to expose the marrow. Melted fat was drunk by the quart; unlike cattle fat, buffalo fat did not upset the stomach. Yards of intestine were squeezed through the teeth to get at the partially digested grass or sucked in like lengths of spaghetti. Many an evening was spent around a campfire eating roasted stuffed intestines, called "boudins" or "boudies." Trapper Thomas Jefferson Farnham recalled such a mountain feast:

> Our friend Kelly . . . seized the intestines of the buffalo, which had been properly cleaned for the purpose, turned them inside out, and as he proceeded stuffed them with strips of well salted and peppered tenderloin. Our *"boudies"* thus made, were stuck upon sticks before the fire, and roasted till they were thoroughly cooked and browned. The sticks were then taken from their roasting position and stuck in position for eating. . . . Each of us with as fine an appetite as ever blessed a New England boy at . . . Thanksgiving Dinner, seized a stick spit . . . and sitting upon our haunches ate . . . these wilderness sausages. . . . The envelopes preserve the juices of the meat with which while cooking the adhered fat, turned within, mingles and forms a gravy of the finest flavor.[17]

Food and fellowship warmed men's hearts and sealed their friendship.

This way of life lasted for little more than a generation. By 1840 the Rocky Mountain beaver streams were so completely trapped out that it no longer paid to hunt the few remaining animals. Moreover, beaver prices had slipped below a dollar a pound, as hats made of Chinese silk became fashionable.

The mountain man's occupation vanished, but he left a precious legacy for his countrymen. In his search for beaver, he explored every corner of a vast territory. In the process, he named scores of mountains, rivers, and valleys after himself and his friends. Yet his greatest achievement was as a pathfinder. As the beaver disappeared, he went into other lines of work. Mountain men became army scouts during the wars against Mexico and the Plains Indians. Some became "pilots," guiding the wagon trains that brought settlers westward to farms in Oregon and forty-niners to California gold fields. Still others led the way to Santa Fe.

It was harder for merchants than trappers to evade Spain's colonial laws; and the few who tried wound up in the Santa Fe calaboose. That changed with the arrival of William Becknell of Franklin, Missouri. A small-time trapper and merchant, Becknell did not set out to earn the title Father of the Santa Fe Trail. In September 1821 he left Franklin with twelve men and a string of pack mules to trade with Indians in the Rockies. Along the way, he met a Mexican army patrol whose commander invited him to Santa Fe. Mexico, the officer explained, had won its independence just a few weeks earlier and welcomed foreign traders into its territories. Becknell accepted the offer and quickly sold everything. When he returned to Franklin, his men emptied bags of silver pesos onto the sidewalk. Becknell never revealed his profits, but one lady made nine hundred dollars on a sixty-dollar investment.

In the years that followed, Americans flocked to New Mexico along the Santa Fe Trail. The route might have been new to them, but it was very old nonetheless. Plains Indians had used it on their westward treks to trade buffalo hides to the Pueblos. Coronado "discovered" it on his trek to Quivira, and Oñate followed it to the same destination. Americans rediscovered it nearly three centuries later; we say "rediscovered" because in the 1830s the history of the Southwest was practically unknown in the United States. From then on the trail's story became an American saga.

The Santa Fe Trail started at Independence, Missouri. Independence lies on the banks of the Missouri River, two hundred miles from its junction with the "Father of Waters," the Mississippi River. Independence was not much of a town during the trail's early days, containing just a few dozen houses, a bank, a printing shop, and three saloons, where rotgut flowed like water. Quiet most of the year, in early spring

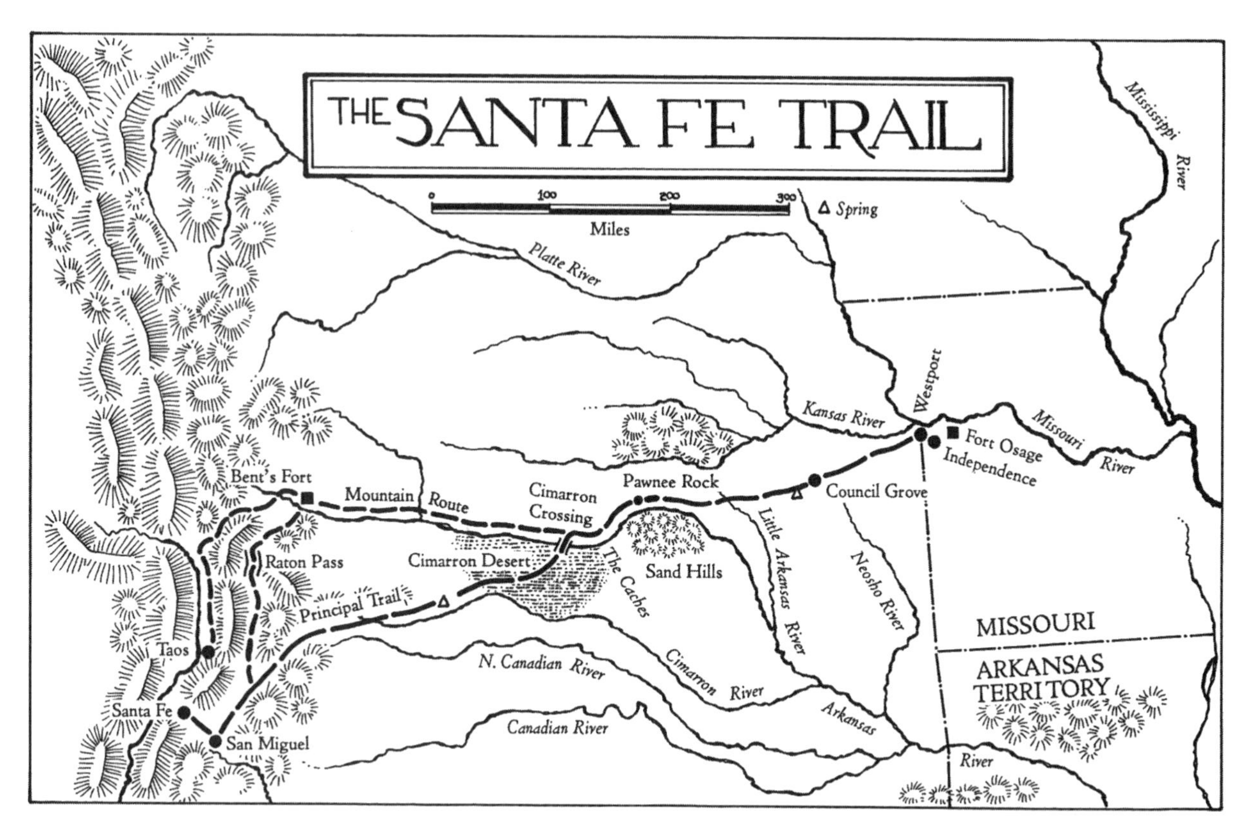

it became one of the liveliest and most colorful places in the country. Fleets of steamboats came upstream belching smoke and tooting whistles, their holds bulging with trade goods. Gangs of sweating stevedores stacked boxes and barrels and bales along the wharves. Brawny packers piled them high on wagons driven by teamsters shouting every curse word in the English language. Waterfront workers, or "wharf rats," were a rowdy bunch. They were fond of fighting and whiskey; when they drank too much, bartenders warned them, "Mind your pints and quarts. Mind your p's and q's." We have been minding our p's and q's ever since.

Success on the trail went not to the brave, but to the cautious. A journey of eight hundred miles, lasting eight to ten weeks, lay ahead of them. This was a long trip to make, and once committed there could be no turning back, for there were no permanent settlements between Independence and San Miguel, the first New Mexican village on the trail.

Before setting out, each member of a trading party stocked up on supplies. He brought the standard rations: fifty pounds each of bacon and flour, twenty pounds of sugar, ten pounds of coffee beans, and a pound of salt. He might also bring a supply of tea, rice, and dried fruits; lemon juice prevented scurvy, a disease caused by lack of vitamin C, which is found in fresh fruits and vegetables. And since there was no doctor, he carried bandages and a vial of opium. An addictive drug, opium was regarded as a cure for many diseases. *Gunn's Standard Medicine,* a basic medical book of the time, praised opium, which "taken in proper quantities, introduces order, harmony and pleasurable serenity."[18] Opium was sold openly in drugstores as a cough medicine and painkiller until early in the twentieth century. In factory towns, mothers unable to afford baby-sitters dosed their infants with "black bottle," a mixture of opium and alcohol, before leaving for work each morning.

Santa Fe traders favored a wagon built in St. Louis by the Murphy family. The Murphy wagon was an animal-drawn version of today's diesel-powered trucks. Built to last, it sold for between two and three hundred dollars, a large sum at a time when factory workers earned under a dollar a day. It was made of oak, stood three feet wide by sixteen feet long, and rolled on wheels five feet tall. The wheels had iron tires five inches wide to support loads of four to five tons. High at the front and back, the wagon had a row of wooden arches covered with white canvas. Seen from the distance, it resembled a ship cruising under full sail, hence the nickname "prairie schooner." And, like a ship, it was brightly painted for greater visibility, with blue woodwork and red wheels. Every seam was caulked with tar to make it watertight when crossing streams.

Prairie schooners were pulled by ten mules or eight oxen. Each animal had its own advantages and disadvantages. Mules were sturdy and did well on the plains. Unfortunately, they were irritable creatures with minds of their own. Mules became stubborn for no apparent reason, and no amount of tugging and kicking could get them moving once they decided to stay put. Oxen, on the other hand, were strong, placid creatures able to pull heavy loads. Yet they were fussy eaters and had delicate feet. It was difficult to make them eat the buffalo grass that was the only forage on the Great Plains; so tender were their feet that drivers shod them with rawhide moccasins. Whatever animal he chose, a smart trader kept an equal number in reserve to replace those that gave out. Oxen suffered most; over the years, their skeletons littered the trail's entire length.

A trader's wagon was actually a country store on wheels. It carried a little of everything, all neatly wrapped and stowed to prevent breakage. Half its cargo consisted of bolts of cloth ranging in value from shoddy cottons to luxurious silks and

The March of the Caravan. A traders' caravan advances in formation on the last leg of its journey to Santa Fe, New Mexico. Drawing from Josiah Gregg's Commerce of the Prairies.

velvets, plus men's and women's clothing: hats, shirts, blouses, shawls, sashes, veils, shirts, pants, shoes, boots, handkerchiefs, ribbons. There were boxes of personal grooming supplies, household items, and hardware. A partial listing of these would include: rings, necklaces, bracelets, earrings, buttons, and beads; combs, toothbrushes, silver toothpicks, mirrors, and razors; clocks and watches; sewing needles, knitting needles, pins, yarn, thread, and thimbles; pots, pans, dishes, and window glass; wax, candles, and candlesticks; pens, pen points, writing paper, ink, and books; lamps, lamp wicks, and whale oil. There was hardware, cutlery, and weapons; butcher knives, pocketknives, hunting knives, scissors, and axes; guns, lead for making bullets, and gunpowder. Drugs included "medicinal whiskey," opium, and mercury, a poison said to cure various diseases. Empty bottles were especially profitable. Pueblo Indians prized colored bottles, giving the value of fifty cents for each. A trader could buy a dozen bottles of whisky for four dollars in Missouri, drink them up, and then get rid of them at a two-dollar profit.

Traders left Independence in mid-April, when the grass turned green. As wagons rolled out of town, citizens gave them a lively send-off. Men cheered and fired guns. Women waved handkerchiefs and blew kisses. "Even the mules," a visitor noted, "prick up their ears with a peculiarly conceited air."[19] Each wagon traveled separately, bound for Council Grove, Kansas, 150 miles to the west. In Missouri you were still close to civilization and help. But only a suicidal fool would venture onto the Great Plains alone. There was safety in numbers; the more men you traveled with and the better they were organized, the safer you were.

Council Grove was the gathering place for the westward journey. There traders rested their teams, repaired their wagons, and united for the trip ahead. Like the mountain men, they were going beyond the reach of the law. So they, too, made their own. A captain was elected, along with two lieutenants, a guide or pilot, a three-member court, and a chief of the guard. The captain knew his way around. Each day he decided on the route, got the wagons moving, ordered the rest periods, and selected the night's campground. His lieutenants saw that his wishes were obeyed, while the court dealt with rule breakers. When, for example, two men feuded over a bad debt, the court ordered the debtor to shut up and pay up. Since he was broke, the court had the money literally taken out of his hide. He was tied to a wagon wheel and whipped, a lash for each dollar owed. The other fellow had to accept the gory "payment" or get a whipping himself. In this way, a personal quarrel was kept from spreading throughout the company.

Having completed its organization, the traders left Council Grove. A few days on the trail were enough for everyone to settle into the routines. At five o'clock in the morning, the captain roused the sleeping camp with a loud "Turn out!" Each man rolled up his blankets and tossed them into a wagon; there were no sleeping bags and few tents. After a quick breakfast of bacon, biscuits, and coffee, the captain gave his second command: "Catch up! Catch up!" Drivers rushed to harness their mules or yoke their oxen, hitching them to the wagons. They prided themselves on being ready quickly, and within minutes the day's first hitched cried, "All set!" When all the teams were hitched and the wagons in their assigned places, the captain shouted the final command, "Stretch out!"[20]

"Stretch out!" meant exactly that: move out in a column. Since a caravan might contain a hundred wagons, it could stretch a mile. The idea was to move together, rather than move quickly; on an average day, a caravan made between fifteen and eighteen miles. Bullwhackers guided their oxen with various calls; *ho-haw* meant "turn left"; *gee-ho,* "turn right"; and *whoa,* "stop." They were not called bullwhackers for nothing. Each walked alongside his team with a "Missouri pistol," a whip that sounded like a pistol shot when snapped. A bullwhip had a wooden stock ten feet long, tipped with an eighteen-inch lash of braided buckskin tapering to the thickness of a man's pinkie finger. A bullwhacker did not beat his oxen, but, holding the whip with both hands, snapped it over their heads in a swift jerking motion. Although he barely touched a lagging ox, droplets of blood appeared wherever his lash nicked the skin. Rattlesnakes did not get off so easily; with pinpoint accuracy, a bullwhacker beheaded any of these "varmints" that came within range.

Everyone knew the trail's landmarks either from experience or store-bought maps. After Council Grove came Diamond Spring, Cottonwood Creek, Turkey Creek, Cow Creek, and Pawnee Rock, a forty-foot-high pillar used by Pawnee braves to scan the horizon for raiders; white travelers carved their names into the soft sandstone, where they can be seen to this day. Western Missouri and eastern Kansas were glorious in the spring. Rolling long-grass prairies were cut by tree-shaded creeks. At the wagons' approach, partridges and quail rose from their concealed nests. Flocks of wild turkeys were measured in square miles, and antelope bounded in front of the caravan throughout the day. As the wagons neared the Arkansas River, the country gradually grew flatter and drier, the grass shorter. They had reached the Great Plains.

Traders echoed Coronado, comparing the Great Plains to the sea. "Greenhorns," or newcomers, told their diaries about prairie schooners "sailing" on boundless "seas of grass" and "the plains ocean." Like the sea, the plains had wild swings in weather. On a calm day, shimmering heat waves rose from the ground, creating optical illusions. Thirsty men ran toward cool ponds, only to have them disappear as they came close. Or cloudbursts triggered flash floods, turning dry streambeds into raging torrents. Lightning struck men and animals dead, igniting fires that burned for days and covered hundreds of square miles until they went out by themselves. Fires might or might not be dangerous, depending on the wind. You were safe if the wind blew the flames ahead of the wagons, allowing them to go forward without danger. But if the wind drove the fire toward the wagons, lives and property went up in smoke. Fire had its own fascination, particularly at night. A trader described it:

> The long sweeping line of fire stretching from one part of the horizon to the other, the lambent [running] flames soaring high into the air, the flitting forms of animals driven suddenly from cover, and the reflection of the brilliant light on the clouds, composed a scene of truly terrible sublimity.[21]

Depending on weather conditions, the horizon might glow red, orange, or purple.

Travelers compared buffalo herds to schools of fish. Centuries of hunting had, thus far, not put a dent in their numbers. It took hours, often days, for a herd to pass a given point, forcing the caravan to halt. Everywhere the ground was crisscrossed by buffalo trails leading to streams. Crossing a stream behind a herd was not a pleasant experience. Buffalo loved to stand in water; it gave them a rest from the gnats that tormented them with their buzzing and bites. Unfortunately, this habit forced thirsty men to drink the yellow "buffalo tea" they left behind.[22] Nevertheless, "stinkers," as Americans called the buffalo, were a blessing. After weeks of eating salty bacon, nothing hit the spot like a sizzling buffalo steak or a serving of hump ribs. Traders were more squeamish than mountain men; they ate the prime cuts and left the rest to rot.

Buffalo country was also the domain of the horse Indians. Pawnee, Osage, Arapaho, Kiowa: All had terrible reputations among whites. The Comanche, however, were in a class by themselves. A traveler wrote:

> They are a people so numerous and so haughty, that when asked their number, they make no difficulty of comparing it to that of the stars. They are so skillful in horsemanship that they have no equal; so daring that they never ask or grant truces.[23]

Traders vowed to die fighting rather than fall into their hands.

"Keep your eyes skinned," old-timers warned as they neared the Arkansas River. Instead of stretching out, as before, the wagons were arranged in four parallel columns. This formation was actually the walls of a moving fortress. At the first cry of "Injuns!" the columns were formed into a hollow square. As bullwhackers unhitched their teams and moved them to the center of the square, others pushed each wagon head to tail, locked their brakes, and chained their wheels together. Everyone then took cover and waited with loaded rifles; for good measure, some caravans had a few light cannons. The square was such a strong defensive position that no Santa Fe caravan was ever overrun. The traders' methods were later adopted by the pioneers who crossed the plains to Oregon and California.

Only eight whites were killed in attacks on caravans during the first decade of the Santa Fe Trail. That, however, did not mellow traders' attitudes toward Indians. They hated them, the Comanche and the others, calling them "red devils" and "two-legged vermin." A Santa Fe trader put it in a nutshell:

> They are the most onsartainest varmints in creation, and I reckon tha'r not mor'n half human. . . . I'd invite um all to a big feast and make b'lieve I wanted to have a big talk; and as soon as I got um all together I'd pitch in and sculp about half of un, and then t'other half would be mighty glad to make a peace that would stick. That's the way I'd make a treaty with the dog'ond varmints.[24]

We can read hundreds of letters and diaries without finding a word of sympathy for Indians or understanding of their point of view.

The worst part of the trail was the Cimarron Desert in southwestern Kansas. Lying between the Arkansas and Cimarron Rivers, it was fifty miles of soft sand without a drop of water. Before setting out, the captain would order every canteen and water barrel filled; the animals were given a good rest, extra time to graze, and made to drink until their bellies bulged. Even so, the three-day trip was hellish. It was a tough pull, and the water quickly ran out. Thirsty men were known to cut off mules' ears and suck the blood. Oxen became frantic. Approaching the Cimarron River, they smelled the water miles ahead. Stampede! The beasts took off, dragging their wagons at top speed. Nothing the bullwhackers did could make them stop or prevent wagons from tipping over.

Comanche war parties passing through the Cimarron Desert usually gave the heavily armed caravans lots of room. Those separated from a caravan or traveling alone, however, were fair game.

The Comanches' best-known victim should have known better. Jedediah Smith was a trapper and explorer, the first white to cross the Sierra Nevada Mountains into California. He was tough as rawhide, and with the scars to prove it, having lost an ear in a "scrape" with a grizzly bear. In 1831, at the age of thirty, he decided to lead his own caravan. That was a mistake. Although he knew the Rockies like the back of his hand, he was a greenhorn on the Santa Fe Trail. While crossing the Cimarron Desert with twenty wagons and eighty men, the caravan lost its way and ran out of water. Apparently Smith thought he could go anywhere. Leaving the caravan, he set out to find the river by himself. He did, but the Comanche found him,

Pecos fell into ruin after marauding Apaches forced its inhabitants to abandon their homes. From a drawing in William M. Thayer's Marvels of the New West, 1888.

too. They shot him full of arrows, scalped him, and left his body for the buzzards.

Once across the Cimarron, a caravan had smooth sailing the rest of the way. Moving quickly, it reached San Miguel, which lay at the head of a regular road. Two days later, it swung past the ruins of Pecos, home of Whiskers and the Chief. Pecos had gone downhill since the great rebellion, thanks to the Comanche. Year after year, raiders swept in from the plains to kill men, kidnap women and children, and steal whatever they could carry. By the 1790s only a few families remained, and these soon left as well. Like the Anasazi cliff dwellings, Pecos was abandoned to the screech owls and scorpions.

From Pecos the trail climbed the long slope to Glorieta Pass. The first man to reach the top shouted at the top of his voice. Below lay their destination, the Royal City of the Holy Faith of Saint Francis. As others came up, hats flew into the air, pistols went off, and whips snapped. The celebration was brief, since everyone wanted to "rub up," look his best for the *señoritas*. Washing the dust from their faces, they slicked down their hair and put on their Sunday best.

The caravan wound its way down the six-mile-long hill that led to Santa Fe. They were expected. All the city's inhabitants, three thousand strong, turned out to welcome them with open arms.

"Los americanos!"—"Los carros!"—"La entrada de la caravana!" they cried. "The Americans!"—"The wagons!—"The entry of the caravan!"[25]

The caravan halted at the customhouse in the central plaza, opposite the old governor's palace. After declaring their cargo, the owners paid an import duty of five hundred dollars per wagon. That was what the law required, but they usually smuggled an amount equal to what they declared; others bribed the customs agents to look the other way. The formalities completed, they sold their goods to local shopkeepers and merchants who visited the outlying haciendas; some New Mexicans,

Santa Fe at last! The capital of New Mexico as it appeared around the year 1846.

called Comancheros, ventured onto the Texas plains to trade with the Comanche. Profits were high. In a good year, traders earned 300 percent on their investments, but usually profits averaged between 10 and 40 percent.

During their spare time, visitors took in the sights of Santa Fe. The town itself was not attractive. Dusty and smelly, it had no sewers and its narrow streets were littered with garbage and horse manure. Streets were lined with one-story houses of adobe brick with tiny windows and flat roofs. The floors of the houses were of adobe, too, which was fine so long as they stayed dry; inside walls were coated with lime "to a dazzling whiteness,"[26] an American recalled. Rich and poor shared one thing in common: a lack of education. Santa Fe had no newspapers, no libraries, and no public schools. Apart from the Catholic priests, few citizens could read. But that did not make the *señoritas* any less attractive.

Like their sisters in Old Mexico, New Mexican girls dressed differently and carried themselves differently than those in the States. A "proper" American girl of "good family and morals" wore no makeup or, heaven forbid, used tobacco. She never showed more of herself than her face and hands. Modesty demanded that she wear dark, heavy stockings and long dresses with layers of petticoats, bustles, long sleeves, high necks, and tightly laced bodices with metal stays that hid her figure. Winter and summer, rain or shine, she wore the same costume.

Señoritas preferred a loose-fitting, low-necked, short-sleeved *camisa,* or blouse; a short skirt; a colorful shawl; and slippers worn without stockings to reveal their legs and ankles. Nor were they strangers to *cigarritos*—little cigars, called "cigarettes" by Americans. Everyone smoked in public. Both women and men carried a small tobacco pouch and could roll a cigarette in a piece of paper or a corn husk with a few twists of the fingers. New Mexican women also wore makeup. They began by coating their faces with a paste of white flour or chalk, then daubed their cheeks and painted their lips with the red juice of the *alegría* plant.

Visitors claimed never to have seen an ugly *señorita.* A trader wrote:

> Their brilliant eyes make up for any deficiencies of feature, and their figures, uninjured by frightful stays, are full and voluptuous. Now and then, moreover, one does meet with a perfectly beautiful creature; and when a Mexican woman does combine such perfection she is "some punkins," as the Missourians say when they wish to express something superlative in the female line."[27]

The best place to find female companionship was at the fandango, or Spanish ball. Everyone danced. And how they danced! It was unlike anything Americans had ever seen. Back home, women's bulky outfits prevented them from moving quickly, much less getting close to their partners. Hispanic dances, however, had lots of movement and personal contact. In La Cuna ("The Cradle"), for example, couples danced with arms locked and their heads thrown back. Other favorites included El Zapatero ("The Shoemaker"), El Sastroncito ("The Little Tailor"), and El Espadero ("The Swordsman").

The Americans watched from the sidelines. After a while, an invitation might hit them in the head; the custom was that if you wanted to attract a partner of the opposite sex, you broke an eggshell filled with cologne over his or her head. Awkward at the beginning, the visitors caught on quickly. James Ohio Pattie was an old hand at fandangos:

> The fandango room was about forty by eighteen or twenty feet, with a brick floor raised four or five feet above the earth. That part of

> the room in which the ladies sat, was carpeted with carpeting on the benches, for them to sit on. Simple benches were provided for the accommodation of the gentlemen. Four men sang to the music of a violin and guitar. All that chose to dance stood up on the floor, and at the striking up of a certain note of the music, they all commenced clapping their hands. The ladies then advanced, one by one, and stood facing their partners. The dance then changed to a waltz, each man taking his lady unceremoniously, and they began to whirl around, keeping true, however, to the music, and increasing the swiftness of the whirling. Many of the movements and figures seemed very easy, though we found they required practice. . . . Be that as it may, we cut capers with the nimblest, and what we could not say [in so many words], we managed by squeezes of the hand, and little signs of that sort, and passed the time to a charm.[28]

New Mexican men were flashy dressers. A gentleman's outfit was topped by a *sombrero,* a wide-brimmed hat to shade him from the sun. His *chaqueta,* or jacket, had large buttons and was embroidered with elaborate designs. For pants he wore *calzoneras,* with the outer leg of the garment open from the waist to the ankle, the edges trimmed with lace and colored braid. In cold or wet weather, he wore a *serape,* a woolen cape with a hole in the center through which he put his head. When out riding, he put on *chaparerras* (American cowboys still call them "chaps"), leather overalls to protect his legs in high brush. Attached to his boots were a pair of spurs, each with a rowel, a rotating disk with points to nudge the horse along. Big spurs and rowels were not meant to frighten anyone or to show off. The rule was: The bigger the rowel, the gentler the rider. A small rowel had few points and dug deep, drawing blood. A big rowel—say two inches in diameter—had many points

Wealthy landowners, or hacendados, as they dressed in the early 1880s.

Carrera de gallo, or "snatching the rooster," was a popular sport throughout the Spanish colonies in the New World. The sport, though hard on roosters, allowed men to prove their courage and show off their riding skills.

close together, which did less damage to the animal's side.

Men's sports were played on horseback. Horse racing was a popular activity, during which lots of money changed hands. Other games tested balance, timing, and eye-hand coordination at high speed. In the *coléa de toro,* several horsemen raced for the honor of being first to "tail" a wild bull. The object was not to kill, as in a bullfight, but for a rider to lean over and grab the tail, throw his right leg over it and give it a sharp jerk, sending the animal crashing to the ground. In *correr el gallo,* "coursing the rooster," a rooster was hung on a tree by his feet or buried in the ground up to his neck. His head and neck were then well greased. The riders charged, each trying to yank off the rooster's head in a single motion, no easy task when you have a handful of grease. Eventually, the bird was torn to pieces and the winner presented the bloody head to his admiring lady.

After a stay of three to four weeks for the traders, the wagons were loaded for the return trip. They were lighter now, carrying about a thousand pounds of cargo each, mostly furs, hides, and wool. Their chief cargo, of course, was gold and silver coins. These were put into bags of wet cowhide, shaken down, and the openings tightly sewn. The hide shrank as it dried, pressing the contents into a solid mass. To avoid the autumn snows, caravans had to be gone from Santa Fe by the first of September. The return trip took about forty days.

So the wagons rolled on, year after year, across the Great Plains. Yet they were only part of a larger story. America was on the move, bringing different ideas and different ways to the Southwest. That movement was compared to the rumbling of an approaching storm. When it finally struck, it would not be in New Mexico, but next door, in Texas.

Texans and All Americans in the World

Commandancy of the Alamo
Feby 24, 1836

To the People of Texas and All Americans in the World–

Fellow Citizens and Compatriots:

I am besieged with a thousand or more Mexicans under Santa Anna. I have sustained a continual Bombardment and cannonade for 24 hours and have not lost a man. The enemy has demanded surrender at discretion, otherwise, the garrison is to be put to the sword, if the fort is taken. I have answered the demand with a cannon shot. . . . I shall never surrender or retreat. Then, I call upon you in the name of Liberty, of patriotism, and everything dear to the American character, to come to our aid with all dispatch. . . . If this call is neglected I am determined to sustain myself as long as possible and die like a soldier who never forgets what is due his honor and that of his country.

VICTORY OR DEATH.

William Barret Travis
LT. COL. COMD'T.

Our future Lone Star State was the last part of the Southwest to be settled by Spaniards. Within a decade of the Pueblo revolt in New Mexico, exploring parties were crossing the Rio Grande farther south. Moving in a northeasterly direction, they met the Hasinai, peaceful farmers who lived in small, scattered villages. When asked to identify themselves in sign language, the Hasinai misunderstood the question.

Instead of giving their name, they cried, "*Teychas! Teychas!*" ("Friends! Friends!") The word came to be spelled two ways in official reports: *Tejas* and *Texas.*

Texas proved to be a disappointment. No precious metals were found, and it was seen merely as a distant wasteland beyond the Rio Grande. Eventually, the land itself would be the real treasure.

In 1682 the French explorer René-Robert, Cavelier de La Salle, descended at the Mississippi River and, arriving at its mouth, claimed all the territory along its course, which he named Louisiana in honor of his king, Louis XIV. La Salle dreamed of an empire stretching from New France (Canada) to New Spain. Using Louisiana as a base of operations, he planned to seize Durango and other silver-mining centers. Although La Salle died before he could put the plan into effect, Louis XIV still hoped to bring the Southwest under French control. In the following years, French agents visited the horse Indians to win them as allies. Among the gifts they brought were guns, making the tribes even more dangerous to the Spaniards. Finally, in 1717 the French began building the city of New Orleans at the mouth of the Mississippi. It was a challenge Spain dared not ignore.

The following summer, construction was begun on a town and four missions among the Hasinai of eastern Texas. The town, San Antonio, was located on the banks of a river with the same name. One of the missions was called San Antonio de Valero in honor of Governor Valero. Locals called it the Alamo, from *los álamos,* a clump of cottonwood trees that grew nearby. Texas, therefore, began as an outer defense for New Spain. Apart from some soldiers and friars, who were sent there by their superiors, the colony attracted few settlers during its first century of existence. It was too distant, too rugged, and too dangerous for any but the bravest, or the most foolish, people to venture into.

The worst threat came from the Comanche, who killed intruders on sight. Having crushed the Plains Apache, they turned on the Spaniards. Not even San Antonio was safe from their marauding bands. Whenever they felt like it, war parties took over the town, making the soldiers hold their horses while they looted private homes. After 1759 no Spaniard ventured west of San Antonio. If anyone wanted to go to Santa Fe from there, they had to recross the Rio Grande and head northwest, a route that added hundreds of miles to the journey.

Another problem arose in the late 1790s. Evading Spanish patrols, enterprising Americans crossed into Texas from Louisiana to capture wild horses for sale in the southern states. They called themselves "mustangers," since they caught mustangs; Spaniards called them *piratas,* or "pirates." Like pirates at sea, they were considered "enemies of the human race," having no legal rights whatsoever. If captured, they could be executed without a trial.

The most daring mustanger was Philip Nolan. Not only did Nolan take horses, he was a top-notch scout and the first English-speaking person to draw an accurate map of Texas. Try as they did, for five years the Spaniards failed to corner him. In 1801, however, a cavalry patrol ambushed his party. Nolan was shot and his ears cut off as a souvenir for the governor of Texas. Every fifth man was sentenced to be hanged and the rest given ten years at hard labor in the jungles of southern Mexico. But a Spanish official ruled that only one should die. The survivors were forced to kneel, blindfolded, and handed two pairs of dice. The fellow who threw the lowest number went to the gallows. The official's action was fair and humane, by the standards of the day. Luck had nothing to do with the outcome; people believed that those who threw a high number had been spared by God.

Wise men warned that Nolan's death would not discourage his countrymen. They were right. The Louisiana Purchase advanced the American frontier to the Sabine River, Texas's northern border. Mustangers swarmed across the Sabine. Land-hungry pioneers built farms, in effect stealing thousands of acres of fertile farmland. Appeals to the government in Washington fell on deaf ears. It would not stop them—*could* not stop them. Indeed, politicians and newspaper editors were claiming Texas as part of the purchase. With barely four thousand whites living in an area nearly a third the size of Mexico itself, it seemed impossible to stem the flood of trespassers. Unless something was done, and soon, Texas would be absorbed by the United States.[1]

The Mexican government decided on a bold scheme. In 1821, just as William Becknell was opening the Santa Fe trade, it offered Americans free land in Texas. Each family would receive 177 acres if it intended to farm, or 4,428 acres if it went into ranching, because cattle needed extra room for grazing. Immigrants would also live tax-free for ten years and pay no duties on imported goods for seven years. All they had to do was give up their American citizenship and swear to be loyal Mexicans. Such generosity was supposed to accomplish two things at once. First, colonies of Americans would form a human barrier between the Mexican settlements and the Comanche. Second, colonists would defend their adopted country against foreigners; that is, against their former countrymen.

The program was given over to contractors, or "empresarios," who received huge tracts of land for bringing in settlers. The leading contractor was Moses Austin, who developed the idea of Texas colonization and chose a site along the Brazos River for his colony. When he died, his son took over the enterprise. A soft-spoken Missouri lawyer, Stephen F. Austin built the town of San Felipe de Austin; shortened to Austin, it was to become the capital of the Lone Star State. Austin's first settlers were known as the "Old Three Hundred," the Texas equivalent of the First Families of Virginia or New England's Mayflower Pilgrims.

In their advertisements, promoters described Texas in glowing terms. This amazing country, said the ads, was as large as the human imagination. In the spirit of democracy, it offered land, liberty, and prosperity to anyone willing to work. People believed and, before long, "Texas fever" was sweeping the United States. Families came from every corner of the nation, particularly the South, bringing slaves to labor on the cotton plantations that sprang up along the Gulf of Mexico. In frontier towns men scrawled *GTT* (Gone to Texas) on their doors and headed for the promised land.

Stephen F. Austin was invited by the Mexican authorities to bring Anglo-American settlers into Texas. A painting in the San Jacinto Museum of History, LaPorte, Texas.

They were not disappointed. The early settlements were located in the most fertile eastern areas, far from the dry plains and the Comanche to the west. The prairies of eastern Texas were seas of waving grass and carpets of wildflowers—Spanish bayonet, Mexican poppy, Texas plume—that stretched to the horizon. Streams teemed with fish and bullfrogs big as a man's head. Along the river bottoms lay rich black soil and stands of fine timber. The soil grew pumpkins that only a strong man could lift and sweet potatoes large enough to serve an entire family. Travelers were swept away by the land's bounty and beauty. Texas, gushed Captain William S. Henry of the U.S. Army, was God's

An Anglo-American family working and playing near their cabin in Texas around the year 1836.

country. "No summer climate can exceed it in loveliness; the everlasting breeze deprives the sun of much of its heat. Such evenings! Such a morn! Young people should come here to make love; the old should emigrate and rejuvenate themselves."[2]

Texas still took a lot of getting used to. It was a land of extremes. As the proverb says: "If it is cold with us, it freezes; if it is hot, it melts; if it rains, it pours." Northers could set teeth chattering as the thermometer plummeted within minutes. On cold nights, you could expect a rattlesnake to join you in bed for warmth. Seven-inch centipedes and quarter-pound tarantulas were marvels of nastiness, particularly when they took up residence in your shoes while you slept.

And then there was the work: months of grueling labor in every sort of weather. Not only must a pioneer family clear the land and "put in" a crop, it had to build a home from scratch. The typical family lived in a two-room log cabin with a "stick and mud" chimney for cooking, heating, and light. Cabins were windowless, with dirt floors and a few pieces of furniture made on the spot or brought from the old house. Women worked harder than men, who could at least take time out for hunting. They also worked longer hours, what with cooking, cleaning, mending, caring for the children, doctoring the farm animals, grinding cornmeal, baking bread, spinning cotton, weaving cloth, turning fat into soap, and molding candles. No woman disputed the remark by pioneer Noah Smithwick: "Texas was heaven for men and dogs; hell for women and oxen."[3]

Settlers prided themselves on being "go-ahead folks" with an inborn "go-a-head-a-tiveness."[4] Their energy and drive seemed boundless. In less than a decade, they developed Texas more than the Spaniards had done in a century. They built towns with names like Goliad, Harrisburg, New Washington, and Washington-on-the-Brazos. New farms, ranches, and plantations dotted the landscape. Roads were laid out and ferries installed at river crossings. Population skyrocketed. By 1830 Anglo-Americans numbered thirty thousand, nearly eight times the Hispanic total.

Mexicans became alarmed. No doubt some were jealous of the newcomers' prosperity. Still, there was genuine cause for concern. Each day made a basic fact clear: Anglos were not part of *la raza*, "the race." This term had nothing to do with "race" as English speakers understood it. For Anglos, race was linked to blood; if you came from "good stock," you were "superior" to those who did not. We call this idea "racism." *La raza*, however, referred to a cultural heritage spread by Spain throughout Latin America. Although Spain had lost its empire, Spanish art, poetry, music, religion, and values continued to shape people's thoughts and outlook.

Americans came out of a different tradition. During the twentieth century, peoples in developing countries spoke of the "ugly American," an aggressive, bigoted bully who boasted of his country's wealth and power. Nineteenth-century Mexicans used similar terms. Anglos were seen as greedy, grasping, and ungrateful. This may not have been true of all Anglos, but it was true enough in too many cases.

Anglos were clannish, rarely associating with Mexicans or bothering to learn the Spanish language. In addition to their material possessions, they brought American ideas of government, politics, morality, and work. Certainly their "go-a-head-a-tiveness" got things done in a hurry, but it came across as pushiness to Mexicans, accustomed to a more relaxed pace. In turn, Anglos scorned Mexicans as lazy and stupid. Captain Henry wrote:

> It certainly was never intended that this lovely land . . . should remain in the hands of an ignorant and degenerate race. The finger of Fate

> points . . . to the time when they will cease to be owners, and when the Anglo-American race will rule with republican simplicity and justice, a land literally "flowing with milk and honey. . . ."[5]

Such statements were seldom challenged by Americans. Racism was an accepted attitude and would remain so for generations to come.

Religious differences added fuel to the fire. To be eligible for land, a settler had to become a Roman Catholic. Few did, or did so sincerely. The majority were Protestants, whose various groups had been feuding with Catholics since the time of Cabeza de Vaca. Back in the States, Protestants were so resentful of the Catholic minority that mobs burned churches and beat up priests. Similarly, Hispanics were despised for their religious beliefs. Catholic priests were accused of paralyzing people's minds with superstition. Stephen F. Austin thought so, and said so in no uncertain terms. Mexicans, he wrote in a private letter, "are bigoted and superstitious in the extreme. . . . To be candid the majority of the people of the whole nation as far as I have seen want nothing but tails to be more brutes than the apes."[6]

For their part, Mexicans were shocked by the Anglos' apparent disrespect for religion. Take, for example, the expression "God damn!" An Anglo would "God damn this" and "God damn that" and "God damn the man in the moon." No offense was intended, and none usually taken, at least by Anglos; it was merely a strong way of making a point. Mexicans, however, were so deeply offended that they invented insulting names for their neighbors. Several Texans together were called "Godamees," a single Texan "Señor God Damn." In return, Texans called Mexicans "greasers," "bean eaters," and "dagos."

Americans had been invited to Texas to prevent its being gobbled up by the United States. Yet, by 1830 Texas was rapidly becoming Americanized. Mexico City decided to slam on the brakes while it still could. A law passed on April 6 closed the border to Americans at the same time as Mexicans and immigrants from other foreign countries were encouraged to settle in Texas. Moreover, settlers would be taxed and duties collected on imported goods before the time originally promised. To enforce the law, soldiers were sent to key locations throughout the colony. Without realizing it, or intending to, the government had set the stage for further trouble. Mexico was about to learn the same painful lessons Great Britain had learned from the American Revolution.

That event was still a living memory. As youngsters, Texans had heard about it from their fathers and grandfathers, many of whom had served under George Washington; there were even some Revolutionary War veterans among the settlers. For these people, liberty was not just a word. It was something to live for, and fight for, and kill for if necessary. Liberty's enemy was no longer British, but he acted in exactly the same way. Taxation without representation! Broken contracts! Tariffs on imports! Military occupation! Soldiers behaving like bullies! Civilian rule replaced by military rule!

Once again the wheels of revolution began to turn. Again, committees of correspondence were formed to keep each other informed about events in their respective part of the colony. Again, smugglers brought in duty-free goods, this time from New Orleans. Again, committees of safety sprang up to organize citizen-soldiers like the minutemen.

In May 1832 seven colonists were arrested for smuggling at the port of Anáhuac on Galveston Bay. Rushing to their defense, local people seized the town and captured the Mexican garrison. Soon word of their action was spreading across Texas with the speed of a prairie fire, as other towns followed Anáhuac's example. The colonists did things that no government anywhere in the world could overlook without endangering its own existence. Yet the Mexican government was powerless, at least for the moment. Civil war had raged on and off since Mexican independence from Spain, with one general after another seizing the presidency, only to be overthrown in turn. On average, a president lasted seven and a half months in office. Rather than provoke a full-scale uprising, the authorities decided to swallow their humiliation. The troops were withdrawn from Texas.

Another general took over within the year. No ordinary thug, he was one of history's complete scoundrels. He would be Mexico's president five times between 1833 and 1855. During those years, he would cause thousands of deaths, unimaginable suffering, and national tragedy. Mexican schoolbooks still treat him as the nation's top criminal. His name was Antonio López de Santa Anna.

Born in 1794, Santa Anna became a soldier at sixteen, rising to the rank of general within twelve years. He was a quiet man, five feet ten inches tall, with pale skin and dark, sad eyes that made him look more like a bookish professor than the scoundrel he was.

Santa Anna was power hungry—no, power crazy. There were no limits to his ambition or the methods he used to achieve it. The more power he gained, the more power he craved. Even the power of God could not have satisfied him for long. "Were I made God," he admitted, "I should wish to be something more."[7] But if he could not be God, at least he could be Napoleon, who, to his mind, ranked a close second. Calling himself the "Napoleon of the West," he collected mementos of the French dictator, even combed his hair from back to front, just like his hero. Yet he was more than a play-actor. Like Napoleon, he had a keen sense of timing, was a brilliant organizer, and was totally ruthless. He cared nothing for human life—except, of course, his own.

Because he was a dictator and led his country to defeat in wars against the Texans and the United States, General Antonio López de Santa Anna is one of the most hated figures in Mexican history.

Santa Anna was a complicated person. As an opium addict, his personality could change in a split second. Brave in battle, he could also be so cowardly that officers had to use all their self-control to keep from laughing in his face. A liar, a bully, and a thief, he robbed churches if he ran short of cash; he once dressed soldiers in burial shrouds and had them hold up a church during Mass, stealing the donations for the poor. Vain and conceited, he demanded his luxuries, though everyone around him was miserable. He wore a uniform heavy with gold braid and carried a sword worth seven thousand dollars. During campaigns, his private wagon train was loaded with luxuries he could not possibly be without: a silk tent, porcelain dishes, fine silverware, wine bottles with gold stoppers, crates of champagne, boxes of chocolates, a silver chamber pot. Preferring not to ride, he went about in a carriage fit for Napoleon himself. Heaven forbid that His Excellency, El Presidente, should raise saddle sores on his tender behind!

During the first years of his presidency, Santa Anna acted as a reformer. It was just that—an act. He never had any intention of sharing power or governing according to laws made by others. Meanwhile, he made allies, put his henchmen into top government posts, and built his power base. Then he struck. Early in 1835 he abolished the Mexican constitution, sent the congress packing, and became dictator. That fall he turned his attention to Texas.

General Martín Cós, El Presidente's brother-in-law, was sent across the Rio Grande with an army. His mission: crush resistance to Mexican authority.

Stephen Austin hoped that the colonists' differences with Mexico could be settled peacefully. But when he learned that troops were on the way, he knew there could be no turning back. "War is our only resource," he declared. "There is no other remedy. We must defend our rights, ourselves, and our country by force of arms."[8] Austin's call sent dozens of "Paul Reveres" pounding down dusty roads to spread the alarm. Everywhere Anglos took guns down from wall pegs, cleaned them well, and checked their ammunition.

A month before Cós's arrival, a cavalry patrol had been sent to Gonzales sixty miles west of San Antonio. The army had once given the town a light cannon to scare off the Comanche. Now it wanted the gun back. The people refused. The patrol left. End of confrontation.

On October 2, Cós sent a hundred-man detachment to Gonzales. It found 160 volunteers waiting with loaded rifles. Mrs. DeWitt, a Texan "Betsy Ross," had made them a battle flag out of her daughter's silk wedding dress. In the center of the flag she'd embroidered a cannon barrel. A red star was embroidered above the barrel and below it were four neatly lettered words: COME AND TAKE IT.[9] The soldiers came. The volunteers fired, killing one man and forcing his comrades to retreat. The Texans got off without a scratch.

Gonzales has been called "the Lexington of the Texas Revolution." The two events *are* similar. Just as the patriots of 1775 fired the "shot heard round the world" at Lexington, Massachusetts, the men of Gonzales fired the shot heard round Texas. A few days later, delegates met at Austin to set up a government and appoint General Sam Houston commander in chief of the (as yet) nonexistent "Texas army." Stephen Austin was sent to rally support in the United States.

The Texans hoped to keep the enemy off balance until help arrived from the States. On October 9, volunteers seized Goliad, ninety miles southeast of San Antonio. One Mexican soldier died and three were wounded in the assault; the Texans had one man wounded, the revolution's first casualty, a free black named Samuel McCullough. The loss of Goliad made Cós lose his nerve. A more able gen-

The men of Gonzales stand by their gun. When troops under Mexican general Cós arrived, they displayed a flag bearing the motto COME AND TAKE IT. *From a mural in the San Jacinto Museum of History, LaPorte, Texas.*

eral, knowing that his force still outnumbered the enemy, would have attacked. Cós retreated to San Antonio to see what happened next. He did not have to wait long.

The rebels moved on San Antonio, gathering reinforcements from farms and ranches along the way. On October 28, they won a major victory at La Concepción mission east of the city. The Mexicans were astonished at how easily Texans handled their weapons. Slowly, deliberately, they took aim, nearly always hitting their mark. Although not trained soldiers, they had a system that allowed them to keep up a steady fire. Working in pairs, one man fired while his partner loaded, so that there was never a time when everyone was loading at once. The Texans' disciplined fire killed a hundred Mexicans and wounded many more.

Now it was the victors' turn to be astonished. As a rebel approached a wounded Mexican soldier, the man begged him not to shoot. Nor was he alone in this request; scores of prisoners were pleading for their lives.

It took a few minutes to figure out this odd behavior. During the revolution and civil wars in Mexico, losers had usually been forced to give up "at discretion"; that is, unconditionally. Not ones to live and let live, the winners often shot prisoners in droves. As a young officer, Santa Anna had routinely executed those who fell into his hands, including the wounded. "Having no knowledge of civilized warfare," a rebel recalled, "the poor wounded wretches thought they were to be summarily dispatched, and it was painful to hear them begging for the miserable lives that no one thought of taking."[10] Texans prided themselves on fighting as "civilized" men—or at least they did early in the struggle.

Meanwhile, volunteers arrived from the United States. As news of the war spread, another form of Texas fever swept the country. "Texas, Texas, Texas," a newspaper reporter wrote from New York City. "Crowded meetings, and gun-powder speeches, calling down vengeance upon the oppressors of the Texonians, is the order of the day."[11] Demonstrators paraded with banners proclaiming, TEXAS AND LIBERTY. Santa Anna was burned in effigy, and money collected for the "liberty-loving" rebels. To many Southerners, however, "liberty" included the right to maintain slavery.

Americans signed up for the rebel army. They did so for various reasons: love of liberty, love of adventure, love of fighting. And pure greed, too; for the rebels offered land to anyone who joined them with a rifle and a hundred bullets. Volunteer units took names calculated to inspire courage in themselves and fear in the enemy. Among them were the New Orleans Grays and Mobile Grays (from their gray uniforms), Kentucky Mustangs, and Red Rovers of Alabama. Arriving in Texas was a moving experience; some men fell to their knees and kissed its "sacred soil" when they crossed the Sabine River.

San Antonio was encircled after the battle of La Concepción. For six weeks both sides pegged away at each other from a safe distance. The Mexicans kept low, fearing Texan marksmanship; the Texans kept their distance, fearful of Mexican artillery. By December 5, the attackers had figured out a way to advance in safety. While one group fired from cover, another rushed a house with crowbars and axes. Breaking down the door, they shot the defenders and went to work on the walls. Like modern row houses, the houses of San Antonio had common walls. Once inside, it was easy to smash through the

The Alamo in San Antonio, Texas. Until the rebel Texans made it famous by dying there, the Alamo was an abandoned mission used for storage. The "hump" at the top was added by the U.S. Army during the Mexican War.

General Santa Anna watches his men marching to the Alamo. From a mural in the San Jacinto Museum of History, LaPorte, Texas.

adobe bricks into the adjoining house, and so on down the line until they reached the town center. Cós retreated to the Alamo, only to find that he had leaped from the frying pan into the fire. Overcrowded and short of rations, the Alamo could not be held. Cós surrendered on the fifth day of the battle. The victors were generous; they could afford to be, having killed or wounded hundreds of Mexicans at a cost of two dead and twenty-six wounded. After promising to leave Texas forever, the Mexicans were set free.

Santa Anna, however, had made no promises. Furious over the setback, he launched a full-scale invasion. By the time he had finished with them, he vowed, no Anglo would dare raise a finger against a Mexican. The rebel leaders must die. Americans found without passports must be treated as pirates. The costs of the operation would be met by selling the Texans' property.

El Presidente headed north with six thousand troops, the largest army ever seen in the Southwest. To those who didn't know better, victory was a sure thing. The army certainly *looked* impressive. With military bands setting the pace, mounted officers led their regiments through the gates of Mexico City. Officers wore elegant blue uniforms with scarlet fronts, high black boots, and felt hats topped by flowing peacock feathers. Oddly enough, these fancy dressers were in the majority; Mexico's army had twenty-four thousand officers and twenty thousand enlisted men! Elite units—gunners, engineers, shock troops—wore red, blue, and green shoulder knots for identification. Common soldiers wore blue cotton jackets with white belts crossed at the chest, white pants, sandals, and tall leather hats with pom-poms.

Apart from its elite units, the Mexican army was an army of the wretched. Enlisted men earned twelve and a half cents a day, barely enough to keep a Mexico City beggar alive, let alone a man with a family to support. Rations, *if* they arrived, were always short; Santa Anna and his staff sold much of the food and pocketed the money. They did not consider this stealing, but a "bonus" earned through faithful service to the republic.

The soldiers' weapons had improved little in the years since independence. Mexico had few gunsmiths, making it necessary to buy outdated weapons from overseas. The best was the Brown Bess musket used by the British during the American Revolution and Napoleonic Wars. A trained soldier could fire two one-ounce lead balls a minute. But since Santa Anna believed that battle was the best teacher, recruits received no firearms training whatsoever! Even if they had, it would have done little good, given the quality of Mexican gunpowder. It was so inferior that cartridges had to be overloaded, which in turn made the soldier fear his own weapon. One Texan learned this the hard way. Putting a captured Brown Bess to his shoulder, he took aim and pulled the trigger. "My first impression was that I had been struck by a nine-pound cannonball," he recalled. "It kicked me heels over head, and I suppose kept on kicking me after I was down, for when I 'came to' I found that my nose was unjointed and two of my ribs stove in."[12] To avoid the recoil, Mexican soldiers fired from the hip or with the musket held above the head. The idea was not to aim, but to send lots of bullets in the same direction at once. In that way, they were bound to hit something.

Only desperate men enlisted in the Mexican army. And since these were never enough to fill the ranks, others were "pressed" to make up the difference. "Press gangs," actually bands of government-licensed kidnappers, plucked peasants from their fields, townsmen from their shops, and students from their classrooms. Long lines of these wretches could be seen shuffling along the roads chained in pairs, bound for regimental barracks. If a unit was still undermanned, the local jail was emptied and the inmates sworn in as soldiers. Officers regarded their troops as scarcely human, saying they "heard only through their backs," like dumb beasts obeying the driver's whip.[13]

Had this been the whole story, Mexico could not have survived as an independent nation. In truth, its fighting men proved to be better than their leaders, training, and equipment. The typical soldier was a little over five feet tall, stocky, and weighed about 115 pounds. Usually a peasant, he was as tough as they came. A life of hard work in the open had made him strong, thrifty, and able to take hardship in stride. So could his woman. Female camp followers, or *soldaderas,* always accompanied Mexican armies; Santa Anna's had three thousand, half its fighting strength, plus an unknown number of children. Apart from giving companionship, women did many necessary chores: carrying knapsacks, preparing campsites, collecting wood, fetching water, foraging for food, cooking, mending, nursing. If *soldaderas* did not help the sick and wounded, few others would; for Santa Anna's army had no doctors, no stretchers, no surgical instruments, and no medicines. And it had a rendezvous with some of the best marksmen on earth!

After capturing San Antonio, most of the Texans went home. It was winter, and nobody expected another fight until spring, if then. Those who remained spent their time flirting with the *señoritas,* drinking the local firewater, and sleeping late. Whenever they felt like it, which was not often, they worked on the Alamo's defenses.

Abandoned by the friars in the 1790s, the Alamo had served as a fort ever since. A rectangular courtyard, or plaza, 54 yards wide by 154 yards long was surrounded by stone walls three feet thick and from nine to twelve feet high. Against these, facing the plaza on three sides, were a line of adobe huts and the "low barracks," a one-story structure on the south side. The hospital and main sleeping quarters were located in the "long barracks," a two-story building on the fourth, or eastern, side of the plaza. Nearby stood the Alamo church, a roofless building with walls four feet thick.

Sam Houston had doubts about the Alamo. The place, he knew, was merely a make-do fortress. Compared to fortresses designed by military architects, it was not even a joke; it was a death trap. There were no observation towers. Its shallow moat was a dry ditch; besides, it did not go all the way around the enclosure. Its walls, crumbling in places, were too low to withstand a determined assault and had no loopholes, forcing the defenders to show themselves while firing.

Early in January 1836, Houston sent James Bowie to San Antonio. Bowie's orders

James Bowie, slave trader, frontier brawler, and hero of the Alamo.

were to salvage whatever he could from the Alamo, blow it up, and evacuate its garrison to Goliad. Yet he was not the sort of man to run from danger; actually, he liked nothing better than stepping into harm's way. The Alamo seemed to be the "shield" of Texas. If the shield was removed, he reasoned, there would be nothing to prevent Santa Anna from marching all the way to the Louisiana border. So, orders or no orders, he decided hold the Alamo at all costs.

Jim Bowie, thirty-nine, was a big, handsome man with reddish-brown hair and gray-blue eyes. A born adventurer, during his boyhood in Louisiana he had broken wild mustangs and ridden on the backs of alligators. He and his elder brother, Rezin, got rich smuggling slaves into the United States by way of Galveston Island; they bought captured Africans from the pirate Jean Lafitte for a dollar per pound (an average slave, called a "unit," weighed 140 pounds) and sold them for a thousand dollars each.[14] Rezin invented the bowie knife, a single-edged blade nine inches long by an inch and a quarter wide. Although intended for hunting, Jim's use of it as a fighting weapon made it a frontier favorite. In savage brawls called "medleys," he chopped, slashed, and stabbed his way to fame. Knife fighting was considered more dangerous, and therefore more "manly," than dueling with swords or pistols. Truly brave men were supposed to go at each other at close quarters. Jim was the best; he won fights in which the two foes held opposite ends of a handkerchief between their teeth, or had their left wrists tied together.

A month after Bowie's arrival at the Alamo, an officer came to check on his progress. William Barret Travis, twenty-six, was an adventurer of a different sort, an educated man who was not afraid of hardship and could earn the respect of hard men. "Buck," as friends called him, had come to Texas to forget about a failed marriage. A lawyer by profession, he had no respect for Mexican law as vested in the person of Santa Anna. In the first days of the revolt, he joined the cavalry with the rank of lieutenant colonel.

Agreeing that the Alamo must not be abandoned, Travis joined Bowie in strengthening its defenses. They sent work crews to close gaps in the north wall with a framework of wooden beams. The barracks were fortified with trenches dug across the floors and the rooms barricaded by packing earth between stretched cowhides. Fourteen cannons, a "gift" from Cós, were rolled into position. Each fired a nine-pound iron ball; one, the largest gun in Texas, could send an eighteen-pound ball half a mile. Loaded with sawed-up horseshoes, at close range the cannons became gigantic shotguns.

The legendary frontiersman Davy Crockett came to the Alamo with eleven followers eager for a fight. Crockett died, surrounded, it was said, by dead Mexican soldiers. From a colored print in the San Jacinto Museum of History.

On February 8, eleven Tennessee "boys" rode into San Antonio. They'd come, they said, because "we heard you were having trouble with the likes of old Santy Anny and we 'lowed as how we might help you, since we like a good fight."[15] Superb marksmen, they were the equivalent of a hundred ordinary volunteers. The Texans threw them a party.

Their leader was David Crockett, and there was nobody else like him on the planet Earth. Crockett, forty-nine, was a living legend. Tall and fair-skinned, he had a big nose, dark brown hair, and blue eyes. "Davy," as everyone called him, had been an expert hunter since boyhood, having killed over a hundred bears in one season. Outgoing and generous, he had a ready smile that made others want to smile, too. He could also look you in the eye and tell the most outrageous story without cracking a smile. He bragged:

> I'm that same David Crockett, fresh from the backwoods, half-horse,

> half-alligator, a little touched with snapping-turtle; can wade the Mississippi, leap the Ohio, ride upon a streak of lightning, and slip without a scratch down a honey locust; can whip my weight in wild cats and . . . hug a bear too close for comfort.[16]

His gift of gab won him two terms in the Tennessee state legislature and three terms as a congressman. Defeated for reelection, he told his neighbors to go to hell; he was going to Texas.

Young Dan Cloud was standing watch in the bell tower of a San Antonio church on February 23. Suddenly, far out on the plain, he saw cavalry in glittering helmets and breastplates. "Jesus God," Dan whispered, scarcely believing his own eyes. "Jesus God . . . there must be hundreds . . . thousands. . . ."[17] He yanked the bell rope with all his might. *Bong. Bong. Bong.* Again and again, he sounded the alarm. The Mexicans had come!

Buck Travis ordered the garrison into the Alamo. Having been taken by surprise, there was no time to lose. "Quick, Sue," cried Captain Almeron Dickinson as he galloped up to his fifteen-year-old wife, "the Mexicans are upon us! Give me the babe and jump on behind me!"[18] She did. Soon they were among a mass of people rushing in the same direction. Not all were Anglo-Americans. One man, Joe, was Travis's slave; given a gun, he turned out to be a courageous fighter. Nine Mexicans joined the defenders as well, men with names like Badillo and Esparza, Fuentes and Seguin. They did so because they despised the Santa Anna dictatorship. There were also ten Mexican women and their children.

William Barret Travis decided to die in the Alamo with his men rather than retreat or surrender.

Santa Anna sent a demand for unconditional surrender. When Travis replied with a cannon shot, red flags rose over the Mexican positions. The red flag was an ancient symbol. Pirates flew it to announce they would kill any ship's crew that fought back. During the Middle Ages, armies raised the oriflamme, a crimson banner announcing "no quarter," a fight to the death. Santa Anna's flags meant the same thing. *"En esta guerra no habrá prisioneros,"* he told aides. "In this war there will be no prisoners."[19] Several officers objected. The Texans, they pointed out, had never harmed a Mexican prisoner. If Mexicans executed captured Texans, they would surely answer in kind. El Presidente would not listen. He was out for blood, and only blood would satisfy him.

Bowie was the Alamo's first casualty, victim of an unknown disease rather than Mexican gunfire. On February 24, he collapsed while helping to move a cannon, leaving Travis in sole command. Desperate, Travis sent a messenger with his famous plea for aid "To the People of Texas and All Americans in the World." Help arrived on March 2, when thirty-two volunteers from Gonzales slipped through enemy lines at night. Others tried, but failed. In all, Travis had 184 men under his command.

The Mexican artillery kept the defenders awake and on edge, but did no harm. Santa Anna had only light cannons, whose shot could not smash even the Alamo's flimsy walls; his heavy guns were still far to the rear, at least a week away. Mexican muskets were next to useless. The Brown Bess was a smoothbore; that is, the inside of its barrel, or bore, was smooth, which caused the bullet to wobble as it flew. A rifle, however, had rifling, spiral grooves cut on the inside of the barrel. Rifling gave "spin" to a bullet, allowing it to travel farther and travel true. Although the rifle took longer to load, American frontiersmen favored it for hunting and fighting. The Alamo's defenders had plenty of rifles; each kept four or five of them by his side, all loaded and ready for action. Mexicans took cover whenever they saw the tall rifleman they called "Kwockey." Davy Crockett seldom missed.

The siege dragged on. Food and ammunition were running out. So was time. Sensing that the end was near, Travis called his men together during a brief lull on March 5. Drawing his sword, he scratched a line in the dust. "Our fate is sealed," he said firmly. "Within a very few days—perhaps a very few hours—we must all be in eternity. This is our destiny and we cannot avoid it. This is our certain doom."[20]

He stepped over the line, turned around, and slowly moved his eyes from face to face. Who would cross over to him?

One by one, they came. Jim Bowie, flat on his back, asked for help. "Boys, I am not able to go to you, but I wish some of you would be so kind as to remove my cot over there."[21] Four men did as he asked.

Now one man stood alone. Louis Moses Rose was a veteran of the Napoleonic

THE ALAMO
Under Fire

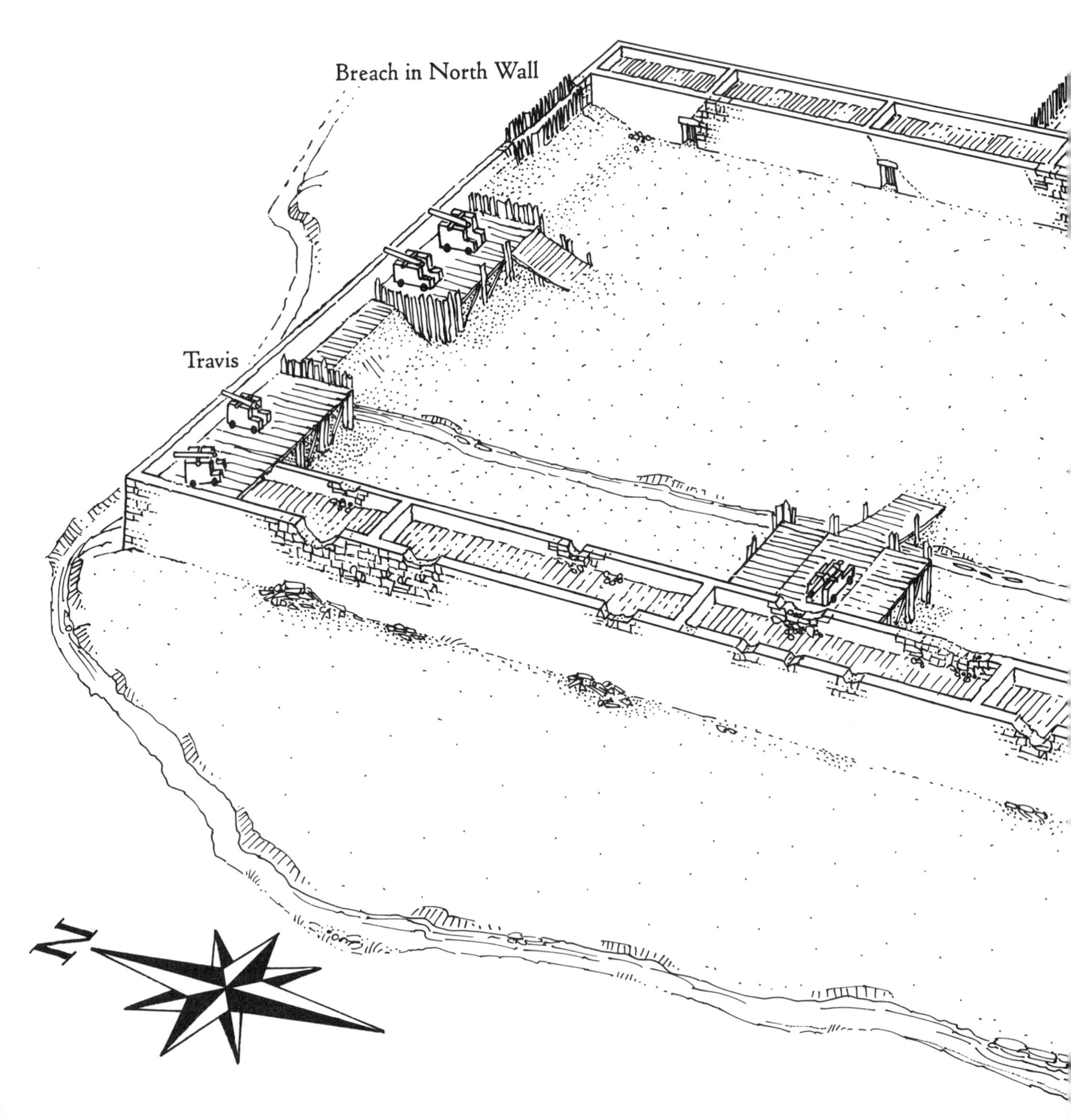
Breach in North Wall
Travis
N

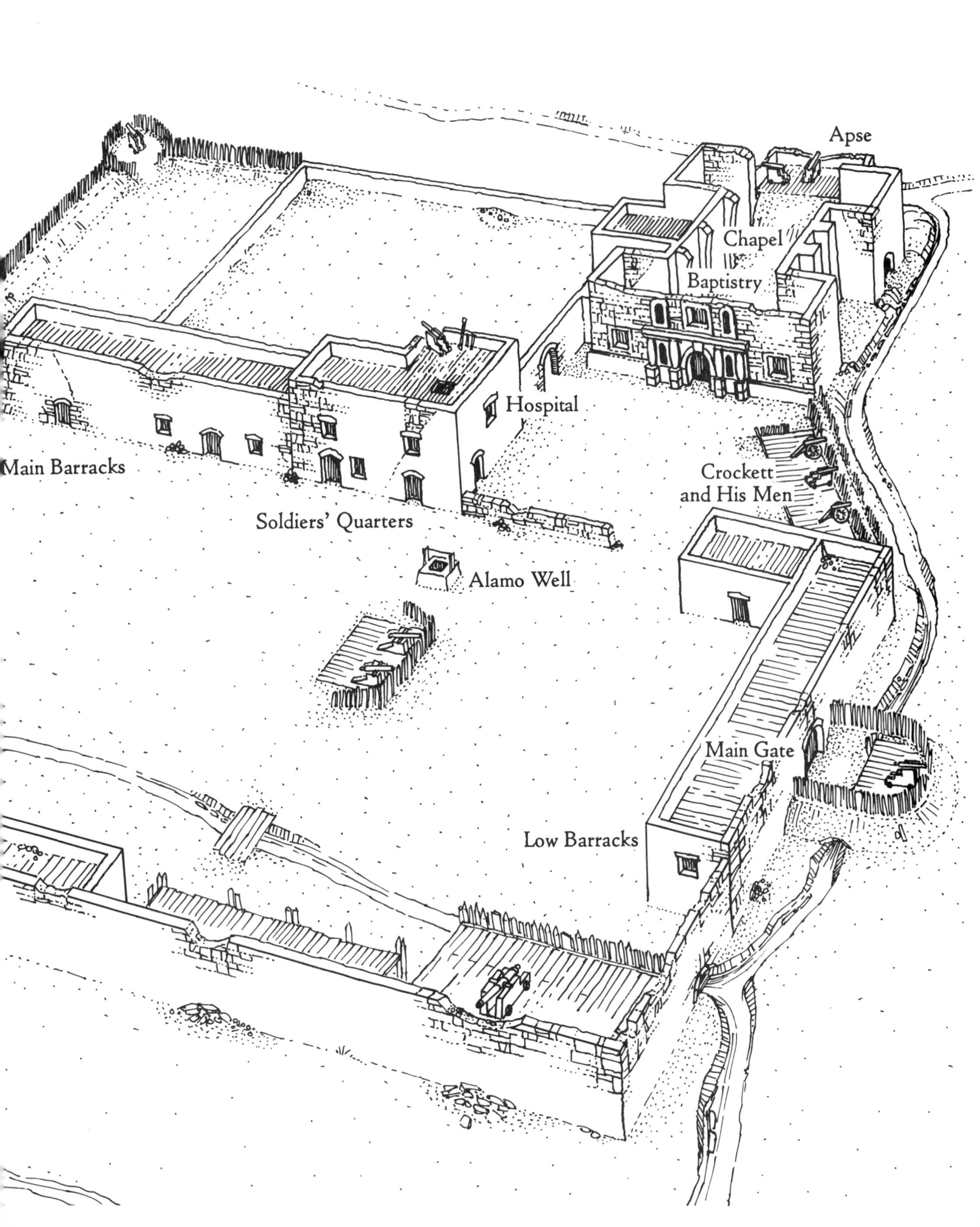

Apse
Chapel
Baptistry
Hospital
Main Barracks
Crockett
and His Men
Soldiers' Quarters
Alamo Well
Main Gate
Low Barracks

Wars in Europe. He had been through it all, seen it all, and knew all about "glorious" death in battle.

Bowie asked Rose if he was willing to die with his friends.

No, he was not.

Crockett reminded him that they were trapped, so he might as well come over and make it unanimous.

No, he would not.

Louis Moses Rose chose life. At sundown he slid over the wall and escaped. As he ran through the darkness, he slipped in a pool of Mexican blood.

Was Rose a coward? No one who hasn't faced a similar situation is qualified to pass judgement. Coward or not, we owe him a debt. He, Sue Dickinson, Travis's slave Joe, and some of the Mexican women left the only eyewitness accounts of the Alamo from the defenders' side.

Rose got away in the nick of time. That night the Mexican guns fell silent. This was no act of human kindness, but the calculation of a killer. Days of stress, exhaustion, and hunger had pushed the Alamo's defenders to the limits of their endurance, so that only raw willpower kept them going. Santa Anna knew they would doze off during the lull; and once a really tired man sleeps, he does not waken easily. While the defenders slept, Mexican assault troops took up their positions. El Presidente knew he would win. Already he could taste victory, feel it in his bones.

His generals felt trouble. Standing before their chief, they argued their case while he ate a chicken supper. They knew what Anglos with rifles could do to troops massed in the open. At the Battle of New Orleans in 1815, Andrew Jackson's frontiersmen had stood behind bales of cotton, waiting in silence. Across the way were veteran British regiments, fresh from defeating Napoleon in Europe. The redcoats charged, only to be mowed down in long red lines. There was no need to do a repeat of New Orleans, the generals told Santa Anna. The Alamo's defenders were not going anywhere. The big guns would arrive soon. When they did, they would blow the walls apart, leaving the infantry not with a battle, but a mopping-up exercise. El Presidente silenced them with the wave of a chicken leg. "What are the lives of soldiers more than so many chickens?"[22] he said sneering. The attack would begin at five A.M. sharp.

March 6, 1836. Sunday, the Lord's Day.

"*Arriba!*" Mexican officers cried. "Up!" Assault troops stood up and stepped out, each unit accompanied by men with scaling ladders. There was no attempt at silence; indeed, Santa Anna wanted to jar the defenders awake, confusing them during the first crucial minutes. So, as his troops charged, bugles blared and bands played a musical version of the red flag. Known as the *degüello,* it was a Moorish battle tune that meant "the throat slitting." The *degüello* sounded throughout the battle, a constant reminder that no prisoners were to be taken.

Travis awoke with a start. Grabbing a double-barreled shotgun, he dashed toward the north wall, shouting for Joe to follow. "Come on, boys!" he cried. "The Mexicans are upon us and we'll give them hell!"[23] Rolling out of their blankets, men rubbed the sleep from their eyes and squinted into the dawn light. Yes, there they were, swarms of Mexicans coming on the run.

The Texans gave them hell. Cannons thundered, spewing iron fragments at the dense formations. Orange flames spurted from rifles. The effect was horrendous. Heads and arms, hats and muskets, flew into the air. Soldiers toppled over, lying quietly in death or writhing in pain.

The attacking lines wavered and broke. Now it was every man for himself. Soldiers dropped their muskets, shouting *"Diablos! Diablos!"*—"Devils! "Devils!" General Francisco Duque, mortally wounded, was trampled to death by his own men.

Yet the Mexicans were soldiers, and brave ones, too. They had to be brave to do what came next. Regrouping, they charged again, only to be broken again. Rising above the savage *degüello* was the sound of Texans cheering.

They were not cheering when the third assault came at eight o'clock. There was no stopping the Mexicans this time. Hundreds of them fell, but those from behind pushed on over the bodies. Ladders went up against the walls. Ladders went down, as Texans shot and clubbed the first men to reach the top.

It was different at the north wall, where troops climbed the beams supporting the damaged section. By ones and twos, then by dozens and scores, they came over the wall. Only then did the first Texan fall. It was Buck Travis. Shot in the head, he rolled down an earthen ramp, coming to rest against a cannon. Seeing the dying man, General Ventura Mora tried to finish him off with his sword. Travis saw him coming. Summoning his last ounce of strength, he plunged his own sword into the Mexican general's chest, and they both closed their eyes for the last time.

Captain Dickinson found his wife in the church. "My God, Sue," he cried, "the Mexicans are in the fort! All is lost! If you live, take care of our child!"[24] Then he

Nearing the end, the Alamo, March 6, 1836. As shown in this drawing, Mexican soldiers have broken into the Alamo and cornered one of its last groups of defenders. The troops obeyed Santa Anna's orders to kill every defender, including the wounded.

kissed her and ran out to join his comrades in death.

There was no hope once the Mexicans came over the north wall. Threatened from behind, the defenders were forced to abandon their positions on the other walls. Fleeing across the plaza, they reached the long barracks, where the bulk of the killing took place.

Had the Mexicans rushed the barracks, they would have been slaughtered. Fortunately, for them, the Texans abandoned their cannons without destroying the firing mechanisms, as regular gunners are trained to do. This allowed the weapons to be used against their former owners. After blasting openings in the barricades, troops cleared the rooms one at a time. They fought *mano-a-mano,* hand-to-hand, the Mexicans with bayonets, the Texans with bowie knives, tomahawks, and clubbed rifles; the fighting was so fast and furious there was no time to reload. In the hospital, the Texans held out until a cannon was dragged in and fired at point-blank range.

Excitement and anger seemed to drive Mexicans out of their minds. Dead bodies were bayoneted over and over again, until they were barely recognizable as human beings. A man seeking refuge in the church was butchered before Sue Dickinson's eyes. She recalled how, "drunk on blood," soldiers stabbed him with bayonets "and lifted him up like a farmer does a bundle of fodder on his pitchfork."[25] Jim Bowie received similar treatment. Lying on his cot in a room near the church door, he was too weak to resist; it is a myth that he slew several Mexicans as they burst into the room. Soldiers repeatedly shot him in the head, splattering his brains against a wall. Soldiers also clubbed a stray cat, shouting, "It is not a cat but an American."[26]

Sue Dickinson and her baby daughter, the Mexican women and their children, and the slave Joe were spared. So was Anselmo Bogarra, a Mexican who lied about having been held prisoner by the Texans. Six of the defenders found hiding under mattresses were dragged before Santa Anna. General Manuel Fernandez Castrillón wanted them spared as an act of humanity. El Presidente refused. Turning on his heel, he ordered the guards to shoot the prisoners. One of them may have been Davy Crockett; Castrillón thought so. Other than the fact that Crockett died in the Alamo, nobody knows how or when the end came. Later stories that he died fighting, surrounded by Mexican corpses, may or may not be true. Surely he would have wished to go out in a blaze of glory.

"It was but a small affair," said Santa Anna, pointing to the heaps of bodies.[27] Small indeed! One hundred eighty-two Anglos and their Mexican allies had been killed. The battle cost Santa Anna sixteen hundred dead and at least half that number wounded. He visited the wounded but could offer only smiles in place of surgeons and medicines. When the town cemetery filled, he had the Mexican dead tossed into the San Antonio River. The Texans' bodies were stacked between layers of wood, doused with oil, and burned. Ever since ancient times, burning enemy dead had been considered the worst insult, and that is exactly what El Presidente intended. When the fires subsided after two days and nights, melted fat stained the earth for several feet beyond the ashes. The ashes were dumped into a pit, whose location has never been found. But this was not the end.

Legend has it that the slain Texans reappeared soon after their cremation. It was said that on dark, moonless nights their ghosts mounted the bullet-scarred walls of the Alamo with swords of fire. So terrible were they, that Mexicans called them *Los Diablos Tejanos*—"The Devil Texans." It was said they would never rest until their deaths had been avenged.

While Santa Anna's army regrouped in San Antonio, strong detachments were sent deep into rebel territory. On March 20, General José Urrea surrounded Colonel James Walker Fannin's command near Goliad. Although Fannin surrendered unconditionally, he had Urrea's promise to do everything possible to save the prisoners' lives. Urrea was an honorable man and fully intended to keep his word.

The prisoners were marched to Goliad and kept under guard in the old Spanish presidio. During the next week, Urrea fought a behind-the-scenes battle for their lives and his own self-respect. The Alamo killings, he wrote his chief, had been of armed men in the heat of battle; killing the Goliad captives would be cold-blooded murder. So be it, replied Santa Anna; if the general wanted to keep his head on his shoulders, he had better follow orders *pronto!* Urrea obeyed. On Palm Sunday, March 27, the able-bodied prisoners were shot on the prairie outside Goliad. The bodies were then robbed, stripped, and burned.

Meanwhile, the wounded awaited the end in Goliad. Hearing the distant shooting, they knew what lay in store for them. Hustled out of their quarters, some on stretchers, others hobbling on crutches, they were mowed down in the street before the eyes of horrified townspeople.

Twenty-seven survived, thanks to brave Mexicans who risked their lives to defy the dictator. One of these was Señora Francisca Alavez, "the Angel of Goliad." The wife of an army officer, Señora Alavez hid several wounded men, later helping them to escape. Colonel Francisco Garay, a combat veteran with no stomach for murder, managed to save others. Mexican soldiers hid prisoners in their own beds, covering them with their bodies during the slaughter. Several officers wept over the day's shameful events.

Santa Anna wanted to terrorize the settlers into leaving Texas. Having regrouped, he sent columns to the north and east. His orders were to burn every town, home, farm, ranch, and plantation in their path. As a result, thousands of families joined "the Runaway Scrape," a mass flight toward the Louisiana border. The work and sweat and sacrifice of fifteen years were often abandoned in as many minutes. Families piled their belongings on wagons and oxcarts or left with only the clothes on their backs. There were more women and children than men, and more old men than men of military age. Women carried babies in their arms, while toddlers clung to their skirts. Heavy rains turned the roads into muddy streams. Everyone was wet and hungry. Shoes wore out. Disease spread. The weak were buried by the roadside.

The Texas army was also on the move. Its commander, Sam Houston, forty-three, had been born in Virginia and raised in the mountains of Tennessee. He stood six feet three, weighed 220 pounds, and had the build of an athlete. A hero of the War of 1812, he was a favorite of Andrew Jackson's. Supported by "Old Hickory," he became a major general in the militia, a member of Congress, and governor of Tennessee. At the height of his career, he might easily have become president had not his teenage bride left for reasons that have never been explained. What is certain is that the resulting scandal ruined his political career. Resigning the governorship, he became an opium addict and went to live with the Cherokee Indians, who gave him the nickname Oo-tse-tee-Ar-dee-tah-skee, or "Big Drunk." Having reached rock bottom, he went to Texas for a fresh start in life. There he quickly got back on his feet and won his fellow citizens' respect.

After the Alamo disaster, Sam Houston led the Texans to a stunning victory over Santa Anna at the battle of San Jacinto.

Houston's retreat was no Runaway Scrape. It was, rather, a calculated move, like a boxer's stepping back to get into position for a knockout blow. Until then, however, there was plenty to do. Troops had to be trained and disciplined. Scouts had to keep tabs on the enemy's movements. Houston's best scouts were a company of twenty-five Mexicans under Juan Seguín, a wealthy San Antonio landowner who despised Santa Anna. Finally, newcomers had to be organized into combat units. Eager to get their hands on Santa Anna, that "bloody tiger," volunteers were arriving daily from the United States. Some recited this little ditty:

> *Vengeance on Santa Anna and his minions,*
> *Vile scum, up boiled from the infernal regions.*
> *Too filthy far with crawling worms to dwell,*
> *And far too horrid and too base for hell.*[28]

Barely eight hundred strong, the Texas army consisted of men from every walk of life. There were shopkeepers and doctors, teachers and soldiers of fortune, farmers and ranchers, lawyers, lawmen, and desperadoes trying to keep a step ahead of the law. The majority ranged in age from their midteens to their early forties. Although "Uncle" Jimmy Curtis, sixty-four, was the oldest man in the army, he was as spry as any youngster. He carried his "fuel" in three bottles: the first contained water, the second whiskey, the third a devil's brew of boiled red ants.

Despite Houston's efforts, Uncle Jimmy and his comrades did not look very soldierly. Yet, upon seeing them, a volunteer thought they would do just fine. He wrote:

"We found the Texian force . . . all unwashed and unshaved, their long hair and beards and mustaches matted, their clothes in tatters and plastered with mud. A more savage looking band could scarcely have been assembled."[29]

Santa Anna's columns destroyed one town after another, but Houston always gave them the slip. Moving eastward, he approached the San Jacinto River at Lynch's Ferry. Santa Anna was thrilled. If he got there first, he believed he could cut Houston off and finish the war with another Goliad massacre. Houston, however, had a plan of his own. From Juan Seguín's reports, he learned that Santa Anna was racing ahead of the main army with a separate strike force. Clearly, El Presidente wanted to head him off. Knowing this, Houston did the unexpected. Turning *toward* the enemy, he took a position along the river, deliberately walking into a "trap."

The Texans took cover in a grove of oak trees. To their rear and right was Buffalo Bayou, a sluggish stream one hundred and fifty feet wide and thirty feet deep. To their left flowed the San Jacinto River, which empties into Galveston Bay ten miles to the south. A marshy inlet called Peggy Lake branched off from the right side of the river. In front of the Texans, stretching for three-quarters of a mile, was a meadow leading to a gentle rise in the ground.

On April 20, Santa Anna reached the San Jacinto with nine hundred men. After a brief skirmish, he camped to await reinforcements scheduled to arrive the next morning. They would be led by General Cós, who had been forced by El Presidente to break his promise to stay out of Texas. A five-foot-high barrier of knapsacks, baggage, branches, and earth was hastily built in front of the Mexican camp. The rise in the ground protected the camp from Houston's artillery, two light cannons known affectionately as "the Twin Sisters." Peggy Lake lay along the camp's right, or eastern, side.

April 21, 1836. Thursday. A hot, muggy day.

"This is going to be a damned good day to fight a battle," said Sam Houston, stepping from his tent. He promptly ordered scout Erastus "Deaf" Smith to cut the bridges over the bayou. Houston was a gambler if there every was one. He was staking everything on a single roll of the dice, a single do-or-die battle. One side or the other was going to lose. And when it did, it would not be able to retreat.

The Mexicans thought it a good day to fight, too. Every man was at his post, waiting either to attack or to repel an attack. Later that morning Cós arrived with four hundred reinforcements and a string of pack mules. Cós had driven his men hard, and they were exhausted from the all-night march. No matter. Santa Anna was in no hurry this time. He had Houston in the palm of his hand, he felt. All he had to do was give the order to squeeze—hard. Rather than go into battle with tired men, at noontime he ordered the army to stack arms and take a siesta. El Presidente also wanted to rest. He put on his blue silk robe, took a few grains of opium, and went to bed. Yet he had forgotten two "minor" details. No additional sentries were posted and no scouts sent to watch the enemy camp.

Charles Shaw's painting Texans Fighting and Dying. Fighting against overwhelming numerical odds, the Texans were victorious in their rebellion against Mexican authority.

As often happens with the military, it was now a matter of "hurry up and wait." Houston's men were ready long before he gave the order to "arm and line" at 3:30 P.M.; he waited so long because he wanted to have the setting sun at his back but shining into the faces of the enemy.

Seven hundred eighty-three men stood at the edge of the oak grove. "Trail arms! Forward!" Houston shouted. Starting as one man, they stepped from the shadows and moved out across the meadow. The general led on his white stallion, Saracen. Immediately behind him gun crews pulled the Twin Sisters with rawhide ropes. Ten yards behind them came the infantry in line of battle and, on their right, a fifty-man cavalry force. How they crossed that meadow without being seen is a mystery. Yet cross it they did.

The Texans grew restless, fingering their triggers. They were not going to hold their fire much longer.

Houston's greatest fear was not of being seen, but of someone's firing too soon, which would bring on a volley followed by a pause for reloading. Nothing must break the momentum of the advance. "Hold your fire!" he cried. "Hold your fire, God damn it!"[30] There would be time for just one volley, and he wanted it to explode in the enemy's faces.

Closer and closer they came, the barricade growing larger by the minute. At

"Remember the Alamo!" Mexican soldiers, taken by surprise at San Jacinto, flee toward Peggy Lake, where hundreds drowned or were shot by Texans as they floundered in the water. From a mural in the San Jacinto Museum of History.

Houston's signal, the gunners halted, wheeled their weapons around, and fired. Cannonballs tore through the flimsy barricade, blowing sections of it sky high.

That woke the Mexicans. Leaping up, those nearest the barricade opened a ragged fire. It was too little and too late. Taken by surprise, they never had a chance to form ranks for battle.

The Texans came on grimly, silently, relentlessly.

One hundred yards. Eighty yards. Twenty yards.

"Halt! Halt!" Houston roared. "Now is the critical time! Fire away! God damn you, fire!"[31]

They fired point-blank, their volley exploding in the enemy's faces. Then, without pausing to reload, they swept through the gaps in the barricade. As they came, a terrible war cry burst from their throats: "Remember the Alamo! Remember Goliad!" Juan Seguín's company gave the cry in Spanish, shouting even louder than their comrades: *"Recuerden el Alamo! Recuerden el Alamo!"*[32]

Five slugs struck Saracen simultaneously, turning its snowy flank into a sheet of red. A private caught a riderless horse and brought it to Houston. He mounted, only to have it, too, shot from under him at the same moment a bullet shattered his right ankle. Ordinarily, a person would have felt excruciating pain after receiving such a

wound. But Houston was so excited, so keyed up by the action, that he hardly felt a thing. He swung into the saddle of a third horse and galloped toward the enemy tents. By then, however, resistance had totally collapsed. Everywhere Mexicans were dropping their weapons and fleeing for their lives. The Battle of San Jacinto was over, having lasted only eighteen minutes. The slaughter that followed took several hours.

Deaf Smith said it all. Firing his pistol at anyone in a blue uniform, he urged comrades to "take prisoners like the Meskins do!"[33] Texans needed no urging. Their anger and anxiety had built up over the last two months, like floodwaters behind a dam. The dam burst at San Jacinto, giving way to a killing frenzy that surprised even themselves.

"Me no Alamo! Me no Alamo!" unarmed Mexicans cried, cringing on the ground. It did them no good. "Remember the Alamo!" became the Texans' version of the *degüello,* and it was the last thing many heard. A quick thrust with a bowie knife, or a clubbed rifle swung at a skull, ended their pleading. Uncle Jimmy Curtis had lost his son-in-law, Washington Cottle, at the Alamo. The old man sailed in with his rifle butt, bellowing at each blow, "Alamo! You killed Wash Cottle!" Panicky Mexicans scattered across the prairie, horsemen galloping at their heels. Leaning forward in the saddle, pistol in hand, the riders dropped them without breaking stride. Some infuriated Texans scalped their victims.[34]

Hundreds of Mexicans were stampeded into Peggy Lake. Pushing and shoving, those who did not drown were shot. It was like a turkey shoot. Texans knelt on one knee, took aim, and fired at the bobbing heads. They kept it up until their ammunition ran out, then smashed skulls with rifle butts. Officers encouraged the butchery. "Boys," screamed one of Houston's captains, "you know how to take prisoners, take them with the butt of guns, club guns, & remember the Alamo . . . & nock [*sic*] their god damn brains out."[35]

The few officers who tried to intervene were ignored or, worse, threatened by their own men. When, for example, Colonel John Wharton ordered a Texan to stop shooting, the fellow stepped back, pointed his rifle at the colonel's chest, and said: "If Jesus Christ were to come down from Heaven and order me to quit shooting Santanistas I wouldn't do it, sir!" Wharton left.[36]

Sam Houston was equally powerless. He tried desperately to halt the mayhem, even ordered a drummer to sound the cease-fire, but no one listened. Nor did they obey direct orders. "Gentlemen! Gentlemen! Gentlemen," Houston shouted in frustration. "Gentlemen, I applaud your bravery. But damn your manners!"[37] Only exhaustion and darkness ended the killing.

Never before had one army destroyed another at so little cost to itself. The Texans had two killed in action and thirty wounded, of whom seven later died. The Mexicans had 630 killed, 730 captured, and 200 wounded; these received no medical attention for three full days after the battle.

Survivors expected to be killed that first night. The Twin Sisters were loaded with sawed-up horseshoes and pointed at their compound. Guards patrolled outside, armed to the teeth and glaring at the helpless prisoners. A woman camp follower begged a Texan for mercy. *"Señor God Damn,"* she said, her voice trembling, *"no me mata por el amor de Dios y por la vida de su madrecita!"* ("Mr. God Damn, don't kill me for the love of God and for the life of your dear mother!")[38] Mr. God Damn turned away; he had done enough killing for one day. From out on the prairie came the howling of wolves fighting over Mexican corpses. Eventually the corpses rotted and local farmers buried the bones.

Santa Anna was not among the prisoners. When the shooting began, he'd run from his tent, wringing his hands and so tongue-tied that he could not give orders. Leaping on a horse, he sped away from the battlefield. It was a case of cowardice in the face of the enemy, the worst offense a soldier can commit in the line of duty. Had anyone else acted this way, he, Santa Anna, would have had him shot without batting an eyelash.

But he lived by another rule: Anything he wanted was good; anything he did was right.

Next morning a patrol found him in some tall grass beside a stream. No, he knew nothing of El Presidente's whereabouts, he said, looking up at the grim horsemen. He was a simple cavalryman who had lost his mount and become separated from his unit, he explained. Still, there was something strange about him. He wore muddy pants and a silk shirt buttoned with diamond studs. Rather than shoot him, as his men wished, the patrol leader decided to bring him back for further questioning.

Prodded by a lance, Santa Anna walked ahead of the patrol. He walked slowly, moaning and whining and begging to ride. After a few miles, he dropped to the ground. As a Texan came up, he rose, seized the man's hand and . . . covered it with wet kisses! "If this crazy son of a [so-and-so] doesn't stop this kissing, I'm going to kill him," the rider snapped, his face red with embarrassment.[39] The leader told Santa Anna to sit behind him in the saddle.

When the patrol reached the prison compound, hundreds of men snapped to attention and cried, "El Presidente! El Presidente!"

"I am Antonio López de Santa Anna, President of Mexico, Commander-in-chief of the Army . . . and I put myself at the disposition of the brave General Houston," he said as he stood before the enemy commander. "I wish to be treated as a general should when a prisoner of war."[40]

Houston was lying on a blanket under an oak tree. Mellow from a dose of opium, he invited Santa Anna to take a seat beside him. His soldiers were less polite. "I'm going to kill him and skin him for Wash Cottle," yelled Uncle Jimmy Curtis. "Shoot him! Hang him!"[41] others chimed in. Houston ordered the guards to clear the area. A statesman as well as a soldier, he was looking beyond victory. Yes, Santa Anna deserved death for his atrocities. Sparing his life, however, might achieve the ultimate victory: peace and independence for Texas.

Santa Anna was trembling with fear and withdrawal pains; he missed his opium. Houston offered him some of his own. El Presidente swallowed a piece of the narcotic.

Regaining his composure, he congratulated Houston on capturing the Napoleon of the West. Having done so, however, he was obliged to treat his prisoner with the utmost generosity.

"You should have remembered that at the Alamo," said Houston politely.

"I was acting under the orders of my government," answered Santa Anna nervously.

"Why, you ARE the government of Mexico," said Houston, his tone not so polite

Santa Anna is brought as a captive to the wounded Sam Houston after the battle of San Jacinto. From a mural in the San Jacinto Museum of History.

anymore. "A dictator, sir, has no superior."[42]

Santa Anna reached for another piece of opium.

Houston had the upper hand, and El Presidente knew it. To gain his release, he would say anything, do anything, sign anything. He ordered the rest of his army withdrawn from Texas and swore never again to fight the Texans. All prisoners still held by the Mexicans were to be set free. Last but not least, he recognized Texan independence.

The agreement looked wonderful on paper, but was worthless in reality. Upon returning to Mexico City, Santa Anna fell from power—for the *first* time. The new government renounced the agreement, because it had been made under threats of death. Texas was not independent, and never would be, if they had anything to say in the matter.

Meantime, the Republic of Mexico and the Republic of Texas glared at each other across a troubled border.

Blood on the Borders

Peace! Peace! Eternal peace among Mexicans! War, war, eternal war against Texans and the barbarous Comanches!
–General Mariano Arista, January 3, 1843

Oh, say, were you ever in the Rio Grande?
Way, you Rio.
It's there that the river runs down golden sand.
For we're bound to the Rio Grande.

And away, you Rio!
Way, you Rio!
Sing fare you well,
My pretty young girls,
For we're bound to the Rio Grande.
—American song, 1845

April 22, 1836.

A group of refugees sat around a campfire, staring into the leaping flames. Bone weary and half starved, they had been on the Runaway Scrape for weeks. Toward sunset a wild-looking woman ran into the yellow circle cast by the fire. "Hallelujah! Hallelujah!" she shrieked, clapping her hands and jumping up and down. Onlookers thought her crazy until, moments later, a man they recognized tore into camp on a sweat-covered horse. Waving his hat, he yelled, "San Jacinto! San Jacinto! The Mexicans are whipped and Santa Anna a prisoner!" His words had a magical effect. Instantly the tension broke, as people hugged, laughed, and wept all at once.[1]

This incident was typical of countless others throughout Texas. San Jacinto was the turning point. Overnight Sam Houston's victory changed the Texans' spirit from terror and despair to confidence and hope. Early in September the young republic elected him president for the first of two terms. At the same time, the city of Houston was founded in his honor near the San Jacinto battlefield.

The first item on President Houston's agenda was the annexation of Texas by the United States. That he should want to put an end to the republic he had just fought so hard to create is not as strange as it might seem. Texans saw themselves as Americans and expected to be admitted into the Union as soon as they won their independence. Yet this would take longer than they hoped—in fact, another decade.

The question of annexation was a thorny one, filled with dangers both at home and abroad. Mexicans found the very idea of annexation outrageous. Not only did they reject Santa Anna's deal, their government promised to go to war should Texas become part of the United States. This threat, however, did not worry Washington, D.C., all that much; if Mexico could not defeat Texas alone, it seemed unlikely to beat Texas *and* its "big brother" to the north. The fact that Mexico made such threats, and repeated them year after year, merely lessened their impact to the point where Americans ignored them altogether.

Slavery was the real problem. Since the first enslaved Africans were brought to Virginia in 1619, the slavery issue had been a source of bitter dispute. Southern states favored annexation because Texas allowed slavery. Northern states opposed annexation for exactly the same reason. Agitators called "abolitionists" thought slavery a sin against God, in whose image every person, regardless of color, is created. Slave-holding Texans insulted the majesty of the Creator, they said. William Lloyd Garrison, a leading abolitionist, insisted: "All who would sympathize with that pseudo-republic hate liberty and would dethrone God."[2] Moreover, admitting Texas to the Union would upset the balance of power in the United States Senate between slave and free states, which might in turn lead to civil war. Given these difficulties, the best Congress could offer Texas was recognition as a new nation, a step followed by the governments of France, England, the Netherlands, and Belgium.

Stunned by the rejection, Texans hoped Congress would change its mind in due time. Meanwhile, their country grew by leaps and bounds. Within a decade, its population rose from 30,000 to 140,000, with scores of families arriving weekly. Thanks to generous offers of land, no other frontier area attracted so many people so rapidly. Gradually, the makeup of the population changed. Although Anglo-Americans were still in the majority, settlers were coming from England, Ireland, Germany, and France.

Texas also grew economically, as cotton growing and ranching expanded. With thousands of wild cattle roaming the brush country south of San Antonio, Texans became cowboys, or, as they liked to call themselves, "cowpokes." The Texas cowboy was basically an Anglo version of the Mexican vaquero. From his hat to his chaps to his spurs, he borrowed the vaquero's clothing, gear, and methods. Like the vaquero, he worked cattle from horseback, roped them, branded them, and gathered them in roundups. He used a rope, known as a lasso or lariat (from *la reata*), and a Spanish-style saddle with a horn to wind the rope around, stopping the animal in its tracks. Every ranch had its wrangler, from *caballerango,* "one who cares for horses"; its horse herd was the remuda, from *remonta,* or "remount." The word *ranch* itself comes from the Spanish *rancho.* Many cowboy songs, such as "The Streets of Laredo," are actually translations of Mexican ballads.

As population increased, so did the amount of land needed for farms, ranches, and towns. From eastern Texas, settlers began moving to the west and south. But as they did, they became involved in a series of ferocious border wars that would last into the early years of the twentieth century.

Western Texas was the domain of the Comanche. The earliest pioneers were not seriously troubled by these horse Indians. Settlements were located mainly outside their hunting grounds, and the Comanche were content to raid their old enemies, the Mexicans. Most bands, indeed, were friendly to the newcomers. Stephen Austin was once captured by a Comanche war party. For a few minutes he feared for his life, but when they learned he was an Anglo, they set him free. The only thing they kept was his Spanish dictionary, not because they wanted to learn the language, but because they used paper to pad the insides of their shields.

Friendship turned to hostility as the line of settlement advanced toward the Great Plains. The first blow fell less than a month after the battle of San Jacinto. On May 19, 1836, raiders struck Fort Parker on the Navasota River in Limestone County. Of the settlement's thirty-one inhabitants, five men were killed and scalped. An elderly woman was speared, raped, and left for dead. Five women and children were kidnapped, four of whom were later ransomed and returned to their families. The fifth, nine-year-old Cynthia Ann Parker, was to become famous in Texas as a "white

Pioneers warding off an attack by "horse" Indians.

Indian." Cynthia Ann was adopted into the tribe and easily adjusted to its ways. At about the age of thirteen, she married a war chief with whom she had three children. Her eldest son, Quanah ("Fragrance"), was to become one of the most stubborn foes of the *tahbay-boh,* or "white men."

Texans formed self-defense units of "mounted gunmen" to meet the Comanche threat. Like the minutemen before them, the first units consisted of volunteers ready to act at a moment's notice. But as the raids increased, they became a regular force—the Texas Rangers. These units ranged far and wide, hence their name. Always on the move, their job was to patrol the frontier areas, warn of danger, and carry the fight to the enemy. This required a special sort of man. "A Texas Ranger," one explained, "can ride like a Mexican, trail like an Indian, shoot like a Tennessean, and fight like a very devil."[3] He had to be good at his trade. Events such as those at Fort Parker had taught him that lowering his guard just for an instant could be the last thing he ever did. That knowledge made him hard and, at times, cruel. Like the mountain man, he was capable of mutilating enemies and using other forms of terrorism to crush resistance.

Like Big-Foot Wallace, the early Texas Rangers had no uniform and provided their own horses and weapons. Drawing from The Adventures of Big-Foot Wallace.

Even so, the early Rangers fought at a disadvantage. Weapons were the problem. Armed with a pistol and rifle, the typical Ranger could plug a prairie dog between the eyes at a hundred yards. Yet the Comanche were not prairie dogs. Unless taken by surprise, preferably while asleep, they were more than a match for Texans. Like the Spaniards before them, Texans had never fought horse Indians until they came onto the plains. And, like the Spaniards, they found that a mounted warrior could travel three hundred yards a minute and keep eight well-aimed arrows in the air at once. Guns packed a terrific punch, but they were heavy, fired only one bullet at a time, and took half a minute to reload—more on horseback. By the time the Ranger was ready for another shot, the warrior had turned him into a pincushion or, dashing in close, ran him through with his fourteen-foot lance.

Yankee ingenuity saved the day. In 1836, the first year of the Texas republic, the inventor Samuel Colt began to manufacture a different kind of gun. Colt's revolver, or "six-shooter," was actually six guns in one; each time you pulled the trigger, another bullet came into firing position. Although there was little demand for the six-shooter back East, within two years it had been discovered by the Texas Rangers. It was love at first sight. Suddenly, they had a lightweight (four pounds, nine ounces) weapon that was easily loaded while galloping across the plains. Colt's gun deserved its nickname: "the equalizer." It allowed the outnumbered Rangers to get close to the Comanches and fire six times in as many seconds; better yet, with two Colts they could pour out a veritable stream of hot lead. When empty, the gun made a handy club. Holding it by the butt, its owner could "pistol-whip" an enemy with the eleven-inch barrel.

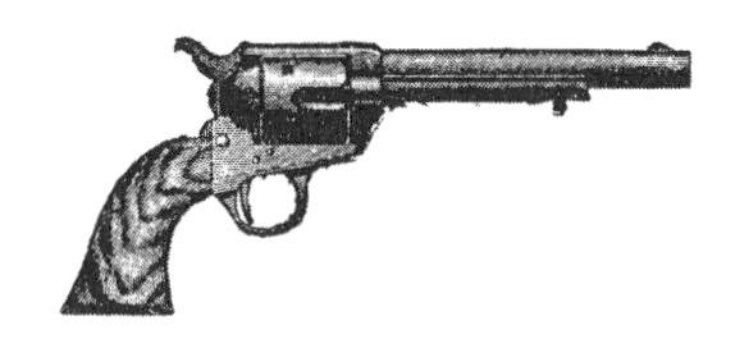

Sam Colt's revolver, "the gun that won the West," cost only twelve dollars and ninety-five cents. For a man on the western frontier, the six-shooter was as much a part of his costume as any piece of clothing.

The equalizer turned the tide in the Texans' favor. The Comanche were still dangerous and would remain so for another two generations. Nevertheless, for the first time whites could fight horse Indians in their own element—on horseback. And once that happened, nothing would drive them off the plains.

It was different with the Mexicans. Indian raids into Mexico reached their peak in the 1830s and 1840s. Crossing the Rio Grande, Comanche and Apache war parties ravaged the states of Sonora, Chihuahua, Durango, and Coahuila. Northern Mexico became known as the *mal pais,* the "bad country." George F. Ruxton, an English traveler, was shocked by what he saw. Each year, he noted, the marauders drove farther into the country's interior. Haciendas and ranches, often entire villages, stood abandoned. "For days together," he wrote, "I traveled a country completely deserted . . . passing through ruined villages untrodden for years by the foot of man."[4] The Mexican army was useless in this kind of warfare. By the time it learned of a raid, the attackers were already gone. If cavalry pursued, the war party either scattered like a flock of birds or set an ambush.

Desperate for relief, state governments began a war of extermination. Professional killers, or bounty hunters, were hired to take the scalps of "wild" Indians. Prices varied from place to place, but generally an adult male's scalp brought two hundred pesos, the scalps of women and children half as much. Captive women and children brought 150 pesos. Warriors were never taken alive.

Both Mexicans and Texans took part in this dreadful business. Bounty hunters cared nothing about innocence or guilt. To them, it was simply a matter of cold cash. Men like John Glanton, Mike Chevallie, and Edward A. Weyman had no qualms about luring "bloodthirsty savages" to their camps with food and whiskey, then signaling hidden gunmen to mow them down.

James Kirker was the king of bounty hunters. A former mountain man and fur trader, he discovered that Indian scalps could be more profitable than beaver pelts, and easier to get. He became one of the most popular men in northern Mexico. After one raid, Kirker's gang returned to Chihuahua city, the state capital, with the scalps of 182 Apache men, women, and children, plus 18 captives. What a triumph! What a blessing! The city fathers declared a day of festivity and thanksgiving in the scalpers' honor. The governor and priests led the procession through the streets, past cheering crowds that lined the route. Opposite the cathedral's main entrance, stretching along an entire side of the main square, were rows of Apache scalps dangling from poles. While bands played gay tunes, Kirker's grisly trophies were added to the display.

Kirker and his kind did not intimidate the Indians; if anything, they made them angrier and more determined to seek revenge. The war parties kept coming. The killings and kidnappings continued. In the long run, however, Texas would cost Mexico more than all the Indian raids combined.

The Texas Republic claimed the Rio Grande as its southern border. It followed, therefore, that all of New Mexico lying east of the river belonged to Texas. Mexico City scoffed at the claim. Six hundred miles of wilderness separated the nearest Texas settlement from Santa Fe. Nobody, it was thought, would be so foolish as to venture into that no-man's-land of buffalo and Comanches.

In June 1841 the Texans decided to do just that. Rather than launch an outright invasion, they sent the "Santa Fe Pioneers." Fifty merchants left Austin with twenty-five wagons loaded with trade goods. The caravan resembled those that used the Santa Fe Trail, except for its escort of 270 soldiers commanded by a general in the Texas army. Officially, the soldiers were supposed to protect the merchants from the Comanche. Unofficially, they had a more sinister mission, as revealed in bundles of printed leaflets stowed in the wagons. These invited New Mexicans to enjoy "full participation in all our blessings."[5] Translation: If the people revolted against Mexico, they could count on support from Texas.

Nothing went right. The caravan got lost. Comanches ran off horses. The sun seemed about to broil everyone's brains. Food ran out. It was a relief to be taken prisoner by troops sent by Governor Manuel Armijo. The captives were marched to Santa Fe, then ordered south to Mexico City. Before setting out, Captain Damasio Salazar, the march commander, received last-minute instructions. "If one of them pretends to be sick or tired on the road," said Armijo, *"shoot him down and bring me his ears!* Go!"[6]

Salazar did as he was told, and more. Captives were made to run barefoot over sharp stones. Captives were deliberately starved and deprived of water. If anybody died of exhaustion, or was shot for lagging behind, his body was not buried, though Salazar cut off his ears and strung them on a strip of rawhide he carried in a pouch. The only relief came during a three-day stopover at El Paso. General José María Elias Gonzáles, the local army commander, was outraged at the prisoners' treatment. He arrested Salazar for murder and made sure the captives were well treated. The people of El Paso opened their homes and their hearts to the miserable men. They fed them, clothed them, even bathed those too weak to help themselves. Yet this was only a brief pause on a two-thousand-mile trek to the Mexican capital. On their arrival, they were put in prison until June 1842, when Santa Anna celebrated his birthday by releasing them.

"'Ole Santy Anno" was back. After losing the presidency, he bided his time, waiting for a chance to return to power. That chance came sooner than expected. In 1838 he joined in the defense of the port of Vera Cruz against a French fleet sent to punish Mexico for a minor insult. Santa Anna led the defenders to victory, but lost a leg in the process. That victory, coupled with the lost leg, wiped away his past errors, crimes, and defeats. A grateful nation dubbed him "the Hero of Vera Cruz." His amputated leg, sacrificed for "duty and love of country," received a state funeral. Enclosed in a crystal urn, it was escorted by an honor guard through the streets of the capital and laid to rest atop a tall marble column. Back in the country's good graces, in 1841 he showed his gratitude by overthrowing the elected president and becoming dictator with the support of the army.

Ever since Texas became independent, its southern border had been a line traced in blood. There were constant across-the-border raids, each raid triggering another in retaliation. Mexican *banditos* waylaid travelers and shot up wagon trains. Mexican *rancheros* splashed across the Rio Grande to "collect grandfather's cattle." Texas cowboys returned the visits. When not fighting the Comanche, Texas Rangers gave the Mexicans a taste of their equalizers; so much so that they trembled at the sight of Los Tejanos Sangrietos, those Bloody Texans. Bitterness deepened. Mexicans mocked Texans, indeed all Anglo-Americans, as *gringos,* from "Green Grow the Lilacs," a popular song. Texans, for their part, thought Mexicans lower than Indians, which was saying a mouthful. "I can maintain a better stomach at the killing of a Mexican," a lawman claimed, "than at the crushing of a body louse."[7]

Santa Anna made things worse. In his eyes, his defeat at San Jacinto had been bad luck, nothing more. He was still the Napoleon of the West, the greatest figure in Mexican history since Cortés. In March and September 1842, his forces took San Antonio and quickly withdrew. During a second raid, they carried away sixty-seven prisoners, including a judge, the members of a jury, and three congressmen. These were not attempts to reconquer Texas, but displays of force to show that he was still a man to fear.

The Texans struck back. In December a detachment of volunteers captured Mier, a town seven miles inside Mexico. They went no farther. Encircled by a large Mexican cavalry force, 186 men surrendered. On orders of El Presidente, they began the long trek to Mexico City.

In retaliating against Mexican army raids, Texans seized the town of Mier. Overrun by Mexican troops and forced to gamble for their lives, seventeen prisoners were shot when they drew black beans from an earthen jar. Big-Foot Wallace drew a white bean, saving his life. Drawing from The Adventures of Big-Foot Wallace.

Every step of the way was torture. Stripped of their clothing, most had only a threadbare blanket to shield themselves from the winter winds. Whenever they reached a town, they were paraded through the streets as living trophies and made to sleep in cattle pens ankle-deep in manure. Swaggering officers boasted that their treatment was mild, compared to what would await American troops should they ever set foot on Mexico's sacred soil. Why, their destruction would be followed by an invasion of the United States itself. Mexico's "irresistible army" (their term) would keep going until its flag flew from the Capitol in Washington, D.C. The Texans were not impressed. "Oh, spare the women and children!" one sang out in mock fear. "You had better whip Texas first before you tackle Uncle Sam!" another chimed in, grinning from ear to ear.[8]

Nobody smiled when the next order arrived from Mexico City. Santa Anna wanted the prisoners decimated; that is, every tenth man was to be executed. On

March 25, 1843, a Mexican officer put one bean for each man, of which seventeen were black, into an earthenware bowl and covered it with a cloth. Each prisoner was to reach under the cloth and take out a bean. Those who drew black beans would be stood against a wall and shot.

Among the last to draw was a fellow named Pat, a recent immigrant from Ireland. "Oh, its for murtherin' me ye are . . . widout judge or jury," said Pat, his face flushed with anger. But since the guards threatened to shoot him if he held back, he drew a bean. It was white. "There . . ." he growled, handing the bean to the officer in charge, "it *was* a black one, but I offered up a short prayer to Saint Patrick, you see, and in the twinkling of an eye, he convarted it into a white one! Hooray for Saint Patrick and Ould Ireland forever!"[9] Moments later firing squads carried out the death sentences. Some Mexican officers turned away from the horrible scene, openly weeping. Atop the execution wall, a Mexican guard was so sickened by the sight that he reeled and nearly fell off, but was caught by his comrades.[10]

Upon reaching Mexico City, the Texans were assigned to various prisons. The rule was: No work, no eat. Each day they were marched out in chains and forced to do odd jobs around the city. They swept the streets. They got down on their hands and knees to scrub cobblestones. They hauled away garbage, harnessed to the carts in place of horses. Passersby gathered around, shouting, "Death to the gringos" and "Texas cannibals." That was too much for one "cannibal." Known as Big-Foot Wallace, from his size twelve shoes, he grabbed a wrinkled old woman "and took a good bite at her neck, but it was tougher than a ten-year-old buffalo bull's, and though I bit with a *will,* and can crack a hickory nut with my grinders, I could make no impression on it whatsoever."[11] Nevertheless, no one called him "cannibal" again.

The Texans were released in September 1844, when Santa Anna declared an amnesty after his wife's death. By then, however, the road to war between Mexico and the United States lay wide open. Once again, the issue was the annexation of Texas.

By 1844 Americans were ready to reconsider annexation. The reason had little to do with Texas as such, but fear of how France and Great Britain might use it against the United States. Both nations wanted to curb American expansion. The United States was becoming a major industrial competitor and, sometime soon, was expected to challenge their influence in world affairs. This most concerned Great Britain, which had set its sights on the Oregon Territory. "John Bull," as Great

President James Polk wanted the United States to expand into the Southwest, even if that meant war with Mexico.

Britain was known, was not shy about flexing his muscles in front of the "Yankee Noodle." Already Mr. Bull had an army stationed in Canada and in posts along the Great Lakes. Let him get bases in Texas, and, at the least, he could cut the trails across the Great Plains. At the worst, he might crush the United States in a gigantic vise. Sam Houston, sly as a fox, encouraged the belief that Texas favored the European powers.

Eighteen forty-four was a presidential election year. James K. Polk of Tennessee won the Democratic Party's nomination and the campaign that followed. The eleventh president was not an impressive figure. Five feet eight inches tall, he was thin as a rail and had gray eyes and gray hair, which he wore shoulder length. Stern-faced, his lips pursed into a scowl, it seemed that his face would crack if he smiled. A sour, humorless man, he banned dancing and liquor in the White House as "undignified." Yet he was shrewd, hardworking, and knew exactly what he wanted. "Jimmy" Polk believed in Manifest Destiny, the notion that God wanted Americans to create an "empire of liberty" stretching from the Atlantic to the Pacific, from the Saint Lawrence to the Rio Grande. Naturally, that empire must include Texas, New Mexico, and California, all of which Mexico either claimed or owned.

Events began to pick up speed after the election. On March 1, 1845, three days before Polk's inauguration, Congress offered statehood to Texas. A few weeks later, the president offered to buy New Mexico and California. Furious over the impending annexation of Texas, Mexico refused to sell. The offer, the Mexican ambassador declared, was in itself an insult to his country's dignity. Worse, Mexico broke diplomatic relations with the United States, traditionally the first step in going to war.

This surprised no one. The Mexican government had always insisted that the annexation of Texas by the United States was an act of war. Once Texas accepted statehood, Mexican guns would go off by themselves.

The Mexican people supported their government's war policy as passions became inflamed. Actually, they wanted to cross swords with those crude gringos, those "Bárbaros de Norte" (Barbarians of the North). Demonstrators in Mexico City marched under banners demanding war. Priests gave sermons urging war against American "heretics" and "enemies of God." Newspapers called for war to erase the humiliation of San Jacinto and restore the nation's pride.

Victory was certain, Mexicans told themselves. Although helpless against the Comanche and Apache, their army was thought to be more than a match for "so contemptible" a foe as the United States. Americans, it was said, worshiped a false god, the Almighty Dollar, and would never pay taxes to support a war for Texas. Mexicans, however, were a nation of heroes and warriors. They boasted of invading the United States, freeing two million black slaves, and lassoing regiments of American foot soldiers! Nor was there anything to fear from a gringo invasion. Mexico was the fourth largest country in the world—only Russia, China, and Brazil were larger. Even if the invader moved inland, he would have to cross vast mountain ranges, barren plains, and waterless deserts before reaching the capital. Let him come; the farther he advanced, the longer his supply lines would stretch, making them easier to cut.

Some Americans who volunteered for service in the Mexican War were little more than bandits.

Empty bluster and wishful thinking: The Mexicans were doing plenty of each. Still, they had a point. The United States was *not* a military power. Its army of 6,562 officers and enlisted men—less than a quarter of Mexico's—was scattered among dozens of outposts, mainly in the West, to watch over the Indians. Whereas Mexico's top generals were combat veterans, no U.S. Army officer had ever commanded a thousand soldiers in peacetime, let alone in battle.

The army's ranks were filled with men fleeing the law and men with nowhere else to go. Although the legal age for enlistment was eighteen, solders were as young as thirteen; they had run away from home and lied about their age, or were juvenile delinquents forced by judges to choose between jail and the army. At age seventy, the oldest enlisted man was a veteran of fifty years' service, having fought in Napoleon's Italian, Egyptian, and Russian campaigns. Many soldiers were immigrants, speaking only broken English, or deserters from British regiments in Canada. Low even by the standards of the day, the soldier's pay ranged from seven dollars a month for privates—"seven-dollar targets" they called themselves—to seventeen dollars for sergeants.

Army discipline was harsh, punishment brutal. Ordinary rule breakers were made to stand on barrels with signs around their necks such as GREAT COAT THIEF. Or their heads were shaved and they were thrown into the guardhouse on a diet of bread and water for two weeks. More serious offenses brought whipping and branding on the shoulders with *HD* (for Habitual Drunkard) or *W* (for Worthless). Offenders were also hung by the wrists while standing tiptoe on the ground, or bucked and gagged, the most dreaded punishment of all. A bayonet was put sideways into the offender's mouth and tied in place with a string. He was then seated on the ground with his knees pulled up almost to his chest, a stick placed under his knees, and his arms tied in front. After a few hours of this treatment, few needed a second dose of the medicine. Nevertheless, it was better to take your punishment than hit back. Striking an officer was a hanging offense, as was desertion; they called it "climbing the golden stair on a rope." Even so, desperate men did desperate things, and desertions averaged a thousand a year in peacetime. A private did not exaggerate when he said: "A soldier's life is very disgusting."[12]

Nor did the army enjoy popular support. Americans did not like professional soldiers; they reminded them of the Hessians, Germans hired by the British during the Revolution. Citizens were expected to volunteer in time of national emergency, but no self-respecting person would dream of a career in the regular army. A professional soldier was said to be little more than a "drilled automaton," a "moving and musket-holding *machine*."[13] Such a person was unfit to defend liberty.

Even the United States Military Academy at West Point, New York, had its critics. Founded in 1802, the academy lacked the public's respect; Congress once came within a single vote of abolishing it. Academy graduates were denounced as snobs, "swells," and do-nothings growing fat at public expense. Lieutenant Ulysses S. Grant learned this after graduating in 1843. Returning to his home in Ohio, he rode proudly down the main street in his brand-new uniform. But instead of being admired as an officer and a gentleman, a little boy jeered him with: "Soldier! Will you work?

General Zachary Taylor used his popularity as a Mexican War hero to become president of the United States.

No, sir-ee; I'll sell my shirt first." Onlookers were amused, "but I did not appreciate it so highly," he recalled forty years later.[14] Nevertheless, West Pointers like Grant were the army's brains. Within twenty years they would command the armies of the Union and Confederacy in the Civil War. In 1845 they were friends serving under the same flag.

War was coming with the speed of an express train. On June 23, the Texas congress voted for annexation. On July 21, Mexico began preparing for all-out war. Ten days later President Polk ordered an "Army of Occupation" into Texas as a precautionary step. Its destination was Corpus Christi at the mouth of the Nueces River, 150 miles east of the Rio Grande. Meanwhile, volunteer units began to form throughout the country. It seemed that everyone wanted a crack at the enemy while the "game" lasted. Americans, like Mexicans, expected a short, glorious war; "an adventure full of fun and frolic" is how one newspaper put it.[15]

The Army of Occupation was commanded by Brigadier General Zachary Taylor. Born in Virginia in 1784, Taylor was the son of a colonel on George Washington's Revolutionary War staff. No West Pointer, he received his lieutenant's commission directly from President Thomas Jefferson. After serving in the War of 1812, he was stationed in frontier outposts, fighting Indians and rising slowly in rank. As a reward for an 1837 campaign against the Seminoles of Florida, he was promoted to brigadier general. Tough and able, he earned the nickname "Old Rough and Ready."

Rough he certainly was. A heavyset man of medium height, he had short legs, deep creases in his face, and gray hair. Unless you knew him, you would never take him for a general, but for a shabby farmer just back from his fields. Taylor was no spit-and-polish soldier. He hated uniforms and never wore a sword or his general's stars unless absolutely necessary, which was seldom the case on the frontier. He dressed comfortably in rumpled civilian clothes, a floppy straw hat, and shoes worn down at the heels. Nor did he sit a horse the way an officer should. Taylor on horseback, a shocked West Pointer wrote, "looks like a toad."[16] His favorite mount was Old Whitey, a big, placid stallion that he treated more as a comrade than an animal. Sitting sideways in the saddle, both legs dangling, he chewed tobacco and absent-mindedly spat streams of brown juice. Staff officers stepped lively at such times.

Enlisted men loved him. "Old Zack," as they called him for short, was a simple, fatherly person who knew what made them tick. There were never any guards posted around his tent, and anyone could drop in for a visit. He always had time to listen to soldiers' problems, or just to chat. Unlike other commanders, he forbade whipping except in the most severe cases. Not that he was a softie; far from it. When his temper flared, he would grab a soldier by the ears and shake him hard. He called it "wooling."

Everyone had a favorite Zack story. One day, for example, a new lieutenant came to pay his respects. Finding the general's tent empty, he went around back, where he saw a gray-haired man with his sleeves rolled up, cleaning a sword.

"I say, old fella, can you tell me where I can see General Taylor?" asked the lieutenant.

"Wull, stranger, thar is the old hoss's tent," said the old fellow, pointing but not looking up.

The lieutenant asked if the sword was the general's. Yes, it was, came the reply.

"Ah!" gushed the lieutenant. "I suppose then, my worthy man, that you work for the General?"

"I reckon, and doggone hard, and little thanks and small pay I get too," the worthy man answered.

"My good man," said the lieutenant, "I would like to have you clean my sword, and I shall come tomorrow to the General and then I will give you a dollar."

General Zachary Taylor was a simple man with simple ways, as depicted in this cartoon from the July 31, 1847, issue of Yankee Doodle.

As promised, he returned the following day. Sure enough, the good man appeared with the cleaned sword. "Come, old fatty," the lieutenant said, poking him in the ribs, "show me General Taylor and the dollar is yours."

Old fatty drew himself up to his full height. "Lieutenant!" he snapped. "I am General Taylor, and I will take that dollar!"[17]

Taylor's men disliked Corpus Christi. A flea trap consisting of twenty-odd shacks, it had fewer than a hundred residents when the troops arrived. There were nearly four thousand of them, more than half the total strength of the U.S. Army. It was the largest gathering of American fighting men since the War of 1812.

Life revolved around the camps built along the banks of the Nueces River. Every activity was governed by the clock. Buglers blew reveille at five A.M. sharp, rain or shine. As soon as the bugle sounded, everyone rolled out of their blankets and dressed. Uniforms were blue—for enlisted men light blue jackets, pants, and caps; for officers dark blue coats, light blue pants, and high hats. After dressing, enlisted men ate breakfast, reported for roll call, did camp chores, and drilled until noon. Lunch was followed by more drills. Hour after hour, troops went through the motions of loading, cleaning, and reloading their weapons. They also practiced marching in formation, a vital skill that enabled large bodies of men to reach the scene of action quickly and deploy for battle.

Gunners used every waking moment to perfect their skills, since artillery was an American specialty. Time would show that no army in the world used cannons so effectively. West Pointers had developed what they called "flying artillery." Usually it took a while to move field guns into position during an action. As a result, they might not be available to support an infantry assault or beat off an enemy attack. Constant drill, however, enabled the flying artillery to get a four-gun battery where it was needed within minutes. Then the guns cut loose with a variety of projectiles, or "shot." Solid shot was a six- to twelve-pound iron ball used to batter fortifications and troops massed more than half a mile away. Shells were metal tubes filled with gunpowder and exploded in midair by a fuse. Canister and grapeshot were antipersonnel devices; that is, used to kill men at random. Canister was a tin can filled with hundreds of musket balls; grapeshot was a container loaded with lead slugs the size of golf balls. Fired at close range, the containers burst, spreading their contents like shotgun pellets. A dose of this dreadful stuff was called a "blizzard." Experienced crews could fire off a blizzard once every two minutes.

Cavalry, however, was a weakness in Taylor's army. Horses were in short supply, and riders needed practice in close combat. Fortunately, mustangs were abundant in Texas; the best could be bought for ten or eleven dollars. Better still, a few units were being armed with Sam Colt's equalizers. Most, however, relied on single-shot pistols and swords.

A company of Texas Rangers taught the fine points of fighting on horseback. They were a ferocious lot, and Old Zack's men were glad to have them on their side, rather than as enemies. Samuel E. Chamberlain, a sixteen-year-old private from Boston, had never seen such fellows before. They reminded him of devils, he wrote in his book, *My Confessions.*

> A more reckless, devil-may-care looking set it would be impossible to find this side of the Infernal Region. Some wore buckskin shirts, black with grease and blood, some wore red shirts, their trousers thrust into high boots; all were armed with Revolvers and huge Bowie Knives. Take them altogether, with their uncouth costumes, bearded faces, lean and brawny forms, fierce wild eyes and swaggering manners, they were fit representatives of the outlaws which made up the population of the Lone Star State.[18]

Oh, but how they could ride! Spectators gasped as Rangers put three silver dollars in a row on the ground and then picked them up riding at a full gallop.

Camp living conditions were "basic." Soldiers were quartered in tattered tents that offered no protection from the elements. Rain leaked through, like water through a sieve, drenching everything. At night men wrapped themselves in soggy blankets and slept in the cold mud. The general shared their misery, but he was such a tough old bird, they said proudly, that there was no sense in complaining. Still, men came down with colds, bronchitis, and pneumonia.

Cleanliness was another problem. Regulations called for washing hands and faces once a day and baths once a week. That was impossible. Soap was always in short supply, and hot water so scarce that units might go weeks without a good wash. Often the water itself was so polluted that passing clothes through it made them smellier than ever. Drinking such water was the same as drinking poison.

Dirty bodies and dirty clothes attracted bugs. In addition to the usual scorpions, tarantulas, and centipedes, soldiers were attacked by some of the orneriest biting, stinging, and sucking creatures in insect creation. Lice were the most common pest. Nicknamed "seam rats," they infested everyone's hair and clothing. Whenever possible, soldiers "read their seams"; that is, ran their fingers along the seams of their clothing, cracking the tiny terrors between thumb and forefinger. Chiggers burrowed into the skin. Ants were a plague. "Last night," a soldier wrote, half joking, "the ants tried to carry me off in my sleep."[19]

Disease spread through the camps. Among the less severe diseases were rashes, boils, chicken pox, measles, and mumps. Although they might put you on the sick list for a week or so, you usually recovered. Dysentery was different. A severe form of diarrhea, it had always been *the* killer of soldiers, deadlier than any battle. Pale as ghosts, dysentery sufferers crowded the latrines, filling them to overflowing. "When we go to drill," Lieutenant Thomas Ewell explained as delicately as he could, "the men have to leave the ranks by dozens, & as the plain is as bare as a table, make an exposé of the whole affair. The effect is unique as they squat in rows about a hundred yards from the battalion & when we deploy . . . we run right over them."[20] At times, more men were down with dysentery than reported for duty.

Until the scientific breakthroughs of the twentieth century, disease killed more soldiers than gunfire. The Mexican War (1846–48) was no exception. For each American soldier killed in battle or died of wounds, eight fell victim to disease. No figures exist for the Mexican army, but they were certainly as high.[21] Nobody knew that dirt breeds germs and that germs cause disease; indeed, few doctors had ever seen a germ, since medical schools had no microscopes. Nor were there such things as X rays, vitamins, blood transfusions, sterile bandages, antiseptics, and antibiotics. A doctor began treatment for most ailments by bleeding the patient; that is, opening a vein to let the "bad vapors" escape with the blood. Drugs were largely useless—or deadly. "Blue mass" was standard for a wide variety of complaints, including stomachaches. Made of mercury, a powerful poison, it killed as many as it cured; and of these "cures," a certain number went crazy, since mercury damages the brain. Camphor and peppermint mixed with alcohol were less dangerous and had a soothing effect, as did laudanum, a mixture of opium and alcohol. Pure opium was an effective treatment for dysentery, except that it resulted in addiction.

Army food was a health hazard, too. The daily ration consisted of beans, vinegar, coffee, and pork or beef pickled in salt to prevent spoiling. The meat was tough, fatty, looked awful, and tasted worse; it took a lot of willpower, or a mighty empty stomach, to swallow this stuff and keep it down. Instead of bread, soldiers ate hardtack, a flat cracker much like a dog biscuit, made of flour and water. At its best, hardtack, or "teeth duller," was difficult to chew. At its worst, it was alive with beetle grubs. "Our food is abominable," a volunteer wrote his folks in Ohio, "when you break a biscuit, you can see it move."[22] For variety, soldiers hunted wild birds and other animals, including prairie dogs; one squad dined on a rattlesnake seven feet long and liked every inch of it. Mexicans gladly sold local delicacies such as tortillas for a few pennies. These, however, did not always sit well in gringo stomachs. Served with chili-pepper sauce, tortillas tasted like burning coals and caused tears to flow.

Taylor's men used their spare time as soldiers have always done. All ranks went fishing, ran footraces, and held wrestling and boxing matches. Officers built a theater and put on plays written by themselves or by famous playwrights; Lieutenant U. S. Grant took the female lead in William Shakespeare's *Othello.* A majority of enlisted men could read and write. They read everything from the Bible to scandal sheets, newspapers that specialized in risqué stories and tales of violence. They wrote letters, but liked receiving them better. Mail call was a time of high excitement in camp. "Last night," a soldier wrote, ". . . I flew through the chaparral, scratching my hands and tearing my clothes, but was amply rewarded by receiving two letters from HOME, which I read over and over again before I turned in. . . ."[23]

Spare time also involved less wholesome activities. Soldiers, it seemed, would bet on anything. Horse races, card games, and dice were popular ways to lose one's pay. So was getting drunk. Drunkenness was the most common offense, and no threats other than a firing squad could get soldiers to mend their ways. Anything alcoholic was considered fit to drink. Peddlers known as "sutlers" followed the army during campaigns. Like the Santa Fe traders, their wagons were general stores on wheels. Their most called-for item was whiskey. The nicknames soldiers gave sutler's whiskey indicate its potency: "tarantula juice," "tonsil paint," "coffin varnish," "lightning flash." Mexican *aguardiente* was known simply as "firewater."

On December 29, 1845, Texas entered the Union as the twenty-eighth state. And since Texas claimed the Rio Grande as its southern boundary, Old Zack was ordered to take up positions along that river. Early in March 1846, his Army of Occupation left Corpus Christi.

A belt of sandy country lay between the Nueces River and Rio Grande. Already it was warm, and the men had a hard time keeping up. Sweltering in his woolen uniform—there were no lightweight uniforms for warm weather—each foot soldier had a blanket roll looped over his left shoulder and tied at his waist. In addition to his musket (nine pounds, twelve ounces), he carried a bayonet (eleven ounces), canteen (eighteen ounces), and leather cartridge box with forty bullets (three pounds) attached to his belt. Tightly strapped to his back was a pack weighing about forty pounds, containing extra clothing, an overcoat, mess kit, half a pup tent, tent pegs, and personal items like tobacco, comb, toothbrush, shaving supplies, writing utensils, and anything else he felt he needed. Normal marching speed was three-and-a-half miles an hour, no fun when you are trudging through sand on a warm day.

The countryside had changed little since Cabeza de Vaca's time. The wildflowers were just as colorful, the antelope, jackrabbits, and birds just as plentiful. One thing, however, was different. Mustangs! As the troops marched, droves of wild horses galloped toward them out of curiosity. Lieutenant Grant was astonished to see one drove as large as a buffalo herd.

> As far as the eye could reach to our right, the herd extended. To the left it extended equally. There is no estimating the number of animals in it. I have no idea that it could be corralled in the State of Rhode Island, or Delaware at one time. If they had been, they would have been so thick that the pasturage would have given out the first day.[24]

Old Zack occupied Point Isabel, a tiny port on the Gulf of Mexico, and built a small fort on the bank of the Rio Grande, twenty-five miles to the southwest. Fort Texas, as it was called, lay opposite the city of Matamoros, Mexico, a major military base. It would have been hard to find a more dangerous spot for a fort.

Two armies stood eye to eye, waiting. Both their countries were spoiling for a fight. A false move by either side would be a match tossed into a barrel of gunpowder; the explosion would be heard all the way to Mexico City and Washington, D.C.

Meanwhile, in their off-duty time, Taylor's men gathered along the riverbank to take in the sights. There was plenty to see. The *señoritas* of Matamoros used the Rio Grande for bathing. Morning and evening, they came down to the riverbank, took off their clothes, and plunged into the stream. Swimming and splashing, laughing and singing, they enjoyed themselves without embarrassment. For the gringos, however, they were an eye-opener in more ways than one. "Nearly all . . . have well-developed, magnificent figures . . . and appear as happy and contented as the day is long," wrote Captain William S. Henry, a prim and proper West Pointer.[25] "Their bosoms," said a brother officer, "were not compressed in stays . . . but heaved freely under the healthful influences of the genial sun and balmy air of the sunny south."[26] Back home, girls did not swim in the nude, let alone in front of members of the opposite sex. Mexican girls did, and no one, not even the strict Catholic priests, accused them of immorality. Perhaps they were not being immoral? Perhaps different peoples simply had different ways? It was a learning experience.

The girls called to the men, and the men called to the girls, from across the river. The girls asked how they were; the men replied "well" and hoped they would be friends. Encouraged by such kind words, some Americans stripped to their birthday suits and swam toward the girls. Seeing them coming, the girls laughed and waved "real friendly-like," as a soldier put it. Mexican sentries did not wave. As they neared the middle of the stream, the sentries fired warning shots. Another lesson learned: When nations feud, there is little room for youthful high jinks.

The Mexicans also fired "paper bullets"; that is, used propaganda to encourage Americans to desert. Leaflets were smuggled across the river at night and left in the camps. Why suffer in the army, they asked, when a life of ease and plenty waited just a short swim away? Anyone who deserted was promised a warm welcome, a cash bonus, and a large tract of land. This was a strong appeal, particularly for Catholic soldiers angry at discrimination in the United States.

Deserters plunged into the Rio Grande each night. And each night American sentries shot to kill. Some deserters sank, leaving a red slick on the water. Most, however, made it to the far shore. Among them was Sergeant John Riley, an expert gunner who had once taught artillery to West Point cadets. Of the 9,207 Americans who deserted from 1846 to 1848, only a handful fought against their own country. Riley was the most famous of these. Soon after reaching Matamoros, he formed the San Patricio Battalion. Since the majority of its recruits were Irish, he named the unit after Ireland's patron saint. On one side of its flag was the Mexican eagle and the motto LONG LIVE THE REPUBLIC OF MEXICO; the other side bore a harp and a portrait of Saint Patrick. After the Mexican War began, it was said the San Patricios fought like men "with ropes around their necks." They did. If captured, they knew what awaited them.

On April 24, 1846, General Mariano Arista, the commander at Matamoros, sent a force of sixteen hundred cavalry across the river. Learning of this move, Old Zack ordered a sixty-three-man patrol to keep tabs on them. The next day, the patrol was surrounded and its members either killed or captured. Its leader, however, escaped.

Old Zack fired off a message to the White House. American blood, he wrote, had been shed on American soil. Nowadays, the message would be received instantaneously. But Taylor did not have access to a telegraph line, much less a radio transmitter. So the message went by mounted courier, then by steamboat, arriving on the evening of May 9, two weeks after the event.[27]

"Shed American blood upon the American soil!" President Polk liked the phrase so much he borrowed it for the war bill he sent Congress. The House of Representatives passed the bill by a vote of 173 to 14, the Senate by 42 to 2. On May 13, Polk signed it into law.

That made it official. It was war.

All on the Plains of Mexico

When Zackarias Taylor gained the day,
Heave away, Santy Anno;
He made poor Santy run away,
All on the plains of Mexico.

So heave her up and away we'll go,
Heave away, Santy Anno;
Heave her up and away we'll go,
All on the plains of Mexico.
–Sailors' song, 1848

My mind wandered in bright dreams of glory and renown in that region of romance,
the land of Cortez and Montezuma.
–Private Samuel Chamberlain

he Mexican War had been in full swing for nearly a week before the formal declaration by the United States. It began with the bombardment of Fort Texas, during which Major Jacob Brown, the commander, was killed; the town that grew up on the fort's site is named Brownsville in his memory. A few days after the bombardment, General Arista crossed the Rio Grande with his entire force. But instead of moving to capture the fort, he circled around and headed for the American supply base at Point Isabel.

Old Zack rushed to meet the threat to his rear. On May 8, the two armies met at Palo Alto, or "Tall Timber," an area of cottonwood trees and thick brush. The

An old drawing of General Zachary Taylor's troops going into action during the battle of Palo Alto.

Americans were outnumbered by better than two to one—2,300 to 6,000 men. Despite the long odds, Old Zack was calm. Sitting sidesaddle on his horse, he chewed tobacco, spitting a brown streak and talking to anyone who passed by. His confidence was well placed. In the battle that followed, the Mexicans sent wave after wave of cavalry against his thin blue lines. The riders were slaughtered. Retreating, Arista took up a position at Resaca de la Palma, a dry streambed near the Rio Grande. The Americans attacked the following day, winning another victory. What is interesting is not the victories themselves, but the casualties, which were far out of line to the numbers involved: 147 Americans killed and wounded to the Mexicans' 1,200, a ratio of more than eight to one.

These battles set the pattern for the entire war. The Americans always won by doing the enemy several times the damage it did them. The reasons were superior leadership and firepower. Not only did American generals prove to be better at their trade, they had a solid core of West Pointers to carry out their orders on the battlefield. They were also backed by artillery that was second to none. Mexican guns were old and worn; their cannonballs struck the ground far short of the American lines, rolling and bouncing forward so slowly that soldiers could easily step aside to let them pass. The Americans' flying artillery, however, lived up to its name. "Flying" to the point of greatest danger, the gunners unleashed blizzards of grapeshot and canister. The result was a slaughter. "It was a terrible sight to go over the ground the next day and see the amount of life that had been destroyed," a shocked Lieutenant Ulysses S. Grant wrote his fiancée after Palo Alto. "The ground was literally strewed with the bodies of dead men and horses."[1]

The aftermath of battle was always similar in human terms. The dead were lucky, if they went quickly. The wounded were unlucky; most died later, often screaming in pain. There were no painkillers during the first year of the Mexican War, nor, for that matter, in any previous conflict. True, in September 1846 Dr. William Morton

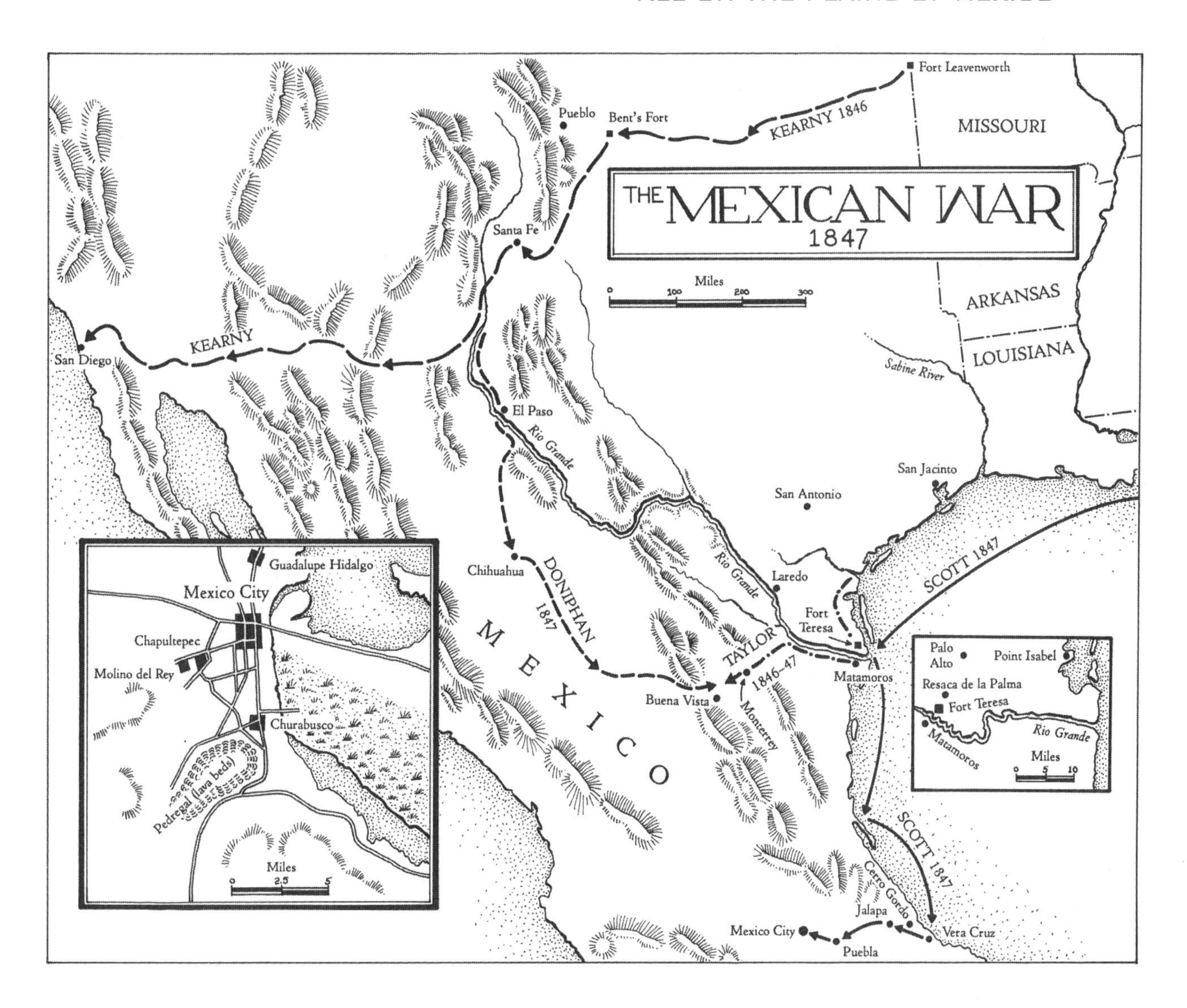

of Boston used ether for the first time during an operation. But Morton's discovery, which was to revolutionize surgery, did not reach army doctors for a full year; and even then there was seldom enough ether to meet the demand. Surgeons, therefore, did as they had always done. It was not pretty. The patient was laid on a table by the orderlies and a stick placed between his teeth to prevent him from biting off his tongue. Then they held him while the surgeon went to work. Often the pain was so severe that the patient died of shock.

Simple wounds were closed with needle and thread and the patient returned to duty. In dealing with bullets, the surgeon searched for the slug with a finger or an iron probe like a dentist's pick, removing it with a pair of forceps. Bullets were not the only things taken from wounds. Bits of leather and cloth, even other people's teeth and fragments of their bones, were also extracted. A cannonball struck with such force as to blow its victim apart, turning pieces of his body into high-speed "missiles" able to kill or cripple bystanders. Frequently, those counted as "missing" after a battle had been blown into pieces too small to be identified.

"The surgeon's saw was going the livelong night, and the groans of the poor sufferers were heart-rending," Captain Henry wrote after Palo Alto.[2] It had to be. A musket ball could shatter bones and tear flesh, creating ragged, gaping wounds. For a serious leg or arm wound, there was but one remedy: Cut it off. Surgeons deserved the nickname "sawbones," since amputation was their treatment of choice. Amputation was fast and neat, avoiding unnecessary loss of blood. On average, a surgeon could take off a limb in under three minutes. The stump was then sewn or cauterized, that is, seared with a red-hot blade to stop bleeding. Deep chest and stomach wounds were almost always fatal; the best that could be done for such patients was to make them as comfortable as possible while they waited for the end. If such men were found on the battlefield, friends as well as foes might finish them off with a bullet or a bayonet. "Mercy killing" might be illegal, but most soldiers believed it was kinder than letting a doomed man die slowly and in agony.

For those who survived surgery, the ordeal had only just begun. Ignorance of how disease spreads made it impossible to prevent infection. Wounds were washed with soiled cloths to give the surgeon a better view, or not washed at all. If an instrument fell to the ground, the surgeon wiped it on his bloodstained smock and kept working. The same instruments, unwashed, were used throughout the day. Surgeons washed their hands *after* operations, not before, and there were no such things as rubber gloves. They also used their saliva to wet their silk stitching thread. Bandages could be anything from bedsheets cut into strips to discarded underwear, even torn-up flags. As a result, every surgical patient came down with an infection of one sort of another. If his body was strong enough, he survived. If not, he "went home to mother"—that is, died.

General Taylor's victories made him a national hero. Congress gave him two gold medals, and there was talk of him as a candidate for the presidency in 1848. His fame also acted as a magnet, attracting volunteers to the army. Every red-blooded American, it seemed, wanted to join Old Rough and Ready. A recruiting poster captured the popular mood:

HERE'S TO OLD ZACK!
GLORIOUS TIMES!
ROAST BEEF, ICE CREAM AND THREE MONTHS ADVANCE![3]

Not everyone was so enthusiastic. Opposition to war is as American as the Fourth of July. Even before there was a United States of America, there were Americans who rejected violence for religious reasons. Pacifists, as they were called, believed that God's word was the highest law. And since He commanded "Thou shalt not kill," fighting could never be right. Nonpacifists, however, held equally strong opinions about war. Although believing that war is proper under certain conditions, they might oppose a particular war as unjust, unwise, unnecessary, or unlawful.

The Mexican War was said to be all of these. Americans were bitterly divided over their first conflict fought on foreign soil. Abolitionists branded it a Southern conspiracy to bring more slave states into the Union. Rather than see that happen, poet James Russell Lowell insisted that the free North "instantly divide" from the unfree South; that is, secede from the Union and form a separate country. His fellow poet, Henry David Thoreau, opposed the war by refusing to pay taxes.

Opposition voices were raised in the halls of Congress itself. An Illinois representative by the name of Abraham Lincoln demanded to know the exact "spot" on American soil where Mexicans had shed American blood. He pushed his demand so hard that he became known as "spotty Lincoln," who would die of "spotted fever." An irate politician challenged Lincoln to a duel, which he accepted, provided he chose the weapons—"cow-dung at five paces." Everyone laughed, forcing the man to drop his challenge.

Now and then, war critics went overboard. Like some opponents of the Vietnam War 120 years later, they praised the enemy and made no secret of their hopes for an American disaster. The most outspoken critic was Senator Thomas Corwin of Ohio. Nicknamed "Black Tom," he advised Mexicans to greet his fellow countrymen "with bloody hands" and to welcome them "to hospitable graves."[4] That was going a bit too far; indeed, it verged upon treason. The reply was swift and nasty. A scarecrow representing Corwin was made of cow dung, dressed in a Mexican uniform, and set on fire. This poem was nailed to a post over the smoking mess:

Old Tom Corwin is dead and here he lies;
Nobody's sorry and nobody cries;

Where he's gone and how he fares,
Nobody knows and nobody cares.[5]

Soldiers opposed the Mexican War, too, only they did so in private. This should not be surprising; American soldiers have never been mindless killing machines. More often than not, they have been men of conscience with a deep moral sense and respect for human life. Take, for example, Colonel Ethan Allen Hitchcock. A brilliant officer, this one-time chief of West Point cadets thought the war unjust. "My heart is not in this business," he wrote a friend. "I am against it from the bottom of my soul as a most unholy and unrighteous proceeding."[6] A fellow officer, a dignified Virginian named Robert E. Lee, said he was "ashamed" that his country should have "bullied" its neighbor.[7] Ulysses S. Grant called it a "wicked war," an "unholy war," and "one of the most unjust ever waged."[8] Yet they agreed on still another thing: they must do their duty. As soldiers in a democracy, they were not free to choose their wars. They were servants of the people, educated at the people's expense. As the people's representative, an officer, having lawfully decided on war, must either obey or resign his commission. Anything else was dishonorable.

Honorable men on both sides were disgusted by certain actions. The Mexican War was fought with all the savagery of the Vietnam War. Some American soldiers committed offenses that, in peacetime, would have meant a court-martial, or military trial, followed by a "necktie party" at the gallows. There were crimes against property, as when Americans looted shops, killed livestock, and pulled down private homes for firewood. Other offenses were due to soldiers out for a night's "funning," having a good time at Mexican expense. Drunken troops, for example, might run through the streets of a town firing their pistols through windows. In Parras, cavalrymen showed no respect for man or God; they rode into the town church during Mass, cursing and yelling as worshipers cringed in terror. Crimes against people ranged all the way from verbal insults, slaps, and armed robbery to rape and murder. Few were punished.

Mexicans helped to raise the level of brutality. As the war continued, guerrillas became a serious problem for the Americans. *Guerrilla* is Spanish for "little war"; that is, war fought by bands of civilians, or soldiers disguised as civilians, operating behind enemy lines. The story of Mexico's "little war" is a tale of horror and atrocity. Guerrillas were a law unto themselves, combining the roles of judge, jury, and executioner. For guerrillas, terrorism began at home, against their own people. Their aim was education through violence. The lesson: Friendly contact with Americans brought certain death. Anyone who sold food to an American, let alone gave him information, was a goner. And becoming an American's lover was a capital offense. There are cases where such women, called "Yankedos," were branded with the letters *U.S.*, raped, and then tortured to death. Sam Chamberlain saw a lieutenant's girlfriend "covered with blood from having both ears cut off close to her head!"[9]

Guerrillas went after Americans, too. Antonio Canales, a notorious border raider, targeted General Taylor's supply lines to the Rio Grande. In his biggest raid, Canales destroyed an entire wagon train, 130 vehicles carrying food and ammunition. The train was a legitimate target, but what he did to the American teamsters was a crime. All 110 of them were killed. The majority were shot after surrendering; the rest were lassoed, stripped naked, and then dragged through clumps of cactus until dead.[10]

Another time, drunken Americans entered a church, lassoed a wooden statue of Christ, and dragged it through the streets by the neck. Townspeople later caught one of the Americans alone, tied him to a cross in the town square, and skinned him alive. A rescue party arrived moments later. Sam Chamberlain recalled:

> As they charged into the square, they saw their miserable comrade hanging to the cross, his skin hanging in strips, surrounded by crowds of Mexicans. With yells of horror, [they] charged the mass with Bowie Knife and revolver, sparing neither age nor sex in their terrible fury. The miserable cause of all this was yet alive and in his awful agony cursed all and everything and begged his comrades to shoot him and end his suffering. He was cut down and finding him beyond hope the . . . Captain put a bullet through the brains of the wretch. . . . The matter was hushed up and kept secret from the world.[11]

Old Rough and Ready got rough. He let the Texas Rangers deal with guerrillas in their own way. The trouble with Los Diablos Tejanos was their long memories—memories of the Alamo, of Goliad, and of countless border raids. Rangers went to war filled with hatred and burning for revenge; they called it "Texan vengeance." After the wagon-train massacre, Mustang Gray, not yet twenty and a captain, led one of the search parties. Canales's gang had butchered his family back in 1840, and he meant to even the score no matter who paid. Surrounding a ranch house, his men broke down the doors, taking the occupants by surprise. None of them, apparently, were guerrillas. Mustang didn't care. He had thirty-six men and boys tied to posts and shot before the eyes of their families. Then he burned every building on the ranch.[12]

Revenge was also the motive in the war's worst atrocity. On February 9, 1847, guerrillas murdered a volunteer in an Arkansas regiment near the village of Agua Nueva, Mexico. Next day, the Arkansans—or "Rackensackers," as they called themselves—decided it was payback time. About a hundred men swooped down on a nearby village. Searching the houses, they found what they took to be some of the dead man's equipment. Without further ado, they opened fire on the villagers, who fled to a cave on a hillside. Following them into the cave, the Rackensackers massacred thirty men, women, and children. They might have killed everyone had not the sound of gunfire brought other Americans. Along the way, they found a Mexican scalped but still breathing. A sword thrust ended his suffering. Although they stopped the killing, the killers could not be brought to justice when efforts to identify them failed. Many officers were ashamed of their countrymen. If only a tenth of the atrocity stories were true, said General Winfield Scott, it was enough "to make Heaven weep, & every American of Christian morals *blush* for his country."[13]

Meanwhile, Old Zack pushed forward. On May 18, 1846, Matamoros fell without a fight. The Mexican army withdrew eighty miles to the west, to Monterrey, a walled city of twenty thousand and the key to northern Mexico. Defended by nine thousand soldiers with thirty-eight cannons, Monterrey was a tough nut to crack. In the five-day battle that followed (September 20–24), Southern units rushed to the attack with a spine-chilling yell. *"Yip-yip-yip-e-e-ee-e-e-e! Yah-ah-ah-yah-e-e-e-e-e-e-e!"* It probably originated as a hunter's call, but there, for the first time, it was used as a war cry. Less than twenty years later, as the "Rebel yell," it would echo across the battlefields of the Civil War.

The battle for Monterrey was a brutal, soldier-to-soldier slugfest. Having overrun the outer defenses, the Americans had to take the city house by house. As the Texans had done at San Antonio, they battered down doors and smashed through shared walls, inching their way toward the main plaza and the cathedral, which had been turned into an ammunition dump. Amid the smoke and dust, soldiers saw a Mexican woman dart among the fallen, bringing water to the wounded of both armies. Maria Josefa Zozaya kept to her errands of mercy until someone, no one knows who, shot

An artist's impression of the worst American atrocity of the Mexican War: The massacre of civilians at the cave of Agua Nueva.

her in the back. "She was dead!" wrote an American soldier who ran over to her moments later. "The waste! The stupidity! That such a fine person should get such a cruel reward was too much even for a strong man to bear. I turned my eyes to heaven and thought, 'Oh God, and this is war!'"[14]

The Americans fought their way to within artillery range of the cathedral. Fearing that a single shell might blow the city to kingdom come, General Pedro de Ampudia, the Mexican commander, surrendered on condition that his troops receive the "honors of war"; that is, be allowed to leave with their weapons and battle flags. Old Zack agreed. As his men marched through the streets, bands played "Yankee Doodle." Halting in the main plaza, they fell silent as they watched the Mexicans depart. These were brave soldiers, and they respected them. But when the San Patricio deserters passed, they turned their backs and jeered. The price of victory was 433 American casualties; Mexican losses are uncertain but were surely twice that number.

After taking Monterrey, Old Zack rested his army and awaited further orders from Washington. While he waited, other operations were underway far to the north and west.

After conquering New Mexico, Stephen Watts Kearny moved westward to California, where he occupied Los Angeles.

President Polk, we recall, wanted to acquire California and New Mexico. To that end, a 1,700-man "Army of the West" was assembled at Fort Leavenworth, Kansas, under General Stephen Watts Kearny, fifty-two, a small, quiet man who had served in frontier posts for thirty years. In June 1846 Kearny set out for New Mexico. Following the Santa Fe Trail, he made no secret of his destination; he even sent messages that the Americans were coming "as friends, not as enemies, as protectors, not as conquerors."[15]

Meanwhile, New Mexico Governor Manuel Armijo prepared to meet the invaders with four thousand men, mostly volunteers. A rich man, described as "a mountain of fat," Armijo boasted that he had made his fortune by stealing sheep. Although he put up a brave front, his motto was, "It is better to be thought brave than to be so."[16] He meant it. As Kearny approached, Armijo abandoned Santa Fe. New Mexico fell on August 18 without a shot being fired.

Kearny divided his army into three units. Five hundred men under Colonel Sterling Price continued the occupation of Santa Fe; Colonel Alexander W. Doniphan was sent south into the state of Chihuahua with a thousand men; Kearny himself led about a hundred men westward to California. After crushing an uprising at Taos, Price forced the Pueblos to take an oath of loyalty to the United States; the Apache gave their loyalty to no white men. By the time Kearny reached California, an American naval expedition had already taken the major towns. Doniphan made the longest march in American military history. Leaving Santa Fe, he led his force over the Dead Man's March, crossed the Rio Grande at El Paso, and captured Chihuahua city on February 28, 1847, after a short, sharp fight. Chihuahua's citizens were then treated to the sight of naked gringos bathing in public fountains and singing "Yankee

Doodle" at the top of their voices. In the spring, Doniphan was ordered back to the United States by way of New Orleans, ending a journey of over six thousand miles.

In the meantime, Old Zack was getting nowhere fast. Despite his victories, it was becoming clear that the war could not be won in northern Mexico. The arithmetic was all wrong. Five hundred miles of mountains and deserts lay between Monterrey and Mexico City—five hundred miles without a decent road. At the rate he was going, Taylor would need years, and a considerably larger army, to smash his way to the enemy capital.

The high command decided to take a shortcut. Since the U.S. Navy already controlled the Gulf of Mexico, an invasion force could be landed at Vera Cruz. With the navy supplying it by sea, the force could make a beeline for Mexico City, 250 miles inland. This route also led across rugged mountains, but these had never stopped Cortés. And if Spaniards could cross, so could Americans! Besides, the way had been improved during the last three centuries. A fine road, the National Highway, linked the coast to the capital.

President Polk approved the plan. But since there weren't enough troops to fight on two fronts at once, it was necessary to take troops from Old Zack's army. Written orders were sent, telling him to release nine thousand men for duty elsewhere by January 3, 1847. He obeyed, although he swore a blue streak. And no wonder. When he counted heads, he found that he had slightly fewer than five thousand men available for action. Before long, he would need every one of them.

A follow-up message had been sent to make sure Taylor knew what he was supposed to do. It never arrived. At sundown on January 11, Lieutenant John Ritchey, the courier, was lassoed by guerrillas, dragged to his death, and his dispatch case rushed to Santa Anna's headquarters in central Mexico. The Napoleon of the West was overjoyed. By a stroke of good luck, he knew the enemy's entire plan. But how should the information be used? There were two choices: move south to strengthen Vera Cruz and the National Highway, or north to strike Old Zack and his weakened army. Santa Anna decided to do both. He would crush Taylor before the landing took place, then defeat the invaders when they came ashore at Vera Cruz.

Like the defenders of the Alamo, Taylor did not expect the Mexicans to advance during the winter. Sleet and snow lashed the thinly clad troops and their *soldaderas*. Scores of men, women, and children froze along the way, but the others kept going. Whatever they might think of Santa Anna, they were patriots first. Foreigners had invaded their country, and they were determined to drive them out.

Not until February 21, when the Mexicans were only thirty miles from his base at Agua Nueva, did Old Zack learn of the danger. With not a moment to spare, he ordered an immediate retreat. The army left in such a hurry that tons of supplies had to be burned to keep them from falling into enemy hands.

The army took up positions near the Hacienda de Buena Vista, a sheep ranch a few miles south of the city of Saltillo. The ranch had a good view, a *buena vista,* of some gorgeous mountain scenery. The Sierra Madres loomed behind the ranch, an unbroken wall outlined against the horizon. Mountain spurs extended like stone fingers to the ranch's right and left, enclosing a wide plateau cut by two deep ravines. Leaving his aides to position the troops, Old Zack went to Saltillo to check on his defenses there. Saltillo was his main supply base, and he worried that Santa Anna might circle around Buena Vista to cut him off.

The Napoleon of the West was in a panic. Finding the Agua Nueva camps deserted, he feared that the gringos might have given him the slip. That was unthinkable; he *must* have his battle. A strong cavalry force was sent ahead to find the enemy, pin him down, and hold him until the main army arrived to finish the job.

The cavalry made contact with the Americans on the afternoon of February 22. Santa Anna breathed a sigh of relief. At dusk a Mexican officer rode up to Taylor with a white flag of truce and a message from his chief. The Americans, the message said, were facing twenty thousand veteran troops. El Presidente, a kindly person, was prepared to treat the invaders mercifully, if they surrendered within the hour. If not, they would be annihilated.

Old Rough and Ready did not scare easily. He gave the officer a long, hard look that made him uncomfortable. It was the calm before the storm.

"Tell Santa Anna to go to hell!" the general growled.

Turning to William S. Bliss, his chief of staff, he ordered, "Major Bliss, put that in Spanish!"

Ever a gentlemen—they didn't call him "Perfect Bliss" for nothing—the major toned down the reply. It said, "I beg leave to say that I decline acceding to your request."[17]

Santa Anna had chosen the worst time to pick a fight. Like their general, the American troops were feeling pretty cocky. February 22 is, after all, the anniversary of George Washington's birthday. Washington was still the nation's most admired figure, its greatest hero, the father of his country. Old Zack's troops considered it a good omen to be facing the enemy on that day, something to make them fight with greater energy. When they turned in for the night, officers gave the password to the sentries: "Memory of Washington."

If Washington's memory warmed men's hearts, it did nothing for their bodies. Buena Vista is six thousand feet above sea level, and it was a bitterly cold night. The Americans had few tents, and the Mexicans none at all. Neither side lit fires, because there was no firewood on the plateau. Soldiers had to be satisfied with a few mouthfuls of greasy bacon and, if they were fortunate, a swig of whiskey. Then, wrapping themselves in their blankets, they shivered through the night.

Tuesday, February 23, 1847. The day dawned bright and clear. While bands played "Hail Columbia," the American infantry checked their weapons, the cavalry took their positions, and the flying artillery stood by, waiting for orders. Across the plain, they heard bugles and saw priests bless the Mexican troops as they marched out of camp. The American army had no chaplains.

Santa Anna hurled masses of infantry and cavalry at the American positions. Throughout the battle, the San Patricio deserters manned their field guns, sending cannonballs ripping into their former comrades.

The pressure was terrific all along the American line. Some men lost their courage. Sam Chamberlain saw a fellow shot through the arm. No sooner did he cry out than eight others dropped everything to take him to a surgeon; one even carried his hat.[18] Seeing men turn tail, officers whacked them with the flat of their swords to remind them of their duty; and if that didn't work, a pistol aimed at the head could be very persuasive. Such threats worked with individuals but were useless when entire units panicked, as happened on the left flank. There the 2nd Indiana Regiment was ordered to pull back to a better position. Seeing it go and thinking the battle lost, regiments from Arkansas and Kentucky broke for the rear. The pullback became a route.

The entire front would have collapsed had Old Zack not returned from Saltillo in the nick of time. The general by himself was a one-man reinforcement. "Calm as a summer's morning" is how an officer described him.[19] Riding into the thick of the action, he reined in his horse. He sat, or rather sprawled, on Old Whitey, bullets popping overhead, cannonballs tearing the ground on either side, without flinching. Calmness, like panic, is contagious. Well, soldiers thought, if "the Old Man" could take it, so could they.

"Stand to your guns and give them hell!" Old Zack cried.

"Give 'em Zack!" they shouted in reply.[20]

The line steadied.

The general, however, had not come alone. He brought several squadrons of cavalry and the First Mississippi Rifles under Colonel Jefferson Davis. Reckless fighters, the Mississippians did not wear the regulation blue uniform, but black slouch hats, red shirts, and white canvas pants. At Davis's signal, they put a volley into the oncoming Mexican infantry, hurling them back with heavy losses. "Well done, Jeff!" Old Zack cheered, waving his hat frantically. "Hurrah for Mississippi!"[21]

While the infantry was retreating, a thousand Mexican cavalry charged. Sitting tall in the saddle, their steel helmets topped with red plumes, their lances decorated with fluttering ribbons, they came like a whirlwind. The cavalry were awesome, but not terrifying—to the Mississippians. Instead of retreating, they fired a volley and dropped their guns. Then they did something totally unexpected. Buena Vista may be the only battle in history where infantry charged cavalry who were charging them. Somehow, they took it into their heads to go forward. Drawing eighteen-inch bowie knives, the Mississippians rushed the astonished riders. Catching the horses by the bridle, they backed them onto their haunches and stabbed the riders. *"Diablos! Camisas coloradas!"*—"Devils! Red shirts!"—the survivors shouted as they fell back in confusion.[22]

The confusion did not last long, however. Regrouping his men, Santa Anna threw the day's heaviest attack at the American center. Once again, the line was about to break when rescue came in the form of a battery of flying artillery. It was like the Mississippians' charge, only with field guns. Galloping toward the oncoming Mexicans, Captain Braxton Bragg, the battery's commander, gave a signal. Suddenly the guns stopped, wheeled about, and spat a stream of hot iron into the Mexicans' faces. At that moment Old Zack rode up. Upon asking what kind of shot was being used, he was told grape. "Give them a little more grape, Mr. Bragg," he is supposed to have said. Perhaps. Most likely, he shouted, "Double-shot your guns and give 'em hell!"[23] Whatever he said, Bragg's battery blew the attack apart. The Battle of Buena Vista was over. The Mexican army retreated under cover of darkness.

But Santa Anna claimed victory! The Americans, he told newspapers in Mexico City, had had two thousand men killed and an equal number wounded. It was a lie. With 746 dead, wounded, and missing, Buena Vista *was* the bloodiest battle in American history up to that time. In his official report, however, Taylor estimated

General Zachary Taylor's camp near Monterrey, Mexico, after the battle of Buena Vista, February 22, 1847. With this victory, Taylor's job in Mexico was done.

Mexican losses at two thousand dead and wounded, plus two to three thousand deserters. The exact figures will never be known, because Santa Anna was too busy running away to count. Whatever the number, American scouting parties knew the enemy had suffered a stunning defeat. The road leading south from Buena Vista was cluttered with the wreckage of battle. La Encarnación, a village where the Mexican wounded were collected, was abandoned to the victors. Sam Chamberlain was an eyewitness:

> All along the way we passed terrible evidence of the complete route and fearful sufferings of the once formidable host of Santa Anna. Bodies of man and beast, partly eaten by Vultures and Coyotes, broken arms, belts and horse trappings lay scattered the whole distance. About noon on the second day our advance [party] . . . dashed into Encarnación. . . . I was with the advance that entered the place. It was a den of horrors! Death was on all sides; miserable wrecks of humanity with fearful wounds lay in the square on the bare ground, and in

> the houses and the little Chapel nearly three hundred more wounded wretches lay without bedding or blankets on the hard cement floors, wallowing in filth, while maggots and vermin crawled in and out of their undressed wounds, and the air was so foul and pestiferous that it seemed impossible to breathe it and live. A detachment of half-starved Mexican infantry was on duty, burying the dead . . . after first stripping them of the few rags that covered them. Some four hundred women were moving around doing what they could to nurse the wounded, but there was not a Surgeon in the place![24]

Buena Vista turned out to be Old Zack's finest hour as a general. Yet, ironically, it put him out of work. Having reached the peak of his military career, there was nothing left for him to achieve in northern Mexico. He returned home to plan for a different sort of campaign—a campaign for the White House.

Two weeks after Buena Vista, lookouts at Vera Cruz gazed out to sea. Moments later they fired their signal guns. Out there, emerging from the morning mist, was a fleet of eighty warships. The invasion had come.

The invasion's leader was Winfield Scott, commanding general of the U.S. Army. A man of sixty, Scott stood six feet four inches tall, weighed 240 pounds, and *looked* like a general. From the barrel chest to the large head set on the short, stout neck, he radiated authority. A career soldier, his daredevil actions had made his name a household word during the War of 1812. At the Battle of Chippewa,where he routed a stronger British force, his troops wore drab homespun gray, the only cloth available when the regulation blue ran out; in honor of the fight, West Point cadets have worn gray uniforms ever since. Soldiers called him "Old Fuss and Feathers," because he was so finicky about details. Unlike Zachary Taylor, he loved dress uniforms; so much so, it was said, that he wore all the uniform and gold braid the law allowed. Tight-lipped and grim-faced, he expected obedience. Once he ordered that any soldier found drunk must dig a grave and then look into it for a while, because he would fill it if he kept drinking. Men stayed sober as long as he led the unit.

The fleet arrived off Vera Cruz on March 8, 1847. Anxious to see the city's fortifications for himself, Scott invited his staff and several junior officers—Captains Robert E. Lee, Joseph E. Johnston, P. G. T. Beauregard, George Gordon Meade—

for a ride aboard the *Petrita,* a steamboat captured from the Mexicans. As the tiny craft drew closer, enemy gunners fired a few shots to find its range. From what the officers could see, the city was surrounded by stout walls bristling with cannons. Those would be a problem, if they ever got ashore, which was growing unlikely, for the gunners were dropping their shells ever closer with each try. Finally, Scott ordered *Petrita* turned around. A few minutes more and a shell might have ended the expedition and killed many future leaders of the Civil War.

Known as Old Fuss and Feathers, General Winfield Scott commanded American forces during the final stages of the Mexican War. The nation's longest-serving officer, Scott fought in the War of 1812 and was commander of Union forces during the first days of the Civil War in 1861.

Scott chose a landing spot three miles up the coast from Vera Cruz. Seasick troops were willing to risk death, even the surgeon's saw—anything to get off those rolling tubs. Clambering into longboats, they cast off and were rowed toward shore by sailors. But as they approached, Mexican cavalry came out of the woods behind the beach. That was no surprise; Scott expected heavy resistance at the water's edge. So when the cavalry appeared, warships turned broadside to the beach and cut loose with their big guns. The cavalry scurried away. By evening over ten thousand men were safely ashore, together with their equipment. The first amphibious landing in American history had been a total success.

Although isolated by sea and land, Vera Cruz was determined to resist. This gave Scott three choices, none of them pleasant. He could order a frontal assault; that promised to be quick and bloody, perhaps even cripple his army's effectiveness. He could besiege the city; that would cost fewer casualties but take more time. And time was precious. Vera Cruz lies in a tropical region plagued by yellow fever or, as Mexicans called it, *"el vómito negro,"* "the black vomit." Caused by a virus carried by mosquitoes, the disease brings high fever, turns the skin yellow, and makes the victim vomit a sticky black goo. Starting in early April, the disease lasted until it became too cool for mosquitoes to breed. Exposed to yellow fever for centuries, Mexicans had built up a resistance to it. Americans had not. Scott, therefore, had less than three weeks to take the city and move his army into the cool highlands. Hence the third choice: a ruthless bombardment to break the defenders' will.

Robert E. Lee was put in charge of the siege guns. A skilled combat engineer, Lee did his best, only to find that it was not good enough. The Mexican guns were not the problem; although they answered shot for shot, their crews were poorly trained and fired wildly. Now and then an American soldier lost an arm or had his head knocked off, but usually the Mexican shells were more of a nuisance than a threat. The city's walls were something else. High and thick, they were too strong for the American field guns, which fired nine-, twelve-, and eighteen-pound shells. So Lee asked the navy for six of its ship-killing monsters, guns able to throw thirty-two- and sixty-eight-pound shells a mile.

Robert E. Lee, later famous as a Confederate general in the Civil War, was in charge of the American artillery during the assault on the Mexican defenses at Vera Cruz.

For eighty-eight hours nonstop, every American gun hammered Vera Cruz. The shriek of shells filled the air, followed by the crash of explosions. A blanket of smoke hung over the city, reddened by the bursting shells and the glare of fires. Fortifications began to crumble. Buildings collapsed, burying whole families under their rubble. Hysterical civilians ran from place to place, trying to find safety if only for a few minutes. Their yells and screams could be heard hundreds of yards away in the American lines.

Captain Lee had mixed feelings about the bombardment. The shells, he wrote his wife, were "so beautiful in their flight," trailing fiery streamers as they sped through the night sky. Their effect, however, was as ugly as could be. "It was awful! My heart bled for the inhabitants. The soldiers I do not care so much for, but it was terrible to think of the women & children."[25] Nevertheless, he had done his duty. Vera Cruz surrendered on March 29. The operation had cost the Americans seventy-four killed and wounded; Mexican casualties numbered between five hundred and a thousand, mostly civilians.

The march inland began on April 8, just as the first cases of yellow fever were being reported. Scott's combat troops considered themselves lucky to be getting away from Vera Cruz. For those who stayed behind to man the supply lines, the following months would be an ordeal worse than any battle.

The first battle was fought ten days later. Santa Anna led the Mexican forces. That in itself came as a surprise, for nobody in Scott's army expected to be facing him anytime soon. During the siege of Vera Cruz, they had received news of Taylor's victory at Buena Vista. The troops were jubilant, firing salutes with live ammunition into the city. "Old Woodenleg's" army, soldiers joked, had been "licked up like salt."[26] Old Woodenleg, however, had worked something of a miracle since Buena Vista. Convincing his countrymen that *he* had won a great victory, he regrouped his forces and headed south with twelve thousand men.

Santa Anna was dug in on two steep hills that formed a narrow pass, the Devil's Jaws, near the village of Cerro Gordo. It was a death trap. Any troops passing along the road below would be blown to smithereens by Mexican artillery. The Napoleon of the West was so sure of victory that he pledged: "My duty is to sacrifice myself and I know how to fulfill it! . . . I am decided . . . to die fighting!"[27] To which a cynic might have replied: "The way you have always done?"

General Scott asked Captain Lee to search for a way to get at Cerro Gordo from behind. Lee found a trail, but the enemy nearly found him. He was returning to headquarters when, pausing to take a drink from a stream, he heard the voices of approaching Mexican soldiers. Lee dove behind a vine-covered log that lay beside the stream. Hugging the ground, hardly daring to breathe, he saw sandaled feet dangling before his face. Soldiers were sitting on the log just inches above him! Hours dragged by. A mosquito landed on his nose. Ants paraded across his arms. He lay perfectly still, itchy and sweaty and anxious to get back with his news. Finally it grew dark. The soldiers left, and he reported to his chief.

The Battle of Cerro Gordo began on April 17. While one American troop column held the Mexicans' attention in front, another looped around to strike from the rear. Seeing that they were about to be trapped, the defenders retreated, Santa Anna leading the way on horseback. He fled so quickly that he left his luxurious traveling coach behind. Inside it an Illinois regiment found a chest containing silver pesos to pay Santa Anna's soldiers, a roasted chicken, and his spare wooden leg. They sent the money to headquarters, ate the chicken, and took the wooden leg home as a souvenir.

By nightfall of the second day, the battle was over. American casualties were 387, among them 64 dead. Mexican casualties numbered over a thousand; an additional three thousand were captured and released after promising not to fight for the duration of the war. For the first time, Old Fuss and Feathers showed emotion in public. "Brother soldiers," he told the assembled troops, tears welling up in his eyes, "I am proud to call you brothers."[28] As he spoke, he held his hat in his hand as a sign of respect. Captain Lee became a celebrity in the army. Fellow officers agreed that he was a born leader with a brilliant career ahead of him. They were right on both counts.

Santa Anna fell back to Mexico City to prepare for the assault that was sure to come. Scott moved ahead, taking Jalapa, Santa Anna's hometown, and Puebla without firing a shot. Puebla was a real prize. Located eighty miles from the capital, it was Mexico's second city, with a population of one hundred thousand. Had they chosen to, its inhabitants could have given the invaders a rough time. The city's Catholic priests, however, despised Santa Anna and discouraged resistance. The Americans made it as easy for them as possible. Even though Scott and his staff were Protestants, they attended Catholic services as a sign of respect.

Scott spent twelve weeks (May 15–August 7) at Puebla. During that time he rested his troops, received reinforcements, and built up his supplies. The last was not easy to do, since Mexican guerrillas had stepped up their activities along the National Highway. To keep tabs on them, Scott hired Mexican spies. His chief spy was Manuel Dominguez, a famous bandit chief. With Dominguez, money talked; he received three dollars a day, his men a dollar less. In return, they were a gold mine of information.

That information enabled Scott to make a crucial decision. His supply line reached all the way back to Vera Cruz. Like a rubber band, the more he stretched it, the thinner it became and the easier it was to cut. This had also been Cortés's problem in 1519. The Spaniard had solved it by sinking his ships and living off whatever he could take from villages along the way. Scott decided to follow Cortés's example, only he would pay for his army's needs with hard cash.

Scott left Puebla with 10,738 officers and men. Although they knew that Cortés's force had been tiny compared to theirs, they saw themselves as latter-day conquistadors, reenacting one of history's greatest adventures. West of Puebla, the National Highway gradually climbed into rugged country varying in elevation from four to eight thousand feet above sea level. These are the Mexican highlands, a plateau broken by mountains into valleys, each separated from the others. The beauty of the place moved soldiers to tears; indeed, it knocked some of them off their feet. "I know not whether I am more susceptible to the effects of fine scenery than others," a Kentuckian wrote his wife, "but this . . . was by far the most glorious picture of nature I have ever beheld . . . and I dropped on earth to breathe a prayer and a thanksgiving to a good God who had made such a glorious world."[29]

The highway curved its way between two snowcapped volcanoes, Popocatepetl, "Smoking Mountain," and Ixtaccihuatl, "White Lady." Cortés had tried to climb Popocatepetl but without success. A group of young Americans, among them Ulysses S. Grant, tried as well, only to be driven back by high winds and snow blindness. Several of them, however, succeeded on their second attempt. They reached the top, gazed into the smoking crater, and planted the Stars and Stripes on the highest pinnacle. The flag, a climber wrote, had been placed where it would catch the rays of the morning sun as it rose from the Atlantic and the beams of the setting sun as it sank into the Pacific.[30] Someday soon, they hoped, an American empire would stretch from ocean to ocean.

Higher, higher, the highway went. The air grew colder and thinner, making it harder to breathe. The sun's rays were intense in the thin air, causing painful sunburns. Scott's army struggled up the 10,500-foot pass of Río Frío, turned the corner of a hill, and halted in its tracks. There it was!

The Valley of Mexico spread out below them like a huge map. Lakes glistened in the sunlight and roads ran through villages in a straight line toward Mexico City. Although the capital was thirty-five miles away, even at that distance they could identify the twin towers of the cathedral in the Zócalo, or central plaza. The immense structure stands near the foundations of the pyramid of the Aztec war god, in whose honor each year priests had sacrificed thousands of victims by cutting out their hearts and making their blood flow in streams down its sides. Cortés destroyed the pyramid, replacing it with a cathedral worthy of any Spanish city.

The capital had upward of two hundred thousand inhabitants and was defended by thirty thousand soldiers, a force nearly three times the size of Scott's. And more—Mexico City was actually an island fortress defended by other island fortresses. It lay at the center of a network of marshes and lakes that spring rains had caused to overflow their banks. A fifteen-mile-wide lava bed called the Pedregal guarded the approaches to two key defense positions: the hill at Contreras to the south and, to its northeast, the stone Convent of San Mateo at Churubusco, Aztec for "Place of the War God." Formed by volcanoes ages ago, the Pedregal was described as hell with the fires out. The ground was strewn with chunks of broken lava and obsidian, a volcanic glass sharp enough to slice through the soles of boots.

Scott called in his "miracle worker," Robert E. Lee. A head-on assault, he said, would be costly and almost certainly fail. But if Lee could do a repeat of Cerro Gordo and find a way through the Pedregal, it might be possible to circle around the enemy positions. The captain promised to do his best, snapped a salute, and left on the double.

Lee and his friend Captain P. G. T. Beauregard set out with a small scouting party. Entering the Pedregal on a stormy night, their way lit by lightning flashes, they discovered a mule trail that came out just north of Contreras on the road leading to Churubusco. The next day, August 20, Lee guided a strike force through the lava field.

The battle that followed lasted exactly seventeen minutes. Seeing Americans coming down the road behind them, the Mexicans abandoned their positions. A mob of soldiers and camp women swept northward, desperate to escape while there was still time. When Beauregard brought the news of the victory to Scott, he received a warmer welcome than he could have imagined. "Young man," said the general, opening his arms wide, "if I were not on horseback, I would embrace you!" Old Fuss and Feathers was almost smiling.[31]

The fight at Churubusco, however, was nothing to smile at. The convent had been turned into a fort manned by picked troops backed by the guns of the San Patricios. The Americans attacked time and again, only to be hurled back with severe losses. Eager to get at the San Patricios, they pushed on, ignoring the cost. They waded a flooded ditch in front of the convent, broke through the gate, and charged with their bayonets. Mexicans began to flee or try to raise the white flag of surrender. The San Patricios shot them down. Knowing what awaited them if captured, they fought like demons. Yet it was hopeless. When the smoke cleared, their battalion was shattered; of its 250 members, only 66 survived to be taken prisoner. The day's "butcher bill" for the Americans was 1,056 killed and wounded, all but 60 of them at Churubusco.

Mexican losses totaled no fewer than 4,000 dead and wounded, plus 2,637 prisoners, among them eight generals and two former presidents of Mexico.

Both sides had been so badly mauled that they agreed to a truce. Each commander meant to use the truce for his own ends. Scott wanted to rest his men and allow Nicholas P. Trist, an American diplomat, to negotiate a peace treaty. Santa Anna was not interested in peace just yet; he needed time to strengthen the city's defenses.

Meanwhile, the San Patricios faced a court-martial. Most of their former comrades would have been glad to see them hanged on the spot, without going through the formality of a trial. Not Scott. A hard man, but also a just man, he insisted that they, like every American, were entitled to their day in court. At his urging, the jury found that although all were guilty of desertion, they were not equally guilty and deserving of death. Twenty *were* executed and thirty others saved for a special fate, as we shall see. One fellow was pardoned; an old-timer, sixty years of age, he had been a faithful soldier until tempted to desert by Sergeant Riley. A deserter whose son had refused to go along also escaped the rope. It was for the sake of the son that the father was spared. "In the hour of the greatest temptation," Scott explained, "the son was loyal and true to his colors."[32]

The remaining fourteen, including Sergeant Riley, were spared as well; they had deserted before the declaration of war and were therefore not guilty of desertion in the face of the enemy. That was the law. Their punishment, however, was as harsh as the law allowed. They were forced to dig the graves of their executed friends, then bury the corpses. Having finished that grisly chore, they received fifty lashes on their bare backs with a rawhide whip studded with knots. "Why those thus punished did not die under such punishment was a marvel to me," an onlooker wrote. "Their backs had the appearance of a pounded piece of raw beef, the blood oozing from every stripe as given."[33] Then a large letter *D* (for Deserter) was branded with a red-hot iron high up on a cheekbone, under the eye but not close enough to cause blindness. After their heads were shaved, iron collars weighing eight pounds with three-foot-long prongs—the same devices used to tame unruly slaves—were fastened around their necks. Finally, they were put to hard labor until the end of the war.

The truce lasted from August 24 to September 7. When Santa Anna rejected the American peace terms, Scott ordered the final assault on Mexico City.

No one expected it to be easy. The chief obstacle was a massive fortress atop Chapultepec, the Aztec "Hill of Grasshoppers." When Cortés first visited this spot, he stayed in the summer palace of the Emperor Montezuma. Spanish viceroys later built the castle of Chapultepec to guard the approaches to the capital. After independence, the Mexican republic gave over part of the building to the National Military Academy, its West Point. Ranging in age from thirteen to eighteen, the academy's hundred cadets were spoiling for a fight with the gringos.

They expected to win, and with good reason. Chapultepec was the strongest fort in the New World. Defended by eight thousand soldiers, it had walls four feet thick and twenty feet high. The castle, however, did not stand alone. It and its hill were at the center of an enclosure surrounded by giant cypress trees, which in turn were surrounded by a twelve-foot stone wall. Cannons mounted on the castle's walls were trained on the open ground between the trees and the hill. The steep incline up to the castle was cut by ditches and studded with mounds resembling freshly dug graves: land mines. Crude but effective, mines were barrels of gunpowder buried in the earth and exploded by long fuses. The western side of the enclosure was formed by the Molino del Rey (the King's Mill), a low stone building a quarter of a mile in length. Finally, the entire enclosure was linked to the city by two causeways, elevated roads that crossed the marshes. These roads ended at the city "gates," stone buildings used in peacetime as guard stations but now heavily fortified.

During the truce, Scott heard that Santa Anna was sending Mexico City's church bells to be melted down and cast into cannons at the Molino del Rey. On September 8, he ordered it taken as a warm-up to the main assault on Chapultepec. He regretted that decision for the rest of his life.

The Americans came in two waves, one a hundred yards behind the other. Nothing stirred within the building. Approaching to within point-blank range, the first wave could hardly believe its luck. Still no resistance. That the Mexicans had retreated seemed too good to be true, and it was. Suddenly, a thousand muskets cut loose at the same instant. The advancing troops, dazed and bloody, fell back—those who were still standing. Those who had fallen, the wounded, stared in wide-eyed horror as Mexicans burst from the building and rushed toward them. Shouting wildly, they bayoneted the helpless men until the second wave struck full force, driving them back and taking the position. American casualties were 786, and all for nothing. Only after its fall did Scott learn that cannons were not being cast at the Molino del Rey. As for his men, they had a score to settle. Their chance came five days later, at Chapultepec.

Scott's plan was to hit the castle from four directions—north, west, south, and

The battle of Molino del Rey was fought on the outskirts of Mexico City. In the background, on the right of the picture, can be seen the fortress of Chapultapec.

southeast—at once. While his artillery softened it up, assault troops were to sweep up the hill and place ladders against the walls. Once over the walls, it would be a free-for-all with victory going to the best, or the luckiest, side.

As with any battle, those who fought at Chapultepec could not see the "big picture," the general's picture of maps and plans and grand strategy. Their battle was personal, limited to what happened to them and to those in their immediate vicinity. Only later, after the guns fell silent and they could compare notes with others, did they understand their role in the outcome.

For Lieutenant Thomas J. Jackson, the assault was a glorious adventure, an emotional high unlike anything he had ever experienced. Assigned to clear a road for the northern advance, he dashed forward with two light field guns and their crews. Finding the road cut by a ditch, they came to a screeching stop, which in turn brought them under fire from a Mexican battery. Horses were blown to bits. Several men were hit by canister shot, while a fellow lieutenant had his leg torn off at the knee. Seeing

Built atop the "Hill of Grasshoppers," Chapultapec housed a military college and was the strongest position protecting the Mexican capital.

this, the remaining gunners dived for cover and stayed there, trembling with fear.

Tom Jackson was not afraid. Danger energized him, making him more determined than ever to prove his ability. Stepping onto the middle of the road, he faced the enemy battery alone. A hail of grapeshot few over his head. A cannonball bounced between his legs. Jackson neither ducked nor flinched. Standing straight as a rail, he bellowed, "There is no danger! See! I am not hit!"[34] A sergeant believed him. Together, they carried a gun across the ditch, wheeled it into position by hand, and blasted the Mexican battery until relief arrived.

To the west, two regiments set out from the ruins of Molino del Rey, joined by others pressing in from the south and southeast. Joseph E. Johnston, recently promoted to lieutenant colonel, led his regiment to the edge of a trench on the western slope, where it stalled under a shower of enemy bullets. But the bullets were less dangerous than the gravelike mounds that dotted the ground. Recognizing them for what they were—mines—Lieutenant Joseph Hooker ordered his men to pick off anyone who tried to touch them off, while he pulled the fuses out of others with his bare hands. It worked. Not a single mine exploded.

Lieutenant Louis A. Armistead, first across the trench, was wounded instantly. Lieutenant James Longstreet, carrying the Stars and Stripes, led his men across and began to race up the western slope. A bullet wound put him out of action. As he fell, the flag was caught up and carried forward by a dear friend, Lieutenant George E. Pickett.

Ladders went up against the wall. Ladders went down, together with the men climbing them, as the Mexicans pushed them away. Other ladders went up, too many for the defenders to push away all at once. Pickett, a dandy with long, perfumed hair,

The raising of the Stars and Stripes over Chapultapec was the signal for executing American deserters serving in the enemy's San Patricio battalion.

was what soldiers called a "fighting fool." Once his blood was up, nothing could make him give in. The first to gain a foothold, he led his men into the fortress, flag in hand. Within minutes, hundreds of Americans were swarming over the walls behind Pickett's troops. They remembered Molino del Rey. Shouting to one another to take no prisoners, they cut down anyone who stood in their way. Among them were the teenage military cadets. Six cadets died, including one who leaped from the walls wrapped in Mexico's green, white, and red tricolor. To this day, they are revered by their country as Los Niños Héroes, "the Boy Heroes."

Pickett stepped over the body of the last cadet, Augustín Melgar, on the stairway leading to the castle's roof. Hauling down the Mexican colors, he raised the Stars and Stripes in their place. That flag-raising meant different things to different people. To the Americans below, it meant victory. The moment it unfolded in the breeze, cheers burst from thousands of throats, including Scott's. Santa Anna and an aide saw the flag reach the top of the staff. "If we were to plant our [gun] batteries in Hell the damned Yankees would take them from us," moaned the dictator. His aide just shook his head and said, "God is a Yankee."[35]

Lieutenant Ulysses S. Grant at Mexico City. The future commander of Union forces during the Civil War hauled a light cannon into a church steeple at a critical moment in the attack on one of the city's main gates.

At the village of Mixcoac, two miles to the south, thirty men watched the flagpole with keen interest. The doomed San Patricios stood in twos at the rear of flatbed wagons parked beneath a long scaffold. Each man had one end of a rope tied around his neck, the other end fasted to the overhead beam. It was the end of the line, for the moment the Stars and Stripes appeared over Chapultepec, they would die. Some cursed the American flag, that "dirty old rag," while others cursed the executioners: "Bad luck to ye!"[36] When Pickett's flag unfurled, executioners, guards, and teamsters cheered. The doomed men also cheered, louder, witnesses recalled, than anyone else. Why they cheered is a mystery. Perhaps it was to relieve the tension, or because they regretted what they had done and were glad to see an American victory. In any case, whips cracked, horses moved, and the wagons rolled. Their bodies hung swinging, twitching, and jerking in the breeze.

With Chapultepec in American hands, the way to the capital lay open. By afternoon, fighting was raging at the city gates. Ulysses S. Grant helped turn the tide at the San Cosme Gate, a key fortification. Searching for a weak point, Grant noticed that the belfry of a church overlooked the gate. Without hesitating, he ordered his men to dismantle a small cannon known as a howitzer. Together they carried the gun up into the belfry and opened fire, forcing the defenders to pull back. American troops burst into the city soon afterward. Although sniping continued throughout the night, Santa Anna was finished. He fled, leaving city officials to arrange the surrender.

At seven A.M., September 14, 1847, a marine lieutenant hoisted the Stars and Stripes over the National Palace, the legendary "Halls of Montezuma." Later that

United States troops, led by Winfield Scott, enter the main square of Mexico City.

morning Scott entered the city with bands playing patriotic tunes. He wore his best full-dress uniform, the one with the gold epaulets and the white-plumed hat. Standing on the balcony of the National Palace, he gazed down at his assembled troops. Like all soldiers after a battle, they were hungry, dirty, and tired. His words brought smiles to their lips and tears to their eyes. Removing his hat, Old Fuss and Feathers bowed low and shouted: "Brave rifles! Veterans! You have been baptized in fire and blood and have come out steel!"[37] Yet victory had not come cheaply. In storming Chapultepec and the city gates, the Americans suffered 863 casualties, of which 130 lost their lives.

Although the enemy capital had fallen, the killing continued. Mexico City had nearly twenty thousand *léperos,* an underclass of beggars, thieves, and murderers, plus two thousand prisoners Santa Anna had released from the jails before he fled. No sooner did the Americans arrive than a reign of terror began. Fires were set. Houses were burglarized. Law-abiding citizens feared for their lives. Snipers shot at gringos from rooftops. When a sniper shot a sergeant, Lieutenant George B. McClellan grabbed the fallen man's gun and killed the killer. One section of the city was nicknamed "Cutthroat," because any American who went there alone would surely have his throat cut.

Scott could not allow this state of affairs to continue. If the population got the idea that he could be pushed around, it might rebel, swallowing his small army in street fighting. So, like Taylor, he sent for the Los Diablos Tejanos.

The Texas Rangers arrived early in December. Citizens lined the streets to see if they lived up to their devilish reputation. They did. When a *lépero* knocked off the hat of Colonel John Coffee Hays with a stone, Hays calmly drew his equalizer and shot the fellow dead. "Colonel Jack's" message was driven home a few days later. Blundering into Cutthroat, one of his men was murdered by a mob. That night a band of Rangers rode into the area. In the morning Mexican police found the bodies of more than eighty *léperos*. They had been shot down in the streets and their bodies left in pools of blood for passersby to see. Scott was stunned. This was more than he expected. But instead of apologizing, Hays defended his men's actions. "The Texas Rangers," he said in his soft drawl, "are not in the habit of being insulted without resenting it."[38] A combination of Texan terror and firm, fair military government soon brought the situation under control. Life returned to normal and few Americans were murdered in Mexico City.

Meanwhile, Santa Anna rallied the remnants of his army to attack the small force Scott had left behind at Puebla. The attack was beaten off by reinforcements from Vera Cruz, among them a detachment of Texas Rangers under Sam Walker, a beloved leader. When Walker was killed in an ambush at nearby Huamantla, his men broke into the taverns and drank themselves crazy. Regular army officers were powerless to stop what followed. A lieutenant reported:

> Old women and girls were stripped of their clothing—and many suffered still greater outrages. Men were shot by dozens while concealing their property, churches, stores and dwelling places ransacked. . . . It . . . made [me] for the first time ashamed of my country.[39]

After Puebla, Santa Anna resigned the presidency and fled the country. Except for small-scale guerrilla raids, the fighting was over. Amazingly, Santa Anna resumed the presidency within a few years, only to be overthrown and sent into exile abroad. Finally, in 1874, the Mexican government allowed him to return. Poor and nearly blind, he was no longer a threat to anyone. The Napoleon of the West died alone and unmourned two years later at the age of eighty-two.

Compared to the wars of the twentieth century, the Mexican War was a small affair. It claimed 11,300 American lives, 1,500 of which died as a result of enemy action; the rest died of disease. In round numbers, the war cost the United States one hundred million dollars. Its results, however, were far-reaching and long lasting.

Diplomats met at the village of Guadalupe Hidalgo to bring the conflict to an end. According to the treaty, signed on February 2, 1848, the United States agreed to pay Mexico fifteen million dollars. In return, Mexico accepted the Rio Grande as its boundary with Texas and ceded California and New Mexico to the United States. The New Mexico Territory was later divided into the present states of New Mexico, Arizona, Utah, and Nevada, plus part of Wyoming and Colorado. Thus, by a stroke of the pen, Mexico gave up approximately one-half of its national territory (counting Texas), while the United States became larger than all of Europe (without Russia), sweeping from the Atlantic to the Pacific. Its unexpected victory made the European "great powers"—England, France, Austria, Russia—sit up and take notice. A new power was emerging, and it would expect its voice to be heard in world affairs.

Not only did Mexico lose territory, it saw the centuries-old dream of a golden kingdom realized by an enemy. In January 1848 gold was found near San Francisco, California. But since news traveled slowly, the discovery did not become widely known until months after the signing of the peace treaty. The "gold rush" that followed only added insult to injury, as Americans headed for the gold fields by the tens of thousands. Mexicans felt cheated. To this day they have a saying: "Poor Mexico! So far from God and so close to the United States." Cross-the-border raids continued. The last was in 1916, when the bandit Pancho Villa attacked Columbus, New Mexico, murdering sixteen townspeople and burning much of the town. Without bothering to get a declaration of war from Congress, President Woodrow Wilson sent an army into Mexico to capture him. The expedition failed. Villa was later murdered by fellow Mexicans.

The last American troops left Mexico City in June 1848. For them, as for their comrades who'd left earlier, Mexico had been an adventure to be shared with their countrymen. It became fashionable for Americans to "go Mexican," that is, adopt Mexican ways. Mexican-style mustaches became popular, with men "parading a moustache in every thoroughfare throughout the country."[40] The vaquero's broad-brimmed hat and cowhide boots were seen on city streets, as were Mexican *cigarritos*. Spanish words came into American speech as never before. Such words as *adobe, sombrero, lasso, corral, guerrilla, hacienda, calaboose,* and *fandango* became common expressions. So did Mexican place-names and the names of Mexican War leaders. By 1859 the United States had eighteen Buena Vistas, sixteen Monterreys, nine Palo Altos, and two Resacas, plus any number of Taylors and Taylorvilles, Polks and Polkvilles. The state of Iowa had counties with names like Polk, Taylor, Scott, Palo Alto, Buena Vista, and Cerro Gordo. Needless to say, there are no Polks, Taylors, or Scotts in Mexico. The San Patricios, however, are well remembered. A stone cross dedicated to their memory stands in a suburb of Mexico City. It bears a fighting cock to symbolize their courage and dice as a token of their gamble with destiny. A skull and crossbones represents their fate.

By stimulating America's westward movement, the Mexican War marked the beginning of the end of the horse Indians' way of life. Gone were the days when small groups of mountain men and Santa Fe merchants came to trap and trade. Gone were the days when a few prairie schooners sailed the grass sea. Free gold and free land brought a flood of white people surging across the Great Plains.

The Comanche and Apache had welcomed the Mexican War. Eager to keep the enemy off balance, American agents had encouraged their raids into Mexico with words and gifts. Peace, however, affected them in ways they had not foreseen. Gold seekers went to California by two routes. One was by ship, around the southern tip of South America. The other was by the El Dorado Trail, which crossed the Rio Grande at El Paso, heading westward through Mexico to California. This trail, like the Oregon Trail across the northern plains, invaded the Indians' hunting grounds. The result was both an ecological and a human disaster. Where the emigrants passed, they left a man-made desert. In their wake lay mounds of garbage, polluted streams, river bottoms stripped of timber, and thousands of rotting buffalo carcasses, many of which had been killed for their tongues alone. Germs were also left behind. For a decade after 1848, white people's diseases—smallpox, cholera, measles—ravaged the Plains tribes, wiping out entire bands. Scholars believe that half the Comanche died of cholera introduced by travelers.

When the United States took over the Southwest, it promised to halt Indian raids on Mexico. The army began by building forts and stationing cavalry regiments along

After the war. A caravan of forty-niners bound for the gold fields of California.

the old war trails. Within a decade, the balance of power had tipped in favor of the whites. The Mescalero, one of the largest Apache bands, were rounded up in a series of hard-hitting campaigns. In 1863 Colonel Kit Carson led an expedition into the Navajo country. Unable to catch up with the "hostiles," Carson killed their sheep and burned their cornfields. Faced with starvation or surrender, the Navajo began their "Long Walk" to a reservation at Fort Sumner, New Mexico. The army then turned its attention to the other Apaches. Under chiefs such as Cochise, Nana, and Victorio, they fought a losing battle for the next twenty years. The last "wild" Apaches, led by Geronimo, surrendered and were sent to prison in Florida in 1886. At the same time, the Mexican army destroyed the Apaches of Sonora and Chihuahua.

The Comanche fought their losing battle against the cavalry and Texas Rangers. Not that these were their only foes. When a way was found to turn buffalo hides into high-quality leather, white hunters nearly exterminated the herds. With their main food source gone, the Comanche had to give up their free life and move to reservations. In 1874 Quanah Parker surrendered the last holdouts at Fort Sill, Oklahoma.

Finally, the Mexican War set the stage for that greatest of American tragedies, the Civil War. Bitterness over the slavery issue had died down after Texas's failure to gain admission to the Union in 1836. Victory over Mexico, however, awakened that snarling dog once again. "Should slavery be allowed in the new lands?" was the big question. It so divided the nation that a simple "yes" or "no" answer threatened a national calamity. Allowing slavery would tip the balance of power in the Senate in favor of the slave-owning South. But not allowing slavery might drive Southerners out of the Union, leading to a breakup of the country. Abolitionists were not backing down. They were in a crusading mood, as we learn from "1848," a poem by John Greenleaf Whittier:

Sound for the onset! Blast on Blast!
Till Slavery's minions cower and quail:
One charge of fire shall drive them fast
Like chaff before our Northern gale.[41]

Zachary Taylor saw the fire rising and tried to douse it in time. When Polk refused to seek reelection, Taylor entered the 1848 race, becoming the nation's twelfth president. He did not serve out his term. On July 4, 1850, he attended the laying of the cornerstone of the Washington Monument. It was a brutally hot day, and Old Zack had to sit in the sun for hours. Returning to the White House, he wolfed down handfuls of cold cherries and gulped down a pitcher of ice milk. Five days later he was dead. Nevertheless, the basic work had been done on the Compromise of 1850. According to this measure, California was admitted to the Union as a free state, while Utah and Nevada were allowed to decide about slavery for themselves when they gained statehood.[42]

The Compromise postponed the split for a decade. But in 1860, after the election of Abraham Lincoln as our sixteenth president, the Southern states decided they could no longer remain in the Union. Eleven states seceded, forming a new nation, the Confederate States of America. Men who had held important commands in the Mexican War did so again. Jefferson Davis became the Confederacy's president. Winfield Scott remained general-in-chief of the U.S. Army until his retirement in November 1861, after fifty-five years of service. By then, however, the Civil War was raging across the land.

The Mexican War has been called the "schoolroom of the Civil War." Its campaigns provided invaluable experience for hundreds of officers destined to become generals in the larger conflict. It has also been called the "brothers' war," because men who had served together and were as close as brothers fought on opposite sides in the Civil War.

Before the shooting began, General Scott offered Robert E. Lee battlefield command of the Union armies. Scott thought the younger man a genius. "I tell you," he wrote a friend:

> If I were on my death bed tomorrow, and the President of the United States would tell me that a great battle was to be fought for the liberty or slavery of the country, and asked my judgment as to the ability of a commander, I would say with my dying breath, "Let it be Robert E. Lee!"[43]

It was not to be. Lee's chief loyalty was to Virginia, his home state, rather than to the United States. He refused Scott's offer, going on to serve the Confederacy as head of the Army of Northern Virginia, one of the greatest fighting forces of all time. Among the Confederacy's other military leaders were Generals Tom "Stonewall" Jackson, James Longstreet, Joseph E. Johnston, George E. Pickett, P. G. T. Beauregard, Braxton Bragg, and Louis A. Armistead. They were opposed by the Army of the Potomac, commanded at various times by Generals George B. McClellan, Joseph "Fighting Joe" Hooker, George Gordon Meade, and Ulysses S. Grant. "Unconditional Surrender" Grant had never forgotten Mexico. During the dark days of the Civil War, he would sit at a campfire for hours, reminiscing with other veterans about that wonderful land. In the end, it was he who saved the Union by destroying Lee's army.

But that is another story.

ENDNOTES

Prologue: The Golden Legend

1. Alexander McKee, *The Queen's Corsair: Drake's Journey of Circumnavigation.* (London: Souvenir Press, 1978), 214.
2. John Upton Terrill, *Journey into Darkness.* (New York: Morrow, 1962), 15–16.
3. David J. Weber, *The Spanish Frontier in North America.* (New Haven: Yale University Press, 1992), 28.

Chapter I: The Long Walk of Cabeza de Vaca

1. Herbert E. Bolton, *The Spanish Borderlands: A Chronicle of Old Florida and the Southwest.* (New Haven: Yale University Press, 1921), 19.
2. Morris Bishop, *The Odyssey of Cabeza de Vaca.* (New York: Century Company, 1933), 37–38.
3. Fanny and A. F. Bandelier, trans., *The Journey of Alvar Núñez Cabeza de Vaca and His Companions from Florida to the Pacific, 1528–1536.* (New York: Allerton Book Company, 1922), 31–32.
4. Bandelier, 40–41.
5. Bandelier, 53.
6. Bandelier, 54–55.
7. Bandelier, 66.
8. Bandelier, 63.
9. Bandelier, 74.
10. Bandelier, 118.
11. Bandelier, 126.
12. Pedro de Castañeda, *An Account of the Expedition to Cibola which took place in the year 1540, in which all those Settlements, Their Ceremonies and Customs are Described,* in George Parker Winship, ed., *The Journey of Coronado, 1540–1542, from the City of Mexico to the Grand Canyon of the Colorado to the Buffalo Plains, Kansas and Nebraska as Told by Himself and His Followers.* (New York: Greenwood Press, 1969), 84.
13. Bandelier, 97.
14. Bandelier, 106–108.
15. Bandelier, 112–113.
16. Frederick W. Hodge, ed., *Spanish Explorers in the Southern United States, 1528–1543.* (New York: Barnes & Noble, Inc., 1953), 97.
17. Bandelier, 158.
18. Bandelier, 144.
19. The arrowheads were probably not emeralds but a mineral called malachite, which is pretty but not precious.
20. Bandelier, 163.
21. Bandelier, 168.

Chapter II: Coronado and the Seven Cities of Gold

1. Herbert E. Bolton, *Coronado, Knight of Pueblos and Plains.* (Albuquerque: University of New Mexico Press, 1949), 18.

2. John Upton Terrill, *Pueblos, Gods and Spaniards.* (New York: Dial Press, 1973), 36.
3. Bolton, *Coronado,* 33.
4. Bolton, *Coronado*, 36.
5. Bolton, *Coronado*, 36.
6. Castañeda, 16.
7. Castañeda, 23.
8. Castañeda, 172.
9. Castañeda, 33.
10. Henry Savage Jr., *Discovering America, 1700–1875.* (New York: Harper & Row, 1979), 315.
11. Castañeda, 35–36.
12. Castañeda, 37.
13. Castañeda, 41.
14. Castañeda, 205.
15. Castañeda, 206.
16. Castañeda, 44.
17. Castañeda 43.
18. Castañeda, 48.
19. Castañeda, 51.
20. Castañeda, 54.
21. Castañeda, 140.
22. Castañeda, 141.
23. Castañeda, 112.
24. Castañeda, 71.
25. Castañeda, 69–70.
26. Castañeda, 219.
27. Castañeda, 219.
28. A. Grove Day, *Coronado's Quest: The Discovery of the Southwestern States.* (Westport, Conn.: Greenwood Press, 1981), 253.
29. Weber, *The Spanish Frontier in North America,* 49.

Chapter III: Conquest of the Pueblos

1. Elsie Clews Parsons, *Pueblo Indian Religion,* 2 vols. (Chicago: University of Chicago Press, 1939), Vol. 1, 27.
2. Paul Horgan, *Great River: The Rio Grande in North American History.* (New York: Rinehart & Co., 1954), 55.
3. George Parker Winship, ed., "The Coronado Expedition, 1540–1542," *Fourteenth Annual Report,* Bureau of Ethnology, 1892–1893, Part I. (Washington, D.C., 1896), 522.
4. Parsons, Vol. 1, 50.
5. Richard Erdoes, *The Pueblo Indians.* (New York: Funk & Wagnals, 1967), 82.
6. George P. Hammond and Agapito Rey, *Don Juan de Oñate, Colonizer of New Mexico, 1595–1628.* (Albuquerque: University of New Mexico Press, 1953), 338–339.
7. Hammond and Rey, 458.
8. Hammond and Rey, 477–478.
9. Horgan, *Great River,* 243.
10. Weber, *The Spanish Frontier in North America,* 113.
11. Terrell, *Pueblos, Gods and Spaniards,* 269.
12. Horgan, *Great River,* 254.
13. Weber, *The Spanish Frontier in North America,* 113.
14. Horgan, *Great River,* 219.
15. Weber, *The Spanish Frontier in North America,* 132.
16. Weber, *The Spanish Frontier in North America*, 133.

17. Castañeda, 112.
18. Horgan, *Great River,* 262.
19. Charles Wilson Hackett, *The Revolt of the Pueblo Indians of New Mexico and Otermín's Attempted Reconquest, 1680–1682,* 2 vols. (Albuquerque: University of New Mexico Press, 1942), Vol. 1, 177–179.
20. Grace Ertel, "Mustangs: The Horses that Won the West," *Persimmon Hill* (winter 1993): 44.

Chapter IV: Mountain Men and Santa Fe Traders

1. R. L. Dufus, *The Santa Fe Trail.* (New York: Longmans, Green & Co., 1930), 40.
2. Dufus, 43.
3. Dufus, 44.
4. James Ohio Pattie, *Personal Narrative during an Expedition from St. Louis to the Pacific Ocean.* (Cleveland: Arthur H. Clark Company, 1905), 83.
5. Dale Van Every, *The Final Challenge: The American Frontier, 1804–1845.* (New York: William Morrow & Company, 1964), 233.
6. George F. Ruxton, *Adventures in Mexico and the Rocky Mountains.* (Glorieta, N.Mex.: Rio Grande Press, 1973), 245.
7. Ray Allen Billington, *The Far Western Frontier, 1830–1860.* (New York: Harper Torch, 1962), 46.
8. Billington, 54; Frederic E. Voelker, "The Mountain Men and Their Part in the Opening of the West," *Bulletin of the Missouri Historical Society* III (April 1947): 159.
9. Erdoes, 46.
10. Stanley Vestal, *Mountain Men.* (Freeport, N.Y.: Books for Libraries Press, 1977), 47.
11. Pattie, 62.
12. Pattie, 94, 137.
13. Pattie, 135.
14. Voelker, "The Mountain Men," 157–158.
15. Billington, 50.
16. Robert G. Cleland, *This Reckless Breed of Men: The Trappers and Fur Traders of the Southwest.* (Albuquerque: University of New Mexico Press, 1976), 32; Pattie, 107.
17. Cleland, 32.
18. Jeff Long, *Duel of Eagles: The Mexican and U.S. Fight for the Alamo.* (New York: William Morrow & Company, 1990), 116.
19. Billington, 29.
20. Josiah Gregg, *The Commerce of the Prairies.* (New York: Citadel Press, 1968), 38–39.
21. Cleland, 143.
22. Stanley Vestal, *The Old Santa Fe Trail.* (Boston: Houghton Mifflin, 1939), 79.
23. Cleland, 143.
24. Dufus, 131–132.
25. Gregg, 102.
26. Dufus, 160.
27. Vestal, 268.
28. Pattie, 167–168.

Chapter V: Texans and All Americans in the World

1. Mexico is 761,830 square miles in area; Texas, 267,339.
2. W. S. Henry, *Campaign Sketches of the War*

with Mexico. (New York: Arno Press, 1973), 121.
3. Walter Lord, *A Time to Stand.* (Lincoln: University of Nebraska Press, 1961), 30.
4. Henry, 121.
5. Henry, 120.
6. David J. Weber, "Scarce More than Apes: Historical Roots of Anglo-American Stereotypes of Mexicans," in Weber, ed., *New Spain's Far Northern Frontier: Essays on Spain in the American West, 1540–1821.* (Albuquerque: University of New Mexico Press, 1979), 297–298.
7. Justin H. Smith, *The War with Mexico,* 2 vols. (Gloucester, Mass.: Peter Smith, 1963), Vol. 1, 42.
8. T. R. Fehrenbach, *Lone Star: A History of Texas and the Texans.* (New York: Collier Books, 1980), 189.
9. Lon Tinkle, *13 Days to Glory: The Siege of the Alamo.* (College Station: Texas A & M University Press, 1985), 163.
10. Long, 72.
11. Lord, 45.
12. John C. Duval, *The Adventures of Big-Foot Wallace, the Texas Ranger and Hunter.* (Philadelphia: Claxton, Remsen & Haffelfinger, 1871), 165–166.
13. Long, 137.
14. After 1808 it was illegal to import slaves into the United States. But since demand was so great and profits so high, slave smugglers, like modern drug smugglers, were willing to take the risk.
15. Tinkle, 81–82.
16. Long, 104.
17. Tinkle, 24–25.
18. Tinkle, 46.
19. Tinkle, 204.
20. Tinkle, 181.
21. Tinkle, 182–183.
22. Long, 222.
23. Long, 242.
24. John M. Myers, *The Alamo.* (Lincoln: University of Nebraska Press, 1973), 224.
25. Myers, 252.
26. Long, 253.
27. Long, 260.
28. Lord, 171.
29. Frank X. Tolbert, *The Day of San Jacinto.* (New York: McGraw-Hill, 1959), 125.
30. Tolbert, 140.
31. Tolbert, 141.
32. Tolbert, 142.
33. Fehrenbach, *Lone Star,* 232.
34. Tolbert, 155.
35. Long, 313.
36. Tolbert, 152–153.
37. Tolbert, 157.
38. Tolbert, 171.
39. Tolbert, 177.
40. Tolbert, 179.
41. Tolbert, 180.
42. Tolbert, 181–182.

Chapter VI: Blood on the Borders

1. Fehrenbach, *Lone Star,* 234.

2. Fehrenbach, *Lone Star,* 264.
3. Walter Prescott Webb, *The Great Plains.* (Boston: Ginn & Company, 1931), 166.
4. Ruxton, 101.
5. Horgan, *Great River,* 571.
6. Horgan, *Great River,*, 577.
7. E. Eugene Hollon, *Frontier Violence: Another Look.* (New York: Oxford University Press, 1974), 41.
8. Duval, 177.
9. Duval, 216.
10. John Edward Weems, *Dream of Empire: A Human History of the Republic of Texas, 1836–1846.* (New York: Simon & Schuster, 1971), 267, 268.
11. Duval, 222–223.
12. George W. Smith and Charles Judah, *Chronicles of the Gringos: The U.S. Army in the Mexican War, 1846–1848, Accounts by Eyewitnesses and Combatants.* (Albuquerque: University of New Mexico Press, 1968), 424.
13. Robert W. Johannsen, *To the Halls of the Montezumas: The Mexican War in the American Imagination.* (New York: Oxford University Press, 1985), 40.
14. Ulysses S. Grant, *Personal Memoirs of Ulysses S. Grant and Selected Letters, 1839–1865.* (New York: Library of America, 1990), 34–35.
15. Smith, *The War with Mexico,* Vol. 1, 126.
16. Charles L. Dufour, *The Mexican War: A Compact History, 1846–1848.* (New York: Hawthorn Books, 1968), 31.
17. Samuel E. Chamberlain, *My Confessions.* (New York: Harper & Brothers, 1956), 140–141.
18. Chamberlain, 38.
19. Smith, *The War with Mexico,* Vol. 1, 210.
20. Smith and Judah, *Chronicles of the Gringos,* 277.
21. John S. D. Eisenhower, *So Far from God: The U.S. War with Mexico, 1846–1848.* (New York: Random House, 1989), 369.
22. Johannsen, 88.
23. Smith and Judah, *Chronicles of the Gringos,* 316.
24. Grant, 61–62.
25. Henry, 70.
26. Johannsen, 169.
27. The inventor of the telegraph, Samuel F. B. Morse, sent the first message from Washington, D.C., to Baltimore, Maryland, on May 24, 1844. Still experimental, the device had a long way to go before the army could use it.

Chapter VII: All on the Plains of Mexico

1. Grant, 910.
2. Henry, 94.
3. Edward J. Nichols, *Zack Taylor's Little Army.* (Garden City, N.Y.: Doubleday & Co., 1963), 101. "Advance" refers to the pay men received as soon as they signed their enlistment papers.
4. Johannsen, 276.
5. Smith, *The War with Mexico,* Vol. 2, 278.
6. Dufour, 52.
7. Nancy Scott Anderson and Dwight

Anderson, *The Generals: Ulysses S. Grant and Robert E. Lee.* (New York: Knopf, 1988).

8. Lloyd Lewis, *Captain Sam Grant.* (Boston: Little, Brown, 1950), 126.

9. Chamberlain, 208.

10. Chamberlain, 175–176; Johannsen, 35–36.

11. Chamberlain, 73–74.

12. Chamberlain, 177.

13. Johannsen, 35.

14. Smith and Judah, *Chronicles of the Gringos,* 90.

15. Dufus, 201.

16. Dufour, 132.

17. Chamberlain, 116.

18. Chamberlain, 120.

19. Johannsen, 116.

20. Alfred Hoyt Bill, *Rehearsal for Conflict: The War with Mexico, 1846–1848.* (New York: History Book Club, 1947), 201.

21. Chamberlain, 123.

22. Chamberlain, 123.

23. Dufour, 181.

24. Chamberlain, 137.

25. Margaret Sanborn, *Robert E. Lee: A Portrait,* 2 vols. (Philadelphia: J. B. Lippincott, 1966), Vol. 1, 171.

26. Smith, *The War with Mexico,* Vol. 2, 35.

27. Dufour, 223.

28. Grady and Sue McWhiney, eds., *To Mexico with Taylor and Scott, 1845–1847.* (Waltham, Mass.: Blaisdell Publishers, 1969), 142.

29. Johannsen, 163.

30. Johannsen, 164.

31. Dufour, 250.

32. Smith and Judah, *Chronicles of the Gringos,* 145–146.

33. Johannsen, 435.

34. John C. Waugh, *The Class of 1846: From West Point to Appomattox.* (New York: Warner Books, 1994), 120.

35. K. Jack Bauer, *The Mexican War, 1846–1848.* (New York: Macmillan, 1974), 318.

36. Chamberlain, 227–228.

37. Waugh, 124. This incident is recalled whenever U.S. Marines sing the opening stanza of their hymn:

From the Halls of Montezuma,
To the shores of Tripoli.

38. Walter Prescott Webb, *The Texas Rangers in the Mexican War.* (Austin, Tex.: Jenkins Garrett Press, 1975), 119–120; John Edward Weems, *To Conquer a Peace: The War between the United States and Mexico.* (Garden City, N.Y.: Doubleday & Co., 1974), 435.

39. Smith and Judah, *Chronicles of the Gringos,* 270.

40. Johannsen, 205.

41. Bill, 327.

42. New Mexico itself was admitted into the Union in 1912 as the forty-seventh state.

43. Sanborn, Vol. 1, 232.

SOME MORE BOOKS

There are hundreds of books on the peoples—Spaniards, Mexicans, Indians, Americans—of Texas and the Southwest. Here are a few of the ones I found most helpful in preparing my own book. Wherever possible, I have tried to use eyewitness accounts in telling the story.

Bahti, Tom. *Southwestern Indian Tribes.* Flagstaff, Ariz.: KC Publications, 1968.

Bandelier, Fanny, and A. F. Bandelier, trans. *The Journey of Alvar Núñez Cabeza de Vaca and His Companions from Florida to the Pacific, 1528–1536.* New York: Allerton Book Company, 1922.

Bannon, John Francis. *The Spanish Borderlands.* New York: Holt, Rinehart & Winston, 1970.

Bauer, K. Jack. *The Mexican War, 1846–1848.* New York: Macmillan Publishing Co., 1974.

Beck, Warren A. *New Mexico: A History of Four Centuries.* Norman: University of Oklahoma Press, 1969.

Bill, Alfred Hoyt. *Rehearsal for Conflict: The War with Mexico, 1846–1848.* New York: History Book Club, 1947.

Billington, Ray Allen. *The Far Western Frontier, 1830–1860.* New York: Harper Torch, 1962.

Bishop, Morris. *The Odyssey of Cabeza de Vaca.* New York: Century Company, 1933.

Bolton, Herbert E. *Coronado, Knight of Pueblos and Plains.* Albuquerque: University of New Mexico Press, 1949.

———. *The Spanish Borderlands: A Chronicle of Old Florida and the Southwest.* New Haven: Yale University Press, 1921.

———, ed. *Spanish Exploration in the Southwest, 1542–1706.* New York: Barnes & Noble, 1959.

Castañeda, Pedro de. *An Account of the Expedition to Cibola which took place in the year 1540, in which all those Settlements, Their Ceremonies and Customs are Described,* in George Parker Winship, ed. *The Journey of Coronado, 1540–1542, from the City of Mexico to the Grand Canyon of the Colorado and the Buffalo Plains, Kansas and Nebraska as Told by Himself and His Followers.* New York: Greenwood Press, 1969.

Chamberlain, Samuel E. *My Confessions.* New York: Harper & Brothers, 1956.

Chidsey, Donald Barr. *The War with Mexico.* New York: Crown Publishers, 1968.

Cleland, Robert G. *This Reckless Breed of Men: The Trappers and Fur Traders of the Southwest.* Albuquerque: University of New Mexico Press, 1976.

Clissold, Stephen. *The Seven Cities of Cibola.* London: Eyre & Spottiswoode, 1961.

Connor, Seymour V. *Texas: A History.* New York: Crowell, 1971.

Connor, Seymour V., and Odie B. Falk. *North America Divided: The Mexican War, 1846–1848.*

New York: Oxford University Press, 1971.

Dale, Edward E. *The Indians of the Southwest.* Norman: University of Oklahoma Press, 1949.

Day, A. Grove. *Coronado's Quest: The Discovery of the Southwestern States.* Westport, Conn.: Greenwood Press, 1981.

De Bruhl, Marshall. *Sword of San Jacinto: A Life of Sam Houston.* New York: Random House, 1993.

De León , Arnaldo. *The Mexican Image in Nineteenth-Century Texas.* Boston: American Press, 1982.

Denhardt, Robert M. *The Horse of the Americas.* Norman: University of Oklahoma Press, 1975.

De Voto, Bernard. *The Year of Decision: 1846.* Boston: Little, Brown & Co., 1943.

Dozier, Edward P. *The Pueblo Indians of North America.* New York: Holt, Rinehart & Winston, 1970.

Dufour, Charles L. *The Mexican War: A Compact History, 1846–1848.* New York: Hawthorn Books, 1968.

Dufus, R. L. *The Santa Fe Trail.* New York: Longmans, Green & Co., 1930.

Duval, John C. *The Adventures of Big-Foot Wallace, the Texas Ranger and Hunter.* Philadelphia: Claxton, Remsen & Haffelfinger, 1871.

Eisenhower, John S. D. *So Far from God: The U.S. War with Mexico, 1846–1848.* New York: Random House, 1989.

Erdoes, Richard. *The Pueblo Indians.* New York: Funk & Wagnals, 1967.

Every, Dale Van. *The Final Challenge: The American Frontier, 1804–1845.* New York: William Morrow & Company, 1964.

Fehrenbach, T. R. *Fire and Blood: A History of Mexico.* New York: Collier Books, 1973.

———. *Lone Star: A History of Texas and the Texans.* New York: Collier Books, 1980.

Forbes, Jack D. *Apache, Navajo and Spaniard.* Norman: University of Oklahoma Press, 1960.

Forrest, E. R. *The Snake Dance of the Hopi.* Los Angeles: Westernlore Press, 1961.

Goetzmann, William H. *Army Exploration in the American West, 1803–1863.* Lincoln: University of Nebraska Press, 1959.

Grant, Ulysses S. *Personal Memoirs of Ulysses S. Grant and Selected Letters.* New York: Library of America, 1990.

Gregg, Josiah. *The Commerce of the Prairies.* New York: Citadel Press, 1968. A classic book on the Santa Fe trade by an eyewitness.

Hackett, Charles Wilson. *The Revolt of the Pueblo Indians of New Mexico and Otermin's Attempted Reconquest, 1680–1682.* 2 vols., Albuquerque: University of New Mexico Press, 1942.

Hallenbeck, Cleve. *Alvar Núñez Cabeza de Vaca: The Journey and Route of the First European to Cross the Continent of North America, 1534–1546.* Glendale, Calif.: Arthur H. Clark Company, 1940.

Hamilton, Holman. *Zachary Taylor: Soldier of the Republic.* New York: Bobbs-Merrill Company, 1941.

Hammond, George P. *Don Juan de Oñate and the Founding of New Mexico.* Santa Fe: El Palacio Press, 1927.

Hammond, George P., and Agapito Rey. *Don Juan de Oñate, Colonizer of New Mexico, 1595–1628.* Albuquerque: University of New Mexico Press, 1953.

Henry, W. S. *Campaign Sketches of the War with Mexico.* New York: Arno Press, 1973. Reprint of a book first published in 1847.

Hodge, Frederick W., ed. *Spanish Explorers in the Southern United States, 1528–1543.* New York: Barnes & Noble, Inc., 1953. This book contains translations of accounts by some of the early Spanish explorers.

Hollon, Eugene V. *The Southwest: Old and New.* New York: Knopf, 1961.

Horgan, Paul. *Conquistadors in North American History.* New York: Farrar, Straus & Co., 1963.

———. *Great River: The Rio Grande in North American History.* New York: Rinehart & Co., 1954.

Hulbert, Archer B. *Southwest on the Turquoise Trail: The First Diaries on the Road to Santa Fe.* Denver: Denver Public Library, 1933.

Irey, Thomas R. "Soldiering, Suffering, and Dying in the Mexican War." *Journal of the West* XI (April 1971): pp. 285–298.

Johannsen, Robert W. *To the Halls of the Montezumas: The Mexican War in the American Imagination.* New York: Oxford University Press, 1985.

Johnson, William W. *Heroic Mexico: The Violent Emergence of a Modern Nation.* Garden City, N.Y.: Doubleday & Company, 1968.

Jones, Oakah L., Jr. *Santa Anna.* New York: Twayne Publishers, 1968.

Josephy, Alvin M., Jr., ed. *America in 1492: The World of the Indian Peoples before the Arrival of Columbus.* New York: Vintage Books, 1991.

Kelly, William H. *Indians of the Southwest.* Tucson: University of Arizona Press, 1953.

Kessell, John L. *Kiva, Cross, and Crown: The Pecos Indians and New Mexico, 1540–1840.* Washington, D.C.: National Park Service, 1979.

King, Richard. *Susanna Dickinson, Messenger of the Alamo.* Austin: Shoal Creek Publishers, 1976.

Lavender, David. *Climax at Buena Vista: The American Campaign in Northern Mexico, 1846–1847.* Philadelphia: J. B. Lippincott, 1966.

Lofaro, Michael A. *Davy Crockett: The Man, The Legend, The Legacy, 1786–1986.* Knoxville: University of Tennessee Press, 1985.

Long, Jeff. *Duel of Eagles: The Mexican and U.S. Fight for the Alamo.* New York: William Morrow & Company, 1990.

Lord, Walter. *A Time to Stand.* Lincoln: University of Nebraska Press, 1961.

Lozano, Ruben R. *Viva Tejas: The Story of the Tejanos, Mexican-Born Patriots of the Texas Revolution.* San Antonio: Alamo Press, 1985.

McGraw, William C. *Savage Scene: The Life and Times of James Kirker, Frontier King.* New York: Hastings House, 1972.

McWhiney, Grady, and Sue McWhiney, eds. *To Mexico with Taylor and Scott, 1845–1847.* Waltham, Mass.: Blaisdell Publishers, 1969.

Minge, Ward A. *Acoma: Pueblo in the Sky.* Albuquerque: University of New Mexico Press, 1976.

Myers, John M. *The Alamo.* Lincoln: University of Nebraska Press, 1973.

Nichols, Edward J. *Zack Taylor's Little Army.* Garden City, N.Y.: Doubleday & Co., 1963.

Parsons, Elsie Clews. *Pueblo Indian Religion.* 2 vols. Chicago: University of Chicago Press, 1939.

Pattie, James Ohio. *Personal Narrative during an Expedition from Saint Louis through the Vast Regions between that Place and the Pacific Ocean.* Cleveland, Ohio: Arthur H. Clark Company, 1905.

Prucha, Francis Paul. *Sword of the Republic: The United States Army on the Frontier, 1783–1846.* Bloomington: Indiana University Press, 1969.

Robertson, Brian. *Wild Horse Desert: The Heritage of South Texas.* Edinburg, Tex.: New Santander Press, 1985.

Ruxton, George F. *Adventures in Mexico and the Rocky Mountains.* Glorieta, N.Mex.: Rio Grande Press, 1973. Reprint of a book first published in England in 1847.

Sanborn, Margaret. *Robert E. Lee: A Portrait.* 2 vols. Philadephia: J. B. Lippincott, 1966.

Sando, Joe S. *The Pueblo Indians.* San Francisco: Indian Historian Press, 1976.

Sauer, Carl O. *Sixteenth-Century North America: The Land and the People as Seen by the Europeans.* Berkeley: University of California Press, 1971.

Savage, Henry, Jr. *Discovering America, 1700–1875.* New York: Harper & Row, 1979.

Silverberg, R. *The Old Ones.* New York: New York Graphic Society, 1965. The story of the Pueblos and their ancestors.

Smith, George W., and Charles Judah. *Chronicles of the Gringos: The U.S. Army in the Mexican War, 1846–1848: Accounts by Eyewitnesses and Combatants.* Albuquerque: University of New Mexico Press, 1968.

Smith, Justin H. *The War with Mexico.* 2 vols. Gloucester, Mass.: Peter Smith, 1963. Reprint of a classic first published in 1919.

Spicer, Edward H. *Cycles of Conquest: The Impact of Spain, Mexico, and the United States on the Indians of the Southwest, 1533–1960.* Tucson: University of Arizona Press, 1992.

Terrell, John Upton. *Estevanico the Black.* Los Angeles: Westernlore Press, 1968.

———. *Journey into Darkness.* New York: Morrow, 1962.

———. *Pueblos, Gods and Spaniards.* New York: Dial Press, 1973.

Tinkle, Lon. *13 Days to Glory: The Siege of the Alamo.* College Station: Texas A&M University Press, 1985.

Tolbert, Frank X. *The Day of San Jacinto.* New York: McGraw-Hill Book Company, 1959.

Turner, Martha Anne. *William Barret Travis: His Sword and His Pen.* Waco: Texian Press, 1972.

Udall, Stuart L. *To the Inland Empire: Coronado and the Spanish Legacy.* Garden City, N.Y.: Doubleday, 1987. A beautifully illustrated book.

Vestal, Stanley. *Mountain Men.* Freeport, N.Y.: Books for Libraries Press, 1977. Reprint of a book first published in 1939.

———. *The Old Santa Fe Trail.* Boston: Houghton Mifflin Company, 1939.

Voelker, Frederic E. "The Mountain Men and Their Part in the Opening of the West." *Bulletin of the Missouri Historical Society* III (April 1947): 151–162.

Waugh, John C. *The Class of 1846: From West Point to Appomattox.* New York: Warner Books, 1994.

Webb, Walter Prescott. *The Great Plains.* Boston: Ginn and Company, 1931.

———. *The Texas Rangers in the Mexican War.* Austin, Tex.: Jenkins Garrett Press, 1975.

Weber, David J., ed. *Foreigners in Their Native Land: Historical Roots of the Mexican Americans.* Albuquerque: University of New Mexico Press, 1973.

———. *The Mexican Frontier, 1821–1846: The American Southwest under Mexico.* Albuquerque: University of New Mexico Press, 1982.

———, ed. *New Spain's Far Northern Frontier: Essays on Spain in the American West, 1540–1821.* Albuquerque: University of New Mexico Press, 1979.

———. *The Spanish Frontier in North America.* New Haven: Yale University Press, 1992.

Weems, John Edward. *Dream of Empire: A Human History of the Republic of Texas, 1836–1846.* New York: Simon & Schuster, 1971.

———. *To Conquer a Peace: The War between the United States and Mexico.* Garden City, N.Y.: Doubleday & Co., 1974.

Williams, John Hoyt. *Sam Houston: A Biography of the Father of Texas.* New York: Simon & Schuster, 1993.

Winship, George Parker, ed. *The Journey of Coronado, 1540–1542, from the City of Mexico to the Grand Canyon of the Colorado and the Buffalo Plains, Kansas and Nebraska as Told by Himself and His Followers.* New York: Greenwood Press, 1969.

———. "The Coronado Expedition, 1540–1542." *Fourteenth Annual Report.* Bureau of Ethnology, 1892–1893, Part I, pp. 329–613. Washington, D.C., 1896.

Note: Page numbers for illustrations are in italics.

B